SEPARATED AT DEATH

LEO AXLER

BERKLEY PRIME CRIME, NEW YORK

SEPARATED AT DEATH

A Berkley Prime Crime Book / published by arrangement with
the author

PRINTING HISTORY
Berkley Prime Crime edition / April 1996

The Putnam Berkley World Wide Web site address is
http://www.berkley.com

ISBN: 0-425-15257-X

Berkley Prime Crime Books are published
by The Berkley Publishing Group,
200 Madison Avenue, New York, NY 10016.
The name BERKLEY PRIME CRIME and the BERKLEY PRIME CRIME
design are trademarks belonging to Berkley Publishing Corporation.

PRINTED IN THE UNITED STATES OF AMERICA

10 9 8 7 6 5 4 3 2 1

ONE

■■■■■■■■■■

NORMALLY, MY JOB is to bury the dead. But sometimes I dig them up. Not often, but sometimes. I've long thought it strange the way people save up their dead in certain parts of town, carefully indexed with marble marker slabs, fenced round with iron and stone, locked tight at night, lovingly tended, or so the cemetery administrators would obviously like us to believe, forever. Being an undertaker, I rarely mention my misgivings about deceased-relative storage, but I think about it from time to time—especially when I'm called upon to disinter.

Paul J. Larson had been buried, against his will, on January 23, 1989. Instead of an in-ground interment, he had made it clear that he preferred to be cremated . . . a request that his wife had refused to honor. Nearly five years later, Mr. Larson's son, Jerome, contacted me with what he thought was an unusual request.

"I'd like him dug up," he had said over the phone. "My mom's in the hospital; her doctors don't expect her to last out the week. Ever since Dad's funeral she's been torturing herself about how he wanted one thing when he died, and she did something else. She made me promise that I'd arrange to have him cremated, like he originally planned. When she dies I'm supposed to put his ashes in her casket so that they can be together forever. I know it sounds weird, Mr. Hawley, but it's what my mother wants."

In my best professional voice, I assured Jerome Larson that his request was anything but unusual.

"We do disinterments all the time," I said. "Usually for the very reason you've just described. The other big reason for disinterring a remains is to move the casket from one cemetery to another, which we do about a dozen times a year, on average. Some parts of town have gotten so run-down that you can't visit a grave without somebody hitting you on the head for your wallet. We move a lot of grandparents to cemeteries in the suburbs so that families can be buried together."

"So what do I do?" he asked. "What's the procedure?"

"Just stop in and sign an authorization form," I said. "I'll take it from there."

"That's where we run into a snag, Mr. Hawley. I'm out of town, in Phoenix. My mom moved here after Dad died. Like I say, she's terminal. She's got a week, maybe ten days. I can't possibly leave her, so I won't be back in Ohio until it's time for her funeral."

"Then we'll take care of it then," I cut in, trying to be helpful. "I assume you're going to have your mom viewed, so we can use that time to take care of your dad. Having his cremains ready by the day of your mother's funeral shouldn't be any problem at all."

"See, if it were up to me, that's exactly how we'd go," Jerome Larson replied, his voice taking on that pained quality of You - know - I'd - like - to - do - it - the - easy - way, - but - Christ, - my-mom's-dying-and-it's-what-she-wants that I so often hear. "But, like I said, this thing's been preying on her mind for years. She wants to know that it's been done, before she dies. She wants me to look her in the eye and say, 'Dad's wishes have been met.' It really means a lot to her."

"I don't suppose you'd consider telling her what she wants to hear, whether it's true or not, just to put her mind at ease?"

"No. I couldn't do that."

"Then we've got a problem, Mr. Larson. I could probably fax the form to you at the hospital, but I don't know what good it'd do. I can't notarize a faxed signature, and the cemetery requires a notarized authorization or they won't honor it."

"Really, Mr. Hawley," he said impatiently, "isn't this all a little silly? Can't you just sign my name to the form and be done with it? You're going to be burying my mom in a few days, for God's sake. How much more assurance do you need?"

I tried to say that it wasn't a question of my needing anything, but he wouldn't give me the chance. Instead, he pushed, hard, arguing so persuasively that finally, against my better judgment, I gave in, saying, "All right, Mr. Larson, I don't normally do this, but I suppose yours is a special case. I'll sign your name to the authorization, disinter your dad, and have him cremated, probably by week's end. Is that all right?"

"It's better than all right," he said. "It's great. Mr. Hawley, you're a saint. You've made a very hard time a little less terrible, both for me, and especially, I'm sure, for my mom. I really appreciate it. Sincerely."

I accepted his thanks gracefully, feeling a little flush of satisfaction in having been able to help. I didn't like the idea of forging the disinterment authorization, but hey, sometimes you need to stretch the rules. My clients are human beings after all . . . human beings stuck in the middle of what will often prove to be one of the most difficult and emotional times of their lives. Sometimes just leading them through it all isn't enough. And, quite truthfully, it's been my experience that those times when I've had to go the farthest out of my way usually end up being exactly those times when I feel that maybe what I do for a living has some value after all.

Three days later, I was still feeling so self-satisfied that by the time Paul J. Larson's concrete vault was pulled, dripping and cracked from its muddy grave, I had all but put my original misgivings aside. Everything had gone so smoothly with the cemetery office, vault company, and city hall, that when the trouble started I was taken almost completely off guard.

Usually in a disinterment, I don't even see the body. But since Mr. Larson had been buried in a steel casket, which doesn't burn, we had to remove him. It was in the Lake Erie Crematory's receiving dock, accompanied by a single, semi-retired funeral director who was picking up a few hours a week part-time to supplement his Social Security, that I made my grisly discovery.

"What the . . . ?" the older gentleman said when, after we had opened the casket, I pulled back the velvet blanket to reveal a substantial lump under the mattress between the dead man's feet.

By the way, I should mention at this point a few details about body preservation:

When a human being dies, *E. coli* bacteria in the intestines begin the process of decomposition almost immediately. In life, this bacteria aids in the digestion of food. In death, it aids in the digestion of the body. That's the way nature works. Embalming, contrary to popular belief, is not so much done to the aesthetic end of making the body more presentable during the viewings. Instead, its concern is mainly hygienic. A dead, unembalmed body is literally alive with degenerative bacteria, some of which can be transferred to a person coming into contact with that remains through the air . . . such as the tuberculosis virus, which has mutated over the past several generations and is making a comeback as a dangerous disease. Embalming sterilizes a body, destroying the bacteria in it, and soaking the tissue through with chemicals that make it unappetizing for further biological action. Also, since bacteria needs oxygen to fuel its work, an embalmed body, left undisturbed in a sealed casket and vault, will last, theoretically, forever.

So when I say that I had disinterred a man who had been embalmed and buried five years before, I am saying that when I opened that casket, instead of a horror show, I simply found an old man in a suit, blanket pulled up to his chin, lying peacefully with a wilted white rose on his chest. It was when I pulled the blanket off so that we could lift him out of the casket that I noticed the bulge in the mattress. And when I pulled that mattress back, the crematory attendant and I bent over, looked inside, looked at one another, and almost simultaneously said, "What the hell?"

Which is pretty much what the cops said when they arrived on the scene.

What the hell?

It was a very good question.

Dr. Gordon Wolf, our county's medical examiner, left me to cool my heels for nearly two hours before he was ready to talk to me. During that time I used a phone in the crematory's front office to call my brother, both to check in and to explain what was taking me so long.

"You found a what?" Jerry asked, sounding more animated than I had heard him sound in quite some time.

Younger than me by only three years, Jerry is so dissimilar from me in personality and appearance that sometimes it's hard to believe that we're really related. Lately he'd been acting even funnier than usual—distracted, uneven, almost surly; which wasn't that tough to understand, given that he's the one who inherited Grandpa's temper. But during the two years that he'd lived with me, the rift between us that dated back to the day an automobile accident left his legs paralyzed, and my guilt fused to my bones, had healed enough for us to begin growing close again.

Still, something'd been bothering him, and even without his coming right out and saying it, I knew what it was: Jerry was having woman trouble, and he was too embarrassed to talk to me about it because the woman in question was one that I had told him not to get involved with in the first place.

"A head," I replied simply. Though I kept my voice even, I was still feeling shaken. "We found a woman's head, in a plastic bag, hidden under the casket's mattress. The cops are here now; they won't let me leave until I make a statement. And I can't make a statement until the medical examiner's ready to take it. So I'm stuck."

"A head?" he repeated. "Christ. What are you going to do?"

"What can I do? I guess I'll wait around until Dr. Wolf's done with me, and then I'll come home. Why, what's happening?"

"We got a body."

"Where?"

Quickly he ran down the details of the death call, finishing with, ''I told the widow that she could come right in if she wanted, but she insisted on making arrangements with you. Something about you burying her parents.''

''Yeah. Okay,'' I said, rubbing my eyes under my glasses as I tried to put the image of a grieving widow, counting the seconds until her phone rang, out of my mind. ''Call her back, apologize for me, and tell her I'll be in as soon as I can. Have her start getting her husband's clothes together, and if he was a vet, tell her to dig up his discharge papers. At least that'll keep her mind occupied. Did you send the wagon for the body yet?''

''Yeah.''

''Good. Okay, call Uncle Joe and sit tight. I should be in soon.''

As I was putting the receiver down, a uniformed police officer stepped into the office and said, ''Mr. Hawley, Dr. Wolf will see you now.''

''Wonderful,'' I mumbled, following him back into the receiving dock, where Dr. Wolf was standing in front of Paul J. Larson's open casket, snapping pictures with a Polaroid camera.

Dr. Gordon Wolf's nickname is the Wolfman, both because of his name, and because of the frightful shock of stark white hair he combs straight back off his looming forehead. His hobby is collecting Beatles memorabilia—plastic figurines, old forty-fives, stuff like that—and he's married to a very rich woman who has some pretty remarkable political connections. With one eye squinted shut and the other hidden by the rubber cup of his camera's viewfinder, he said, ''So, Mr. Hawley, what do you think?''

''What do I think about what?'' I asked.

Once the Polaroid had flashed, the Wolfman indicated the open casket with a nod of his head, distractedly waving the developing picture as if drying it.

''Offhand I'd say that it looks like somebody was trying to hide a body,'' I said. ''Or at least a part of a body. Somebody, maybe, who's in the business.''

''Meaning?''

''Meaning, maybe a funeral director. Or even an embalmer.

Who else would have had unobserved access to the casket before it was closed?''

"To hold up this well, I'd say somebody embalmed that head before they packed it in a compound," Dr. Wolf commented, checking the photograph's progress. "Something drying, I should think. We'll know better once I get her to the lab. I wonder where the rest of her is."

"So do I."

"Okay, guys," Dr. Wolf announced. "Take her downtown. Is there anything you'd like to say about this, Mr. Hawley? Any mysterious details you noticed along the way?"

"None that I can think of. Is that the question you kept me waiting two hours to answer?"

"Yup. Irritating, isn't it?"

"Very."

"As long as you're still here," the Wolfman added, a little too cryptically for my taste, "and considering your predilection for this sort of thing, maybe you'd like to accompany me downtown."

Despite myself, I was flattered by his offer. Dr. Wolf, for whatever else he might be, is a top-drawer pathologist. He also owes me, big time. About a year back, I got him off the hook in what could have turned out to be one righteous mess involving both him and his wife. For a time, things between us were tense. But suddenly, about six months ago, he unilaterally decided on a cease-fire. Since then he's been my buddy, more or less. Though I do get the impression that he would love nothing more than to catch me doing something wrong so that he could privately let my transgression slide. Dr. Wolf is not the kind of man who likes owing someone a favor. I think he's looking to pay me back, once and for all.

"Though I appreciate the offer," I said, watching the doctor's face as I did, "I've got a prior commitment. But could you call me when you know something? Could you maybe let me in on what's what?"

"Certainly." He handed me the Polaroid and added, "For your scrapbook." Then he walked away.

I glanced at the photograph, finding, in graphic, flashbulb-whitened detail, the woman's face, gazing back at me, looking very much as she had when I had first pulled that mattress back earlier in the day. She appeared to be between fifty and sixty years old, had short, salt-and-pepper colored hair, remarkably smooth skin, and no teeth. Through the clear plastic in which she was wrapped, her partially open eyes were rolled back in their sockets in a strangely expressionless, almost fish-like way. Only her mouth seemed affected by what she had been through, for her lips, pink with makeup and rubbery with preservative fluid, formed an absurdly startled expression that seemed to say, "What happened? What did they do to me? Who are you?"

That was a person once upon a time, I thought, looking up in time to catch a final glimpse of the head as a cop carried it away like a bowling ball in a bag. That was a person . . . there just had to be a story here. Then, looking at where Mr. Larson was lying quietly in the casket he and the lady had shared for the past five years, I whispered, very softly to myself, "What the hell?"

Nat was sitting with Mr. Larson's file opened on the kitchen table before her, his death certificate in one hand, the Polaroid of the woman's head in the other. Her deep blue-grey eyes were troubled. She was frowning.

Nat's my wife. We've been together almost constantly from very nearly the first day we met, over thirteen years ago, in the same college where she now works as the director of the library's reference section. Of all the couples married from our graduating class, we're the only one that made it. Everybody else got divorced. I can't even imagine getting divorced from Nat. That would be like deciding that I could get along better without my hands. It's that simple. Together we make a whole person; apart, we're incomplete.

Nat looks more exquisite today than she did when I first met her. She is of predominantly German origin, but her great-grandmother was an American Indian. The Native American tinge to her features, the darker skin, the long, straight, jet-black hair, the serene, almost almond-shaped eyes, give her appearance an exotic flavor that has mellowed as she's aged.

I'm biased, but I think my wife is the most beautiful woman in the world.

Sitting at the kitchen table in our apartment over the funeral home, she was still dressed in her work clothes: a black dress covered with pink roses, a pearl necklace, and black, high-heeled shoes. I was leaning against the kitchen sink, drinking citrus-flavored carbonated water from the bottle, waiting for her to speak as I watched Quincy, our cream-colored, male Persian, do his "I'm so happy you're home" dance around her legs. I could hear him purring all the way across the room. Nat was studying the picture of the woman's head, eyes narrowed with concentration, lips pressed tightly together. It surprised me a little that she was looking at it so closely. Normally, Nat doesn't get along with the dead. She's sensitive and cries easily, even for strangers.

"Tell me again what the police found out," she said, laying the photograph aside and turning her attention to the Xeroxed copy of Paul J. Larson's five-year-old death certificate.

It was just after five-thirty. True to his word, Dr. Wolf had called about an hour before to fill me in on his findings. As succinctly as I could, I related those findings to my wife.

"Well," I began, screwing the cap back on the water bottle before placing it on a shelf in the refrigerator, "the Wolfman said that they don't have the faintest notion about who she is. But apparently her teeth weren't extracted after she died, like I thought. They were pulled before . . ."

"While she was alive?" Nat exclaimed.

I raised a placating hand.

"It's not what you're thinking. Her gums had started healing after the teeth were pulled; there were marks, here, along the ridge."

I showed her where by running a finger along my own gum line.

"She had had her teeth extracted professionally, probably in preparation for a dental plate. It was done just a few days, maybe even as much as a couple of weeks, before she died. Other than that, there's not a hell of a lot."

I sighed, thinking aloud.

"Her head was removed from the body fairly neatly. Not

'surgically,' which is Dr. Wolf's term. But it wasn't hacked off—that's the point. It wasn't an ax or anything like that. The incisions were clean, indicating a very sharp instrument, a scalpel probably, and scissors.''

"You can cut someone's head off with scissors?'' Nat asked, surprising me again with the graphic nature of her interest. This wasn't like her.

"You can if you know what you're doing, and have a place, and sufficient time, to do it.''

"So you're saying someone had a private place and plenty of time?''

"That's the implication.''

"And they had surgical instruments?''

"Yes.''

"Go on.''

"Well, there's not much else to say.''

"Where's the rest of her?''

"I don't know.''

"Are they going to look?''

"I suppose. But where can they start? It was just by the wildest coincidence that we found her head. If Mr. Larson's son would have left his father be, we never would have even known it was there.''

Nat fixed me with a peculiar, penetrating stare as she said, "So they aren't going to look, are they, Bill?''

I shrugged, trying to demonstrate that I didn't have anything to do with what the authorities did or didn't do with the case.

"Dr. Wolf said that they'll make all the right noises,'' I said, as Quincy, failing to get Nat's attention by rubbing himself against her legs, took matters into his own hands and jumped up onto her lap. As I spoke, she rubbed the cat's head, making his eyes squint with pleasure.

"They'll do an artist's sketch of her face and run it in the newspaper to see if anyone comes forward who recognizes her. They'll also go over the missing persons' file for the year Mr. Larson was buried, and the years immediately before and after. But other than that, they can't invest too much time or manpower. They've got enough to do that's a lot more likely to turn out right.''

"Meaning?"

"Meaning that once a case is more than a few months old, the percentages drop exponentially as to its likelihood of ever being solved. Something like this—a five-year-old decapitated head . . . no identity . . . no motive. It's like one in a million that anything's ever going to come of it."

"Because they aren't even going to try," Nat observed, looking at me as if it were my fault.

"Hey," I said, "I didn't do it."

"No," she agreed, again lifting the photograph with one hand while continuing to stroke Quincy with the other. "But someone really should do something, Bill. Can't you just feel how wrong this is?"

I exhaled slowly, saying, "Yeah, I know what you mean. I've been thinking about her all day. Maybe it's because her eyes were open. When I pulled back the blanket, there she was, looking up at me like she'd been waiting."

"She was a beautiful woman," Nat commented.

"I suppose."

"And somebody cut her up and buried the pieces in other people's coffins."

"You don't know that."

"It was your idea. If a funeral director wanted to make someone disappear, you said, all he'd have to do is cut up the body and put the pieces in the caskets of his next five or ten funerals. Remember?"

"Yeah. We were talking about that girl's body they found in the park last year. Somehow they always manage to trace things back to a suspect, and I said that if you could just rig things so that the body would never be found, then, for all practical purposes, you wouldn't have a murder."

"But you would have a murder," Nat corrected.

"But nobody would know about it," I said. "So that's like it never happened."

"A tree falling in the woods, huh?"

"That's not what I mean. It's just that the cops need something to go on. They need a corpse. No corpse, no case."

"Well, now you have a corpse . . . or at least a part of one. And you still don't have a case, according to you."

"Not according to me. According to Dr. Wolf."

"You've got a private investigator's license, Bill. It's hanging on your office wall, right next to your funeral director's license, and your gun permit. What if you were to ask around a little, as a supplement to the police? Just to make sure that somebody at least tries, at least makes some kind of effort on her behalf."

I had a hunch that this was where she was going. But I still found it a little hard to believe, even after she'd arrived.

"Private investigators usually have a client," I said. "In this case, I don't."

Nat held the photograph so that I could see the dead woman's face as she said, "What about her? She could be your client."

"She can't pay," I said, trying to soften things with a little joke.

But Nat didn't bite.

"Is that what determines your attitude?" she asked.

"Come on," I returned. "What's eating you?"

I hadn't understood, I guess. Even after so many years together, Nat can still surprise me. Which is exactly what she did that afternoon. I had been functioning under the assumption that she was simply interested in a perplexing circumstance. Instead, she was genuinely emotionally involved.

"I'll be your client," she said, as Quincy jumped to the floor and headed for his dinner bowl. "I'll pay your fee. How about that?"

I stepped forward, took the seat across the table from her, and held both her hands in mine as I looked her straight in the eye and said, "This is really upsetting you, isn't it? It hit home?"

She nodded grimly. Then she took her hands away, stood up, and flipped her long, dark hair back, saying, "Well?"

"Tell me why," I returned.

"You really don't get it, do you?"

"No."

"That woman was a human being, Bill. She probably had a husband, maybe even a family. Someone must have missed her. Someone somewhere is probably still wondering what ever became of her. God . . . if they only knew.''

She paused.

Then, ''She was a human being, and someone chopped her up and hid the pieces . . . like a little kid hiding the pieces of a broken plate. But she's not an object. She deserves better. She deserves more than some police file stuck in a drawer. If they don't identify her, what will they do with her head?''

''Eventually they'll bury it.''

''Where?''

''Potter's Field, I suppose.''

''In an unmarked grave?''

''Look, Nat, I understand how you feel. I feel the same way. But in this particular instance, I'm afraid there's nothing I can do.''

''Not even for me?''

Her eyes were dark, and open very wide. Her features were set in an expectant expression that made me want to do anything she asked, forever. One of the things I have always loved about her is her capacity to feel compassion for others. I also love her spirit . . . that fire in her heart. But still, this time, I was stuck.

''Without a legitimate client to sign a contract, I can't get involved,'' I said, as gently as I could. ''There's too much at stake; we've got too much to lose.''

''So what you're telling me is that you're not even going to think about her anymore, right? You're just going to put her right out of your mind.''

''I doubt if I'll do that,'' I admitted.

''Good,'' Nat said with a satisfied nod. ''You think about her.''

''What's that supposed to mean?'' I asked as she walked past me toward the bedroom.

Over her shoulder she replied, ''Nothing. I'm going to change my clothes, and then I'm going to make dinner. Why don't you relax in your office for a while? Maybe you can think in there.''

Dammit, I thought, realizing what she meant. She knew me better than I did myself.

''I know what's going through that mind of yours,'' I called down the hall after Nat had disappeared around the corner. "You think I can't do it. You think it's going to drive me nuts until I have to try and work it out. Well, not this time, sweetie. No way. I'm stronger than you think. If I say no, it's no. You just watch."

"Fine," she called back. "Dinner will be ready in about an hour."

"You don't believe me, do you?"

"Whatever you say, Bill," she replied.

I picked up Mr. Larson's file from where she had left it on the kitchen table. Removing the Polaroid Dr. Wolf had given me of the woman's head, I stared at it, saying softly, "When I say no, it's no."

TWO

■■■■■■■■■■■

AFTER DINNER, JUST as an intellectual exercise, I went over Paul J. Larson's death certificate, since it was the one really solid piece of information I had in my possession. As such as I hated to admit it, Nat had been right in her implied conviction that I wouldn't be able to leave this thing alone. It was going to nag at me, I knew. It was inevitable. So, after I finished washing the dinner dishes, just for something to do, I sat myself down in my office and decided to look things over. I wasn't going to get involved, I reiterated to myself . . . not without a paying customer to justify my efforts. But there certainly wasn't any harm in thinking things through.

I started with Nat's notion about someone in the funeral business having committed murder before disposing of the body by dismemberment and scattered burial in the graves of strangers. Immediately I saw that, even though it fit the circumstances, her conclusion was nothing but conjecture based on the flimsiest evidence. Not that a severed head hidden in a casket is flimsy evidence . . . but extrapolating a whole series of supposedly related events from a single object, no matter how suggestive that object might be, is a definite no-no when it comes to an investigation.

My mentor, and the master P.I. under whom I had sort of served my apprenticeship, Larry Fizner—who was supposedly dying of cancer, although he didn't act like it—would have been the first person to point out the inherent fallacy in Nat's reasoning. If I had presented her conclusion as my own, Larry would have lit a cigarette, paused, and then, using a lot of swear words, proceeded to construct a flawlessly logical case for my being a perfect moron.

That's Larry Fizner.

That's not me.

First rule of poking your nose where it really doesn't belong:

Don't jump to conclusions, take your time, do it right.

Second rule:

Keep it low-key, let the evidence speak for itself.

Third rule:

Take whatever help you can get.

My first impulse, in line with rule number three, was to call to see what Larry Fizner had to say. During the nine months since I had officially received my private investigator's license, we had been working as a kind of half-assed team on a fairly regular basis. We had even placed a joint advertisement in the yellow pages. Since my brother Jerry had decided to serve his apprenticeship in preparation for taking the test for his own funeral director's license, I had been finding more time to devote to things outside the funeral home. But still, I let Larry pretty much take care of almost all the calls we got for investigations, since most of those calls were the kind of bullshit, wayward-husband-or-wife-surveillance jobs that Larry does so well, and seems to enjoy so much. I find such work both boring and, to be brutally honest, luridly pathetic.

Private investigating, it has been my experience, isn't a very romantic profession. It involves a lot of long, uneventful hours spent sitting in a car, clutching a camera equipped with a telephoto lens, waiting to get a shot of some cheap motel that can be used in one divorce case or another. But every once in a while a case comes along that's special, that resonates, that calls out, perhaps because of its subtlety, or its portent, for attention. Every once in a while a case comes along that, try as I might, I simply can't ignore.

Was this such a case? I wondered. Was there really something here, or were my wife and I reading more into it than there could possibly be? Was this even a case of actual murder? Despite the implied violence inherently contained within the circumstances of my discovery, there still wasn't a single, solid piece of evidence that pointed positively toward a capital crime.

At least not yet.

Once the coroner determined a cause of death, perhaps I'd know better. But given that she was working with a disembodied head, I had my doubts as to how accurately she could determine anything, short of the obvious—like the race of the deceased, her approximate age to within five years or so, and maybe even her height, roughly. But unless the terminal trauma, assuming there even was a terminal trauma, was delivered to the skull, the coroner might not be able to say more about what had killed her than that the capillaries in her eyes were ruptured, indicating that she had died of asphyxia . . . which is a fancy way of saying that she was strangled or otherwise deprived of oxygen. Or that her skin showed residual signs of poisoning. Arsenic stays in the hair, so I supposed there was always that. . . .

But so what?

What was I doing?

What was the plan?

I had to admit that I really wasn't sure exactly where I stood. Even with the image of that woman's sunken, imploring eyes seared, as it was, into my memory, I still couldn't decide if there was anything here that I could actually *solve*—which is, I think, the central root of what I do when I get rolling in an investigation. It's the brass ring, I suppose . . . the goal. I'm a very goal-oriented person; I need an object toward which to strive. Until I could organize my impressions into a more cognizant whole, I lacked, at the deepest level possible, a sense of direction. At present I was groping, which, I have found through experience, is a time when it is best for me to allow my mind to wander, to observe while resisting the urge to judge, to meander instead of march. I do that better when I'm on my own.

So, despite my inclination to ask Larry Fizner for his opinion, I decided to hold off until I had had a chance to do a brain work of my own because I knew once Larry was given an opportunity to sink his teeth into a problem, he would have some very definite notions as to what course of action was appropriate.

An Ohio death certificate provides a lot of information, such as the deceased's name, age, birth date and place, Social Security number, place of residence, schooling, occupation, parents' names, next of kin or person responsible for the disposition of the body, attending physician's name and diagnosis as to a cause of death, and any pertinent factors thereto, the place of the deceased's final disposition, and, most importantly at that moment as far as I could tell, the name of the person who embalmed the body, as well as the firm that took care of the funeral.

As much as I hate to admit it, and at the risk of sounding like the moron Larry Fizner would have surely accused me of being, I have to confess that I agreed with Nat's conclusion about it being someone related to the funeral business who had disposed of our mystery woman's body by chopping it up and sticking part of it in a stranger's casket. So . . .

Death certificate line number 23:

The Noland Funeral Home, 9844 Scranton Road, Cleveland, Ohio 44109.

I looked it up in the phone book, only to find that it wasn't listed, making me think: out of business.

The Noland Funeral Home—God, that took me back.

My first job in high school had been carrying bodies for a private ambulance company, which served to familiarize me with virtually every hospital and funeral home in the area. The Noland Funeral Home, as I remembered it, was one of those old-fashioned establishments that had started life as an opulent, sprawling private home, ending up as a funeral parlor after the addition of sliding doors, public bathrooms, and a parking lot. It had a set of six or seven stone steps leading up to a pair of leaded-glass doors that emptied into a towering foyer in which hung an immense chandelier on a black steel chain. Inside there was lots of dark paneling, booming hardwood floors, and an ever-present air of genteel mourning that overhung the place like a shadow. You just wanted to whisper in there, whether you knew the deceased personally or not. It was the kind of place that made you want to take off your hat and keep your voice down.

Much like its owner, Marshall Noland.

Old Marsh: what a character.

When I was sixteen, he must have been seventy, so that meant that if he was still alive he would be close to ninety years old today. He was, as I recalled, your stereotypical undertaker of his generation—tall, lean, with stooping shoulders, a balding head, and the grim, long-faced, subdued-tone-of-voice demeanor that just dripped insincere sympathy. At least that was how he came off to his families, who ate it up because, back then, that's how they expected a funeral director to act.

But in contrast to his professional facade, in private Marsh Noland was a genuinely nice man who loved a joke, loved to laugh, and was always ready to buy a drink, lend a hand, or slip a sixteen-year-old kid delivering a body to his funeral home for a private ambulance company in the middle of the night a five-dollar bill as a tip, winking conspiratorially as he did and whispering, "That's for you. Don't tell the boss." He was the kind of guy you just couldn't help but like. And I did like him, making it all the more difficult for me to imagine what in the hell he could have to do with murder.

There was that word again.

Murder.

I rubbed my eyes.

The desk at which I was sitting was the same one upon which my grandmother had taught me to read. When we were kids, Jerry had a nervous condition that affected his stomach so badly that he only kept down about a third of what he ate. The doctors wanted to operate, but my mother said no, deciding that all he needed was a little special attention. So, while I was still too young for school, she farmed me out to her mother during the day so that she would have more time to devote to him.

Grandma believed in books, not TV. Instead of parking me in front of the tube to watch cartoons, she sat me down at her writing desk and taught me how to read when I was still only about three years old. I remember being bored out of my mind my first two years of school, sitting there staring out the window while the other kids learned their letters. They probably should have skipped me a couple of grades, but instead they decided that it was more important that I learn social skills among children my own age. What a crock. My school experience, I maintain to this day, is at least partially responsible for me turning out twisted.

Anyway.

I was sitting at my grandmother's desk, which I refinished after she died, staring at Mr. Larson's death certificate, when I noticed the embalmer's name:

Edward Craig.

License number 6514-C.

Edward Craig?

Why did I remember that name?

Snapping my fingers I jumped up and called to where Nat was sewing in her workroom that I was going out for about an hour. She looked up from the quilt she was working on— Nat's *always* working on a quilt—and said that she hadn't heard the phone ring. Which was verbal shorthand for, we didn't get a body call, so you're not going out on business. And you never go out without taking me along unless it's on business. So where are you going?

I kissed her on the forehead, responding to all her unasked questions by saying, "I'm taking the Miata. I won't be long."

"Can I come?" she asked, eyes bright with triumphant knowledge.

I shook my head, making her ask, "Why not?"

"Because," I replied, "you wouldn't like where I'm going."

"Oh." She shrugged, returning to her work and adding, "Well, have fun."

That's another thing I love about Nat:

When she's right, she doesn't gloat.

In the funeral home's triple-car garage I dropped the ragtop on our Mazda Miata—a 1990 model, bright red with a black interior, two seats, automatic transmission, and a Ford V-8 engine that a friend of mine stuck under the hood in place of the four-cylinder installed at the factory—buckled up, and hit the automatic door opener clipped to the sun visor.

The place I was heading—just to ask a few harmless questions, nothing more—is called Greenleaf Mortuary Shipping, and is located in the "valley," which is a fairly new industrial park complex not far from my funeral home. In the front of the building there's a shipping and receiving department with about six secretaries busily tapping away at clicking computer keyboards twenty-four hours a day. In the back there's a crematory retort in a room adjoining a ten-table embalming facility in which there's always somebody being embalmed, no matter when you visit, day or night.

Their main business is picking up, embalming, and shipping remains from one city to another. They have a network of funeral homes with which they work, so that if a person should pass away in, say, Seattle, and the family in, say, Nashville wants to bury him in Tennessee, Greenleaf Mortuary Shipping will contact the funeral home with which they are affiliated in Seattle, have the person picked up, embalmed, and flown to Nashville, all paperwork squared away. I've used them myself, and they do a nice, professional job.

They also do trade embalming, which means that they will, for a fee, pick up a remains, take it to their shop, embalm, cosmeticize, dress, and deliver it to your funeral home. It used to be that practically every funeral director in Ohio either was an embalmer or had an embalmer on staff. Not so anymore. As a matter of fact, things are kind of leaning away from embalming on the premises, since it probably won't be long before, for environmental reasons, funeral homes aren't going to be allowed to use the sewer system to dispose of their liquid waste. Pretty soon, the prep room's slop sink is going to have to empty into an underground, hazardous materials holding tank, which will cost like fifty grand to install. Since most places won't be able to afford a tank, the time will come when there will be central embalming facilities, like Greenleaf Mortuary Shipping, that will serve all the funeral homes in a particular area.

The reason I was going there was that the embalmer's name on Mr. Larson's death certificate, Edward Craig, was one that I recognized as belonging to a trade embalmer I had met a couple of times over the years. Though I happened to know that he didn't presently work for Greenleaf M.S., if anybody knew his particulars, it would be Greenleaf's embalming room supervisor, a man named Bob White, who knew absolutely everything about absolutely everybody even vaguely associated with the funeral business anywhere in the state.

To look at it, you wouldn't pick Greenleaf Mortuary Shipping out of the crowd as being any different than any of the other buildings on its street. It looks rather like some kind of small, manufacturing facility, with blond brick walls, tinted windows on the office area, and bay doors around back. You have to buzz to get in, which I did.

It was pushing nine o'clock, so it was dark outside, and, even though it was already late May with summer coming on fast, the evening air was still northern-Ohio, close-to-Lake-Erie, turn-up-your-collar cold. Too cold really to have been riding with the convertible top down. But in Cleveland you get so few months when you can really enjoy a convertible, I tend to push it. Consequently, my face was stinging from the freezing wind I had endured on the way over—with the stereo blasting an Oingo Boingo tape and the heater blowing full go. My nose was a little numb and runny. And when they saw me, the girls in the office all smiled at once.

There's a strange camaraderie among people in the business that I'm not sure I understand. I suppose it exists in all professions, but in the funeral industry it seems particularly strong. Maybe it's just that, since we're perceived as being so weird by the general public, we tend to band together in self-defense. Or maybe it's because the business attracts a specific kind of person, so therefore we all get along. But the tendency is for all the local funeral people to know each other. I don't. I'm lousy with names. But I smile a lot and act enthusiastic, so I usually get by.

As I expected, Bob White was in. He's always in. I think he lives there. You can stop by any time and find him, dressed in his stained white smock, either just peeling on or just peeling off a pair of rubber gloves, with the ''World's Greatest Dad'' coffee mug at his side that he uses as an ashtray. The guy just embalms. That's all he does. Actually, thinking about it, I don't believe I've ever seen him outside of an embalming room. I've never seen him, say, in a restaurant. Maybe he's like a vampire and would turn to dust under anything but fluorescent light.

He grinned when he saw me, peeling off a rubber glove so that he could shake my hand as he asked, "Is this a social call, or are you playing detective again?"

Playing detective.

That's a term I don't hear a lot anymore. Ever since my last "case," things have changed for me, both publicly and in the business. There was a time, and it wasn't so long ago, that the O.O.F.P., the Ohio Organization of Funeral Professionals, which is our industry's state oversight committee, disapproved of my ancillary activities. But after the governor's office contacted them to say what a wonderful job I had done in the last situation I unraveled, the organization's attitude mysteriously changed. Suddenly I'm an item, and little articles about me have started popping up in trade magazines and newspapers, all endorsed, and sometimes even written, by members of the group. I've been asked to give talks outlining some of my activities, and people tend to know who I am . . . which can be both a blessing and pain. But the bottom line is that, at least in the funeral community, I'm no longer an anonymous entity. When I show up, just about anywhere, someone is sure to know my name.

Shaking Bob's hand, I admitted that I was looking for information, asking if we could talk in private. Bob got serious as he led me to his office, leaving on his bloody smock and one rubber glove.

"Coffee?" he asked, closing the door and snapping a wall switch that flooded the tiny room with way too much fluorescent light.

"No, thanks," I said, deciding to get right to the point. "Bob, what do you know about a trade man named Edward Craig?"

Bob sat down behind his desk and shook an English cigarette out of a box, which he then lifted my way. I declined with a quick movement of my hand, making him ask, "Quitting again?"

"Yes."

He smiled.

Bob White is a short, rather round little man, with a jocular smile and a tiny, Oliver Hardy moustache that makes him look positively jaunty. He looks like anything but an embalmer. If it weren't for the bloodstains on his clothes, I think most people would peg him as an ice-cream store owner. Even with the bloodstains, you'd probably be more inclined to think of him as the friendly butcher than someone so intimately associated with human death. He has short, grey hair, bright, tiny green eyes, and a wide-open smile that makes you want to trust him. Which I do.

"Edward Craig," he said, leaning back and inhaling smoke. "Has he been naughty?"

I shrugged, indicating, I hoped, that I had yet to decide.

"I'd believe it if you said that he has," Bob said, smiling. "Guy's a germ. I never liked him."

This took me a little aback since it's been my experience that Bob White likes just about everybody. I sat down in a chair in front of his desk.

"I think he's in jail," Bob continued. "Or in Florida. So what did he do?"

"I don't know," I replied. "Nothing, probably. His name just came up on a death certificate, and I kind of wanted to chase him down."

"Good luck," Bob said, shaking his head. " 'Cause he's long gone—from around here, anyway. So, are you going to tell me the dirty details or not?"

After a moment's consideration I explained about the woman's head.

"Ooh," he said, looking me straight in the eye. "That's nasty. And Ed was the embalmer?"

I nodded, asking, "What about Marsh Noland? Is he still around?"

Bob frowned as he replied, "Nope. Marsh died about three years ago."

"That's about what I expected. But what makes you say that Edward Craig's in jail?"

"It's nothing to do with anything professional," Bob replied. "It was domestic, more like. I don't know the details, but there was something going around a couple of years ago about him beating up on his wife. Or else she was beating up on him. His picture was in the paper. I remember that."

"Did he ever work at a funeral home? You know, anything regular?"

"Nah." Bob killed his half-smoked cigarette in an ashtray that had the name of a local vault company stamped all over it. "He was strictly a trade man. Moved around. Didn't really like people all that much. He stayed in the back. You know, the Igor type."

That's an inside joke since there seem to be two kinds of people involved in the business. One is the front man, the glad-hander, the guy who chats up the mourners and puts people at ease . . . the Marsh Noland types who can make friends at a fire. Then there are the guys in the back, the embalmers and pencil pushers who do better with their heads down—not much personality, though they end up doing most of the work.

"Why was his picture in the paper?" I asked.

Bob leaned forward as he said, "Craig was a drunk with a gambling problem." He paused and looked at me kind of cockeyed, asking as an aside, "You still sober?"

"Yes," I replied. "For almost five years now."

"Good. You made a lousy drunk."

"Thank you."

"Anyway, Craig's the kind of asshole that gives everybody in the business a black eye. If I had to bet, I'd lay odds that he hasn't spent more than like a week of his adult life out of debt. He was always short of cash. And he was always either just coming off or just climbing on to a drunk. Eventually it got to the point where there wasn't really all that much difference anymore.

"But he was a crackerjack embalmer, even stiff. You couldn't take that away from him. Which I suppose accounts for how he got away with it for as long as he did. Eventually, though, it started catching up with him. His work got sloppy. Bodies were purging; guys were complaining. Last place he worked trade that I know about was out of Roper's, downtown. I was doing independent trade myself about that time, and Ed came to me asking maybe if I could use a hand covering my accounts. I knew he was on what amounted to a probation at Roper's, just this far from getting pink-slipped, so I turned him down—even though God knows I could have used the help. The next thing I hear, he's been arrested.''

Bob peeled off his other glove and dropped it in the wastebasket behind his desk. From where I was sitting, though, it looked as if he just dropped it on the floor.

"It was kind of a bad scene," he said, folding his hands.

"About when was this?" I asked.

"1989."

"You sure?"

He nodded.

"How come I don't remember anything about it?"

"I'm surprised you don't."

"Wait a minute. Was this that guy . . . yeah, it had to be!"

Bob was nodding.

Suddenly, I remembered the story:

In the newspaper Edward Craig was reported to have been arrested on a count of domestic assault stemming from an altercation he and his wife had on their front lawn, very late at night. It was in the local papers, and wouldn't have been all that interesting if it weren't for the fact that Craig's name was linked to another, more serious incident that was, at that time, an ongoing, potential scandal.

Supposedly, an unnamed local funeral home had been charging families for services they weren't performing. The details were fuzzy, but the gist was that unembalmed bodies were supposedly being cosmeticized and shown at viewings. It was exactly the kind of crap that makes every funeral director in the world cringe. Tabloid fodder of the worst kind. The makings of a smear that we would all be living down, whether the allegations proved to be true or not, for years.

Edward Craig, though never charged, was implicated because he was the trade embalmer this particular firm used to do its work. Eventually there were rumors of quiet settlements out of court between the funeral home and some of the concerned families. There were even rumors that the whole thing had been one big scam by a particular family to extort money from the firm, using the threat of character assassination as the stick. Even those of us on the inside were never sure exactly what had happened, and ultimately we didn't much care. All we cared about was that the newspapers finally stopped hammering on the reputation of all funeral homes in general so business could get back to normal.

"It's a little hazy," I said, after having recalled what I could. "I can't seem to nail down whether Craig got popped or not."

"He did and he didn't," Bob White said. "His wife dropped the assault charges, but from what I heard she still raped him on the divorce. Got everything, which wasn't much. But it left Ed with like nothing at all. After his name was in the paper, and with his drinking becoming so flagrant, nobody would touch him as an embalmer. He was really down-and-out. That's why I said that I thought he was probably in jail. That was the rumor. Though there was another one that said he moved to Florida, which, now that I'm thinking about it, is the one I would tend to believe."

"Why Florida?" I asked.

"I don't know. Maybe so he can sleep outside year-round."

"Was he really that bad off?"

"Pretty damned close."

"And this was in '89?"

"Yup."

"About when?"

"Early on, I guess. I remember there was snow on the ground when he and his wife had their misunderstanding on the lawn, because Ed was supposedly so drunk that he didn't notice that he wasn't wearing any shoes."

As Bob was speaking, I was remembering the date of Paul J. Larson's burial, which was in January of that same year.

"Are you sure it wasn't later on in 1989, maybe the following winter?" I asked. "Like maybe November or December?"

"No," Bob said, shaking his head. "It was early in 1989. I'm positive."

"Why?"

"Because we didn't get snow for Christmas that winter until after New Year's. My kid had just turned four, and it was like the first Christmas she could really understand. She wanted snow real bad, but it just didn't happen. So, to keep her from being too disappointed, I bought a bag of that phony snow and sprinkled it all over the carpet around the tree. It took us a month to vacuum it all up.

"Why? Is that important?"

I frowned, rubbing my chin as I thought, did Edward Craig's personal and professional problems have anything to do with the woman's head I had found hidden in a casket coincidentally buried during that very year's first dependably cold month?

"I don't know," I said finally. "But thanks."

Bob stood up, apparently taking the hint that we were through. Sticking out his hand to shake, he said, "So, are you going to give that seminar they've been talking about? That 'Dick Tracy of the Funeral Home' thing? Sounds like an easy two credits."

Funeral directors and embalmers in Ohio have to complete eleven hours of continuing education credits every two years in order to renew their licenses. The O.O.F.P. had decided that, if I agreed to give it, the seminar to which Bob referred would be worth two hours to anyone attending.

"I don't know," I said. "I don't really want to. But then again, I don't think it's a good idea to antagonize the officers of the O.O.F.P., now that I'm back in their good graces."

We made a little more small talk, and then I left, wondering all the way home—ragtop up this time because now that it was nearly eleven at night it was downright freezing outside—what, if anything, Edward Craig's bad luck really meant.

And what about Marsh Noland? I remembered him as being a nice enough guy to give a down-on-his-lucker like Edward Craig a break by throwing a little work his way. I could certainly see that, knowing Marsh. I really could. It would be just like him.

But a severed head?

No.

That was way off the scale.

I took the long way home, swinging down Scranton Road to see what kind of shape the old Noland Funeral Home was in. It was a depressing sight, putting it mildly. The windows were all broken, the yard was overgrown, and on the whole it looked as empty and downtrodden as Edward Craig's reputation.

The Miata's engine was idling smoothly, a low rumble that vibrated the entire car with an underpinning of power, patiently anticipating its opportunity to run. I was sitting by the curb, looking at the old building, with two thoughts hammering in my head, which were:

Who was the mystery lady hidden in the casket of a stranger?

And . . .

Where was Edward Craig now?

For some reason that I would have been hard-pressed to put into words, I was suddenly convinced that an answer to either one of those two questions would lead, inevitably, to an answer to the other.

THREE
■■■■■■■■■■■■

THE PHONE RANG at exactly eight o'clock the next morning. I took the call, wrote down a name on the pad I keep on the night table next to my bed, and stumbled into the kitchen, where Nat laid a computer printout on the table before me at the exact same moment I sat down. While I was out asking Bob White questions the night before, she had fired up my computer's modem, tapping into the store of information contained in the college library's mainframe, following a track I myself had inadvertently set her on before I left.

"Not that you're interested," she said slyly. "But in case you are . . ."

But before I looked at the printout, I asked where my brother was, since he hadn't been in when I got home the night before.

"Jerry's out," Nat said.

"Out," I grumbled, hands wrapped around a coffee mug that had a caricature of Sherlock Holmes printed on its front. I was wearing a pair of black boxer shorts and a "Batman Returns" T-shirt. I hadn't showered yet, so my hair was standing straight up on my head—a little trick it has started performing recently. Isn't the aging process fun? And I needed a shave. "Out where?"

"He's in love." Nat shrugged, dropping a tea bag in the garbage pail under the sink and adding, "Who was on the phone?"

"The morgue. Dr. Wolf thinks he's got a name on the dead woman. It's only, what, like eight a.m.? When did Jerry leave?"

"I don't think he ever came home last night."

"Dammit."

"Come on, Bill," Nat said, sitting down across the table from me. "Cut him some slack."

"She's going to bite him on the ass, Nat," I said, feeling the anger rising and having a truly hard time doing anything about it. "She's a screwed-up, recent widow with a kid . . . and I think she's still on dope. Jerry's just asking for trouble with her. He can do better."

"He's in a wheelchair," Nat apparently found it necessary to remind me. "In his mind, he probably doesn't think he can do at all."

"Ellie Lyttle is a flake," I said definitively. "If Jerry thinks that he's got to settle for somebody like her because of his handicap, then he deserves whatever crap he gets."

"She's had a hard time," Nat said, referring to the fact that Ellie Lyttle's husband had been mauled to death by a dog, and that, not so very long ago, when she had been my client, I had been inclined to overlook her emotional shortcomings. The trouble was that now, with her being involved with my younger brother, I had taken to judging her harshly, dismissing her out of hand as a disaster simply waiting to happen.

"She's got a kid," I said again. "And she's an addict."

"So, you're an addict too."

"I straightened up."

"Maybe she'll do the same."

"Because of Jerry?"

"You never know. You've said yourself that I was responsible for you getting sober."

"You're the love of my life."

"Thank you. But if you'll recall, Jerry wasn't exactly enthusiastic about me when we first got together."

"I never gave a damn what he thought about you. You were none of his business."

"Maybe Ellie's none of yours."

"He's my brother, Nat. I've got a responsibility."

"Because you put him in that wheelchair?"

"No," I said, because I knew if I said anything else, she'd jump on me with both feet. "Just because."

"He's thirty-two years old, Bill. He can do what he wants."

I lifted the printout she had placed on the table, saying, "Tell me about this," in hopes of changing the subject. Whether Nat liked it or not, Jerry and I were going to have it out just as soon as he came home.

Nat couldn't hide the pride in her voice as she described what she had done while I was out the previous evening. Since I had mentioned Edward Craig's name before I left, as well as the name of the Noland Funeral Home, she had used our computer's modem to tap into the college library's reference section, running through the *Cleveland Plain Dealer*'s death notices for the month corresponding to the funeral of Paul J. Larson. The printout was a list of all the services that the Noland Funeral Home had advertised during the months of January, February, and March 1989.

"So," I said, folding the printout back up, "you think the rest of her is hidden in these caskets?"

Nat looked grim as she replied, "I think it's possible."

"So what am I supposed to do, start digging?"

"I was just trying to help," she grumbled. Then she added, "How did the morgue put a name to her face so fast?"

"Some new missing persons' computer program that scans the features of a case into its memory. Apparently, the thing matches specific reference points to establish a mathematical probability when comparing an unidentified subject to the photographs of known missing persons."

"Who do they think she is?"

"They didn't say. But apparently they've got some guy named"—I glanced at the notepaper—"Younger, coming down to talk to me."

"About what?"

"I don't know."

"Is he a policeman?"

"I should think so," I said. Adding, "Nat? Tell you what. Do you want to know what would be even more interesting than what you found out about Edward Craig last night?"

She nodded, quite seriously.

"If you were to use your library computer to look into the county's vital statistics record, you could find out exactly how many bodies Edward Craig embalmed, where, when, and for whom."

"How could I do that?"

I lifted the printout, saying, "While it's true that the funerals the Noland Funeral Home advertised in the paper around the same time as they did Paul J. Larson's were a good place to start, the fact remains that Edward Craig was a trade embalmer. If he was working for Marsh Noland, he was probably working for somebody else. Now, given what I found out about the state of his personal life at the time, the chances of his having a lot of other accounts are probably pretty slim. But who knows? Guys get in a pinch, need an embalmer fast, and take whoever they can get. But if you were to go over all the funerals in the county during those target months, looking for his name, that would tell us a lot more than what we already know."

"All of them?" Nat said. "How am I supposed to tell if he was involved or not?"

"He'll be listed on the death certificate as the embalmer. It'll probably take some time . . . but what you'll have to do is hook up to the public records kept by the division of vital statistics and scan down the line. I'd figure that you can count on looking at a couple of hundred certificates."

Just then the doorbell rang.

"Jesus," I said, glancing at the clock over the refrigerator to find that it was barely 8:15. "They're not messing around."

"I've got to get to work anyway," Nat said, rising from her seat. "You get dressed, and on my way out I'll set whoever it is up with a cup of coffee and tell him that you'll be right down."

"Thanks," I said, kissing her as she left.

I was shaved and dressed in one of my many black suits in less than twenty minutes. When I descended the stairs to my office, I found a middle-aged man standing with his back to me, looking out the window next to my desk. He was wearing a smoke-grey, three-piece suit, and his grey-blond hair was immaculately cut. An empty coffee mug stood in the crystal ashtray I've got on my desk. And there was a brown leather briefcase leaning against the leather recliner in the corner.

The man turned when he heard me come in, revealing a nicely proportioned face, with clear green eyes, a thin, rather harsh-looking nose, and a stern, even cruel mouth, half of which was trying to smile. "Mr. Hawley," he said, stepping around the desk and offering me his hand. "I'm Truman Younger, New American Life Insurance. It's a pleasure to meet you."

I shook his hand and offered him more coffee, which he accepted. After I had mixed us both a cup of instant at the wet bar in the cabinet next to my desk, we took our seats, and Mr. Younger got to it.

"Our company would like to hire you to investigate the disappearance of Madeline Chase," he said, speaking to the floor as he opened his briefcase and fished out a fat file folder, which he placed on the desk before me.

"Madeline Chase," I said, glancing at the file without touching it. "That must be the name they came up with for the woman I found—right?"

"Correct," he replied. "We've had a missing person's report open on her for nearly five years now, which is partially why the coroner was able to identify her so quickly. We were just about to declare that file closed, so your discovery couldn't have come at a more opportune time."

"How so?"

"Madeline Chase," he explained, "maiden name, Parker, was reported missing by her husband, Everett, in February of 1989. An investigation ensued, conducted by both the police and our own private investigative staff, turning up a couple of interesting leads, but nothing solid that would indicate Mrs Chase's whereabouts. After six weeks without a word, Mr. Chase filed for payment of the life insurance benefits due him in the event of his wife's death, which, as you might well imagine, was a substantial amount."

"How much?" I asked, pulling the file to me and opening it to the first page, which had a black-and-white photograph of Mrs. Chase paper-clipped to a sheet describing her vital statistics. She looked considerably better in the photo than she had the last time I'd seen her.

"Exactly one million dollars," Mr. Younger replied, reaching to the file I was examining and extricating a sheet from the bottom of the stack. It was the benefits schedule on a term life insurance policy taken out in the name of Madeline Ackermann in December of 1980.

"Maiden name, Parker; insurance policy name, Ackermann," I observed. "So this Everett Chase was what, her second husband?"

"Yes," Younger agreed, "Her first husband, Daniel Ackermann, was a high-powered, heavy-equipment salesman who blew himself out at the age of forty-two. Died of a stroke. I guess his blood pressure went through the roof and he ignored everything his doctors said. When it finally happened, he was dead before he hit the floor. He made a ton in his lifetime, and spent money like he was mad at it, from what I've been told. But he took out two matching policies, one on himself and one on his wife, both for a million a piece. When he died, we paid. Then Mrs. Ackermann married Everett Chase, and the couple continued paying the premiums on her existing policy, without initiating similar coverage for her new husband."

"Did you settle up on her second husband's claim?"

"Not exactly. Without a death certificate, we aren't obligated to deliver any benefits directly. But, by law, we do have to secure the funds in an escrow account until that time when the insured party is either located or declared legally dead."

"So, even without a body, you'd have to make good eventually."

"Correct."

"In Ohio, it's what, like six years that a person has to be unaccounted for before they can be legally declared deceased. Right?"

"Correct again."

"So you've got just a little less than one year before the trust fund reverts to . . . whom?"

"Originally, the first beneficiary was Everett Chase, the lady's second husband, since at the time the policy was redrawn she apparently considered her children, a son named Ronald and a daughter named Allison, too young to take possession of so much money,'' Younger said, pointing at the benefits schedule. ''But that changed when Allison, the oldest, turned twenty-one. As a legal adult, she assumed the position of primary beneficiary. Once Ronald reaches the same age, which will happen in just a few weeks, he'll take over the number two spot, bumping Everett Chase, the children's stepfather, down to number three—or, depending on your point of view, effectively eliminating him from the list of potential heirs.''

I glanced at the benefits schedule, drank some coffee, and thought about trust funds, asking, ''Is this escrow account interest-bearing?''

The gleam in Truman Younger's eyes told me that I had hit upon something important.

''As a matter of fact, it is,'' he said, shuffling more papers. ''Five years, so far, at a very tidy, fluctuating annual interest rate. The eighties were a good time for investments.''

''So we're not talking about a million dollars anymore.''

''No,'' he agreed. ''We're not.''

''How much are we talking about?''

''Close in on a million five.''

I took this in, imagining a long row of zeros.

''Okay, Mr. Younger, spell it out.''

''Obviously, Mr. Hawley,'' he said, ''considering the amount of money involved, it's vital that our company verify the circumstances surrounding the death of the insured party, as much for the protection of our clients, as our own.''

''Is murder covered?'' I asked.

''Yes.''

''Then what's the problem?''

''It all depends on who did the murdering.''

''What's that supposed to mean?''

''Not long after Madeline Chase disappeared, her daughter Allison turned up dead.''

''Accident?''

''Hardly.''

''What are you implying, Mr. Younger?''

''I'm not implying anything. But what I am proposing is that, before our company releases 1.5 million dollars as payment for the death of one of our clients, we would very much like to make certain that the circumstances surrounding her death didn't directly involve any of the beneficiaries. Does that make sense, Mr. Hawley? Without pointing any fingers, suffice it to say that the amount of money in question can be a tremendous motivator, and that a company like ours, a company responsible for paying claims on demand, has a right to certain assurances. Let's leave it at that, shall we?''

''All right,'' I said, leaning back in my chair. ''Leaving it at that . . . what exactly is it that you want me to do?''

''Pick up where our investigator left off five years ago. Everything he found recorded is in this file, so you can start from there.''

''Why don't you just have the same person finish the job he started?''

''He's no longer with us, and, quite frankly, your name was supplied to us by a very respectable source, with a recommendation of the highest order.''

''Really? Now who would do that?''

''Your county's medical examiner. Dr. Gordon Wolf.''

''Dr. Wolf recommended me?''

''Forcefully.''

I thought about that, and then said, ''I noticed that there wasn't anything about Mrs. Chase in this morning's paper. I thought they were going to run her picture?''

''Madeline Chase was tentatively identified early yesterday evening. Since the missing person's report on her listed our company as one of the concerned parties, we were contacted immediately after Everett Chase was informed. Since we already had a reliable identification, there wasn't any reason for further publicity that we could see, so we asked that the newspaper not be involved.''

''How did Mr. Chase feel about that request?''

''He concurred with our assessment.''

''You've spoken to him?''

''Yes.''

''What's he think about his wife's head being found?''

''He's appropriately upset.''

''That's an interesting choice of words.''

"It's accurate."

"Did he say anything about releasing the funds now that his wife's been verified as deceased?"

"No. But I expect he will."

"When?"

"Soon."

"How soon?"

"Well, that all depends. The computer program that first called up Mrs. Chase's name as a possible match to the specifics of the remains you found is not recognized, legally, as an independent, impartial authority."

"Which means," I cut in, "that technically Madeline Chase still isn't dead."

"Technically, that's correct."

"When can Everett Chase start the claim process rolling again?"

"As soon as the county coroner signs an official finding verifying the identity of remains number, uh, 100945-F as that of Madeline Chase. Until that time, the identification is strictly unofficial, and therefore in no way legally binding."

"When will the coroner sign the million-dollar document?"

"I don't know."

"Guess."

"It could be this afternoon, or tomorrow, or next week. She could have done it already this morning, and I've just yet to be informed. I simply don't have any way of knowing how many of the ten or so items of physical evidence she needs for her determination to stand up in court she's actually compiled."

"So we're working on a deadline, so to speak," I said.

"It's more of a ticking time bomb, Mr. Hawley," Truman Younger replied.

After draining the last of my coffee, I folded my hands atop my desk and stared at them for a moment. Then, glancing up, I said, "As interesting as all this sounds, Mr. Younger, and frankly, as interested as I am, isn't it all besides the point? It seems to me that your company's clearest course would be to verify the alibis of each of the beneficiaries to determine, categorically, that they couldn't have had anything to do with

Mrs. Chase's demise, and then, once the coroner signs her finding, release the funds you're holding to the appropriate party.''

''What about apprehending the culprit?''

''I don't see where that fits into whether or not New American Life Insurance makes good on a legitimate claim for benefits.''

''What if the police fail to find the guilty party?''

''Again, what's that got to do with you paying up?''

''We would prefer to be sure.''

''And the judgment of the police wouldn't be enough?''

''No.''

''That's a pretty cynical attitude, Mr. Younger.''

Rising, Truman Younger reached into the inside breast pocket of his jacket, withdrew a tan leather booklet from which he produced a business card, and said, handing the card to me as he did, ''Our standard payment schedule is ten percent on recovered funds.''

Glancing at the card he had handed me, I read:

New American Life Insurance, Incorporated
TRUMAN WHITEHEAD YOUNGER, ESQ.
President

''Normally, I prefer an hourly billing scale,'' I commented, eyebrows raised. ''Expense plus a fixed per-hour fee.''

''Please bear in mind, Mr. Hawley, that funds slated for payment are considered as recovered if they remain in-house,'' Younger said, returning the leather billfold to its place in his pocket.

''I know this might sound blasphemous, Mr. Younger, but what if I find that none of these beneficiaries did anything wrong? As unlikely as it sounds, what if I find that Mrs. Chase's death was entirely unrelated to her insurance policy?''

''Then we would naturally release the funds.''

''Meaning what?''

''Meaning that Hawley and Fizner, Inc., would then submit an account of our expenses and hours billed to the slime balls in their disbursements office, and they would pay about half of what we claimed," a voice cut in from the doorway leading to the funeral home's main foyer.

Looking up, I found Larry Fizner standing, both hands in his pockets, looking leaner and meaner than ever.

Truman Younger turned and smiled amiably. Like old friends, the two men shook hands. Looking at me as he did, Larry explained, "I've done work for this guy before, Bill. With him, you gotta watch your ass."

How Larry had known to show up wasn't hard for me to figure: Nat had called him. For some reason, Nat holds Larry Fizner in very high regard, which I've always found perplexing, since Larry and Nat are so diametrically dissimilar. If you imagine a scale, with class, elegance, and taste being represented on the right-hand side in the person of Natalie Hawley, a perfect ten, then crass, crude, and boorish would be designated as the scale's left-hand side, where Larry Fizner would score a zero. Yet when it comes to certain things, Nat trusts Larry's judgment more than she does mine. Her explanation for this is that sometimes I get so dazzled by an intellectual challenge that, in her estimation, I resemble a blind person crossing a street: I need somebody to watch for cars. Since she can't always be with me to serve that function, she turns the job over to Larry because, and this is the weird part, she trusts him.

"He's like a faithful dog," she's said more than once. "No matter what's going on around him, he keeps his nose to the ground and his eyes wide open. I just know that he'd cut his arm off before he'd let anything bad happen to you, Bill. He's as straight as they come."

Candidly, I'm not positive I share Nat's conviction concerning Larry's intrinsic virtue. But I do have to admit that there's a certain sense of synchronicity between him and me. We're a team . . . the whole being greater than the sum of its parts . . . whether I necessarily like it or not.

Larry's arrival changed the mood in the room, and before I knew it, Truman Younger and I had signed the contracts that officially designated the New American Life Insurance Company as the clients of Hawley and Fizner, Private Investigators,

Inc. This done, Younger had excused himself with a jaunty, "Gentlemen, good luck."

Once we were alone, Larry, in his red-and-black plaid pants, white shirt, and canary-yellow sports coat, I grinned, rubbed his hands, and said, "This one sounds like a dilly. Shit. If T. W. Younger, in person, was forced blinking from the upholstered womb of his limousine, there's gotta be a buncha gunk goin' on."

Behind me, the fax machine started buzzing, then it beeped, and then it started printing. I ignored it, preferring to watch Larry as he turned Madeline Chase's file folder around to face him on the desk, moistened one thumb with his tongue, and started skimming pages.

I don't know how old Larry is; he refuses to tell me. But my estimate is sixty-five to seventy. He is shorter than my five feet eleven by about four inches, and his build is light to the point of being birdlike. He can't weigh more than a hundred and forty pounds. His bald head is shiny on top, with a ring of thinning grey hair running around the sides. He wears thick-lensed, gold, wire-rimmed glasses, loudly colored, usually mismatched clothes, and, something new, the occasional hearing aid, which, at least as far as I can tell, he doesn't really need, since it drifts from one ear to the other. But Larry's big on appearances, telling me once, "I look a certain way because I want to be taken as a certain type." Though precisely what type he wanted to be taken as he never specified.

In my experience, he only achieves his goal superficially, because, once you get to know him a little, you are forced to realize, almost immediately, that he's a hell of a lot smarter, more observant, and certainly more clever than he looks. After knowing him for a few minutes more, you will come to understand, almost despite yourself, that he must deliberately dress inappropriately, because, and this is the key to his personality as far as I've been able to tell, he doesn't do anything without a reason.

Calculating . . . that's Larry Fizner. Calculating to the point of being cold. He can make you nervous, my partner. He makes me nervous, even when I know he's watching my back. But in the end, having him on my side is usually a comfort.

"Tell me about it," he said, leaning on the desk with both hands and looking at me over his glasses.

Tearing the sheet off the fax machine, I ran my eye over the information printed there, sighed, and sat down. Quickly, but in detail, I filled Larry in, concluding with the fax that Nat had just sent from the library, at the bottom of which she had scribbled, "Had a couple of student workers do it for me. Didn't take as long as I thought. Love you. N."

There were only two names on the page.

Larry looked at it, one eyebrow raised as he said, "So this embalmer, this Edward Craig, was only involved in three of the eight funerals that this Noland Funeral Home conducted around the time Madeline Chase went missing?"

"Right," I concurred. "And out of all the funerals that happened in the entire county during that same period," I added, laying the fax paper on top of Mrs. Chase's file, "Edward Craig was listed as the embalmer on just two other funerals, for two other funeral homes."

Larry looked more closely at the two names.

"One of the two was buried out of town, in Chardon," he observed. "And the other . . ."

"Yeah," I agreed. "And the other."

I took my glasses off and rubbed the bridge of my nose. I was developing a headache. When I put my glasses back on, Larry was holding a pack of Camels my way, saying, "Yes or no?"

I sighed.

"You usually do when we start one of these things," he prompted. "You can always quit next week."

I took a cigarette, put it in my mouth, and leaned forward to accept a light off his battered old Zippo. It was one of those fat Camel filters . . . the ones that feel like you're smoking a little cigar. Nat would be pissed. I was already pissed. One of these days I'm going to leave those goddamn things alone for good.

"You settled on this embalmer awfully fast," Larry was saying, cutting in on my self-condemnation.

I exhaled smoke and admitted that, yes, I had.

Larry was holding the fax sheet loosely in his left hand,

shrugging as he said, "We could nail it down tonight, couldn't we?"

I stared at him, amazed by his enthusiasm. It only takes about ten seconds for him to get his hackles up, and then he's off and running.

"Do you know the shit that would come down if we got caught?" I asked.

He looked at me, saying, "You already came up with a place to start . . . a name, immediately . . . and you weren't even on the job. That's good. But knowing for sure, yes or no, was it Craig or not, would be better. We could find out in like an hour."

I frowned.

On the sheet Nat had faxed to my office were listed the two other funerals with which Edward Craig could be linked that had been conducted at about the same time Madeline Chase disappeared. One of those two had ended in a standard in-ground burial, effectively putting that casket out of reach. But the other involved a mausoleum entombment. And an entombment, for our purposes, was an entirely different proposition.

"If there's another piece of Madeline Chase inside the casket in that mausoleum," Larry said, "then that would really nail it down. Edward Craig would definitely be our best bet, since the funeral home that originally buried the guy whose casket had the lady's head inside was different from the one that took care of this entombment thing. Craig would be the only common link between the two, and it would save us a hell of a lot of time knowing one way or the other, Bill."

I knew that Larry was right. Entombed in Peaceful Knoll Cemetery's mausoleum, the casket in question was accessible by means other than securing a disinterment order, which necessitated a signed affidavit by the family, as well as a certified copy of a death certificate, and an authorization from the cemetery administration . . . none of which we could get, I knew, in the case of the other, buried casket. But it would be risky.

"They've got guards in a cemetery," I said, a little feebly.

"All night?" Larry asked.

"No. Usually just until nine or so."

"You could take a nap this afternoon."

"The cops keep an eye on cemeteries."

"I'll bet they do," Larry said skeptically. "I'll bet that cemeteries are their first priority. They probably park their cruisers inside and run around with flashlights all night long."

"Okay," I said, cutting him off. "Let me think about it."

"Yeah." Larry smiled. "You do that. While you are, what would we need exactly . . . like a screwdriver?"

"Yes," I said. "And a razor knife."

"I'll be right back," Larry said, leaving me to finish the cigarette I knew I shouldn't have taken, while contemplating doing something that I knew I shouldn't do.

For reasons that were entirely practical, we settled on midnight as the best time for our approach, which left me with time to kill. So early that evening I did something I've sporadically taken to doing during the past nine months or so: I hit an A.A. meeting.

When I first quit drinking after the accident that left my younger brother's legs paralyzed, I did it cold turkey, without outside help. Alcoholics Anonymous never even entered my mind. But after having been sober for a few years, I started going. At first I did it out of curiosity. And truthfully, even after attending as many meetings as I have, I've yet to become a card-carrying believer. I'm not putting them down, it's just that, for me, A.A. wouldn't have been enough to keep me dry. Praying, and twelve steps, and listening to horror stories are all well and good, and confessing all your past transgressions while juiced might ease the conscience of some, but for me, being the intrinsic loner I am, it was all just too clubby, too buddy-buddy, too sticky-sweet. I freely admit that the problem is entirely mine . . . that I just don't fit with their program. But I had to stop drinking my own way, depending on myself to do the changing instead of hoping that some outside entity could come in and do the dirty work for me.

Now that I'm sober, there's something about the meetings that I can appreciate that I missed while I was still craving booze every day. There are good people gathered in those "rooms," surrounded by a true sense of acceptance and concern. They'll help you if they can, and they'll leave you alone if you choose. I tend to remain pretty much anonymous when I go: I haven't got a hell of a lot to say. I've never led a meeting, meaning that I've never gotten up and told my story. I just sit there and recite the prayer, listen to the others talk, drop my dollar in the hat, and leave, feeling ... I don't know ... better somehow. Just better knowing that I'm not the only one whose got the taste, and that, if I really, really needed it, there would be someone whose name I might not even know, who would be ready to come and talk, or intervene, as they call it, any time, day or night. It's like an extended family in a way. Unconditional support ... though I've never been able to make the commitment to them that they implicitly make to me every time I go to a meeting. It's a confusing relationship that I'm still exploring.

Larry pulled up in his big old Dodge conversion van at eleven-thirty. I was waiting in my office, lights out, standing at the window. Nat was asleep. Though her reaction had been characteristically subdued when I told her that Larry and I had been hired by New American Life Insurance to do the very thing that she had suggested I do without a client, her satisfied nod had served as my green light. I had her support. All systems were go. Jerry, on the other hand, was still out. He hadn't come home all day, and he hadn't called. I was fuming. It was lucky for him that my mind was occupied elsewhere, or I might have gone looking for him, which would really have caused some sparks.

"Ready?" Larry grinned, stepping into the alcove, his face lit pink from the glow of his cigarette, his hand clamping itself firmly on my upper arm.

I said, "Sure," and locked the door.

Larry was dressed in a dark sweatshirt, dark sweatpants, and tennis shoes, also dark. I checked his profile in the glare of our parking lot's streetlight as we headed for his van, making him ask, "What's wrong?"

"I just wanted to see if you've got shoe polish smeared on your face," I replied.

"Screw you," he said.

The only reason I had agreed to his crazy scheme was because it was the most expedient way to establish the accuracy of my suspicions. The police, who were surely conducting an investigation of their own, would probably have concluded, as had I, that either the funeral home, or the embalmer, or both, that had taken care of Paul J. Larson's funeral would be a good place to start their inquiries. But they would be limited in what they could do. IF they wanted to disinter, they'd have to do it legally, with all the red tape and delays that I could avoid . . . though I'd have to be careful about what I did with anything I found. That's the major problem with acting outside the boundaries of what's normally considered acceptable behavior—though you can often get away with the actual deed, you've got to watch how you proceed thereafter so as not to implicate yourself in a crime by inadvertently letting on about things you have no business knowing.

"The mausoleum's door is going to be locked," I said, climbing into the passenger's seat of Larry's van. I was dressed in a pair of black dress slacks and my knee-length, black, cashmere topcoat. I was also wearing a tie . . .

Ask me why.

Larry said that I should just leave the lock to him as he started up the van and pulled out of the lot.

In the second-floor window that was our bedroom, I could have sworn I noticed, as we hit the street, the dark form of my wife, watching, though I had been sure she was asleep when I left the room.

The Peaceful Knoll Cemetery is one of those contemporary facilities that disallow upright tombstones. So, instead of a cemetery, the grounds look more like a golf course than anything else. It's surrounded by a sandstone wall, five feet high, topped with wrought-iron spikes; and there's a beautiful, arched, scrollwork gate in the front, near the red brick building that serves as an office.

The night was cold, and overcast, which was good. The mausoleum building itself is located near the rear of the cemetery, in a clump of trees, mostly evergreens, which are thick, and ideal for hiding behind, with some thin, spidery birch trees reaching their bare, spindly branches up here and there. From the back wall to the mausoleum is a span of about sixty yards of clear running, which Larry and I would have to cover as inconspicuously as possible, which would be a trick in itself considering that he would be carrying a metal toolbox and I'd have an aluminum stepladder under one arm. But that was the plan—simple and direct.

"This is asinine," I said, as he parked the van down the street from our point of entrance and glanced around, looking, I assumed, for police cars.

"Huh?" he asked, distracted.

"I said that I can't believe I agreed to this. If we get caught you can kiss my funeral home good-bye. My business will be shot."

"Oh, quit worryin'. We'll be fine."

He opened the van's door, making the dome light come on.

On the sidewalk I caught him by the arm. "What about a lookout?" I asked. "Did you think of that? Shouldn't we have somebody watching our backs?"

"To do what?" he asked in return, opening the van's side door and withdrawing his toolbox. "If we left somebody back by the fence, and they did see somebody, what would they do, shout?"

"We could have walkie-talkies," I suggested. "We need to plan this better."

"Bill," he said. "It's a cemetery, not a bank. Nobody gives a shit whether we're in there or not. Kids jump the fence and drink beer on the graves all the time."

"Kids don't have a million dollars invested in a funeral home," I pointed out.

"Bahh," he replied, waving his hand and leaving me to pull the stepladder out and follow.

In my office, the idea of breaking into a mausoleum had sounded outlandish enough. Actually doing it, trotting across the wet grass as I was, approaching the cemetery wall with the moon hidden behind dark blue-grey clouds, and the sounds of nighttime traffic, sporadic on the streets beyond the trees, seemed positively unreal . . . like it was happening to someone else. My heart was pounding, and my breath came in short gasps, exactly as if I were doing something that was truly dangerous in a physical sense, instead of what essentially amounted to a college prank.

Except that we weren't, as Larry had already suggested, simply going to jump the fence and down a few nervous beers amid the tombstones. We were actually going to break into a sealed mausoleum niche, which, considering my age, and what I had to lose, and also considering the reality of what we would look like should we be caught, standing in the dark with muted flashlights in the middle of the night, opening a casket we had just pulled from the wall, made things considerably more serious than Larry wanted to admit.

Larry had reconnoitered the area earlier in the day and had chosen a spot near the wall where there were trees growing closely enough together to hide us as we went over. Quickly we scurried up to that point, leaving the van parked rather conspicuously, I thought, behind us on the street. I had no sooner planted the stepladder next to the wall when Larry was up and over the wrought iron. I handed him his toolbox and he jumped down, landing almost soundlessly on the other side and whispering, ''Wait for my signal before you follow.''

I didn't bother to reply as I climbed up the ladder's first three steps and watched his dark shape move across the manicured lawn toward the trees surrounding the mausoleum. Our plan called for his picking of the lock before I joined him inside. There was no sense in both of us standing exposed on the great marble steps while he fiddled around with probes and picks. When he had the door open he'd . . .

There: one blink of his flashlight.

So fast? I thought. Could he really have gotten the door open that quickly?

Without further debate I was up and over the fence. Standing atop the stone and reaching carefully back over the wrought-iron points, I pulled the ladder up, settling it on the ground and climbing down before folding it under my arm and making my way to the mausoleum. My shoes whispered on the grass, and I could hear my own breath in my ears. But other than that, I felt as alone and detached as if I were on the moon.

''Piece of cake,'' Larry said as I joined him atop the steps.

"The lock gave up when it saw me coming."

The mausoleum's front doors were twelve feet tall and made of some kind of metal that looked green during the day and dull black at night. Larry had opened one of the doors just enough for me to slip through, and as I did I waited for him to follow. Finally, when he didn't, I stuck my head back out to find him folded in behind one of the great granite pillars that adorned the front facade of the building. When I whispered, "Come on," I could see his silhouette shaking his head in the negative as he replied, "I'll wait here."

"You're kidding!" I said, astonished.

"I don't like dead things."

"But this was your idea!"

"You're the undertaker."

"What's that got to do with anything?"

"Just go."

"But . . ."

"We haven't got all night."

"I'll remember this."

"Fine."

"I'm not kidding."

"Fine. Now get on with it."

I turned, swallowed, and hefted the ladder under my arm. I had Larry's toolbox in my other hand, and the location, Aisle of the Martyrs, Row 10, Niche 15, reverberating in my head. My heart was booming so hard that it pulsed in my jaw. My shoes snapped in decaying echoes off the marble walls and floor as I walked. There were tiny little windows way up along the very top of the thirty-foot walls, set about ten feet apart, through which the pale grey light of night was brighter by degrees than the absolute darkness inside the rows. After about a minute, my eyes adjusted to that nearly perfect gloom enough for me to make my way along without having to pull out my flashlight, which, despite the apparent impossibility of anyone else seeing while I was inside, I wanted to use as sparingly as possible.

Described in washes of grey on grey, the mausoleum was a cavernous maze of straight aisles that branched off one another in perfect right angles, pocketed with "prayer corners" that were little alcoves filled with black shadow. Littered here and there were suspended vases that jutted eerily along the walls, dangling the limp and wilted remains of flowers that had long since died. Puffing air through my cheeks, I ran my tongue—as rough and dry as Quincy's—over my lips, tasting the decaying, freezer-burn smell of the place, and briefly turning on my flashlight, just long enough to get my bearings, make a quick turn to the left, then to the right, and then to the left again, into the aisle for which I had searched.

I paused, wondering what Larry was doing. Then I wondered what I was doing. Then I pressed on, figuring that the quicker I got it done, the quicker I'd be out of there.

Flashlight again:

Roberts, Kleam, Peters, Jones . . .

1908, 1991, 1917, 1990, 1952 . . .

Beloved Wife, Loving Husband, Dearest Son . . .

Markowitz, Rushelbache, Blaughman . . .

Torrington.

Bingo!

The memorial wall was perfectly flat, constructed of three-foot by three-foot slabs of marble engraved with the names of the occupants in classic, Roman style letters. Mr. Samuel Torrington was one row up from the floor, to my left. I wouldn't need the ladder, I thought, laying it on the ground. Running my hands over the niche's cool surface, I found four bolts, the heads embellished with fancy washer-type things that made them look like the tops of flowers, with the screw head hidden in the center. A regular screwdriver would be all I'd need then to pop the slab out and prop it on the floor. It would be heavy, but there'd be a wire handle on the top . . .

I paused.

What was that?

Listen.

Listen.

Nothing.

Okay.

Try to swallow the dryness in my throat, find the proper screwdriver, pull on my gloves, set to work . . .

• • •

Later, when I would step back up to the mausoleum's front door, pausing inside to say, "Is it okay to come out?" my heart would no longer be racing, and my hands, which had shaken almost uncontrollably the entire time I worked the four screws free, heaved the heavy marble slab loose, and lowered it as gently as I could onto the floor, would be rock steady and dry, no longer sweating.

Later, as I would step onto the mausoleum's front step to the sound of Larry's voice saying, "Well? What did you find out?" I wouldn't be hyperventilating as I had been as I traced the razor knife carefully along the edges of the plastic sealer panel that was epoxied over the opening to the mausoleum niche behind the marble slab I'd already taken out. My breathing would be calm and easy . . . resigned, you could even say. Resigned, because now I knew.

And later, as Larry and I scrambled back across the lawn and over the cemetery's stone wall, with its wrought-iron spikes, my mouth would no longer be sandpaper dry, as it had been as I slid the casket of Mr. Samuel Torrington out on its rusted rollers, unscrewed the end cap, and pulled it open with a tiny *pop*! that was the pressure of five years letting go. People think that entombment in a mausoleum means that the casket is spared all the mess of burial—the water and the dirt. But in truth, entombment is harder on a casket than an in-ground burial, because an in-ground burial places it beneath the frost line, where the temperature is more or less constant. In a mausoleum wall, the temperature fluctuates with the seasons, so there's a lot of condensation with which to contend. Consequently, metal caskets tend to rust, and the interiors on the non-seal ones can get really sloppy. They also stink of mildew.

I was wearing latex gloves.

And a surgical mask.

I had my flashlight in one hand, the lid of the casket, the end of which I had pulled two feet out from the wall, propped barely open in the other. A Polaroid camera similar to the one I had seen Dr. Wolf use dangled from my wrist on a cord. My eyes blinked rapidly as I reached in, carefully, groping for the mattress between the body's legs, glad it had been placed in the wall headfirst, feeling around, under the mattress, through the springs, free space inside, damp and cold. . . .

"Well, goddamn it!" Larry said as I held the ladder for him to climb down on the outside of the cemetery's wall. "What the hell did you find out?"

I handed him the stack of Polaroid pictures I had taken before sealing the reeking casket back up and returning it to its place. There were six of them. That's all the film I had in the camera. If I would have had more, I would have stood there, flashing explosions of blue-white light, oblivious to how those explosions must have made the little windows thirty feet over my head look from the outside, until the roll was finished. As it was, before I ran a fresh bead of epoxy over the slit I had made, replacing the plastic sealer sheet as I had found it before heaving the marble slab back up into place—nearly giving myself a rupture in the process—I took six pictures, which I handed to Larry Fizner, there, on the grass next to the stepladder by the cemetery wall, under a moonless sky.

"What did I find out?" I said as he took the pictures and held them up, trying to catch some light from the distant street lamp.

His face was blank for a moment as he held up the pictures and lifted his glasses off his eyes to examine them more carefully. Then his expression changed, and when it did I said, "Uh-huh. That's what I found out."

He looked at me, pictures in hand, still holding his glasses up on his forehead like goggles, saying, "What did you say his name was again?"

"Craig," I replied. "Edward Craig."

And, as I took the photographs back from him and started folding the ladder, slipping the pictures, all six of them depicting a woman's arm severed at the shoulder, bare skin fishy-white beneath the harsh flash of my Polaroid's bulb, pink nail polish on the fingers all but glowing, clear plastic bag held shut at one end with a serrated yellow fastener that came out surprisingly vivid in each and every shot, Larry said, "We're gonna have to find that son of a bitch."

I didn't bother to reply, since I was thinking:
Florida or in jail.
Probably Florida . . .
The son of a bitch.

FOUR

■■■■■■■■■■■

BY DAWN, LARRY Fizner was snoring in the leather recliner in my office, feet up, empty Scotch bottle on the floor next to him, crystal ashtray on my desk filled with cigarette butts. My nerves, which had been supercharged and vibrating when we had returned, were finally settled after four hours worth of reading. Nat wasn't mad at me anymore either. She brought me a cup of Earl Grey tea at six and kissed me, running her hand over my stubbled jaw and saying, "You look tired."

When we had first gotten back, my emotional state had been such that when I found Nat waiting for me in my office I had snapped at her instead of taking her into my arms as I should have done. We went a few snaky, verbal rounds before she realized that I was way too keyed-up to be very good company. Leaving me to do whatever I was going to do, she said, "We'll talk in the morning," in a tone that was cool, and a little hurt.

"Where's the booze?" Larry had asked, settling himself into the recliner.

"Gimme a cigarette," I had demanded.

He pitched the pack onto the desk, pressed the recliner's booster handle forward, lifting up the padded section for his feet, and leaned his head back before taking a shot of Scotch straight from the bottle and releasing a long, satisfied sigh. He was asleep in minutes.

The cigarette butts in the ashtray were almost exclusively

mine. By morning my chest hurt and my heart was pounding from nicotine. As the first rays of dawn cut through the haze in the office to land in swirling notes on my desk blotter, I rubbed my eyes under my glasses and yawned.

"Well?" Nat asked, dressed for work, holding her own tea-cup, voice low so as not to rouse Larry, whose snoring sounded as if he were about to strangle.

"Want to walk?" I asked in return.

She nodded, and we headed outside.

Compared to the noxious smog I'd created in my office, the cool morning air tasted sweet on my tongue. I coughed a couple of times, and then inhaled deeply. Nat was watching me from the corner of her eye, saying nothing. She disapproves of my smoking, but since I don't do it very often, she usually lets it slide.

We strolled down the sidewalk from the funeral home's side door, Front Street rolling with morning mist that all but obscured the movie theater across the street. The traffic light on the corner of Front and Seminary was still blinking its nighttime amber-yellow caution though there wasn't a moving vehicle in sight. A woman in a long, neon-blue raincoat stepped from Dick's Bakery holding a white, waxed paper bag and a Styrofoam cup emitting steam from its sipper spout. A police car sat in the Dairy Mart lot, the cop leaning casually on the counter inside the store, talking to the Lebanese guy who worked the graveyard shift selling whatever people buy late at night. The Clark gas station's big orange ball was just flickering to life as Mr. Masterson opened for the day.

We were passing Lawrence-Wynn University's ancient music conservatory building, five blocks down, before I decided on a place to start. Once I did, I didn't stop talking until I had described everything I had learned from the file Truman Younger had left for me about the investigation New American Life Insurance, and the Cleveland Police Department, had conducted into the disappearance of Madeline Chase some five years before. By the time I was done, we had completed one circuit of town and had ended up in the college's quadrangle, sitting on the great sandstone sundial in front of the observatory, across from North Hall, the dormitory where we had originally met, me sharing a second-floor double with a guy I had known in high school, Nat in a third-floor single directly overhead.

"So," I concluded, finishing the last of my tepid tea and rolling the cup between my palms, "that's it. The gist of it is that New American Life's private investigator did a lot of interviews but didn't really come to any solid conclusions. He seemed to think that all was not well in the Chase household, but he couldn't specifically say who, or what, was the problem. 'Suspicious comments,' he called them, 'rumors' concerning Madeline Chase's emotional well-being, but nothing concrete. The cops stopped at pretty much the same spot. Reading through the reports, there were a couple of times when things seemed to be falling together, but it never quite jelled."

Nat was sitting with her legs tucked up under her on the sundial next to me, holding her empty teacup on one knee. When she exhaled, steam hovered languidly in silver grey swirls that bejeweled just the very tips of her long hair with droplets of condensation.

"So, who do you suspect?" she asked.

"Suspect?" I asked in return. "Who is there to suspect? Edward Craig, the embalmer, obviously. But beyond him, Christ . . ."

When I trailed off, I expected Nat to ask another question. Instead she simply looked at me, saying, "Go on, Bill. Talk."

I ran my tongue over my lower lip, glancing up at the dorm across the quad where she and I had first made love and feeling a brief, sharp pang when I realized that that magic night had occurred almost fourteen years ago. I could almost feel myself getting old, and it saddened me on a very intimate, almost physical level.

"Okay," I sighed. "I don't expect that this'll make much sense; it's just impressions. Okay?"

She concurred silently, her dark eyes sparkling in what light the overcast morning had to offer.

"According to the file, Madeline Chase was only married to Everett, her second husband, for like two years before she disappeared. There was no obvious, prior connection established between the embalmer, Edward Craig, and anyone in the Chase family. As far as that goes, it seems unlikely that any family member ever even met Craig. So I guess one of our first questions has to be, how did he become involved?''

I paused, correlated, continued:

''Specifically concerning Madeline Chase's death, on a strictly surface level, my gut reaction is to zero in on the insurance money as the prize that made the alleged murder happen. It's a big, big pile of dollars. That being the case, my gut also says that we should take a careful look at Everett Chase, the dead lady's second husband, since, of the three beneficiaries to the life insurance policy, he's the only one who isn't a *blood* relative to the deceased. The other two were the woman's own children, and, for absolutely no reason other than sentiment, I just tend to believe that a second husband, briefly married later in life, is more likely to bump off a woman for cash than her kids. Call me a romantic.

''Or maybe my misgivings are driven by statistics; though I got a C minus in stats, and that was a gift. But even the notion that she was probably murdered doesn't really sit too well in my mind.

''Contrary to popular belief, murder's not all that common an occurrence. Statistically, a good seventy-five percent of people die natural deaths due to a combination of old age and disease. Fifteen to twenty percent of deaths are accidental— car wrecks and stuff like that. And five percent are homicides and suicides, with suicides probably claiming more lives than officially recorded since in a lot of cases a coroner will rule an obvious suicide as natural or accidental to save the family further pain and embarrassment. The cause of death in the last little bit, two to five percent of all deaths recorded, remain undetermined, even after the police and coroners look them over.

''So, statistically, the chances of running across a homicide—especially a homicide involving a victim in Madeline Chase's age and income bracket—are fairly slim to start with . . . and then, add to that the way this body was mutilated . . .''

Sigh.

''Dismemberment is messy,'' I observed, stating the obvious. ''It doesn't happen by accident. I took the Polaroid of

Mrs. Chase's head that Dr. Wolf gave me and I tacked it up inside the door to the big cabinet next to my desk back at the office. Then I took one of the shots of the arm I found and tacked it up roughly where it would go, anatomically, under and to the left of the head. Then I sat and looked at it for a long time, imagining the rest of her, in pieces.

"From what I could figure, there's probably going to end up being six parts all told—her head, two arms, two legs, and a torso. We've located two of those pieces, leaving four missing. I bit the eraser right off the pencil I was chewing while I was staring at that empty spot where the rest of her would go, thinking—that was major surgery. Nat, you've never seen an embalming in person, but that's exactly what it is—surgery on a dead person.

"But chopping her up like that?

"Somebody meant business. Even for a million bucks, it's hard for me to imagine a husband doing, or having that done, to his wife. Even his second wife. Even a wife he doesn't like very much. Anybody . . ."

"Maybe she was the victim of a serial killer or something," Nat cut in. "Maybe her death doesn't have anything to do with the insurance money."

"You mean like Edward Craig picked her at random, or because she was convenient in some way, and killed her as part of an ongoing sex-crime thing?"

"You never know."

I considered that for a moment, saying finally, "I don't buy it, and again, it's my gut talking statistics. But if you take paperbacked books and mystery movies as your working sample, then sure, the media makes it look like every other school bus driver's a mass murderer. But in real life those people are certifiable freaks. How many bona fide monsters can you think of? The Boston Strangler, Manson, Bundy, John Wayne Gacy, Jeffrey Dahmer, and maybe what, like a dozen more? Two dozen? Three? Now say that for every screwball that we know about, there's ten more we don't. What would you be talking about then? Three hundred active, mad-dog killers out of a population of a hundred and some odd million people? Sounds like a lot, but think about it. What would the statistical chances be of that kind of crap ever touching our lives?''

''You're the one who's always telling me never to let anyone in the house, never to trust anyone,'' Nat observed. ''Are you saying now that you don't believe there's really any danger?''

''Not at all. Children do get snatched out of parking lots, and rapists do get in houses posing as the gas man. It never hurts to be safe. What I am saying is that the notion that we're dealing with a Jack the Ripper type embalmer guy who's been chopping up victims and burying them all over northern Ohio isn't real high on my list of possible explanations.''

''But you do have a dismembered corpse on your hands, which reminds me. How are you going to tell the police you found her arm?''

''I'm not.''

''Why?''

''How can I? At least for now I'm going to have to keep what I know to myself. That arm's not going anywhere, so there's no harm leaving it right where it is.

''What's more important is method this time. This is a five-year-old mess. The cops and an insurance company both had their cracks at it when Madeline Chase first went missing, and they both came up empty. The cops are going over it again, and they'll probably go at it pretty hard this time because they know that sooner or later it's bound to wind up on the news, and they won't want to look like they don't know what they're doing. But I've got a stronger motivation than they do . . . one hundred and fifty thousand stronger motivations.''

''Is that how much that insurance man said he'd pay?''

''Yup. Ten percent of the trust fund's value if I can keep the company from having to release the cash. And Lord knows we could use it. The funeral home's been open for business for almost two years now, and there hasn't been a single month yet that we've broken even. If it weren't for that money we've got stashed in Dad's safe to pay the bills, we'd probably be declaring Chapter Eleven by the end of this year. The money I'll make from New American Life would keep us afloat for a long time. Maybe even long enough for us to finally get a grip in this town. God, people are slow to take to a new funeral home.''

''You knew that when you first decided to build.''

''Yeah, I know. But now that it's two years later and I'm still having trouble meeting the monthly electric bill, my point of view's a lot more immediate. That's the thing about being an entrepreneur: the bills keep coming, whether you have any business or not.''

''Well, good,'' Nat said, climbing to her feet and glancing at the gold pendant watch she had hanging on a chain around her neck. The library where she worked was just across the quad, and the time was almost eight, which was when she was supposed to be at her desk. ''Walk me over,'' she said. Then added, ''So what's the plan?''

''The plan,'' I said, as if talking off the cuff, though this was a part of what I had been chewing on all night, ''is to start at square one and really go over what we have. It's ground that's been searched once already, and is in the process of being searched again. But if we're going to get anywhere, I think it's going to come only if we really get methodical and conduct a true, casebook investigation, complete with interviews, personal visits, and a lot of legwork. It's going to take some time.''

''Can I help?''

''When you can, you can bet that I'll let you know. But for right now, no, I don't think so. I think Larry and I are just going to have to start digging and knocking on doors.''

On the library steps I kissed her, and she held me, making the kiss last. When she drew back, she looked deeply into my eyes and said, ''I love you, Bill. You're a good man.''

''Thanks,'' I said, pulling her to me and feeling her hair against my face. ''I needed that.''

''Have they decided on a cause of death yet?'' she asked incongruously, making me smile as I broke our clinch.

''Christ,'' I said. ''You're getting to be as bad as me with this stuff. But the answer to your question is no. I called Rusty at the morgue's receiving desk this morning, and he said that they've still got 'pending' listed both as to a cause of death and a final, legal ID.

"What Rusty did say that was interesting, though, was that the head was definitely embalmed prior to its being hidden in Paul Larson's casket—which points us directly at Edward Craig yet again. Also, the coroner didn't find any evidence of ligature marks on what was left of the neck, which tends to rule out both manual and mechanical strangulation as a possible cause of death. Rusty also mentioned that all but one of the blood serums they ran came out negative. Which is understandable since she's got all that embalming fluid in her system.

"But still, from what Rusty said, Madeline Chase's blood alcohol content was pretty high—like .21, which could mean that she was either pretty drunk when she died, or that the foreign compounds and intervening years since her death have skewed the test. Sometimes degenerative agents can produce alcohol as a by-product creating an artifact or false reading that only a specialized toxicology lab can accurately identify. So who knows? And since Edward Craig shot her the juice before he gave her the knife, that makes it all the harder to get a true reading on any lab tests the coroner decides to do.

"I sure wouldn't want to be the tech responsible for making a determination on this one. And when the story hits the newspaper, which it's bound to do sooner or later, look out. The pressure's really going to be on."

"Well," Nat said, glancing to her right where there was a newspaper vending machine, "I guess we're off and running."

The morning copy of the *Cleveland Plain Dealer* that was displayed in the dispenser's front window had, not as a headline but as a secondary front-page article, a feature headed, "MYSTERY WOMAN FOUND: AUTHORITIES SEEK PUBLIC HELP." Fishing a coin from my pocket I bought a paper, ran my eye over the first few sentences of the article, and said, "Dammit."

Nat kissed me again, saying, "Let me know, okay?"

I nodded, walking away distractedly, still reading the article about the dead woman, and finding the part where it said that the remains had still not been officially identified gratifying. It meant that I had a little breathing space.

Though just how long the slack would last was anybody's
guess.

Jerry was waiting for me in the funeral home's office, which
was like the very last thing I needed right then. Stepping in I
found him in his wheelchair, parked next to my desk, with
something obviously on his mind. I glanced around, asking,
"Where's Larry?"

He blinked as he replied, "I don't know. He wasn't here
when I got in."

On the desk I found a note reading, "I'll start with Craig.
You take her family. Happy hunting. Fizner."

"Bill?" Jerry said, making me lift my eyes from the note
to look at him. "Can I talk to you?"

Oh, Christ, I thought. Here it comes. I had been dreading
this moment and hoping against all hope that it would never
come. But I could tell by the tone of his voice that this was
the moment of truth. The moment that I was going to have to
do something I didn't normally do with my younger brother—
which was turn him down when he asked me for a favor,
because the favor I knew he was about to ask was one that I
absolutely didn't feel qualified to give. I just couldn't do it . . .
and I was already a little pissed off, just knowing what he was
getting ready to ask.

"Do you know where I've been for the last day and a
half?" he said, looking down at his hands, which were folded
in his lap.

"No," I replied, though I suspected that that wasn't strictly
true. "All I know for sure is that you haven't been here, and
you haven't called, and we've got a body in the back so there's
been work to do, and you haven't done a thing to help."

He looked up at me, eyes narrow with restrained emotion.
"I've been taking care of a baby," he all but hissed. "That's
what I've been doing. I've been feeding and burping and bath-
ing and diapering a baby."

"I assume she finally showed up this morning?" I said,
referring to Ellie Lyttle, the wayward mother of the baby in
question—a little boy, less than one year old, christened Jerry
William, named after both my brother and myself.

He nodded glumly.

"Two days she was gone," he said, shaking his head. "Two days, and not a word. If I hadn't gone over . . ." he trailed off, his eyes unfocused, seeing, I was sure, a baby left alone. "If I didn't have a key . . ."

"Jer," I said, lowering myself into the seat behind my desk. "She needs help."

That's when he hit me with it.

"Would you talk to her?" he asked plaintively.

I steeled myself for the storm.

"Jer," I began, "what good could I do?"

"You've been there," he insisted. "You've gone through it . . . you'd understand. I'm not like that. I just don't get it. I don't have the need, I guess. Or the compulsion, or whatever it is. But I've been reading about it . . . about the illness theory of addiction. It sounds so complicated that I don't even know where to start."

"Listen," I said, lifting a hand to slow him down. "I'm a drunk, not a therapist."

"You're not a drunk anymore."

"Yes I am. I'm just not drinking at the moment."

"See? You do understand. That's exactly what the books I've been reading say."

"So what?"

"Goddamn it, Bill!" he exclaimed, suddenly doing something I had never seen him do before. Jerry is three years my junior, has blond hair, cut short, and a trim, muscular body that he has all but reclaimed from the accident that ruined his legs by untold hours of chin-ups, push-ups, sit-ups, and barbells. His arms look like a wrestler's. His neck looks like a bulldog's. His hands grip with bone-splintering force. But now he was crying . . . the tears rolling down his cheeks as his mouth worked helplessly, chewing air but producing not so much as a single, comprehensible sound.

"Hey, hey, hey," I said, jumping from my seat and moving around the desk to kneel at the side of his wheelchair. "Jerry, man, come on . . ."

Perfect.

Absolutely perfect.

The trained professional: grief counseling at its finest—genuine compassion. Fifteen years consoling widows and widowers, and the best I could come up with when my own brother was hurting was, "Hey, man, come on." Sometimes I think I should just turn in my black necktie.

He was looking at the ceiling, talking to himself as much as to me.

"I've tried everything, Bill. I've threatened, and pleaded, and promised, and screamed. I've smashed bottles. But no matter what I do or say, she just keeps right on fucking up. And it's getting worse. This one was the worst so far. Two days, man! Two fucking days! When she did finally come home she looked like death. She's killing herself, Bill. She's flat out killing herself, and she just doesn't care. I don't know what else I can do. I'm at the end of my rope."

"As hard as it might be for you to accept, you've got to understand that it's not your responsibility," I said, biting back hard on the "I told you not to start up with her in the first place" that was trying its best to come out of me.

"I love her," he said simply, looking me straight in the eye. "I love her, and she's killing herself."

I said nothing.

"She won't see a professional," he went on. "She says that she wouldn't open the door even if I sent one over. She says that she'd call the cops and make them keep me away from her . . . get a restraining order, or whatever . . .

"Maybe she'd talk to you."

"Jer, I wouldn't know what to say."

"Just talk to her."

"I don't want that responsibility."

"Please, Bill."

"Jerry . . . no."

"Come on, Bill. Just talk."

I knew he had me. Goddamn it! I had gone into this prepared to stand firm, to keep my distance, to stay out of it. It wasn't my problem. It wasn't my job. But I also knew, even before I opened my mouth, that he had me. So when I said, "Okay. I'll see what I can do," it really didn't surprise me all that much. I probably just should have agreed to do what he asked at the outset of all this and avoided the charade of putting up a fight. I can't say no. I know I can't. Or if I do, I can't stick to it. So why didn't I just fess up to the fact and save myself and everybody else a whole lot of time and trouble?

I didn't know.

But what I did know, even though I didn't say it to my brother at that moment, was that no matter what I did, no matter what I said, no matter what . . . his girlfriend wasn't going to listen. He was right about at least one thing: I had been there, almost exactly where Ellie Lyttle was now. And what that experience had taught me, more clearly than anything else, was that it was a place so far away that the only voice you can hear when you're there is your own.

FIVE
■■■■■■■■■■

ACCORDING TO THE New American Life Insurance's case history, Ronald and Allison, Madeline Chase's children by her first husband, had both retained their original last name of Ackermann. Everett Chase had never legally adopted either of them, and, in what I took to reflect a veiled reference to tension in the family, both children had chosen to decline their mother's invitation to reside with her after she and Chase were married.

Born in 1971, the older child, Allison, had been killed three years before, in what the police had reported as a robbery-motivated, late-night attack. A student at Ohio State University at the time, Allison Ackermann had been working as a nursing assistant at Columbus General Hospital, where she had apparently been jumped at eleven-thirty in the evening as she made her way to her car in the hospital's parking garage after her shift. The assailant, probably using a baseball bat—judging by the compression fractures left in her skull, the details of which were contained in the copy of her autopsy protocol therein included, but were not immediately relevant, or so I thought—had struck her from behind with such force that two of her teeth had been dislodged. Though the autopsy showed no signs of sexual assault, the authorities, for their own unexplained reasons, never completely dismissed intended rape as a possible, secondary motive. In all, from what the police could ascertain, the thief got away with a paltry seventy-two dollars and the girl's brand-new Visa card, which he never even tried to use.

Born in 1973, fifteen months after his sister, there was surprisingly little personal information about Ronald Ackermann listed in the New American Life report. Just an address— referred to as, "Current as of August 1993; confirmed by Agent 12-D," who had apparently included the rather cryptic footnote: "Overtly hostile to interview: refer for further study. Legal standing vis-à-vis personal responsibility? Competent? Not competent? Who makes the call? Is there a guardian?"

Stapled to one of the Xeroxed pages of Allison's history was a newspaper clipping obituary, showing the girl's scrubbed and shining, brightly smiling face next to a list of her achievements, a list that was impressively accomplished considering her youth:

Cum laude graduate from Magnificat High School, an all-girl Catholic institution known for turning out superior, college-bound young ladies; this that and the other Pre-Med society, sorority, and volunteer group; cheerleader; sky diver; downhill skier; athlete; Catholic Youth League leader; member of the local Big Sister program; lead soloist in the college's choral group.

Stapled to Ronald's vital statistics sheet were copies of at least six municipal court records, listing dates, fines, and fees for transgressions ranging from D.U.I. to lewd and lascivious behavior—urinating off a freeway overpass onto the traffic below.

Allison had been in the process of applying to Ohio State's medical college, having expressed an interest in a concentration in Pediatrics, specifically dealing with research concerning terminal childhood diseases such as juvenile leukemia.

Ronald had just squeaked through an undistinguished public high school, and had since been sporadically enrolling himself in history and philosophy classes at the local community college, where he rarely completed a course, achieving mediocre grades, at best, when he did.

The two kids were like night and day, I thought. And naturally it had been the overachiever who was senselessly murdered, leaving her brother, who, at least according to the file, had never held down a job for more than eight months at a stretch, to go his merry, apparently aimless way.

Then there was Everett Chase, the deceased woman's loving hubby number two.

I wanted to start with him, but when I called the office number listed in hopes of making a morning appointment, I was told that Everett Chase was tied up straight through the afternoon, though he could probably squeeze me in if I could arrive at precisely four-thirty. When I asked if it would at least be possible to speak to him, briefly, over the phone, I was informed by his secretary—or at least I assumed that she was his secretary—in no uncertain terms, that Mr. Chase was far too busy to just pick up a telephone and speak to whoever happened to be on the other end. The Ivy Spring Restaurant was *the* hot item in town at present, and Everett Chase was its driving force . . . its focus . . . its personality, if you will. He was in such constant demand that every moment of his time was strictly rationed.

Four-thirty then, I finally agreed.

I hung up.

Dialed the morgue.

And learned that the ID on Madeline Chase was still not official. No, the lady's only remaining living child, Ronald, her son, had not yet been notified of her death by the county. As a matter of fact, it had been pretty much decided that such notification would be left to the young man's stepfather, seeing that Ronald Ackermann apparently didn't have a phone, and that the morgue's investigators certainly had better things to do with their time than chasing around looking for lost relatives when there were other, more accessible relatives available to do the same job. As far as they were concerned, the family had been notified in the person of the dead woman's husband. Who that husband chose to tell was entirely up to him, and not the morgue's responsibility.

Didn't have a phone?

As I checked the address New American Life had down for Ronald again, the street name finally clicked:

Standish Drive.

I rubbed my chin, deciding that Nat had been right about me needing a shave.

Standish Drive wasn't exactly millionaire's row, I thought, lathering up and selecting a new disposable razor from the bag under the bathroom sink.

Then the rest of it:

Mrs. Madeline Chase, formerly Ackermann, nee Parker, had, according to the insurance company holding the policy, been the recipient of a one million dollar claim after the death of her first husband. I couldn't help but wonder what she had done with the money.

Before she was killed in an apparent robbery attempt, Mrs. Chase's daughter, Allison Ackermann, had been a Pre-Med student, living in her own apartment, but working nights at a hospital, begging the question: Was she doing it for the money, or the experience?

Mrs. Chase's son, Ronald, presently resided on Standish Drive, an unabashedly bohemian part of town, didn't have a telephone, and, unless he'd read about the disembodied head in the newspaper and had jumped to the perfectly unjustified, awesomely unlikely conclusion that it directly affected him in some way, probably didn't even know that part of his mother's body had been located ... effectively putting him, since he was still not quite of legal age, at the back of the line behind his stepfather to inherit a substantial load of cash.

Everett Chase, stepdaddy to the boy and, as of the moment, numero uno in the inheritance lotto, owned the Ivy Spring, one of Cleveland's ritziest restaurants. But despite his having already been contacted by the country coroner's office, when contacted by me, he refused to be rushed into discussing what certainly appeared to be his missing wife's murder.

The thought occurred to me at that moment, not for the first time, but finally in a sufficiently nagging way to bring it to the forefront of my mind, that the way Madeline Chase had set up her estate was a little on the peculiar side. Favoring one child—her daughter Allison—to the exclusion of the other— her son Ronald—strictly on the basis of age, struck me as an almost deliberate formula for family conflict. Wouldn't it have been better, if she sincerely felt that her son wasn't mature enough to handle a large amount of money unsupervised, to have specified that he receive half the settlement in, say, a trust fund that he wouldn't be able to access until he reached the age of thirty? Or thirty-five? Or something? Didn't just giving all the money to Allison, and leaving Ronald—screwup or not, he was still her son—high and dry, smack not even so much of favoritism but of outright vindictiveness?

Jerry didn't mention my promise to visit his girlfriend as I exited the funeral home later that morning. Instead he just agreed to watch the phone, telling me not to worry about that afternoon's visitation since he'd have it covered. I took my Dodge Grand Caravan—dark blue with smoke-grey windows in the rear and a newly acquired sliding floor panel in back to which a pair of one-man cots was clipped, allowing me to transport two bodies at the same time—and headed for the I-71 North entrance ramp. The morning had cleared since the walk Nat and I had taken, with a bright white sun having burned off the fog, pushing the temperature up toward fifty degrees. For the first time in months, there was actual warmth in the air. And despite the tangle of questions running through my mind, the act of driving actually made me feel kind of good.

But my mood darkened as I got off the freeway and headed down Detroit Ave., looking for Standish Drive. These houses had been at one time in the not so distant past the stuff of middle-class dreams. I have a great uncle who never tires of telling me how wonderful the old neighborhood was when he lived there as a boy. Culling images of corner grocery stores, horse-drawn milk wagons, and friendly cops walking their beats, twirling their nightsticks and patting children on the head, he depicts a world that, though obviously attractively nostalgic to him, leaves me kind of cold. Personally, I find all that wholesome good feeling a bit much to swallow.

Since those erstwhile glory days, the area has slid into a more threadbare condition. The big, two- and three-story houses, with their voluminous front porches and tall, narrow windows, have gone from looking cozy, standing as they do so close together, to appearing cramped to the point of claustrophobia. Their once-gleaming trim has been reduced to peeling, rotten boards. The front stoops upon which the old folks whiled away their time now sag in sorry, soon-to-buckle depressions. And the red brick streets, formerly the shady lanes of Norman Rockwell paintings, are now lined with rusty, precariously late model cars that leak oil, billow exhaust on those rare occasions when they do run, and hardly ever seem to move.

Ronald Ackermann, oblivious heir to a minor fortune, lived in a particularly neglected house on a particularly neglected street. There were two cars in the gravel drive, one of which, a light green, late model Buick Skylark, appeared as if it might actually be ambulatory, given sufficiently favorable circumstances, while the other, a cream-colored Ford Fiesta, was streaked with rust and drooped in the middle so sadly that the frame support beneath the side doors nearly touched the ground. I decided to risk parking my van on the street in front of the house, as opposed to leaving the ass end sticking out from the drive. As I stepped onto the front porch, I paused, listening for the inevitable resident dog.

A little girl answered the door, blinking in the sunlight streaming over my shoulder, dressed in a dirty, knee-length, pajama/T-shirt kind of thing with Big Bird on the front. She had jelly smeared on both her cheeks. Behind her the house was dark, but I could just make out the hunched form of what I took to be a man—Ronald Ackermann, I assumed—positioned with his back to me in front of a glowing computer screen, which was part of a whole array of computer-type things that included a number of boxes, printers, and floor-standing attachments, the function of which I could hardly hope to guess.

"Is your mommy home?" I asked, leaning in close to the storm door in hopes of getting a better look inside the house.

"Can I help you?" a voice asked from behind the little girl, who, after having pulled open the door, hadn't said a word or moved from where she had planted herself, looking up at me with big, baby-cute eyes.

As if materializing from the gloom—there were no lights on in the house save for the computer screen way on the other side of the front room—a strikingly pretty woman appeared, placing one hand on top of the little girl's head. The woman had long blond hair and was dressed in an unusual-looking garment kind of thing. "Garment" is the only word I can think of to describe it. It was a sort of one-piece combination dress, robe, shirt-looking arrangement, white or some other light color—it was hard to tell from where I was standing, looking into shadow through the screen door—with an embroidered, scoop front cut square, and long sleeves that hung from her wrists like the robe of a monk. My immediate impression of the woman had something to do with her being out of time . . . as if she had recently stepped out of an old painting.

The man at the computer didn't so much as glance over his shoulder. As far as he was concerned, I apparently didn't exist.

I was all ready for a question and answer session culminating in the man by the computer's admitting that he was Ronald Ackermann, who I would then prepare for the coming bad news with a friendly handshake and conciliatory overtures. But things didn't work that way. The fairy lady . . .

That was the word:

Fairy.

Even though the woman was skipping just along the line between just plain pretty and beautiful, there was a worn, sleepy look to her face that I suspected either came from hard living or hard work. But the way her golden hair hung, combined with her "garment" and bare feet, imparted a kind of semi-contrived atmosphere of the extraordinary that seemed to hang about her the way a suit and tie can sometimes give an otherwise dim man an unearned air of prestige.

She would be the "Fairy Lady" to me from then on. It was simply how her appearance made me feel.

After I had identified myself, I asked to speak to Ronald Ackermann, expecting the man at the keyboard to perk up at the sound of his name. Instead, the woman said that Ronald wasn't home. Then she asked me why I wanted him. It was personal, I replied. How personal? It involved his mother. Had she finally turned up? After all these years? Ah, so you know about his mother being missing? Oh, she isn't missing. She just isn't around. Where's Ronald? Try Brookside Park.

"Is that where he works?"

"No. He's probably practicing. His weapons are gone, and he took his car a couple of hours ago."

"Weapons?"

"His sword and stuff."

"Sword?"

"He usually stays at the park until about two, weather permitting. Try there."

Without a word, the little girl closed the door, leaving me on the porch.

And still the man at the computer hadn't so much as looked at me. Even at the mention of Ronald Ackermann's sword he hadn't expressed the slightest, discernible interest. I hadn't even seen his face. All I saw was the back of his head, which was fuzzy with long, uncombed hair. Around him on the bare hardwood floor of the house's front room, I had seen baby toys, empty pizza boxes, dirty dishes that were days old from the looks of them, newspapers, ashtrays, videocassettes, and an assortment of other junk that had to be a foot deep. At first I hadn't noticed it. But after my eyes had adjusted enough for me to pick up a few details through the screen door, I had realized that the Fairy Lady was standing amid an absolute pigsty of a living room, with her hand resting atop the head of a little girl who looked like she hadn't had a bath in a week—while a big, hairy guy hunched in front of a computer, ignoring everything but the video game he was playing, and that he continued to play. I could see through the curtainless window, even after I left.

The only person who seemed at all interested in me was the little girl, who had taken up a position in the front window. I waved to her from my van's driver's seat. She didn't move. Her mom (?) hadn't been very impressed with my mention of Ronald Ackermann's lost mother. Ronald wasn't working, at eleven a.m. on a Friday, because he was at the park, "practicing" with his "weapons."

I have to admit, I was getting curious.

Brookside Park is located on the grounds of the Cleveland Metropark's Zoo, under the Dennison Avenue Bridge. Since time immemorial, it's been the home of the public softball diamonds most of the area's little and amateur leagues use for their games. I hate softball. Always have. They used to make me play it when I was in grade school, and my performance was unwaveringly miserable.

As a fat kid, I couldn't run very fast. Since it wasn't discovered that I needed glasses until I was twelve, my depth perception before that time was so thoroughly twisted that I couldn't catch for spit. Even when I did get my hands on the ball—usually after having chased it in an awkward duck-shuffle across the outfield as the rest my team yelled at me—I could never seem to figure out where to throw it quickly enough to make a difference. Consequently, I was always the catcher, the thinking apparently being that catcher was the position from which I could do the least damage. But if anything important looked like it might be about to happen at the plate, the pitcher—usually James Plazitski, the best athlete in our class—would invariably run over and take charge before I got the chance to mess things up.

One ball game was in progress on a diamond near the concession stand. I saw, as the van dipped onto the steeply inclined hill leading into the valley beneath the ancient, crumbling bridge spanning both the zoo and the park. The rest of the fields, ten or twelve of them, were unoccupied, except for one, where there were some people kind of running around, waving their arms, doing what I couldn't yet tell. But as I parked nearby, their actions suddenly took on a kind of sense to which Ronald Ackermann's "weapons and stuff" were logically related.

They were fighting.

I got out of the van, standing next to it and watching the three separate fights that were going on between three pairs of what I took to be men, dressed in sweatshirts, big, leather weight-lifter belts, leggings made of something that I took to be chain mail, leather gloves, elbow pads, and metal helmets that covered their faces. They each had a round, wooden shield on one arm and were going at one another with wooden "swords" that looked to be wrapped with some kind of cushioning material, like foam rubber pipe insulation, that was secured with tattered lengths of silver duct tape.

They were playing knights in armor, I realized, taken a little aback. A kids' game, for Christ's sake. Adults yet. But from the way they grunted and groaned, from the dull, wacking impact of their blows, and from the way the man, who I took to be a coach, standing on a stepladder off to one side shouted instructions and encouragement, they were playing this kids' game with vehement intensity.

After about ten minutes, I strolled over to the perimeter of the combat field, to where there was a line of men and women watching the fights. The men were all in various stages of dress, with helmets cocked up on their heads, their elbow pads dangling loosely as they leaned on their sticks/swords, nodding and pointing things out to each other. The women were all dressed in a similar fashion to the Fairy Lady I'd met earlier— lots of flowing dresses with long, billowing sleeves, as well as a preponderance of flowers interwoven into their hair.

"Excuse me," I said. But no one responded. So I said it again, louder, making a man turn to face me.

"I'm looking for Ronald Ackermann."

The man pointed to the field, saying, "The one with the red and white standard."

I followed his direction, spotting a knight in a white helmet painted with a red cross on the front.

Being close to the knights emphasized the homemade quality of their equipment in a way that distance served to hide. I decided that the helmets would have required the most effort, seeing that they were made of metal. Most of them had screws and bolts studded all over, holding the panels together. The man who had pointed Ronald Ackermann out for me was sweating. There was a big, plastic Gatorade cooler on the grass at his feet, like you see on the sidelines at football games. And one of the women was making notes in a book.

"What's going on?" I asked, because I thought it was a reasonable question.

"Practice for the war," the man replied, eyes on the field.

"What war?"

"This weekend."

"Oh," I acknowledged, thinking, Okay, I'll buy that.

It took almost an hour before the men on the field called it quits and the ones standing on the sidelines lowered their helmets and trotted out to take their place. In that time I learned that this was a club, of sorts, called SWORDS, which stood for "Swords, Wizards, Ogres, Renegades, Demons, and Sorcerers." They were what one of the women described as a "medieval fantasy society," that met at different campgrounds periodically during the year. The idea was that the group's members were all role players. "Kind of like really serious D&D," one warrior, named Sir Grand-Ore, offered.

D&D is "Dungeons and Dragons," a game I had tried and found infuriatingly pointless in college. The idea is that each player chooses a persona, playing the game in the person of that character as they face and overcome various challenges as described by the "dungeon master," who oversees whatever quest the players are on, controlling events and making judgments as to the outcome of confrontations by rolling a set of peculiarly shaped dice. I remember having trouble finding any pleasure in the act of creating a character to play; but I also recall that the people who really enjoyed the game often got into it completely—sometimes to the point of obsession. It has a tendency of attracting the pot heads, particularly the ones who got off on J. R. R. Tolkien's *The Hobbit* and *The Lord of the Rings* trilogy.

The idea of the SWORDS group, I was told, was similar, though more involved:

Each member was expected to research a particular historic period and then to assume the role of either a real or fictional character corresponding to that era. When the group got together, they all dressed up, talked in what they called "prithee" speech, and generally pranced around pretending that they were entirely different people, in an entirely different time, engaging in feasts, jousts, and quests. Ronald Ackermann, I was told, was a "stick jockey," or a knight who fights. He was a good one too, according to the people on the sidelines.

By the time he trotted over to where I was standing, I felt that I had enough of a handle on things to understand something about what the material in his New American Life Insurance personality file meant. The history classes, the philosophy courses, the questions about his mental competency, and maybe even his mother's reluctance to endow him with a large amount of money all fell into place when viewed in the light of his activities . . . or, I should say, the dedication he apparently had to his fantasy life. No job, no phone, no college, no ambition . . . just playing knight all day. I was developing a mental picture that was strengthened as I watched the man remove his helmet and throw back a cup of Gatorade handed to him by one of the women, who said something that made him look my way.

"Mr. Ackermann?" I said, stepping closer.

He looked me up and down, then he finished his drink.

He was a large man, taller than me at about six foot two. Like the man playing computer games at his house, he had long, thick hair—his was brown—which cascaded moistly from beneath his helmet, giving him a flamboyant, adventurous air. His rugged face was covered with beads of sweat, the thick eyebrows absolutely hanging with it. He had widely spaced, brown eyes; full, almost feminine lips; and a fine, long nose that came to an abrupt point, giving his face an angular, hatchetlike shape.

He accepted a second cup of Gatorade from the same woman as I again asked, "Mr. Ackermann?"

"Yeah," he said. "Who are you?"

I told him my name.

"You a reporter?" he asked.

To which I replied, "No. Why would you think I was a reporter?"

"We get a lot of reporters hanging around before the spring war. We make for good targets. They like to write funny articles about how weird we are."

"Are you weird?"

I don't think he had quite expected that question. Placing his helmet atop his sword before standing the whole arrangement in a golf bag near an equipment pile, he shrugged and said, "I suppose it depends on which side you're looking at things from."

"Meaning what?"

"If you're watching from outside, you won't understand.

But if you're in a role, it all makes perfect sense. It's all a matter of control. Voluntary, disciplined, focused control.''

"I already told you that I'm not a reporter," I said. "You don't have to throw me any sales pitch."

"You asked," he replied. "So if you're not a reporter, who are you?"

"Is there someplace we could speak in private?"

"Why?"

"It's about your mother."

"What about my mother?"

"I really think it would be better in private."

He looked at me, and there in what was about the first spring sunshine of the coming season I caught just a flicker of a kind of personality I understood. There was anger there—anger suppressed, like my father suppresses his anger, and my grandfather, and my brother. You could see it in their faces the same way you could see it in Ronald Ackermann's. It came up from inside involuntarily, like a shudder, flashing through the eyes. And, despite any effort they made to quell it, despite what was probably a lifelong struggle to mask and control it, I had lived with this kind of person long enough to recognize the brief, telltale indications that this was a man who felt first and thought afterwards.

Despite my being my father's son, I'm not like that. Actually, I'm the exact opposite, or so I like to believe. I think first and feel second. And that, it seemed to me at that moment, gave me an advantage over a man like Ronald Ackermann . . . and my brother too, truth be told. It gave me an edge. Or so I liked to believe.

If he wanted it this way, then I decided to give it to him.

"It's my unpleasant duty to inform you that your mother's remains have been located," I said, right into those hard, revealing eyes. "I'm afraid she's dead, Mr. Ackermann. I'm sorry."

"Dead?" he said, speaking softly, his mouth remaining open after he'd said it. "But . . ."

"Now can we speak in private?"

"Are you sure it's her?"

Not: How did it happen?

Or: Where was she?

Or: Where has she been all this time?

Or: My God, my mother's really dead!

But: Are you sure it's her?

I marked that one in my mind.

"They haven't declared her identity officially yet," I said. "But it's only a matter of time until they do. I felt that you should know, so I decided to speak to you personally. I'll be seeing your stepfather at four-thirty this afternoon at his restaurant, to extend the same courtesy."

Again Ronald Ackermann's eyes gave him away, affording me that split second's worth of warning that I needed. Just as he screamed, "NOOOO!" and barreled toward me. I stepped to one side, and he ran past, full steam, like a bull charging. But he hadn't been charging me. He was just running, like an animal, overcome with emotion, moving, trying to get away. The other people in the group all stepped in closer to me, watching him run, not speaking, though I could feel their collective curiosity. I stood there feeling a little like a snake, but convinced also that I had done well.

Ronald's reaction had been a good one, one I could accept. I've been an undertaker for a long time, so I've seen plenty of grief. I know it. It's a part of my life.

Ronald Ackermann's grief, what I had seen of it, felt genuine, which, as cruel and cold as it might sound, was pretty much what I had wanted to discover when I first decided to talk to him. Though I'd only been able to see his face for an instant, he'd passed the test as far as I was concerned. I felt that I had an idea of where he stood regarding his mother's death. As I watched him run first across the parking lot, and then across another softball diamond, arriving at last at the concession stand, I was thinking: His stepfather's next.

I wanted to see his stepfather's grief. It wouldn't be as fresh as Ronald's, since Everett Chase had already been informed of his wife's death the previous day. But I'd know. Looking at him, talking to him, feeling the vibrations in the air around him, I was confident that I'd know the truth about his sorrow . . . and, more to the point, I felt certain that I'd know the truth about how deeply he grieved.

Somewhat embarrassed, I glanced at the others standing near me, shrugged, and followed Ronald Ackermann to the closed concession stand into which he had disappeared. It was a little brick building, painted white, with a large front window covered with sheets of plywood. I tried the door, which was the one Ronald had accessed, but found it locked. I knocked, called his name, and pressed my ear to the door.

A murmuring voice.

He was talking to himself.

I knocked again, finally giving up and walking away, leaving him contained and alone, to feel whatever he felt. Whatever it was, I was certain that I understood enough about it, and him, to be sure that it was deep, intense, and genuine. It was exactly that sense of understanding, that sense of having made a first step in the right direction, that made what happened later that afternoon all the more awful.

Everett Chase received me at 4:45, emerging from his office with an extended hand and apologies on his tongue. He didn't look like I had expected him to look, although I suppose I didn't have any rational reason to have expected him to look one way or another. I was distracted anyway, having spent the hours leading up to our meeting thinking about my first encounter with his stepson Ronald and the things the young man had said when he finally came out of the little brick building where he had spent nearly a quarter of an hour composing himself.

"It's nice to meet you, Mr. Hawley." Chase said, pumping my hand and smiling broadly. "I've heard a lot about you. You're kind of a celebrity."

He was almost exactly my height, but fat. Really fat. Probably pushing three hundred pounds. His face was heavily jowled, creating a kind of harmless, hound dog countenance that, when combined with the grin and the bright, happy blue eyes, went a long way toward explaining his popularity with the patrons of his restaurant. I could just see him going from table to table, greeting the regulars by name and asking, with the sincerity that only a fat man can muster when discussing the topic, "How's your dinner?"

After a few preliminaries, he took me on a quick tour of the Ivy Spring's premises, pointing out the new, white marble fireplace in the "Lovers' Nook" that he had just put in, the falling water in the grand ballroom that was generated at the top of a clear glass fountain to gurgle and plummet two full floors before joining the boiling roil in the illuminated pool beneath, and the marvelous painting he had commissioned for the ceiling in the "Touch of Romance" room that depicted a group of chubby little angel-like cupids aiming their arrows at each other through the clouds.

I have to say, all in all, the restaurant was quite impressive, but not half as impressive as its owner. Everett Chase displayed all the stereotypical jollity of the fat man, without so much as a hint of the slowness of motion that one might expect from someone his size. He practically radiated energy, scurrying here to point out this interesting feature, rushing there to make sure I didn't miss another, talking a mile a minute all the while.

I should probably stick a disclaimer in at this point about the way I've been describing Everett Chase as a "fat man." I feel entitled to bluntness on this topic since, up until about six months ago, I was fat too. Not as big as Mr. Chase to be sure, but I was up there at about two hundred and thirty pounds before I finally decided to do something about a problem that, I discovered once the weight was gone, had been causing me a great deal of self-image trouble all my life. I lost fifty-five pounds on a combination diet and workout program I bought at one of those health food stores in a local mall, and, at least so far, I've kept it off. As a consequence, I've developed a new confidence in myself, as well as discovering an appetite for physical exercise that I never even knew I had. The stair machine I've got down in the funeral home's basement and I have become very good friends.

"When do you eat dinner, Mr. Hawley?" Chase asked.

"My wife gets off work at 4:30, so we usually eat by 5: 15," I replied.

"So precisely?"

"At the funeral home, evening viewings start at 7:00," I explained. "But the immediate family usually shows up anywhere from 6:15 to 6:30. That gives them some time alone and me a chance to fix anything that might not be exactly to their liking before their friends arrive. So, with setting up flowers, putting on the coffee, and double-checking the body, I've got to be dressed and ready to go by 5:45 at the latest."

"Do you work the afternoon viewings too?"

"Yes. I also make arrangements and removals. I do everything but embalm. For that you need a separate license."

"When do you have time for a life?"

"The funeral home is my life."

"And these investigations I've read about, the ones for which you're so infamous, where do they fit in?"

"I consider those a natural extension of my job."

"Just another service?"

"Something like that, though not quite."

"Well, then, since you eat early anyway, may I offer you dinner as my guest? It'll give you a chance to sample a little of what I do."

As tempting as I found his offer, Nat wasn't with me, so I declined, making him frown. As an excuse I cited the fact that as a vegetarian I almost never eat in restaurants.

"You eat no meat at all?" he asked with interest.

"None," I replied.

"No chicken, or fish?"

"Especially no chicken, and I must admit, there haven't been many days in my life ruined by a lack of salmon. Though in a pinch, like when I'm out for business, I'll have tuna or scrod, just to be polite. Also, it helps me avoid having what I eat become a topic of discussion."

"According to the restaurant trade magazines," Chase said, extending his arm to indicate that I should precede him up a long, winding set of stairs while ignoring my hint about not making my dietary idiosyncrasies an issue between us, "vegetarian cuisine is the next in thing. The chef and I have been dabbling a little with it here. We're even planning an all vegetarian section of the menu. When it's ready, you'll have to come and tell us how we did."

I thanked him and assured him that my wife and I would

be glad to oblige. At the head of the stairs we crossed a lobby that led onto an outdoor patio with tables and umbrellas. Edward Chase sat down at a table right next to the patio's railing, fanning himself with a menu after the climb, and telling the waiter, who appeared almost instantaneously, that he would like a sloe gin fizz, and that his guest would like, ''What?''

''Diet Coke.''

''No alcohol either?'' he asked as the waiter departed.

''No.''

''Can I ask you why you're a vegetarian, Mr. Hawley?'' he said. ''Is it philosophical?''

''No.'' I replied. ''It's practical. I just don't like meat.''

This was my standard answer to his question, which was one I heard quite often. The truth was a little more personal, and therefore, I assumed, would have been more likely to be misunderstood, necessitating a long explanation that I didn't feel like going into at the moment.

I had become a strict veg the day the first cat Nat and I had shared, Leonardo, a purebred, snow-white, long-haired male Persian with blue eyes, who was deaf, since all over-bred cats like him are born that way, died. I had lived with that cat for almost nine years. When he died, I cried. Sincerely. Then it struck me that I was crying over an animal . . . an animal I had grown to truly love. What was the difference between him and any other animal? I wondered. What was the difference between him and me really? We were both alive. We were both warm-blooded, had emotions and moods, likes and dislikes, quirks and charms, problems and talents. We both loved the same woman. We both pretty much just wanted to be left alone. Just because Leo couldn't talk didn't make him an object. He was animate, and in his own unique way, very beautiful.

Then I realized that it wasn't strictly necessary for any other living creature to die so that I could continue living. Maybe, thousands of years ago, people needed to kill in order to survive. But I didn't need to do it. So why should I? Why should I kill, even indirectly? I wanted no part of it. So I stopped eating animals.

It's a nebulous explanation, I know. It's also probably illogical, impractical—considering that I wear leather shoes, and that animal fat is used in making all sorts of things, including, believe it or not, the tin cans in which vegetables are often packaged—and it may even prove to be a rationalization for another completely unrelated and, as of yet, unarticulated motivation. But it's my own personal decision regarding my own personal behavior, and it's nobody else's goddamn business.

Sorry.

Back to Everett Chase:

"So where's the ivy?" I asked as the waiter set down our drinks.

Chase looked at me blankly for a moment, and then his eyes lit up and he laughed.

"Oh, that's right. You didn't go past the reception desk. I've been asked that question so many times that I've got a plaque on the wall there to explain it. My wife, not I, actually started this restaurant. I just sort of fell into running it."

I watched him as he said this.

Not a flicker.

"The story behind the restaurant's name is that Madeline once went white water rafting with her first husband. They were on vacation in one of those rugged states—Utah or something. But the trip was a disaster. They dumped, got drenched, had to drag this lousy canoe up on a bank while all their provisions went rushing out of sight. While lying on the sand, soaking wet, half-drowned and thoroughly pissed off, my wife's husband looked at her and said, 'White water, I don't need. I think my speed would be more an ivory spring.'

"Madeline always remembered the sound of the words, 'ivory spring,' and when she had the opportunity to start this place, that's the name she chose."

"So where's the ivy come in?"

"When the sign makers misspelled 'ivory,' leaving out the *o* and *r* to leave 'ivy,' Madeline just let it go. I think she thought it was even better this way . . . more artsy and personal. So the place has been the Ivy Spring ever since. She had a very private sense of humor."

From where we were sitting next to the patio's railing, I

could see straight out across about twenty yards of lawn. Running past the restaurant was a street, and as I considered my next question, a car trolled by, turned into the restaurant's driveway, kind of stuttered, and then sped up. A moment later the same car exited the parking lot and drove away in the opposite direction from which it had come.

Before I could speak, Everett Chase really broke the ice. Actually, he didn't just break it, he smashed it when he said, "So, Mr. Hawley, is this an objective interview or an adversarial interrogation?"

"New American Life Insurance must have told you that I was working for them," I said.

"That's right. So am I a suspect, or a victim?"

"How would you describe yourself?"

"In my mind, I'm a victim. Absolutely. But there are those, my wife's son Ronald, for instance, who might think otherwise."

"Tell me about Ronald."

"Ronald is a unique individual. What, specifically, would you like to know?"

"Well, for a start, how long has he been running around at the zoo, hitting other unique individuals over the head with a stick?"

The smile that blossomed on Everett Chase's face was wide and infectious. Suddenly, and quite against my better judgment, I realized that I actually liked this man. I certainly hadn't liked Ronald, with whom I had anticipated at least a sense of empathy, given that it was his mother's disembodied head I'd found. But Everett Chase, who I had already predetermined as my most likely suspect in the crime, after the embalmer Edward Craig, and who I had therefore expected to mistrust, I found effortlessly endearing. Still, his lack of apparent distress over the discovery of his wife's remains troubled me.

"Ronald's been a member of SWORDS for as long as I've known him," Chase said, leaning back in his seat and folding his hands atop his generous stomach. His glass sat empty on the table before him, making me wonder when he'd drained it since I hadn't seen him so much as touch it.

"As opposed to the S.C.A., the Society for Creative Anachronism,'' he continued, ''that started in Berkeley, California, about twenty years back, SWORDS was begun more recently, on the East Coast somewhere. Long Island, I think. It's a much more complicated experience. Though the members deny it, I've heard that the club involves a lot of drugs. And other things. Leave it to Ronald to find something like that. He's truly his mother's son, which has caused him simply no end of grief.''

''You mean getting along in the world?''

''I mean getting along with his mother.''

''He and his mother fought?''

''It wasn't so much that,'' Chase said, signaling for the waiter to bring him a fresh drink. ''A gin and tonic, this time, I think. And another pointless glass of bubbles for my guest.'' Then, returning his full attention to me, he continued, ''Madeline saw quite a bit of herself in Ronald, and, by contrast, everything of her husband in Allison. There was always such a strange dynamic going on in that family. The kids belonged absolutely to one parent or the other. And you could tell which it was after about five minutes' worth of casual interaction.

''Allison was her father's daughter—ambitious, driven, sharp. While Ronald was endowed with every one of Madeline's personality traits—an artistic nature, a taste for a certain amount of chaos in his personal space, and a spontaneous streak that made him unpredictable but fun to be around. Unfortunately, he also inherited every single one of Madeline's less constructive attributes. He has absolutely no discernible ambition, is an unapologetic dreamer, is hopelessly lazy, and, most of all, he's as stubborn as hell.''

''So she favored her artistic son over her type A daughter,'' I observed, ''since they were so similar as people?''

Chase gulped his new drink quickly before responding. ''No way. That boy drove her crazy.''

''But you just said they were exactly alike.''

''That was the problem. Opposites attract, similarities repulse. Isn't that the rule of magnetism?''

''So they fought?''

''No.''

''What then?''

"They were close, loved each other deeply, and got along great, at least on the surface. But Madeline didn't trust Ronald as far as she could throw him. Knowing what she did of her own nature, she was convinced that he was doomed to live a life just as directionless as hers had been. She always said that if she hadn't married two men who knew how to provide for her material needs, she'd have been lost."

"Is that why she excluded Ronald from the insurance money?"

"More or less."

"What's that mean?"

"You never answered my first question, Mr. Hawley. Is this a friendly interview, or what?"

I thought about that for a moment and decided to take a shot.

"I truly don't know, Mr. Chase."

"Call me Everett."

"All right, Everett. But I still don't know. You strike me as an intelligent man. You've got to see how this whole thing stacks up."

"Certainly," he agreed. "If I were you, I would be the first person I would suspect."

"And, if you were me, suspecting you as I do, how justified do you think those suspicions would be?"

Everett Chase smiled, raised his glass, and said, "To candor, then." After he drained his drink, he added, "Mr. Hawley, I loved my wife very, very much. As much as any man could love any woman, I suppose you could say. I would never have done anything to harm her, especially, as the inimitable insurance man T. W. Younger so obviously thinks, for anything as inconsequential as money."

"You consider a million bucks inconsequential?"

"Yes, I do."

"I'm jealous."

"Don't be."

"Is it because of the restaurant?"

"Partially. And partially it's because of some other things that aren't really any of your business. The point is that I was fifty-three years old when I married Madeline. I was financially fine. I didn't need her money. And I certainly didn't need a failing restaurant.''

''Failing?''

''Listen, Mr. Hawley . . .''

''Bill.''

''Listen, Bill.'' He leaned forward. ''Madeline's lack of direction bothered her deeply. She often said that she wanted to try setting a goal for herself, like she saw other people do every day. So when her first husband died, and she received that big insurance settlement, she used the money to start this restaurant. But she just wasn't a businesswoman. She didn't have the right temperament. As a matter of fact, she was a disaster. If I hadn't taken things over, we wouldn't be sitting here today because there wouldn't be anyplace to sit. It's that simple. I've pumped a great deal of my own money, and God knows how much of my time, into this place. It's been a real trial.''

''Why'd you do it, Mr. Chase?''

''Everett.''

I nodded.

''I did it because it's fun,'' he said contentedly. ''At first, to be frank, I did it because I was angry. There's a puritanical streak in me that just couldn't sit idly by while a business as valuable as this one had the potential to be went down the tubes. But after I got involved, I realized that this was a great deal. I'm at an age now where I need something like this. I've always been one of the grey men in this world—the fat guy at the corner desk who everybody dumped on. Here, I'm a big shot. It's like a reward.''

''How did your wife feel about you taking over?''

''I don't know. I didn't do it until after she disappeared.''

''Tell me about that.''

''There's really not much to tell,'' he said, standing up and taking a few steps before turning to face the street. Leaning forward, with both his hands on the wrought-iron railing, he continued, as if speaking to himself.''She just didn't come home one night. I did all the typical, legal things a person does, called the police, took out ads in the newspaper, called friends and relatives, worried myself half to death. But when it was all said and done there was still no sign of her. Then the rumors started. When the condition of the books for the restaurant were leaked to the insurance company, I came under scrutiny by an absolutely awful man named Huff. He was a real jerk. No tact. Not like you. But I weathered it. That was five years ago. Five years, which is a long time.''

Yes, it is, I found myself agreeing, suddenly understanding a little of his point. If I had expected tears or emotional outbursts from him, I was going to be rightfully disappointed. His grief had happened already. He was past it.

''For me,'' he said, turning back to face me as he leaned on the railing and crossed his arms over his chest, ''my wife died a long time ago. Your finding her now only verifies what I've known all along but never dared admit to anyone.''

''What's that?'' I asked.

But I never got an answer.

Instead, over Everett Chase's shoulder, coming from his right, the car that had turned around in the restaurant's driveway at the beginning of our conversation reappeared, barreling down the road. Just as Chase was about to answer my question, the driver downshifted, making the car's back wheels squeal on the pavement as they spun in response to the engine's winding roar.

It was a Camaro, I noted, my attention directed at it because of the abrupt noise it made. It was a Camaro, dark blue, maybe black, with gold, wire wheels. But that's all I saw.

Traveling in the lane closest to the restaurant side of the street, its passenger window facing us, the Camaro blasted past. I was halfway out of my seat. Everett Chase was half-turned, saying, ''What the . . . ?'' just as the sound came, the new sound, not the engine or the squeal of racing rubber, but a fast, tight, brutal sound that I don't think either of us recognized. I figured it out later, with the benefit of hindsight clarifying the memory fragments in my mind, but I don't think that Everett Chase ever even knew what hit him.

It sounded like a giant zipper on a giant pair of pants far away. I know that's a dumb analogy, but that's how it sounded. Two bursts, *THHRRRIPPP THHRRRIPPP*, and the Camaro kept on going. Two bursts . . . two eruptions of light in the passenger's window, at the hand of a dark form, holding something and just letting loose. At absolutely the same instant that I heard the sounds, and saw the fire, Everett Chase pitched backward toward me, something dark and wet splashing on the front of him in such a way that it looked like a spray, as great dark patches flowered on the back of his sweaty white oxford shirt. All around us there was noise. Something snapped off the bricks behind me. Glass shattered, also behind me. Everett Chase hit first the table, and then me, taking the whole damned thing, pastel-striped umbrella and all, down as I tried to stand, and then folded beneath his weight.

I swear it felt as if time had slowed and the shooting went on for an hour. I swear it felt as if a thousand bullets slammed into Everett Chase's bleeding body, and the building behind us. I swear it felt as if I was suddenly involved in a war.

But it wasn't true. Actually, the shooting lasted just long enough for the person in the car to get off two brief bursts from what I would later be told was an Encom MP-45 Assault Pistol, which was an unusual weapon for a drive-by shooter to be using. But it did have the advantage of a clip that held fifty 9 mm shells, so in all it was probably close to that many bullets that spattered around me as I fell beneath the dead body of a man to whom I had been speaking just seconds before. They ricocheted everywhere, and did an incredible amount of damage, not only to Everett Chase, but also to his restaurant.

It was a miracle that no one else was killed. Especially me. But in an entirely involuntarily act of heroism, Everett Chase essentially saved my life by taking all the bullets that came in our direction, shielding me with his girth, and dragging me down as he died, which effectively pulled me out of the line of fire.

But that's not saying that I came away unhurt, either physically or emotionally. Both those aspects of myself were damaged: my emotions by the immediacy of seeing, for the first time in my life, a human being die violently. It is a vision that I will never forget. Physically, two of my fingers first felt as if they had burst into flames, and then went absolutely, ominously numb. My dignity was also bruised when, after it was all over and I stood up, completely without thinking about it, just stood up like a puppet coming up on a string, I found, to my unyielding dismay, that I'd wet my pants.

Then the world started moving again. . . .

And I was screaming.

SIX
■■■■■■■■■

WHEN THEY PULLED me off Everett Chase, I was giving him C.P.R., like I'd learned as an orderly in the emergency room at Southwest General Hospital, where I had worked all through college. It was a futile waste of time, but I wasn't exactly firing on all cylinders at just that moment. As a matter of fact, there was a sound like rushing wind in my ears that I would later decide was my inflated blood pressure. A weird, silver sparkle was dancing along the periphery of my vision, as if it were snowing, just out of sight, everywhere I looked. And I was trembling. Really trembling. Like I was cold.

It was a cop who pulled me off. I don't know how much time transpired between the actual event of the drive-by shooting and the arrival of the police, but the fire department wasn't far behind. The cop was a young guy, maybe twenty-two or -three, and at first he was rough with me. Not that I could blame him, since as soon as he pulled me to my feet I started shouting at him to look at the bullet holes, and the broken glass, and why wasn't he chasing the Camaro?! Which was where he wanted to start.

"What Camaro?" he asked.

And I called him an asshole.

Later, in the hospital, I told him that I was sorry, and he forgave me, sort of. He was a cowboy, and didn't take to the shenanigans of civilians very well . . . even civilians who were obviously in shock. Sitting with a blanket thrown over my shoulders in the E.R., with my left hand wrapped in a towel, and my right hand balancing a cup of something hot, vending machine tea or coffee—even after drinking half of it, I still wasn't sure which—I thought that, if this young cop was so cynical at his tender age, he wasn't going to make it to retirement, knowing what he was in for as the years went by. I felt like telling him that he should get out, get another job—one that wouldn't bring him into contact with people under stress—but I didn't. He wouldn't listen to me anyway. That's probably the one defining aspect of being a cowboy: you don't listen to anybody. So I just answered his questions, and eventually he went away.

His replacement was a detective who I vaguely recognized. He accompanied me into the treatment area and talked to me while the doctor looked at my busted fingers. At the time I thought it pretty insensitive that he would persist in asking me questions while I was being treated by the doctor. But later I realized that the reason he had done it was to take my mind off how much my fingers were hurting. He'd meant it as a kindness; the guy was cool.

I'd been shot, as it turned out. And I didn't even remember it. I'd been shot in such a way that I was going to lose the tip of the middle finger on my left hand, nail and all—unless the plastic surgeon could do something about saving it. They gave me two shots, one in the arm, the other in the thigh. The next thing I knew, everything felt just fine.

The plastic surgeon kept me waiting for an hour since he was coming in all the way from Hinckley, where he had a surgery clinic of his own. The hospital had a plastic surgeon on staff, but the guy from Hinckley was better, and, seeing that I was John Hawlinski's son—my dad only changed his name after retiring from the Parma Fire Department and going to work full-time at the funeral home he and his younger brother had built—it was decided by the emergency room staff that nothing but the best would do. So I had to wait, and while I did they gave me shots, and the detective, named Karl, "with a K," Rubins—whose nickname was Special K, I would eventually learn—kept what was left of my attention fixed on him, instead of on my mangled hand.

So that's why the guys in the ambulance had wrapped it up and told me to keep pressure on it and not to let it go. It wasn't so that I would stop the bleeding, since the fingers weren't really bleeding that badly, it was so that I wouldn't see what a 9 mm shell, traveling at like two thousand feet per second, had done to the soft flesh and brittle bone of the most delicate and arguably most important feature of my anatomy. It also explained why the driver, a guy named Sevnik, said that now I really was Wild Bill. I'd earned my nickname the hard way.

Caught in the cross fire, as they say.

No way.

Caught in the *line* of fire. Somebody had known exactly what they were doing, and I was just damned lucky to be alive.

"Did you get a look at them?" I remember Detective Rubins asking at one point.

As much as I'd like to get it exactly right, there's no way I can. That conversation, immediately after the nurse gave me my two shots—to "Calm me down," as she put it—is forever locked in my mind inside a kind of bubble of confusion. It doesn't feel real even now. It feels like a dream, and I remember it in snatches. No linear connectiveness at all. No real motion. No continuity. Just the bouncing of the white linoleum around me as I lay on the gurney and moved my head while the plastic surgeon, a little man with a thingamajig wrapped around his forehead that sported an articulated arm at the end of which was a magnifying glass and also with what looked like a jeweler's glass stuck in one eye, hunched over my hand, telling me two things over and over again. The first was, "This isn't going to be as bad as you think. I'm sure we'll save quite a bit." And the second, equally as reassuring, given the context, was, "Please, look over there. Don't look at what I'm doing."

"But it's my hand."

"Please, look over there. It isn't as bad as you think."

At one point Nat came in, looking pale and scared. I smiled in what I hoped would be a reassuring way. Only to give her, as she described it days later, a death's head grin. She said that I was covered with beads of sweat, that my skin was a pasty white that scared her even more than did the spots of red splattered over my white shirt, and that my eyes were so glassy that she sincerely doubted if I could see her at all.

Later, we were together in what the nurse called, "the recovery room." I was already hurting, despite the shots. Nat never cried, though she later admitted that she had wanted to. And Detective Rubins never left us alone.

The skeleton of our conversation, conducted during my anesthetizing, surgery, and recovery, occurred along the following lines. Detective Rubins asked the questions. I gave the answers.

Did you see the car?

Yes.

What kind was it?

A black or dark blue Camaro with gold, wire wheels.

Did you see the shooter?

Not really.

Man or woman?

Man, I think. But I'm not sure.

Did you see the gun?

I saw fire.

It was a modified Encom MP-45 Assault Pistol, upgraded to a full automatic. We found it on the side of the road about a mile down. They just pitched it. No serial numbers. No manufacturer's ID marks. No prints. That's a weird gun for a gangbanger to use, Mr. Hawley. An Uzi, or a Mac 10, that's more the speed. An MP-45's an exotic weapon, a collector's weapon. Are you sure you didn't notice anything about the shooter?

Not a thing. He was just a dark shape, with fire in his hands.

He?

Figure of speech.

You spoke to Ronald Ackermann earlier in the day. Did he say anything that made you think that he might be involved?

Ronald Ackermann!

At this point I remember trying to sit up, making Dr. Don't-Worry-You're-Only-Going-To-Lose-Part-Of-Your-Hand really get snotty about lying still and not looking at what he was doing, although it wasn't that bad. Really.

"You've got to protect him," I said, after a nurse pushed

me back down. "He's going to be next!"

"Why?" Detective Rubins asked excitedly. "Why do you say that, Mr. Hawley?"

"Christ!" I exclaimed, licking my lips a lot because for some reason, probably the shots, my mouth felt as dry as the inside of a vacuum cleaner bag. "First his sister got greased by a mugger. Then his stepfather got bumped in a drive-by. Everybody that's in line for that insurance money's gotten it in the neck. It's just logical that he would be next."

Detective Rubins looked like he was thinking that one over but couldn't quite bring himself to buy it.

From there it gets kind of hazy. And by the time I got home, at sometime around midnight—the plastic surgeon had worked on my hand for nearly four hours, leaving my index and middle fingers wrapped so thickly in white gauze that I looked like somebody had stuck two golf balls on my fingers—I was really hurting and thoroughly sick to my stomach. My dad had shown up at the hospital too, and, after setting me up on the couch in the living room at the funeral home, he and Nat went into the dining room, where I could hear their subdued voices, earnestly hashing something over. Meanwhile Jerry sat next to me in his wheelchair looking so grim with concern that I eventually told him to lighten up because his facial expression made me think that he had to go to the bathroom.

Finally, I caught a clear sentence from the dining room. It was Natalie's voice, and she said, "Well, Dad, despite all that, I really think we ought to tell him."

"Tell him what?" I called, and when I did my head boomed inside, the veins in my temple throbbing in time to my heartbeat, making me wonder whether or not you can get a hangover from doctor-prescribed anesthetics. Briefly, I remembered a kid I used to work with at the hospital when I was an orderly. We called him Dr. Gas. He was an anesthesiologist. Eventually they booted him for sniffing his own product. So, who knew?

Nat and Dad appeared in the living room looking serious. Everybody was looking serious. How come nobody was looking angry? I was angry. I wasn't showing it right that second because I had too many Demerols in me, not to mention whatever else they'd dripped into my arm through that IV tube, but I was mad all right. For the first time in a long time, certainly since the time someone tried to kill Nat by throwing her down the funeral home's side staircase, I was pissed to my shoes. Why was I the only one?

When I tried to get up my head spun and I had to immediately sit back down. Nat hurried to my side and I asked her again what she had been talking about in the other room. What was it that she thought I should know? She glanced at my dad, either for direction, or as an acknowledgement that she was going to defy his wishes, and said, "Larry called while you were in the hospital. Jerry took it. He's found something. . . ."

"Jerry found something?" I asked, blinking, trying hard not to be confused.

"No, Larry Fizner did," Nat said gently. "He's been looking for that embalmer you were so worried about. Edward Craig . . ."

"He found Craig?"

Nat pressed her lips together, then she said, "He's not sure. But he thinks so."

Again I got up, but this time I was ready for the dizziness and was able to beat it. That's one benefit of having been falling-down drunk as many times as I've been: you develop sea legs, so to speak. Nat wanted to help me, but I brushed her aside. The same with my dad. They both looked hurt, but there was something going on in my head that I couldn't afford to have them interrupt. "Just gimme a minute," I kept saying, staggering toward the door. "Just gimme a minute. Gimme a minute."

I navigated the stairs very carefully, snapped on the green-shaded banker's lamp on the desk in my office, opened the cabinet door next to my leather chair, and seated myself so heavily that for a split second I thought I'd go over and land on my head. The office was dark, my skull was pounding, and my eyes, though not exactly unfocused, were kind of distorting things, forcing me to concentrate very hard on what I was looking at . . .

Which was the photograph of Madeline Chase's arm that I

had taken the previous evening in the Peaceful Knoll Cemetery's mausoleum.

I've seen shit in my life. Nasty shit. Shit that other people—normal people—wouldn't believe goes on in the real world. Doctors, firemen, cops, and undertakers see it all. Even in Cleveland—which isn't exactly Los Angeles or New York—if you're in the business long enough, you'll see it, all of it, the stuff that sticks.

Like the black transvestite found in the trunk of a car in a junkyard in the middle of August, bloated and horrible, having died as a result of sixty-six stab wounds inflicted with an ice pick . . . which, according to the pathologist next to whom you're standing in the morgue's freezer, holding on to your lunch by flexing every muscle you can think to flex, is, "Overkill, since sixty woulda probably done the job just fine."

Or the baby placed in the clothes dryer by her mother.

Or the lady who drank Clorox bleach, because, as the note she left explained, she missed her cat.

Or the ninety-year-old man who wanted to die, but was prevented from taking his own life by the son with whom he lived. That man had found an old ax head in the vacant lot behind their house—the son had hidden everything sharp—which he had honed on the driveway before he cut his throat. His son hadn't been surprised that his dad had finally punched his own ticket . . . it was the way he had done it that startled him. After all, his dad had a history . . .

A history.

I was sitting in the dark, looking at a Polaroid photograph of an embalmed arm in a clear plastic bag. The fingers were curled slightly in toward the palm, which was facing me, so that I could see the arm's wrist.

Nat placed herself behind my chair, laying her hands on my shoulders as she said that maybe it would be a good idea if I went to bed.

I shook my head, eyes locked on the picture of Madeline Chase's arm. Maybe it was the adrenaline of anger and pain still charging through my blood. Maybe it was the painkillers the doctors had pumped into me. Maybe it was both, or neither, or anything. But something in my mind had clicked just then. Something which I had seen before, but had not seen, had just clicked. It was right there, but I didn't know what the hell it meant.

"Look," I said, pointing at the photograph. "Do you see? Right there. See?"

Nat glanced first at me, and then at the picture, asking, "What am I looking at?"

I picked a felt-tipped pen up off the desk and leaned forward in my chair. Using the pen as a pointer, I said, "There. Right there, on the wrist. What do you see right there?"

Nat looked again, saying finally, "They look like scars."

"How many scars?"

"Oh, I don't know. A couple."

"What do they look like?"

"What do you mean?"

"How would she get scars like that?"

"From cuts?"

"What kind of cuts?"

"I'm not following this, Bill. You're not making much sense."

Turning the pen around and uncapping it, I drew three lines across my wrist and then showed my wrist to Nat, saying, "What does that look like? If those lines were scars, what would you think?"

"I'd think that you had tried to slash your wrist," she said.

I pitched the pen triumphantly back onto the desk, saying, "Exactly."

Nat nodded vaguely, paused, and then asked, "So what does that prove?"

"Statistically," I replied, "it takes most people who succeed in killing themselves several tries before they get it right."

"So?"

"Why was she embalmed?"

"What?"

"Embalmed," I demanded. "She was embalmed. You know about that. I told you what Rusty said about the head I found. The coroner determined that Madeline Chase's body had definitely been embalmed prior to its having been dismembered. Why would that be?''

"Because she killed herself?'' Nat asked, putting my two separate inferences together to no good end.

I could feel the muscles in my face go hard.

"Bill?'' she said.

"What?''

"What's the connection?''

My facial muscles felt positively rigid as I admitted, "I don't know.''

"But you think there is one?''

"Yes.''

"You think Mrs. Chase killed herself?''

"I sure think she tried at one time or another.''

"Which means what?''

"That she was likely to try again.''

"What's that got to do with her having been embalmed?''

"I don't know.''

"But they're connected?''

"I think maybe.''

"Will you come to bed now?''

"Yeah,'' I said, placing both my hands on the arms of my chair and pushing myself to my feet with a heavy, heartfelt sigh. "But I doubt if I'll sleep.''

Boy, was I ever wrong.

Larry Fizner showed up bright and early the next morning, positively thrilled about my wounds. I was so awesomely sore that I found it very difficult to share his enthusiasm.

"Here,'' he said, standing in my kitchen while I sat hunched at the table, inhaling the steam rising off the mug of vegetable soup Nat had warmed for me in the microwave before, at my insistence, she had gone to work. Larry had his back to the window over the sink so that his form was defined by sunlight sent directly from hell to fry my tender eyeballs. "Look at this.''

I squinted as he pulled the front of his shirt out of his pants and showed me his stomach.

"What's that?'' I asked indifferently.

"That's ninety some odd stitches,'' he replied. "Guy used

a bayonet on me. You know why a bayonet's blade is shaped the way it is, with its top being flat and the sides tapered? It's shaped that way so that the triangular puncture wound it makes won't close.''

"That's nice," I observed.

"Most of my stitches were internal," he continued, "but you can follow the cut line up from my crotch to my left bottom rib. One long slash and three stabs. Fucker almost took me out on the last one. Nicked my spleen. That's bad shit."

I swallowed some soup.

"And this," Larry added, leaving his shirttails out and pulling up his left pant leg, "was a rifle slug. Went right though my calf. Boom! In one side and out the other. See? Two little red dots. Luckily, it missed the bone."

More soup.

"And . . ."

I placed the mug down and lifted one hand, saying, "Mr. Fizner, what's your point?"

Planting himself on a chair, Larry stared at me from across the table. On the countertop near the sink behind him, a yellow Winnie the Pooh cookie jar smiled confidingly over his shoulder, contrasting his words in an almost surreal way.

"You know how they temper steel?" he asked. "They put it in the fire. That's what happened to you yesterday, Bill. You were tempered."

"Yeah," I agreed unhappily. "By gunfire."

"How does it make you feel?"

"Lousy."

"I don't mean physically. How does it make you feel, here, inside?" He tapped his chest.

I looked at him, leaned forward, and said with exaggerated emotion, "It makes me feel lousy."

He frowned.

And I said, "Okay, it did something to me. I'm just not sure it's the same thing you're looking for."

"What's that supposed to mean?"

"We're different, you and I, Mr. Fizner. I'm not a macho guy. I'm a wimp at heart. You know, even after, Christ, what, like a total of twenty years in and around the funeral business,

I still hate the sight of a dead body. I'm still squeamish. There are times when I've honestly got to force myself to go on a pickup. Twenty years, and it's worse now than when I started. Death bothers me, Mr. Fizner. Death and all its details just bug the shit out of me. And it's getting worse as I get older. It's getting me down. I feel like I've spent my whole life in a goddamn cemetery; and yesterday somebody came pretty friggin' close to putting me in one for good. You wear your scars like badges. I don't think I'll ever have the urge to show mine off like you show off yours.''

''You think I was showing off?''

''Weren't you?''

He leaned back in his chair, pointed at my bandaged hand, and said, ''Hurts, doesn't it?''

''Yes.''

''You coulda got killed. Right?''

''So?''

''So the next time, would you rather feel that kind of pain again, or would you rather die?''

''What kind of question is that?''

''It's legitimate. What would you rather have, more pain, or your chips cashed in?''

''Since when did you turn into my Zen master?''

''Answer the question.''

''I'd rather have all my fingers shot off than get killed. Okay? Is that what you wanted me to say?''

''Me too,'' he concurred, lifting his left hand to show me his palm.

I stared for a moment before asking, ''What happened?''

There were five scars crisscrossing the palm that I had never noticed before now because they more or less blended in with the rest of the wrinkles.

''About ten years ago a guy pulled a knife on me,'' he said.

''Was this before or after the bayonet?''

''After, which is exactly the point. I had already been cut once in my life. It was about the worst thing that ever happened to me, but I survived it. It was a bitch, but I beat it. Goddamn if I didn't.''

''So when this guy pulled the knife,'' I said, completing,

or so I thought, his story for him, "you reached out and took it away from him, even though you knew you'd cut up your hand. You're saying that since you had a choice between getting cut and dying, you chose getting cut, even though you knew exactly how getting cut would feel."

Larry shook his head, saying, "No, I didn't take the knife away from him. You can't take a knife away from somebody by grabbing the blade. That's movie bullshit. A knife blade feels so slippery that, no matter how hard you try to grab it, you can't. Actually, that slippery feeling is the steel slicing up your skin."

"Then how'd you get the scars?"

"I grabbed the knife with one hand, while I shot him with the other."

"You know, Mr. Fizner, my head really hurts. And my fingers are throbbing like crazy. What in the hell are you trying to say? Simply. Use little words so I won't miss anything."

Larry used his scarred hand to pull out his cigarettes.

"What I'm saying," he growled, "is that, at first, you're gonna feel gun-shy after what happened to you yesterday. You'll jump at every sound. You might even start having nightmares. It happens, and there's no shame in it. But later, after you've had some time to get used to it, you might be tempted to say to yourself, you know, I almost bit the big one, and it wasn't so bad. Sure, it hurt, but it didn't hurt *that* much. And the next time, you might do something stupid."

"Like trying to grab a knife out of somebody's hand?"

He shrugged.

"It only takes a second to change your life forever, Bill. But you've got two advantages. One is that you know what a dead body looks like. You've seen more than your share. You don't have any illusions about death being noble or glamorous. You know that it stinks, and that it's ugly, sad, and lonely."

I didn't respond at this point because I thought that essentially he was right on the mark.

"Your second advantage is me," he continued, lighting a Camel.

"I'm certainly a lucky guy," I said.

"You think I'm kidding?" he asked, frowning through his smoke.

"I think you've read too many Mickey Spillane novels," I replied.

And that's when it happened: Larry Fizner lost his cool.

"Goddamn it!" he thundered, standing up so abruptly that his chair crashed backward and bounced on the linoleum behind him. "I've been shot, stabbed, burned, and run over by a fucking taxicab! For real, no shit! I'm tryin' to tell you something important here . . . something nobody ever bothered tellin' me! But you ain't interested 'cause I ain't as articulate as you; I ain't had your fuckin' college; I ain't got your kinda class. I can keep what I know to myself 'cause William Goddamn Hawley don't like my fuckin' vocabulary! Jesus . . .''

He turned and hurled his lit cigarette into the kitchen sink. When he faced me again, his voice absolutely quivered with emotion.

"That's the one thing about you that's just bugged the shit outta me ever since we got together: you think I'm *stupid.*"

Looking down at the table, loath to meet his eyes, I said in a contrite tone, "That's not true, Mr. Fizner."

"Isn't it?"

"Listen, my head's not on straight right now. Okay? Stuff's a little messed up."

Larry turned and busied himself running water in the sink to rinse away the ashes from his cigarette, saying over his shoulder, "Right."

"I'm serious," I insisted. "Maybe it's all the dope they got me on. But I'm not thinking straight. Okay? So I'm sorry."

"Stick your sorry."

"Then you stick your sermons."

"It wouldn't have killed you to listen a little for once, even if you didn't give a shit. It wouldn't have killed you to keep your mouth shut and act like you was at least lettin' some of it in this one time."

"Since when have you ever listened to me?" I asked.

He turned, and we faced each other again.

Finally, he said, "You're so fuckin' stubborn it ain't even natural.''

"I had a good teacher," I replied.

Which made him smile . . . crookedly, grudgingly, but definitely, which made me feel about ten pounds lighter.

"So you wanna hear about Edward Craig or what?" he asked.

"First let me tell you about Ronald Ackermann," I returned.

"You still woozy, or could you ride in the van? I don't want you pukin', so be honest."

"I can ride."

"You sure?"

"I said that I can ride."

"Good," Larry said, sliding his cigarette pack into his shirt pocket. "Then let's do it. We can talk on the way. The sooner we get moving the better."

I stood up, feeling light-headed enough when I did that I needed a second to get my bearings.

"I'm tellin' you, Bill," Larry said. "No pukin'. I mean it."

"Mr. Fizner?" I asked.

"Yeah?"

"If you had a gun, then why did you try to grab the knife?"

"Because I didn't want to shoot."

"Why not?"

"I wanted to be a hero and bring the guy in alive."

"Then why didn't you?"

"Because it took me like a second to realize that once the son of a bitch was done choppin' up my hand, he was probably gonna cut off my ears."

"Oh."

Just as we pulled out of the funeral home's parking lot, a Chevrolet Imperial pulled in behind us. Detective Karl "Special K" Rubins, the cop who had sat through my surgery the previous evening, was at the wheel, which came as no surprise. I understood enough about standard police procedure to know that after the initial interview he had conducted with me immediately after the shooting, he'd be expecting a follow-up session in which he'd ask me to run through it all again, just in case I'd missed something the first time. It wasn't that I didn't want to be helpful to the police. After having seen Everett Chase gunned down like I had, I was prepared to do just about anything I could to make sure that the shooter ended up cuffed and in the backseat of a squad car. It was just that, at that particular moment, I felt an absolutely overpowering urge to move, to take some kind of action, to do the things I do. So . . .

"What did the Ackermann kid have to say?" Larry asked, noting the unmarked cop car we had just missed with a squint at his rearview mirror.

"That his stepfather was a skunk," I replied.

"Is that how you felt about him?"

"Who, the stepfather?"

"Uh-huh."

"No." I leaned back in the van's plush captain's chair, cradled my sore hand in my lap, and described how Ronald Ackermann had locked himself in the Metropark's concession stand after I had told him that his mother's remains were almost certainly about to be legally identified.

"Before he went in," I concluded, "his big concern was whether I was absolutely sure that it was his mother we were talking about. But when he came back out, he tried like crazy to convince me that Everett Chase was the biggest asshole on the planet, that he had married Madeline Ackermann for her money, and that he was, in Ronald's own words, quote, 'Your typical, opportunistic, low-life gigolo type guy, who was preying on a grieving, rich, recent widow by romancing her into his evil clutches,' unquote."

"But that's not the impression you got once you actually met the guy?" Larry asked as he maneuvered us onto the freeway.

"Not even close," I replied. "Actually, when it was all said and done, I liked Everett Chase one hell of a lot better than I did Ronald Ackermann. Chase struck me as a genuinely nice man. I can't believe . . ."

I trailed off, and Larry gave me a quiet moment to feel what I was feeling as I recalled my last image of Everett Chase's body, battered and torn, lying faceup on the concrete patio floor with a bloody handprint on the white dress shirt over his heart where I had been pumping his chest with my own bleeding fingers.

"Anyway," I said, blinking my way out of it. "Now it's your turn."

"You sure you're done?"

"Yes."

"Okay."

Larry's story was brief but informative. Missing persons, he said, weren't as hard to run down as most people seemed to think. Unless a man or woman who wished to drop out of one life and start over with another really knew what they were doing, it was his contention that they left a trail that could be easily followed by someone who was motivated enough to try. Starting with a Social Security number and a driver's license, and leading right through to a person's health insurance and need for credit, all it took was a few phone calls to the right sources, and Larry maintained that he could run just about anyone to earth, no matter how hard they tried to hide. And, as it turned out, Edward Craig hadn't really tried to hide very hard at all.

"It's not like he went underground or anything," Larry concluded, a little smugly. "He just had some problems and kinda dropped out of sight. Not as a way to hide, you understand. More like he wanted to start over where it was quiet."

"How does that fit with him being the one who chopped up Madeline Chase?" I asked.

Larry shrugged as he said, "Who knows? All I know for sure is that he had a messy divorce, a booze and drug problem, gambling debts, and he was publicly implicated in some embarrassing professional bullshit that got his name in the newspaper. Psychologically, that would be heavy enough to cave in almost anybody's roof. He let his embalmer's license lapse, got divorced, and pulled the ladders up behind himself. After what they wrote about him in the paper, nobody would take a chance on him as an embalmer anymore anyhow . . . or at least not often enough for him to make a living at it. So, he had to start his life over, doin' something new."

"Which was what?"

"What's a logical job for an ex-embalmer?"

"I don't know."

"How about taxidermy?"

I blinked, feeling admiration for the astute simplicity of Larry's thinking. Finally I said, "You didn't chase down any credit card numbers or driver's licenses or anything else, did you?"

"No," he admitted. "I didn't."

"What did you do?"

"I looked in the yellow pages and called the four taxidermy shops we've got in town askin' for Eddie. I hit on the second call."

"Are you sure it's him?"

Shrugging, he said, "We'll know in a minute. Would you know him by sight?"

"Probably."

"You think he'd remember you?"

"I don't know. We shook hands at a few funeral director dinners, but that was a long time ago. I guess it would all depend on what kind of impression I made at the time. Craig was usually pretty stiff at those things—he always seemed to have an after-dinner drink in his hand, even before dinner. So, no, I don't think he'd remember me at all."

Larry nodded, saying, "Good," as if I had provided him with some sort of an edge. Then he said, "You know how it looks, don't ya? I mean Everett Chase gettin' waxed right after you talked to Ronald Ackermann?"

"Yeah," I agreed. "Although it took a while before it finally sank in. While I was in the hospital, I was worried that the Ackermann kid was going to be the next name on the 'coming soon, to a cemetery near you' list. I even said as much to Detective Rubins. I asked him to set up some kind of police protection for him, just in case. But after I had a little time to think it through, I saw things in a new light."

"And?"

"And now it looks like maybe Ronald Ackermann hurried up and killed his stepfather before the coroner could officially identify his mother's remains. With Chase out of the way, when that ID does come down, instead of being last in line behind his stepfather, Ronald's going to be the only beneficiary to his mother's life insurance policy left alive—even if he is shy of being twenty-one years old by a couple of weeks. I'm no lawyer, but I'd be willing to bet that even if Everett Chase had died ten minutes after Madeline Chase's body was officially IDed, he would still have been declared her legal heir. If that had happened, then his wife's life insurance money would have ended up as a part of his estate, which I'm sure is earmarked, not for Ronald Ackermann, but for Everett Chase's biological kid.''

''Then you know about Chase's son from his first marriage?''

''Sure. He was mentioned in New American Life's file.''

''And you're convinced that the insurance money is the bottom-line motive to all this?''

Adjusting my sore hand in my lap, I replied, ''Right now I don't know of anything else important enough to be worth the effort. Although, with Everett Chase dead, there's also the value of the Ivy Spring Restaurant to consider, as well as anything else he owned. It all might be up for grabs now that he's gone. . . .''

''No way,'' Larry interrupted.

''Why not?''

''Because of what you just said about Chase having a kid of his own. A guy like Chase, with those kinds of assets and two marriages to worry about? He'd at least have a will, and probably a prenuptial agreement too. If I were him, I'd have the prenuptial tattooed on my chest.''

''His son's name is Brian,'' I said, for clarity's sake. ''He's twenty-eight years old.''

''Do you think he's in the picture?''

''Do you mean do I think that he's been sneaking around, bumping off heirs? No way.''

''You sound awfully sure.''

''What would be his point? His old man was worth a ton even before Madeline Ackermann came along. And you know damn well that, marital assets aside, what was Everett Chase's before the marriage is legally the property of his biological heir. Why would Brian Chase risk a life sentence just to rush an extra million bucks over and above the load that's already in the bank with his name on it? That would be stupid.''

"Is Brian living locally?"

"Not hardly," I said. "He's in New Zealand. According to the file, he's a schoolteacher or something."

"We should probably talk to him anyway."

"Good luck." Then, returning to my original thought, I added, "Which leaves us with Ronald Ackermann as the only person left breathing who stands to gain a dime from his mother's life insurance."

"Unless there's another name on that policy that we don't know about," Larry said cryptically.

"What's that supposed to mean?"

"How do we know that there were only three beneficiaries?"

"Don't you think that Mr. Younger would have mentioned somebody else when he first brought us on board? Why would the president of the company hold back on something like that?"

Larry shrugged, saying, "I didn't say that he would. I'm just brainstorming." Then, as we exited the freeway and parked on Carnege Ave. in front of Sammie's Taxidermy and Trophy Shop, he added, "I cased the place yesterday. It looks like there's only two guys who work here. One comes and goes. But I haven't seen the other one so much as leave the building. How you wanna play it?"

"Gently," I said, checking the inside breast pocket of my suit coat before opening the van's door. "Let me do the talking."

The inside of the shop bothered me immediately. Covering the walls were the heads of a number of deer, a boar, a couple of cougars, and, behind the counter over the cash register, a moose, with antlers that must have been eight feet wide from tip to tip. Everywhere else, mounted on stands, shelves, and pedestals, were other dead animals: squirrels, beavers, raccoons, a couple of skunks, a goat, something that was either a wolf or somebody's dog, a lynx, opossum, fox, and, stuck in the spaces, a bunch of fish, including one of those swordfish things with the big fin on its back that was so hard and stiff that they had it propped up in one corner. The place was so small and dimly lit that I immediately felt cramped. And, something more . . .

I've always hated taxidermy—philosophically as well as physically. I'm probably starting to sound like a broken record on this point, but isn't there enough death in the world already without actively going out and killing something for sport? And what's the point in collecting dead things? Where is the pleasure in having a corpse in the house? Animal or not, it's still a corpse, a carcass, a remains . . . how is that a trophy? Exactly what does it prove? I think that it's morbid and more than a little primitive in its symbolism.

Which leads me to an uncomfortable admission—especially considering my profession—which is that I've always seen embalming as an advanced form of taxidermy. At least we don't keep the bodies around for more than a few days, although, with a little more care, we probably could. And, come to think of it, some people do—like in the case of Lenin, who I understand is lying under glass in a closet in Moscow somewhere. He's supposedly hard, leather-tough, and dusty. Another trophy, commemorating what, I'm not exactly sure.

A little bell jangled brightly overhead as we stepped inside. There was a musty smell in the air, and our shoes clumped harshly on the worn, hardwood floor. A glass counter was located along the shop's back wall, displaying a selection of exotic goodies—including a dozen or so rattlesnake skulls, some bear claws set into necklaces, and at least two silver belt buckles with amber centers into which a number of black widow spiders had been set. There was an ancient cash register positioned at one end of the counter, gold-colored, with a lot of ornate scrollwork like they used to put on just about everything years gone by. At first I thought the place was unattended. Then I saw the eyes.

They were small, black, and shiny . . . just like the glass eyes of the dead animal faces all around us. But these were blacker, and shinier, and they blinked as they rose from where their owner had been sitting behind the counter. As the figure lifted itself to its feet, still indistinct in the gloom near the rear of the shop, its face came into view, causing a catch in my throat.

I swallowed, and said, "Hello," as brightly as I could manage. "I'm looking for a Mr. Craig."

The figure blinked again, slowly, almost painfully, making me wonder, what does skin like that feel like? I've got a couple of scars on my body, and they don't feel like the rest of me. The scar tissue itself is more sensitive. Once you really damage an area of skin, it never feels quite the same again. And this man's skin had been damaged all right. By fire, I assumed. Only fire could do that to a man's face.

He looked as if he were made of wax and had been held too close to a flame. The skin on his face was unnaturally smooth, pink, and stretched, so that his eyes were pulled into narrow, Oriental-looking slits. His nose was freakishly small, with predominant nostrils, also resembling slits. And his mouth had no lips . . . yet another slit in his skin, which bore not so much as a single line or wrinkle, but that seemed to pucker when his tongue flicked back saliva as he prepared his reply. His ears were all but completely gone, and he had no eyebrows. As he stood and placed his hands on the countertop, I noticed that they too had been burned.

What did his skin feel like? I couldn't help but wonder again, involuntarily cradling my wounded hand across my stomach. How did it feel to talk?

His eyes flicked from Larry's face to mine, and in that brief moment of silence, I realized that he was afraid.

"Ed's not here," he finally said, his voice breathy and wet. "Can I take your names?"

I reached into my jacket pocket and laid what I had brought carefully on the counter, saying as I did, "My name's Bill Hawley. You might remember me. This is my associate, Larry Fizner."

The man's eyes glanced down at the two photographs I had placed facedown on the glass, and then back up at me as he said, "Why should I remember you?" with a sucking sound that punctuated his words with nervous emphasis.

I didn't reply, standing, waiting. Larry Fizner positioned himself near the cash register as the clerk said with a slurp, "You'll have to come back. Mr. Craig's not here. I don't know anything. I just watch the place . . ."

His words faded as I turned over first one Polaroid, and then the other. He looked, swallowed, and then, as if he were an automaton that had just been unplugged, he simply collapsed in his seat. His eyes were closed, and his hand, which in contrast to his preternaturally smooth face was lumpy and discolored, went to his forehead where it trembled as he ran his fingers through his sparse, wispy brown hair, pulling it back and pausing. He opened his eyes, looked up at me, and closed them again, his tongue working at the corners of his mouth, his entire being reposed in a physical resignation to defeat.

"Thank God," he said finally, shaking his head and working his fingers deeper into what was left of his hair. "Thank God it's finally over."

I glanced at Larry, who shrugged and said, "Well, that was easy," just as Edward Craig jumped up and disappeared through a curtained doorway behind where he had been sitting.

I looked at Larry, who shot a look back at me. Then, as if moving as a single unit, we pushed our way through the curtain, only to find ourselves in a place of perfect darkness.

SEVEN
■■■■■■■■■■■■

"EDDIE?" I SHOUTED, both my hands out before me as I
turned a corner and stumbled to a halt, causing Larry Fizner
to bump into me from behind. "Eddie, it's Bill Hawley. I'm
not a cop!"

Somewhere ahead I heard footsteps going up, it sounded
like. Then came a clumping on the floor overhead. I took a
tentative step into the blackness, going no more than a couple
of feet before I bumped into something that made me shout
and draw back. Whatever it was, it was big, heavy, and covered with fur.

There was a dry, scraping sound behind me, and then the
hallway turned so bright that my eyes reflexively closed. When
they opened again I found Larry with one hand on the light
switch he had located by rubbing the wall, his other hand
clutching his gun. Overhead, the clumping footsteps shuffled
to a halt. "Come on," Larry said, moving into the lead and
running carefully through the junk-crammed hallway.

The thing I'd walked into turned out to be a bear, standing
a good seven feet tall, arms upraised, lips pulled back in a
perpetual snarl that revealed a plaster tongue and teeth. Stepping around it and tasting the dust I had inhaled from its
mangy fur, I followed Larry through the obstacle course of
cardboard boxes, stacked newspapers, owls, pheasants, and
furry, frozen creatures, down the hall, and up the ratty staircase
at the end. On the second floor we found an open doorway

leading into another cluttered hallway, at the end of which was a door with an apartment number on it. Larry tried the knob, found the door locked, and glanced at me. Without thinking I moved him aside with a brush of my good hand, fixed my attention on the keyhole, and placed a hard kick, just like my fireman father had taught me, right below the knob.

The old wood splintered and the door flew open, banged against the wall, and came bumping back. Larry, gun held out stiffly with both hands, was through in an instant, and I intended to follow. But I didn't. Instead I took a step back, felt the wall behind me, and slid down it, my head swimming as all the blood seemed to rush to my watery legs. Too much exertion, I decided through a brain fuzzy and unbalanced. Please . . . I thought, don't let me pass out.

Please, I can't pass out . . .

Inside the apartment I heard someone shouting over the harsh sound of skin slapping skin. The shouting then turned to a scream, which lasted what seemed an inordinately long time before it finally faded into a series of sobs. I was sitting on the floor with my two injured fingers thrumming in my lap as Larry Fizner appeared in the doorway, looming over me with a pink plastic safety razor in his hand, saying, as he holstered his gun, "You okay, Bill?"

His voice sounded like he was speaking through cheesecloth. I nodded, searching for my glasses, which I finally discovered hanging on one of my knees. The sensation of pressure inside my skull was rapidly subsiding, but my fingers bumped inside their dressings so hard that I sincerely expected blood to start spurting out from between the bandages in little red jets. Larry helped me to my feet, and, with the doorjamb for support, I wobbled into Edward Craig's efficiency apartment—one room, a kitchenette off to the side, and a bathroom straight ahead. Craig was sitting on the bathroom floor, I saw as I slipped my glasses back on, my head clearing by the minute.

"Jesus," I said at last, sitting myself down on the sofa under the main room's only window. "Looks like I'm more screwed up than I thought."

Craig looked like a little kid, sitting Indian fashion on the old linoleum, head down, hand on his knee, palm up. For the first time, I noticed that he was bleeding, and, as I focused my eyes more carefully on him, I also noted that his shoulders were rising and falling in a silent, sobbing rhythm.

I looked at Larry.

"What happened?"

Larry dropped the safety razor on the coffee table, where it ricocheted off an empty Pepsi can and came to rest in a dirty ashtray.

"He was trying to slash his wrist with that," he replied with an expression of obvious disgust.

I looked first at the safety razor, and then at Craig.

"Who viewed her?" I asked, having mentally edited way too much of what I was thinking.

Craig looked up, his black, glassy eyes fixed on me, his smooth, waxy face streaked with tears. Under his right eye there was a bright red discoloration shaped like an open hand, which explained his screams, and answered my original question about how sensitive his scarred flesh actually was. When he spoke, his voice sounded weak.

"I can't go to jail!" he implored. "With this face and all . . . you know what they'll do to me . . . I just can't. I can't go to jail! I . . ."

His voice faded into sobs again as he looked me straight in the eye.

"Please," he almost whispered. "I'm afraid . . ."

His wrist had a single gash running not across but up and down. From Larry's expression it was obvious that he thought that Edward Craig was making a show of cutting himself with the safety razor, and that he couldn't have done any real damage. But I knew, from the way the cut was positioned, that Craig, with his embalmer's knowledge of the human body, had been going for the brachial artery. If he'd gotten to it before Larry had stopped him, he'd have probably bled to death before we could have gotten him into an ambulance.

"Eddie," I said, proud of my sudden clarity, "I asked you who viewed Madeline Chase's body before you cut it up?"

As Craig's eyes blinked, tears leaked from their corners.

"It was what she wanted," he said, his scarred face wrinkled with emotion. "I have a contract spelling it all out. I swear to God. I did it exactly like the contract said I should."

"You have a what?" Larry asked harshly, his tone indicating that he wasn't in the mood for nonsense.

"Over there, in that drawer," Craig said, pointing with his good arm to a dresser.

Larry followed his direction, indicating one drawer, then another. He finally withdrew an envelope which he handed to me. I opened it, unfolded a legal-sized piece of paper, ran my eye over it, and returned my attention to Craig, saying, "She made a pre-need contract with you?"

He nodded, using the bathtub as support as he climbed to his feet, took a roll of toilet paper from the windowsill, and began winding it around his bleeding wrist.

"Are you saying that she *hired you* to kill her?" Larry exclaimed.

"NO!" Edward Craig shouted, his head snapping around, eyes wide. "I swear to God! That's not how it happened . . ."

He was just stepping through the bathroom door, the toilet paper roll in one hand, his other hand, palm up, connected to it by a fluttering sheet, when I said, "He's telling the truth, Mr. Fizner. Madeline Chase was obviously dead long before Eddie even stepped into the picture."

Larry looked at me, a question registering in his eyes. But before he could speak, I asked him to go back downstairs, lock the door so that no customers could wander in and interrupt, and, "Bring those Polaroids I put on the counter back up when you come." He asked me if I was sure that Craig wouldn't try anything funny while he was gone. To which Craig insisted that he wouldn't hurt anybody. He was just scared, he said. Just plain scared. And, more than anything else in the world, he didn't want to go to jail. . . .

"I can't, Bill," he said, acting suddenly as if we were old friends. "You can't turn me in . . . I didn't . . ."

"Didn't what?" Larry cut in aggressively. "You didn't chop up an old woman's body and hide the pieces?"

"Just go lock the door and bring me the pictures," I said, my eyes never wavering from Edward Craig's face. "We'll be okay while you're gone."

Larry frowned but did as I asked. As soon as he was gone, Craig became adamant, talking quickly.

"Look, Bill," he said, nervously wrapping more toilet paper around his wrist as he did, "you gotta believe me. I didn't hurt her; I was just doing what she wanted me to do; I was just doing my job. You knew that I didn't kill her when you first came in here, didn't you? You just said you did. You knew I didn't . . . that I couldn't kill her. Tell me that you know!"

To his obvious disappointment, I didn't say anything.

"It's been hell, these past five years," he said, trying a different tack. "Sheer hell. Everybody that walks through the door, everybody I see on the street . . . just everybody . . . I look at each of them and wonder, Is that the one who's going to blow the whistle? Is that the one who knows? When am I going to get caught? When will it be over?"

"If you thought you hid her body so well, what made you think you'd get caught?" I asked.

"It's just the way things go for me," he said, his misshapen eyes filling with tears again. "I don't ever get a break."

Just then Larry stepped back into the room, handed me the pictures of Madeline Chase's head and arm, and asked what he'd missed.

"Not much," I told him. Then to Craig I said, "Eddie, right this second I'm the only chance you've got. Mr. Fizner here would just as soon see you in Lucasville as look at you. So it's me or the razor . . . which was a dumb thing to grab if you really meant to hurt yourself. With a kitchen knife you would have probably been gone by now. Or what about the workroom where you stuff the animals? You must have a scalpel in there."

He winced, looking at me hard.

"Don't try to shit me anymore, okay, Eddie?" I said. "I'm tired of the act."

He opened his mouth, but I stopped him with one raised finger, saying, "Think about it first. Think about your every word. I'm allergic to bullshit, and the first time I get the urge to scratch, you belong to Larry. Understand?"

He nodded.

"Then sit down."

When I pointed to the battered recliner positioned across the coffee table, Edward Craig lowered himself into it.

"So what happened to your face?"

"I was freebasing coke, and the ether went up. Like what happened to Richard Pryor. Remember?"

"When?"

"Almost three years ago. But I've been clean ever since. Honest. I found Jesus . . . in the burn unit. I found God . . . and Jesus became my own, personal savior."

"How did Madeline Chase know that you would be willing to dispose of her body after her suicide?"

"You sayin' that you knew she killed herself, and that you didn't tell *me*?" Larry Fizner interjected.

Without looking at him, I shrugged and said, "It was a hunch."

"A hunch, huh?" he grumbled.

I waved him off, directing my full attention at Edward Craig as I said, "So let's have it, Eddie. Why would she pick you?"

Craig's face was simultaneously hard for me to look at and hypnotizing. The skin appeared to be so tightly stretched over his facial bones that I could have sworn that it would tear. Consequently, any tiny flicker of his muscles registered immediately in his expression . . . but the way it registered was unpredictable. The wrinkles and creases that rippled over his face as he apparently worked through his response in his mind created incongruous grimaces that didn't seem to have any bearing on the emotions he might have wished to express. They looked unrelated somehow, almost comical—though hardly funny.

Finally, he said, "I don't really know how she knew I'd go for it. But she did. Right from the start she just seemed to know."

"Know what?"

"That I was an embalmer."

"So?"

"And that I needed money."

"How badly did you need money?"

"Bad."

"What for?"

"I had debts."

"And Mrs. Craig knew enough about these debts to understand that you'd be willing to do just about anything for cash?"

He frowned . . . or, that is to say, he did what he could do to approximate a frown. Then he said, "My wife, Jane, and me, we were on our last leg. Our divorce wasn't but a couple of months away. Jane had already started listing the stuff she wanted . . . which was just about everything I had. Not that I could blame her. I mean, I wasn't exactly what you'd call a prize package back then." Finishing with the toilet paper, he placed the roll on the floor at his feet and chuckled to himself sadly as he glanced over the tiny apartment's Salvation Army furnishings. "Not that I've come up in the world much since. But I'm clean now, Bill. I swear to God. I am clean!"

"I think you better call me Mr. Hawley," I said, deadpan.

He nodded, anxiously examining his hands as a way of breaking our eye contact.

Larry was rooting around in Craig's refrigerator. After a moment he came strolling back toward the couch, cracking the tab on a can of Sprite and offering me a slug, which I declined, before seating himself on the sofa next to me.

Returning my attention to Craig, I said, "Did you see that article on the front page of yesterday's paper about me finding her head?"

He nodded.

"So you must have known that eventually it would get back around to you."

"I suppose."

"Then, if you were so terrified of jail, why didn't you do something about it before now?"

"Like what? I don't have much money. With this face, where am I going to get a job? It was just by sheer luck that I fell into this one. I'm not exactly what you'd call Mr. Marketable. If I tried to leave Ohio, and the cops should figure me for having something to do with Mrs. Chase's body, then suddenly I'd be a federal case, since they'd say I was fleeing the state to avoid prosecution. As soon as I tried to apply for any kind of assistance, my name would ring a bell in the computer, and they'd have me cold. So what exactly was I supposed to do—steal cars? Live under a bridge? What? All there was for me was to sit here and pray for a miracle.''

''How much did Mrs. Chase pay you to dispose of her body?''

''Thirty thousand dollars.''

''I'll bet he put that up his nose right quick,'' Larry interjected, looking at Craig coldly as he did.

Craig shook his head. ''That's not true,'' he said. ''I haven't even got it yet.''

''What?'' I asked.

''Look at the contract,'' Craig replied. ''It's a standard preneed . . . nothing funny. I might have jazzed it up with a mahogany casket and a copper vault so that I could itemize up to the total, but just like with any prearrangement, I don't get paid without a D.C.''

I ran my eye over the contract more carefully, finding that, just as Craig had described, it was a standard, irrevocable preneed funeral arrangement—which meant that the money Madeline Chase had paid was presently sitting in a trust fund somewhere. The only way Craig could collect was to provide a certified copy of a death certificate as proof of her passing.

Real quick, because it's important:

The way prearranged funerals work is that a person will choose everything related to their own funeral, including how many viewings they want, what kind of casket, what kind of vault, et cetera. Then they pay for it. The money that the funeral home collects is then placed into what's called an ''irrevocable trust fund,'' where it stays until the person passes away, accumulating interest that is supposed to offset the effects of inflation on the funeral price. There are three reasons why a person might choose to preplan their own funeral. The first is so that their spouse or kids won't have to do it. The second is because once a funeral is prearranged there are never any price increases for what that person chose. And the third, and most important reason, involves government assistance.

Since no one can pay for an extended nursing home stay out of their pocket for very long, considering that nursing homes can cost two or three thousand dollars a month, most folks end up needing help eventually. But before a person receives any money from the government, they have to qualify, which means that they must be unable to pay for their own care. So, an applicant for assistance must "spend down" their assets, meaning that they must liquidate everything of value they own—sell the house and car, cash in the insurance policies, empty the bank accounts. They use that money to pay their own nursing home bill each month until all they have left in the world is fifteen hundred dollars, at which point Uncle Sam starts picking up the tab. The fifteen hundred dollars that remains is set aside for the funeral bill.

But due to a recent change in the law, when a person preplans their own funeral, the money they spend is locked in an irrevocable trust fund, becoming what they call a "nonassumable" asset. Which means that even after the rest of their value is liquidated, the prearrangement account remains sacrosanct. This allows a person to spend their own money, which they were going to spend on nursing home care anyway, on their own funeral, which takes the burden off their heirs.

Since the money stays in a trust fund until the person dies, the funeral home doesn't have access to it until they are able to provide a certified copy of a death certificate as proof that they have fulfilled their obligations according to their agreement.

That was where Edward Craig had run into trouble getting his hands on his thirty thousand bucks.

"I did it that way deliberately," he offered, taking me somewhat aback. "I was so screwed up at that time, mostly from drugs—my marriage was falling apart, my health was suffering. Lord. I didn't know where I was half the time. When Jane and I split up, she took everything I had: the house, our savings, my car, even my baseball cards. She took it all, knowing that I had to agree, because if I didn't she'd go after my embalming business too.

"Since the business was incorporated, she knew that it would be my ongoing source of income. If she pushed for a piece of that, I'd be stuck paying her alimony for whatever the courts said: five, ten, fifteen years. Whatever. She'd be entitled to a percentage of that income since we were married while I was still in embalming school, and she could claim that she helped me get the license since she worked to support us while I wasn't able to.

"But she said that if I forked over the goods up front, she'd let me off the hook on the alimony. Meaning, basically, if I gave her more or less everything I had, she'd be satisfied. She justified this by saying that I could work and replace everything I gave her, while she didn't have the skills to do the same for herself. At that time she was working as a receptionist in a doctor's office, and her paycheck was only about half of what I could drag down per week.

"But her real reason for settling like she did was more practical. She knew I was basically a wash as a person, and that after she was gone I probably wouldn't be able to keep myself straight enough to work. By taking her cut up front, she made sure she got everything she could, since, left to my own devices, there wasn't any guarantee that I'd even have an income that she could share. Half of nothing is still nothing, and Jane was anything but naive. She took hers, and ran, thinking that she'd really made out."

Up to this point, Edward Craig's tone of voice had reflected resignation, but with his next sentence, it went foxy.

"But what she didn't get was my pre-need account. Since she was leaving the embalming business alone, she never had her lawyer check my books. Not that he didn't want to. She just wouldn't let him. See, she didn't know that I could even make prearrangements, since I didn't have my own funeral home. And technically I really wasn't supposed to. But I had Mrs. Chase's thirty grand tucked away, so that at least was money my wife couldn't get.

"Plus, I was thinking that since Mrs. Chase was going to disappear, I wouldn't get the money for six years, or until they declared her legally dead. That gave me time to straighten up. Back then, I would have just thrown it all away on enough coke to OD. But I thought, six years . . . man, by then I'd be almost forty years old. If I really tried, I knew that, in the end, I'd be better off."

"But wouldn't you have to account for the service when

you cashed in the trust fund?'' Larry asked, his tone, for the moment, sounding more interested than confrontational.

"No," Craig explained. "The finance company that set up the trust is based in Chicago. Once Mrs. Chase is declared deceased, all I have to do is get a copy of the declaration from city hall and mail it to them. They'll take her name off the account, which will leave my name as the sole owner. I'll be able to do whatever I want with however much is in there, no questions asked."

"Okay," I said, folding the pre-need contract and placing it on the coffee table next to the Polaroids I had taken of Mrs. Chase's head and arm. "Now tell me exactly what Madeline Chase paid you to do."

Resignedly, Craig told the following story:

He had been sitting in a bar one night. "This was before I took Jesus into my heart," he explained. "So my behavior was still degraded." Madeline Chase showed up, singled him out, and took a seat next to him. To his utter amazement, she spoke as if they were old friends, explaining that she knew about his financial troubles—this was also right at the time when the story about the unethical practices at one of the funeral homes for whom Craig worked had broken, splashing his name all over the print and TV news. She had a proposition that might help him out, she said; and Craig couldn't help but listen.

"See," he explained, "the saddest part of it was that the reporters were right about most of what they were saying about what was going on. Lechowski's Funeral Home was charging their families for embalmings they weren't doing, and a lot of other stuff besides. I don't know how it all got hung exclusively on me, since all I did was trade embalm for the guys. But once those articles were printed, it didn't matter anymore. No matter what I said, I was the bad guy. And Mrs. Chase knew it. She had hired a private detective to check me out, and his report confirmed that I was righteously on the rocks. By the time she sat down next to me in that bar, she had me in her pocket. I just didn't know it yet."

She was a manic-depressive, she said. Adding that she had attempted suicide three times previously, but had, fortunately as it turned out, failed at each attempt. Then she dropped her bomb:

She had just realized that if she killed herself and her body was found bearing the evidence of her fatal act, her kids would lose out on the substantial insurance policy her deceased husband had taken out on her life, and which she had maintained specifically so that those same kids would be taken care of after she was gone. But, if her body were to disappear, well, things would be very different.

"I almost died," Craig said. "No kidding. Here I am, sitting in this joint, watching my own life go down the tubes, and along comes some broad who's got more money in diamond rings on two of her fingers than I've got in the whole world, with this horror movie proposition, talkin' like she means it."

Apparently, the deal had not been finalized during that first encounter because Craig was far too cautious.

"I thought she was nuts," he said. "Or maybe even part of a setup for one of the local TV news teams . . . you know, a sting, like they do on *60 Minutes*."

But Madeline Chase was persistent, backing up her proposition with an initial payment of a thousand dollars, in cash, out of her purse, no strings attached.

"As a sign of goodwill," Craig said. "And Jesus, did that money get my attention. If she was willing just to give me a thousand bucks . . . just give it to me, as in, 'Here, take it and think about what I said,' then she must have had some pretty big bucks to throw around. That's when I finally seriously started listening to what she had to say. She was a really nice lady, you know. After I got to know her a little, I genuinely liked her."

"If you liked her so much, how could you chop her up like that?" Larry Fizner growled.

"It was what she wanted," Craig replied earnestly. "I mean, come on. That's my job. Right? Or at least that was my job, back then. I did for people what nobody else could do. I mean, isn't that what embalmers are? That's why we were called undertakers, once upon a time—because nobody else would undertake the job."

What Mrs. Chase truly wanted was to die, Craig went on to explain, but she couldn't take her own life because certain financial circumstances were standing in her way. The only thing that would allow her to die peacefully was knowing that her kids would be okay money-wise after she was gone . . . especially her daughter.

"What about her son?" I asked.

Craig shrugged, saying, "Her son was another story." He paused, narrowed his already narrow eyes, and continued, "She was really hurting, that lady. I mean really. You know, Mr. Hawley, as hard as it is to understand sometimes, there are some people who just get tired of being alive. They don't find any pleasure in it anymore. I could see in her eyes that she was one of those people. We met five or six different times, and I listened to her talk for hours about all the things she'd tried, all the therapy and drugs, the restaurant she'd started, thinking it would make a difference by giving her a sense of purpose, her kids, her friends, her second marriage . . . but none of it mattered. All she wanted was to get out, but she was tethered by the fear that her children would be cheated out of the money they had coming.

" 'If it weren't for that, I'd be gone by now,' she must have said a thousand times.

" 'And if I agree to this,' I said, also about a thousand times, just to be clear, 'then you're not going to expect me to help you actually do the deed, right?'

"She promised me that I would have absolutely no part in that. All I would be expected to do was embalm her, and conduct her disposition in any way I thought would keep her body from ever being located."

"And you embalmed her so that someone could see her before you made her disappear, isn't that right?" I asked, getting back to the original point that I had found especially important. "You set things up so that someone could have a real, final viewing, with all the trimmings. You even did her hair . . . isn't that true?"

He nodded.

"Who was it who viewed her?"

"Her husband."

"Everett Chase knew about this?!" I exclaimed, thunder-struck, remembering, in that instant, the big, jovial man who had smiled and beamed with pride as we sat beneath the fresh spring sun on his restaurant's patio.

"It was a joint decision . . . made between the two of them."

"And he approved of what you did to her body?"

"Not exactly. He knew she'd killed herself. But he didn't want to know the details of how I was going to dispose of her. He just had a private viewing late one night, said his good-byes, and left me to it."

"What about her kids?"

"They weren't involved because Mrs. Chase thought they were too young to handle it. My wife said that Mrs. Chase was so overprotective of her kids that her shrink thought she was transferring part of her self-destructiveness onto them in the form of a morbid fear for their safety."

"How did your wife know what Mrs. Chase's psychiatrist thought about her condition?"

Craig blinked uncomprehendingly, saying, "Didn't I just say that she was his receptionist?"

"Your wife worked for Madeline Chase's doctor?"

"Yeah."

"Her therapist?"

"That's right."

"Christ," I whispered, thinking, well, at least that explains where Madeline Chase came up with Edward Craig's name.

Suddenly Larry Fizner leapt to his feet and thundered, "BULLSHIT!"

Craig was up and out of his chair in a flash, standing behind it so that the recliner would be between him and Larry.

"This is absolute, unmitigated bullshit!" Larry exclaimed. "I've never heard so much crap in my life." In his hand, he had the pre-need contract that Edward Craig had originally offered as proof of the veracity of his claim. Now he was waving that same contract as a way to contradict everything Craig had said. "This thing doesn't say a single fucking word about you cutting her up! Not a fucking word! She made a prearranged contract with you for her funeral, and since you needed money for your divorce, you decided to speed up pay-ment . . . that's what I say.

"I say you offed her, Mr. Craig. I say that you offed her, and then, when you sobered up and realized what you had done, you panicked. Chopping her up was your last ditch shot at saving your own sorry ass. You've had almost five years to think up a cover story . . . couldn't you have come up with something a little more convincing than 'I vas only followink orders'?''

"Wait," Craig said, walking carefully around the recliner, giving Larry a wide berth, until he had arrived at a picture of Jesus kneeling by a rock which hung next to the entrance to the kitchen. After crossing himself and bowing his head briefly in the picture's direction, he took it off the wall, removed an envelope which had been taped to its back, rehung the picture, and handed the envelope to me, saying, "It was awful, Mr. Hawley. You have no idea. For as long as I was an embalmer, I never saw anything like it. I didn't think it would be so bad. But it was worse than you can even imagine. It's been haunting me ever since. I've seen it in my dreams. I've prayed, night after night, just to be shed of its memory. I don't know how else to explain it . . ."

I took the envelope he offered, listening to his words dis-tractedly without reading what was inside. Instead, I was star-ing at another picture I had just noticed on the wall next to where Jesus hung. The picture was a portrait of two people, one a man, and the other a woman. With that envelope still in my good hand, and Edward Craig babbling on about the internal peace he had finally found in the burn unit of Cleve-land's Metro Hospital, with a young man "ministering" to him over his bed, my face started tingling with something that I wouldn't exactly describe as excitement—but that was pretty damned close.

"Eddie," I said, interrupting his tale of religious salvation, "tell me more about your wife."

Following the direction of my eyes, Craig looked from my face to the photograph and back before saying, "I haven't seen her in years."

But I have, I thought, marking her in my mind.

In the picture, Craig's face was as I remembered it from before he was burned. His hair was full, cut short, looking professional and neat; his skin was smooth; he was handsome. Exactly the kind of man one would expect to see standing next to the lovely girl who was his bride, twenty or so years old, fresh and clean, free of the implied psychic scars she would soon bear as life beat her down with its dual hammers of time and trouble. She positively beamed at the camera, looking radiant in her long, white gown. Her blond hair was either cut shorter than she wore it now, or it was pulled back from her face; the gown itself reflected the style of the times, and she was holding a bouquet of spring flowers. But even through the intervening years, she had retained her lithe figure, and there was no mistaking her face . . .

She was the Fairy Lady.

I'd seen her in Ronald Ackermann's house.

She was the Fairy Lady . . .

And she had worked for the psychiatrist to whom Madeline Chase had confided her deepest secrets.

Just as things were really beginning to churn in my head, the cellular phone in my front shirt pocket started ringing.

"Hello?" I said, after unfolding the phone and extending its short plastic antenna. Craig's eyes were watching me with suspicion.

"Mr. Hawley?" a voice replied. "This is Ronald Ackermann. Remember? I've got something to tell you, if you're interested."

"I am," I replied, still watching Craig. "But how did you get this number?"

"What number?"

"For my phone?"

"I looked in the book."

If Ronald Ackermann had dialed the number he had found in the telephone book, then that meant that Jerry had put my portable phone on the call forwarding, which meant that there was no one at the funeral home, again. Briefly I wondered where Jerry had gone, decided that I probably knew, and returned my attention to what I was doing.

"Can we meet?" I asked.

To which Ronald Ackermann replied, "I haven't got time. I'm leaving for the war like right now. Actually, I'm late as it is. What I've got to say doesn't require us to actually see each other anyway. It's more of a hunch, really. It's about my stepfather . . ."

"What about him?"

"Well, the police talked to me this morning, asking all sorts of questions . . . which is why I'm late getting out of here. But the one thing they were really hot about was that car . . ."

"What car?"

"The Camaro I guess you saw."

"What about it?"

"I've seen it too. But I didn't tell the police I have."

"Why not?"

"Because I didn't put it together until like five minutes ago, and because I'm not a hundred percent sure."

"About what?"

"About whether it's the same car or not. Look, I really can't go into it right now, but depending on whether it is or isn't the same car, I think that somebody I know might be in a lot of trouble."

I was looking at Edward Craig's wedding picture again, hearing Ronald Ackermann's voice, and seeing the Fairy Lady, all at the same time.

"Who are you talking about?" I asked. "Who might be in a lot of trouble?"

"George."

"Who's George?"

"Don't be tedious, Mr. Hawley," Ronald Ackermann said irritably. "I know you were at my house before you came out to the park."

"The guy at the computer?" I asked.

"His name is George Sacks. He pays me rent to live in my basement."

"And it's his car you're talking about?"

"Not exactly. But he does part-time body work at this garage, and sometimes, when I'm not too busy, I'll save him the bus fare by driving him to work."

Busy doing what? I wondered, without saying so.

"The last time I drove him was like two or three days ago," Ackermann continued. "And that's when I saw it: a dark blue Camaro with gold wire wheels. That is the car you told the cops you saw, right?"

"Where is this garage?" I asked.

Ronald Ackermann told me, then he hung up.

"Ronald?" I said into the phone, climbing up off the couch. "Ronald? Are you still there?"

Nothing.

"Ronald?"

Silence.

Depressing the disconnect button, I folded the little phone back up before sliding it into my shirt pocket. Both Edward Craig and Larry Fizner were studying me, neither making a sound. Licking my lower lip, I sighed and said, "Well . . ." Then I stopped, gave myself a moment to think, and continued, quite gravely, reflecting exactly my frame of mind.

"Eddie, before Mr. Fizner located you, I visited Bob White at Greenleaf Mortuary Shipping. You remember Bob, don't you? He's an excellent judge of character; plus, it's been my experience that, with that big heart of his, he likes just about everybody. But he doesn't like you. As a matter of fact, he called you a 'germ.' "

Craig opened his mouth, but I closed it for him by lifting my bandaged index finger.

"Just listen," I said. "I know you're going to tell me that Bob was talking about the old Edward Craig, the one who didn't know Jesus, or whatever. But all I'm doing is repeating what he said, and mentioning that I value his opinion . . . both because I respect him, and because of another little circumstance that neither you nor the newspapers chose to mention.

"Did you know that Madeline Chase had had her teeth surgically extracted before she died?"

Craig's face went blank, and I could see him thinking about it. Finally, he admitted that he couldn't remember. When he had embalmed her, he had been so preoccupied with the image of what he was going to have to do to get rid of her body that he hadn't really been paying all that much attention to what he was doing. And besides, he said, "As a funeral director, you know how many bodies come in without their dentures. How many times have you gotten a little blue plastic Tupperware container with somebody's teeth inside at the same time they give you the clothes they want that person to be laid out in? The body's already embalmed in the back, and they're just now giving you the teeth.''

''My point,'' I interjected, ''is that you've been telling me that Madeline Chase had been seriously planning her own death for at least a month before she actually took her own life. Correct?''

He nodded.

''Then why would a woman who knew that she was about to die go through the misery of having all her teeth pulled in preparation for dentures that she knew she'd never live to wear?''

Craig's open mouth closed, and his expression went totally flat. But only for a moment. It contorted itself dramatically as I slid the envelope he had handed me, as of yet still unopened, into my suit coat pocket.

''Hey!'' he said, automatically reaching out one hand. ''You can't take that! That's the only proof I've got that I'm telling the truth. What if the cops show up? You guys found me . . . so they will too! You've got to leave that contract here!''

''How did she do it?'' I demanded, silencing him with my voice, which broke as the anger that had been so much a part of my reaction to seeing Everett Chase shot to death bubbled back up from whatever secret recess of myself it had chosen as its own. ''What are the details?''

For an instant, I don't think Craig really knew what I was talking about. He had gone off in one direction, while I had pursued another. Finally, as his expression settled, I could see in his face that he'd come back around, and, swallowing nervously, he said, ''Carbon monoxide. She sat in her car and let the engine run.''

''Where?''

''What . . . oh. Uh, well, I don't really know.''

''What do you mean, you don't know? How'd you get the body?''

"Her husband brought it to me. I mean, he drove the car and met me at Noland's Funeral Home."

"Did Marsh Noland know anything about this?"

"No." Craig was shaking his head. "Marsh was out of town and I was covering for him."

"So Everett Chase drove her over?"

"Right. She was slumped down in the passenger seat, and he was driving."

"How did you know she'd killed herself with fumes?"

"That's what she said she was going to do, and when Mr. Chase brought her in, she reeked."

I don't know why, but at that instant I saw it in my mind so clearly that the crispness of the image startled me a little:

It is January, cold, dry, with heavy clouds of exhaust and steam rising from cars, people, and sewers. There is a dusting of that sandy snow on the ground that slithers over pavement in patterns. There is a dark building. It is late at night. There are no lights to be seen save for the blue-white fluorescent glow emanating from the building's interior as a side door opens and a silhouetted figure waves clandestinely to a car with its headlights turned off rolling slowly across the parking lot. The figure at the wheel is swaddled in scarves and a hat, the other is wearing a dress but no coat, slumped over so that her head rests against the passenger door window, which is closed.

On the backseat of this car there is a piece of garden hose, with one of its ends tattered with lengths of silver duct tape from where it had been attached to the car's exhaust pipe, its other end having been run into the car's rear window.

The driver has his window open a few inches, despite the cold, because the interior of the car smells so powerfully of spent gasoline.

Edward Craig, the silhouetted figure, is wearing a rubber apron and latex gloves, which virtually glow in the dim, late-night light.

I saw it all.

I just wasn't sure whether I believed it.

"Did her blood glow?" I asked, looking Craig straight in the eye.

His reply was a blank stare.

"Was Madeline Chase's blood bright red?" I said, a little more emphatically. "You know how blood that's been saturated with carbon monoxide goes practically fluorescent, don't you, Eddie?"

He nodded, slowly, saying. "That's right. It does."

"Did Madeline Chase's blood look like that?"

I thought he was going to cry again. The skin around his eyes actually trembled, and his slit of a mouth quivered as he considered his answer for a moment, licked saliva from its corner, and said, "Honest to God, Mr. Hawley. I can't remember."

It was time to go, and I said so.

"But what about the cops?" Craig demanded as I headed for the apartment door, Larry Fizner in tow. "You guys showed up. What should I do if the cops do too?"

I paused in the hallway, looked back at Edward Craig through the apartment's open door, and shrugged in what I hoped was a casual way, saying, "Maybe you oughta pray."

EIGHT
■■■■■■■■■■■■

"WELL, THAT WAS fun,'' Larry Fizner said, a cigarette jutting defiantly from the corner of his grinning mouth, his hands firmly on the steering wheel as he aimed us at Brookside Park, the first stop we needed to make.

"I thought you'd like it," I replied, dialing my cellular phone.

"But just so we both understand what's going on," Larry added. "We're probably never going to see him again. I predict that by tonight, tomorrow morning at the latest, Edward Craig's going to gather his pennies into a bunch and drag them off to Mexico."

"Who cares?"

"That's an interesting attitude."

"Come on, Mr. Fizner. Do you really think that Edward Craig is intellectually capable of conning anybody out of anything? He's nothing but a gullible dork who got himself manipulated into doing somebody else's dirty work, and who's been regretting it ever since. At the time he agreed to hide Madeline Chase's body, he was practically brain-dead from booze and junk. Now he's hiding in that rodent museum, so wracked with guilt and paranoia that he's wearing his knees out praying for forgiveness.

"And even if the cops should trace it back to him before we get a chance to wrap things up, which I doubt they will, but even if they do decide to pick him up, what can they do to him without this?'' I lifted the envelope Craig had extricated from behind Jesus' picture, which I had already read aloud to Larry, and which described, essentially, the same thing that Craig had said about Madeline Chase's intention to take her own life, as well as his reciprocal assurance that he'd dispose of her remains in such a way as to insure that they would go unrecorded by the authorities forever. Both parties had signed it at the bottom.

Larry thought for a moment and said, ''I guess if he's smart, he'll keep his mouth shut. Then the cops couldn't prove anything.''

''That's right.'' I agreed. ''Without a confession, their evidence is strictly circumstantial. So what if Craig was the embalmer listed on the death certificates of the people who were used to hide the pieces of Madeline Chase's body? That coincidence might have been enough to motivate you and me to shake him down, but in court, what's it going to mean? If he's smart enough to play dumb, chances are good that he'll walk.''

''But he ain't smart . . .'' Larry began.

I stopped him with a motion as I listened to the phone beep a busy signal. I had dialed the funeral home, and since I had been getting the same busy signal for the past ten minutes, I had to assume that the call forwarding was still kicking my signal back to the phone from which I had dialed. As I tried Nat at work, Larry said, ''So, what did the Ackermann kid want?''

I told him about the Camaro Ronald Ackermann claimed to have seen. Then, as someone said, ''L-W Library. Reference. Cheryl speaking,'' I turned my attention to the phone, asking for my wife.

There was a second's worth of silence before the girl said, ''Mrs. Hawley's not here today, sir. She stopped in earlier, but since it's Saturday, and we're so slow, she decided to run some errands. . . .''

Saturday?

Since when was it Saturday?

I thanked the girl, hung up, and worked backward in my mind until I realized that she was right: it was Saturday, which meant that the funeral I had originally arranged when this

whole mess had first started was scheduled for this morning
. . . and I hadn't been there! That explained why the call forwarding was on: I had left Jerry alone without telling him
where I was going, and, since he didn't have anyone else to
cover the phone while he was gone, he had put the diverter
on me, and had then taken the funeral out himself . . . in a
wheelchair, with no license . . .

And Nat hadn't said a word when I had told her that she
should just go to work and not worry about me. She had said
something about taking care of me all day . . . and now I knew
that she had been talking about being home because of the
weekend. But I'd told her that I'd be fine and insisted that she
go to work.

Which she had . . .

Or so I had thought.

So, what kind of "errand" had she decided to run?

At Brookside Park I left Larry in the van while I checked
the concession stand that Ronald Ackermann had used as his
powder room while composing himself after I had told him
that his mother's body had been found. Seeing that it was
suddenly Saturday, the park was more crowded than it had
been when the SWORDS group had been using one of the
softball diamonds as their practice field. The concession stand,
instead of being boarded up and abandoned, was open for
business. It only took me about a minute to find out what I
wanted to know. As I climbed back into the van, I said,
"Here," handing the foot-long hot dog I'd bought to Larry,
who took it without comment and immediately started eating.

Around a mouthful he said, "So? Was a wienie the point
of this trip?"

"There's a phone in there. It's on the counter next to the
door," I said. "Can you eat and drive at the same time?"

Larry did, saying, "Okay, so there's a phone."

"I thought he was talking to himself," I mused. "But he
wasn't. He was talking to somebody else . . ."

"So who'd he call? And why?"

"Who, I'm not sure. The why, I think I know . . . though I
hope I'm wrong."

As we reached the top of the hill coming up out of the park,

Larry unceremoniously handed me his hot dog, made the tight right turn onto the Brookside Bridge, and then took back his frankfurter, saying, "Thank you."

"The one thing that's really bugging me," I said, trying to rub the mustard off my bandages, "is Everett Chase. Not only did he lie to me about his wife's disappearance . . ."

"Assuming that Craig told us the truth, that is," Larry interjected, making me nod once and continue immediately so as not to lose my train of thought.

"Not only did Everett Chase lie, but now I know for sure that Ronald Ackermann called somebody from the concession stand after I'd told him that I was going to talk to Chase later that same afternoon. Before he locked himself in that little building, I told Ronald exactly when and where I was going to meet with Chase. And then, when I got to the restaurant, Everett Chase decided we should sit outside for our interview. Of all the places in that barn of a building, he decided that we should sit outside, on the patio . . . which was the one place that somebody driving by with an automatic assault pistol could get a clear shot."

"So what, you think he committed suicide too?" Larry almost laughed.

"No." I frowned, feeling a chill for the second time that day. "Not exactly. Right before the Camaro rolled by the second time, Chase got up and walked over to the railing . . . leaving me sitting alone on the other side of the patio."

"So you think he was setting you up?"

"It's crossed my mind."

"Why?"

"I don't know."

"Assuming that it was you they were really after, why'd they bump him?"

"I don't know. Maybe they double-crossed him. Or maybe they were going for both of us, and I just got lucky."

"Who?"

"I'm not sure."

"Well, at least you've worked this all out ahead of time."

"Fuck you."

Larry spit chewed bun on his dashboard as he barked with

laughter. I scowled all the way to the gas station, which, according to Ronald Ackermann, was located only a couple of blocks from the park, and about two miles from where the Fairy Lady lived.

The station was small, with a tiny glass lobby on one side and a pair of garage doors on the other. Behind the counter in the lobby sat a single attendant, reading a magazine. Both pump islands out front were empty, and a row of cars that were apparently awaiting repair lined a dusty patch next to where the attendant resided, though none of them were the Camaro. There was a sign taped to the front window declaring that not only didn't the attendant have a key to the safe, but the building was rigged with surveillance cameras, for the customer's "protection."

When I asked for George Sacks, the young man sitting behind the cash register with his feet on the counter pointed to the closed door immediately to my left without even lifting his eyes from the page of his *Omni* magazine. Glancing at Larry, I shrugged, pushed open the door, and stepped into a garage filled with suspended clouds of rolling paint over-spray and the harsh, almost deafening pounding of an air compressor that pumped and banged in one corner.

Everything in the room was covered with plastic and fabric sheets except for a workbench area at the far end of the room that was littered with odds and ends that looked as if they had been over-sprayed a thousand times. The hulk of a car was positioned in the exact center of the double garage, sitting on concrete blocks, wheels off, windows and chrome covered with sheets of newspaper held on with carefully trimmed lengths of masking tape. A man was hunched near the front of the car, holding a spray gun that was connected to the straining compressor by a long, red rubber hose. The man was large and dressed in bib overalls. He had a clear plastic shower cap on his head, a white surgical mask over his mouth and nose, and plastic goggles over his eyes. With all the racket the compressor was making, he didn't hear Larry and I approach, even after I had shouted his name twice.

Larry looked curiously at ease as he strolled over to a

mound of something and lifted a corner of the sheet under which it was hidden from the over-spray. Allowing the sheet to drop, he moved along to another sheet, lifted its corner, and then moved along again. The man in the shower cap had still not heard us, his attention consumed by the corner of the front fender he was presently painting. As he depressed the sprayer's trigger, the nozzle hissed and the compressor kicked on even louder, threatening, it seemed to me, to jump right off its mount. At the fourth sheet corner Larry lifted, he paused and pointed for me to look. I did. Nodded. And tapped the man in the shower cap on the shoulder.

If he was the person in the Camaro who had murdered Everett Chase the day before, he certainly was playing things cool. He wasn't keyed-up or on edge, waiting for the cops to pick him up. He didn't jump when I tapped him. Instead he simply turned and looked at me, eyes myopically indistinct behind the paint-speckled goggles, both hands holding the sprayer near his waist. The compressor was still clattering, and I didn't feel like competing with its din; so, without a word I lifted an old bath towel that was lying on the floor at my feet and very casually wiped it across the Camaro's freshly painted passenger's door, creating a sweep of dark blue as the wet white paint the man had just applied smeared off on the towel, revealing the old color beneath.

That got him.

"Jesus Christ!" I could hear him shout as he slammed the paint gun down on the bench and killed the compressor. "What the hell do you think you're doing?!"

He obviously didn't recognize me, nor had he even noticed Larry. When the compressor stopped, the silence that flooded the room was so abrupt that it felt as if it had actual weight on my skin. The man turned, caught sight of Larry for the first time, and then looked back at me.

I don't know what it was that clued him in. It might have been the way Larry was standing there, sheet hanging from his hand, the four gold wire-wheeled tires that had been removed from the Camaro stacked neatly next to him. Or it might have been the way I stood, towel in one hand, bandaged fingers plainly visible. Or it might have been something else,

some mental communication to which the man was attuned
. . . but something happened, right then, and instead of continuing in the vein of indignation my vandalism of his paint-job
had elicited, after he had looked from Larry to me, he lifted
his goggles and said, very seriously, ''What's going on here?''

I had been wrong, I realized. His tone of voice plainly revealed that he had, in fact, just been waiting for something to
happen.

When I raised an eyebrow very slightly, Larry caught the
signal, picked up the ball, and ran with it.

''This your car?'' he asked, dropping the sheet so that it
fell not on top of the gold wire wheels but away from them.

''No,'' George Sacks replied. ''Who are you guys?''

Larry produced his badge, making me suppress a smile.
Larry keeps it in a very official-looking leather wallet, which
he invariably flips open and closed just a fraction of a second
too quickly for anyone to actually read the word printed on
the also very official-looking gold badge contained inside. The
word on the badge is SPECIAL, which doesn't mean a thing.
Larry bought the badge in an Army/Navy store. But you'd be
amazed at how many people take a badge at its face value,
just assuming that since you've got one you must deserve it.

George Sacks lowered the cotton surgical mask off his
mouth, and I saw his face for the first time. He had a clean
area shaped like his goggles around his eyes, and another corresponding to the shape of the surgical mask around his mouth
and nose. The rest of the skin on his face was covered with a
pale white shading of paint over-spray, giving him an odd,
patterned appearance . . . as if he had markings, like a raccoon.
His nose was large and bulbous. His eyes were also large, dark
brown, and rimmed with long, thick lashes that served to em-
phasize the whites. And his lips were full over his fine, straight
teeth. His was a strong, strangely proportioned appearance
that, despite the implied dissimilarity of some of the individual
features, came together in a kind of balance that was, if not
handsome, certainly striking. In a blink, I realized that he was
mulatto, making me briefly wonder, as I always do, which of
his parents was black and which one white.

He was looking at me. Despite Larry's badge, and his question, George Sacks was looking directly at me. Maybe it was because of my suit and tie, or maybe it was for reasons that were strictly his own, but he had apparently chosen me as the boss. So, if that was how he wanted it, I decided to give it to him, saying, "Is this your car?" as I used the paint-stained towel I was still holding to open the Camaro's side door. As I did, newspaper rustled and tape tore. Sacks flinched but didn't move. Nor did he speak. To fill the silence, I said, "I would imagine you were careful to sweep it out once you got back. I probably shouldn't waste my time looking for shell casings, right?"

"What?" he said, very softly.

Larry stepped up and took Sacks's wrist. Lifting his unprotesting arm he examined the hand and said, "He's got a couple paint specks on his skin, but I think a paraffin test might still pick up a little glycerin."

"What?" Sacks said, now looking at Larry.

"Good," I confirmed, even though I knew Larry was full of shit. A paraffin test will lift trace amounts of glycerin, a chemical by-product of gunpowder combustion, off the skin of the hand a person used to shoot a firearm only if the test is conducted shortly after the shooting, or if the hand has been protected from further contamination. But it was a good ploy, and from the look on Sacks's face, I decided to go with it.

"How about on the car seat?" I asked.

Releasing Sacks's arm, Larry pulled open the driver's side door and looked at me through the car as he said, "Good idea. Fifty shells musta thrown a lot of dirt. We're bound to pick up something off the upholstery."

Returning my attention to George Sacks, I said, "Do you have a lawyer?"

And that did it.

"What in the hell are you two talking about?" he exclaimed, stepping quickly around the car and ripping the shower cap off his head.

"Is this your car?" I asked again.

"No!" he shouted.

"How long did you borrow it?"

He pulled up short.

"Coupla days."

"Were you the only one who drove it?"

"No."

"Who'd you loan it to?"

"Why?"

"Would you rather tell me here, or downtown?"

"Wait a minute . . ."

"Where's the phone?" Larry said from behind Sacks.

Lifting his hands, Sacks said, "Come on. Let me in on it, just a little. Okay? Who are you guys? What's going on? All I did was use the damn thing for a coupla days. What's the federal case here?"

"Drive-by killings aren't federal yet," I said. "Although they're pushing for it."

"Killing?" Sacks mouthed, all the blood draining from his face. "What the hell are you talking about?"

"Fifty shots is a lot of shell casings, you want to bet you missed at least one when you cleaned it out?"

"I don't know . . ."

"Where's the phone?" Larry asked again.

And Sacks shouted. "Goddamn it! What is this?"

I thought for sure the kid by the cash register would pop his head through the door to see why Sacks was shouting so loud, but he didn't. Just out of curiosity I went over to the door and looked into the lobby, just in time to see him get into one of the cars that was parked along the side of the building and drive away.

"Smart child," I said. Holding the door open, I added, "Why don't you step this way, Mr. Sacks? The atmosphere out here's less thick."

Sacks sat down in a chair next to a pop machine. Larry stepped up to the counter, smiled when he found the pay phone, and said, "Now all I need's a quarter."

I leaned against the wall and looked at George Sacks, saying simply, "The Camaro you were just painting was used in a drive-by shooting, Mr. Sacks. I saw it. I was shot." I lifted my bandaged hand. "If you weren't driving, who was?"

He shook his head.

"Who did you loan it to?"

"I . . ."

To my right, the cash register went *CA-CHING*! as the drawer popped open and Larry exclaimed, "Now look at all the quarters in here."

"Her name's Jane!" George Sacks said, abruptly standing up. "She's my landlord's girlfriend. I let her use the car."

"So you what, just took it off the lot?"

"Yeah."

"Do you do that often?"

"Sometimes."

"You just lift the keys?"

"Sometimes."

I turned and examined the Peg-Board behind the counter where Larry was standing. Suddenly I was struck by a very strange thought that motivated me to remove my cellular phone and dial Detective Karl Rubins's office. A gruff-sounding secretary answered, telling me that, though Rubins was in the building, he wasn't at his desk. "Gimme a numba." I hung up, looking more closely at the Peg-Board as I said, using the portable phone's plastic antenna as a pointer, "How often do people leave you all their keys like this?" I lifted a key ring that had a fob shaped like a little tennis shoe and that jingled with all sorts of keys other than the one that would fit a car's ignition.

"Sometimes they do," Sacks replied. "Most people got somebody following 'em when they drop off a car, so a lot of times they'll just leave the whole ring."

The phone rang and I replaced the key ring as I said, "Bill Hawley."

The first words out of Detective Rubins's mouth were, "Hawley, where the hell have you been?"

"I'm fine, Detective. The reason I'm calling is that I have a question about the murder weapon used in yesterday's drive-by."

"What the fuck are you talking about?" Rubins said in my ear, while I pulled a serious face for Sacks's benefit and nodded once, importantly.

"The Encom MP-45, have you traced it yet?"

"Hawley . . ."

"Have you?"

"Sort of," Detective Rubins said, sighing as he did. "We've got a report on file of one that was stolen from a collection about three months ago. I've got a coupla uniforms checking it out right now. The serial numbers were filed, but, like I said, that's an unusual weapon. Maybe we'll get lucky and the owner will cop to it. Why? What did you find out?"

"Have you got the owner's telephone number handy?" I asked.

"What for?"

"Call him, Detective, and then call me back. Find out if the man who reported the gun stolen ever had his car serviced at Lefty's Autoworks on the corner of Scranton and West Forty-third. I'll wait."

"Hawley . . ."

"Please, Detective. Just call me back."

I killed the connection and turned back to George Sacks. I think the phone in my pocket must have bothered him, because he didn't take his eyes off it as he balled his left hand into a fist and casually smacked the side of the pop machine next to which he sat. The machine shuddered, and dispensed, instead of a soda, a can of Budweiser, which he opened and drank from, deeply. Then he leaned his head back and said, "Ahh," blowing air so that the bangs hanging over his forehead moved. Then he said, "So, what's the deal?"

"So far," I replied, "the deal looks like at least a couple of counts of burglary, probably possession of stolen property—once we get a search warrant for your basement apartment—and, as soon as Detective Rubins traces the gun, which he's doing right this minute, accessory to murder in the first degree."

"How do you figure all that?"

"Because these keys lead me to believe that you've been borrowing a lot more than cars, Mr. Sacks. I think you've been supplementing your income with a little breaking and entering, using the house keys these people leave in your possession, while you know that they're stuck at work without a car. That was an expensive piece of computer equipment you were playing with when I stopped by the house. More than just a P. C.

I'm no computer geek, but I noticed the bells and whistles. Somebody laid out some pretty big bucks so you could play Pac-Man.''

"That computer isn't mine," Sacks insisted. "It belongs to Ron, my landlord. He bought it."

"With what? Ronald Ackermann doesn't even work."

"Why should he work when he's got his stepfather to pay his bills?"

"Not anymore he don't," Larry put in from the periphery. Sacks glanced his way before he looked back at me and said, "What's he talking about?"

I examined his expression carefully, finding his eyes dull with what I took to be genuine confusion. Instead of answering his question, I decided to keep our conversation running along a linear path. So I asked, "Are you trying to tell me that Everett Chase contributes to Ronald Ackermann's upkeep?"

"Huh?" Sacks laughed, slamming his Budweiser in three deep gulps before crinkling the aluminum can in one big hand. "Contributes? Man, you don't know half of what you think you know."

My cellular phone rang, and when I answered it, Detective Rubins said, "Yeah, Hawley, the guy who reported the Encom stolen had his car fixed at Lefty's. As a matter of fact, on the day of the burglary, the car was still at the garage. Somebody broke in during the day while he was at work. They got in through a basement window. Why? What have you got?"

"Sit tight, Detective," I said. "I'll be calling you back in ten minutes."

Again I disconnected the phone. Repeating what Detective Rubins had just said, I leaned on the cash register counter, slid the phone back into my shirt pocket, and crossed my arms over my chest, saying, "Mr. Sacks, I think you've got a problem."

"Oh, I don't know," Sacks replied, rather smugly. "Sounds to me like I could have a coupla options here."

"How's that?"

"Well, for instance, there's always the possibility of a trade."

"What for what?"

''What I know for a 'get out of jail free' card.''

''For that we need the prosecutor's okay.''

''Fine.''

I shot a questioning look Larry's way. He shrugged, indicating it was my call.

''How do we know the trade's fair?'' I asked, buying time to think.

''You wouldn't even be considering it if you weren't ready to deal.''

''I can't promise you anything; that's up to the D.A.''

''Then maybe we should talk to the D.A.''

Dammit, I thought, knowing that the bastard had me, since if I wanted to hear what he had to say, I would have to share it with the authorities, which, for reasons of my own, I had been hoping I wouldn't have to do just yet. Chewing my lip, I lowered my head as if examining my shoes. Then, lifting my eyes to look at Sacks from under my brows, I said, ''You know, it was Ronald Ackermann who tipped me off about you. He called me about an hour ago and told me about the Camaro.''

A red hue flowered over Sacks's cheeks, and his eyes went bright. He stood up, and as soon as he did Larry Fizner stepped lightly around the counter to position himself at my left side.

Playing on Sacks's anger, I said, ''How long has Jane Craig been living in Ronald Ackermann's house?''

No reply.

''Did Ronald Ackermann get money from his stepfather on a regular basis or only when he needed it?''

Not a word.

''Who filed the firing pin on the MP-45 to upgrade it to full automatic—you or Ronald Ackermann?''

Nothing.

''Fine,'' I said, unfolding my portable phone again. ''You're on your own. We'll see what kind of deal you can cut without me.''

I was just starting to dial when Sacks reached out his hand, I think to stop me from calling Detective Rubins, although I can't be certain because Larry grabbed the young man's wrist long before he got anywhere near me. I disconnected the line and looked Sacks in the eye. Taking his hand back from Larry's grip, he said, "Tell me one more time what you said about Everett Chase."

"Somebody used the dark blue Camaro you were just trying to paint white, and an automatic pistol stolen from the house of a man who just happened to be having his car serviced in this garage, to kill him."

"And Ron Ackermann told you that I did it?"

"Not exactly. He just told me that he had seen you with a dark blue Camaro, which was exactly the kind of car the police were looking for. I think he got scared."

Sacks smiled wryly.

"Right. Ron got scared."

"Have you got a different opinion?"

"Maybe. But like I already said, I need to cut a deal."

"And like I already said, I can't make you any promises."

"Ron talked about you, undertaker. I recognized your name. Every time he'd find an article about you in the paper he made sure to point it out. He finds you fascinating. How about that?"

I didn't say anything, watching Sacks's face.

"Ron ain't scared," Sacks reiterated, as if to keep things rolling. "Bein' scared means that you don't know what to expect. Ron always knows what's gonna happen next—in each and every way. His whole life's part of one big scenario, one big plan he's got, all written up in his computer."

"What's that supposed to mean?"

"Look," Sacks said. "You've got me on this burglary thing. It was a dumb thing to do. I'm screwed and I admit it. Okay? But this drive-by shooting stuff . . . no way. I ain't takin' somebody else's fall. I don't care what Ron said . . . Ron's got his own troubles. You promise me that my charge stays at burglary, and only burglary, and I'll tell you everything you want to know."

"What kind of deal is that?" I asked, surprised.

"The kind that leaves my options open," Sacks replied. " 'Cause if what you say is true, then the cops are gonna need my testimony to put the car, and the gun, where they say they were. To get it, they're gonna have to drop my charges. No pay, no play. Okay?''

George Sacks's voice was unsettlingly calm and cool. Far too composed for someone who was discussing his own possible involvement in a murder. But along his upper lip there had formed a faint pattern of shimmering beads of sweat. As hard as he fought to maintain his tough-guy facade, his body was betraying him.

As much as he might have liked to believe differently, George Sacks was nothing but a small-time crook who boosted stereos and TV sets for pocket money, thinking he was clever when he kicked in a basement window to cover up the fact that he had let himself in the side door using a key he shouldn't have had, probably justifying what he did by convincing himself that his victims could afford the loss since they were sure to have insurance anyway. He was a hustler, and a liar, a thief, and a jerk . . .

And right now, he was scared stiff.

''I can't make you any promises,'' I said again, sliding my hands into my trouser pockets. ''But, if you play me straight, I think I just might be able to work something out.''

''I'll play you straight,'' Sacks replied, just a little too fast, betraying how anxious he was to get on my good side.

''Where do you want to do this?'' I asked.

''I think we better go to my place.'' He absentmindedly reached up to the Peg-Board behind the counter before catching himself, drawing his hand back from the car keys hanging there and adding with a contrite half smile, ''Uh, maybe you better drive.''

NINE

■■■■■■■■■■

"WHAT ABOUT JANE Craig?'' I wondered aloud on our way to the house on Standish Drive. ''If she's home, we got a problem.''

With a casual wave, Sacks said, ''Don't worry about her. With Ron at the war . . . she'll be with him for sure. She don't let him go no place alone no more. She's like his shadow, man. She don't hardly let him out of her sight.''

''How long has she been living with him?''

''A little less than a year. He didn't really want her to move in, but she was stubborn about it. Wouldn't take no for an answer.''

''Where is this war?'' Larry asked from the van's driver's seat.

''South of here. This construction company's got some land, like a hundred acres or something . . . I don't know. But they've got a bunch of storage barns set up for their equipment, and for renting out for boat and R.V. storage, off-season. They've even got a helicopter pad. The owner lets SWORDS hold their spring war there every year.''

''How long does this thing go on?'' I put in.

Sacks shrugged.

''Usually a couple of weeks. Although it's taken as long as a month once or twice. It all depends on the turnout, and how the scenario goes.''

The scenario, Sacks went on to explain, was devised by

Ronald Ackermann, who spent the majority of his time writing on his computer until he had developed a suitable reason for the various Lords and Kings to confront one another, twice a year, once in the spring, another in the fall, using the armies of stick jockeys each was able to amass from their particular area of the country. To my surprise, it turned out that the people who attended the wars weren't all local, but traveled from as far afield as California and Canada to camp out, engage in "prithee speech" with each other all day, dance, sing, tell stories, feast at night, and either fight in or watch the battles that would rage on the open stretches of field starting on the first Sunday afternoon and lasting until one army emerged as victorious.

"The Lords usually start arriving either on Friday night or Saturday morning," Sacks concluded. "With their entourages in tow. Like a caravan."

"And these people camp out for two weeks at a stretch, sometimes longer?" I asked.

"Yup."

"Who can take a month off work?"

"Who says they work? This is SWORDS, man; its members are dedicated."

"I guess. And Ronald Ackermann is the one who cooks up the reasons for the fight?"

"Yeah, he plots it all out. Calls it, 'The Tale.' He writes up which Lord is mad at which other one, and why, and what it would take to settle things—which piece of land, or flag, or member of which noble family needs to be captured. On Saturday night the Lords meet and choose up sides as to which one is loyal to which other, divide up the available land, move their armies around, and get ready. On Sunday sometime, they start things off, usually with one Lord having his army invade another Lord's territory. After the first charge, it just goes from there."

"Since he comes up with the story they're all acting out, Ron Ackermann must be one of the Lords, huh?"

"No. He likes to fight, so he's a knight. You should see his armor."

"I have. Yesterday, at Brookside Park, when he was practicing."

"That's just his workout stuff," Sacks said as we pulled into his driveway. "He had the stuff he wears at the war special made. Cost him a ton."

We entered the house through the front door, and as soon as we did the little girl I had previously seen with Jane Craig came running out to throw herself into George Sacks's arms. Sacks, for his part, said, "How's my big girl?" lifting "Julie" up over his head and bringing her back down in a bear hug that folded her in tight against his chest. I mentioned that I had assumed the child belonged to Jane Craig, to which he replied that, nope, she was his. The girl's mother and he had never been married, so he had assumed custody of their daughter after the mother "took off" with another man. Sacks didn't know where she was presently residing, nor did he care. Adding, as he patted his daughter's bottom and told her to, "Get Daddy a beer," that Jane Craig was really nice about watching the child when he was at work, which was part of the reason he had been so willing to loan out the Camaro after Ron had called the previous morning, all in a panic.

"Ronald Ackermann called *you*?" I asked, standing in the center of the cluttered living room. "Where were you?"

"I was home."

"Here?"

"Yeah."

"But I thought Ronald Ackermann doesn't have a phone."

"Ron doesn't," Sacks said, accepting a bottle of Rolling Rock from his daughter. "I've got one, downstairs."

"Billed in your name?"

"Yeah."

"When was this? What time did he call?"

"I don't know. About noon, I guess."

"And he asked for Jane?"

"Yeah. He was all worked up over something, and when Jane was done talking to him, she looked worked up too. She asked me if she could use the car for a couple of hours, so I got her the keys, and off she went."

"To pick up Ron?" I offered.

"No," Sacks said, shaking his head after taking a swallow of beer. "Ron showed up about twenty minutes after Jane left. He stayed home the rest of the day."

"You can vouch for that?" I said. "You'll swear to it?"

"Why not? It's true."

"When did Jane get back?"

"Not late. Like six o'clock. Dinnertime."

I thought that through:

I had found Ronald Ackermann in the park, where I had told him that his missing mother's body had finally been located and was about to be identified by the county coroner, presumably at any moment. If that identification occurred before Ronald's twenty-first birthday, the one-million-dollar life insurance policy which was essentially all that was left of his mother's estate—since Everett Chase had invested his own money in, and had assumed responsibility for, his second wife's restaurant—would end up going to Ronald's stepfather, leaving Everett Chase with both the restaurant and the insurance . . . which would total Ronald Ackermann's inheritance up to a big fat zero.

Ronald, who knew that I was planning to meet with his stepfather later that same afternoon, had locked himself in the park's concession stand, where he had used the telephone, I had now been told, to call his "girlfriend," Jane Craig, the former Mrs. Edward Craig, who immediately took off in a "borrowed" dark blue Camaro, which just so happened to be precisely the model of car I saw gun Everett Chase down right before my eyes. And all this after Everett Chase himself had suggested that we sit outside, on the patio, almost as if he had deliberately wanted to expose himself to the street.

"Did Jane Craig call anybody after she talked to Ronald Ackermann?" I asked.

"How should I know?" Sacks replied, sitting himself down in an easy chair next to the desk upon which Ackermann's impressive computer setup was located. "She closed the door."

So, what if she had? I thought. What if Jane Craig had called, oh . . . Everett Chase? As unlikely as that sounded, it fit . . . just barely, but it did fit. What if she had told him who

I was, and that I was sticking my nose in their business? What if she told him that I was going to expose them all . . . tell the whole world the truth about what Madeline Chase had done, as well as their subsequent attempts to defraud an insurance company out of a million dollars by hiding her body? What if she convinced Everett Chase, who, it must be remembered, had himself delivered his wife's dead body for dismemberment, that he had to help her do something about me? To scare me so badly that I'd go away. Or . . .

What if she had convinced him that more drastic measures were in order?

I stopped, feeling my heart skip.

Was it actually me who had been the target of that shooting all along? Had I really come that close? Did Everett Chase so fear the complications that might arise should I ever expose his part in his wife's disappearance that he would agree to help Jane Craig gun me down? I let the idea sink in for just a moment, which was exactly how much time it took for my stomach to turn over and my knees to go weak.

Stop it!

The fat bastard!

Shake it off!

That bitch!

Then I realized that, with both Everett Chase and myself standing on the Ivy Spring's patio, if it were Jane Craig in the Camaro, she had come just that close to removing everyone in the world who stood between Ronald Ackermann and his mother's insurance money.

But it was all conjecture, yet to be proved. For now, at least, I needed to concentrate on what I knew for sure.

Sacks had stolen the Encom MP-45 automatic pistol—he had already admitted as much, adding that Ronald Ackermann had kept that gun as "protection" for the house, giving Sacks two months free rent in trade. Sacks hadn't so much as seen the gun since.

No, he also maintained, as far as he knew, Jane Craig hadn't taken it along when she left in the Camaro, but then again, he really hadn't been watching since it wasn't his habit to peek through windows in case his landlord's live-in girlfriend was packing iron. He had just handed over the car keys and gone to play with the computer.

Larry and I left Sacks sitting in the living room as we went to search the house. On the way up the stairs, Larry said, very softly, ''So, it was that embalmer's ex-wife, huh? She did the shooting.''

On the second floor landing I shrugged, saying, ''Looks that way.''

Jane Craig, I thought, was the one person we had found so far who could connect Madeline Chase (suicide) to Edward Craig (crooked embalmer), since she had been the receptionist in the office of Mrs. Chase's psychologist during the same period that she had been married to Craig. She also connected Edward Craig (crooked embalmer with something to hide) and Ronald Ackermann (potential heir to a fortune) in that she had first been married to the one, and was presently shacking up with the other. And finally, Jane Craig linked the blue Camaro I had seen shoot Everett Chase down in broad daylight to Ronald Ackermann's mystery phone call, which I had heard through a locked concession stand door as a mumbled series of indistinct words, since it was apparently she who Ronald Ackermann had chosen to call.

But why did he call her?

Had he sent her out to kill for him?

Or had she decided to do it on her own?

Either way, the job had ended up sloppy . . . but what could you expect on such short notice? Everett Chase needed to be removed before the coroner's ID was official, which as far as Robert Ackermann knew, was about to happen at any moment. There wasn't much time to concoct a plan. If it hadn't been for the disinterment that had led to the discovery of Madeline Chase's head, he would have had all the time in the world . . . or at least he would have had the two weeks he needed before his twenty-first birthday. But that two weeks had vanished the instant I found his mother's remains. And I do mean vanished. And I do mean at that instant. If Ronald Ackermann was to inherit anything, then something drastic had to be done about his stepfather immediately.

That is, if Ronald Ackermann was really counting on the money. . . .

But how could he not be?

How could he not be just sitting there thinking, "Just two more years," or whatever. "Just two more years, or months, or weeks, until I get a check. A million bucks, gaining interest, just sitting there with my name stamped all over it. And all I've got to do is wait just two more years . . ."

Or weeks.

Or whatever.

Who wouldn't be doing that?

And then to suddenly be told that the whole thing was off? To have me, Bill Hawley, a stranger meddling where he didn't belong, just come strolling up to him in the park one day and say, "Hi. You don't know me, but guess what? Any second the county coroner's going to sign a paper that will send all that dough you've been dreaming about over to your stepfather, to whom you're not even technically related except through your mother's second marriage, and who doesn't really need it since he's got your mom's business and God knows what else. You're living like a bum, and he's as rich as a hog. But he's going to hit the jackpot, and you're gonna get squat."

Can you imagine how that must have felt? No wonder he went running like he did. No wonder he asked me, "Are you sure it's her?"

No wonder.

"So what are we looking for?" Larry interjected.

Blinking my way back to the present, I replied, "Anything that would connect Jane Craig to murder, I suppose. Or anything that would explain why Everett Chase would be giving Ronald Ackermann money."

"That one's easy," Larry said.

I looked at him.

"Think about it, Bill. Edward Craig must have told his wife about hiding Madeline Chase's body. A guy like him? He couldn't keep a secret like that to save his life. Once she knew what was going on, Jane Craig must have turned around and filled the Ackermann kid in as to what really happened to his mom. But instead of running to the cops, Ackermann used what he knew to shake down his stepfather, who could afford to pay, but couldn't afford to get smeared in public.''

I nodded, thinking, so there it was. Larry Fizner had come right out and linked it all together in a chain:

Jane Craig, all of forty years old, and Ronald Ackermann, who was not quite twenty-one—which would have made him about sixteen when his mother died—had made each other's acquaintance sometime, according to George Sacks, within the last year. Even though Ronald Ackermann had initially resisted, Jane Craig eventually moved in. Once she did, Ronald Ackermann started receiving money from his stepfather. And now, just to add a little spice to the stew, both people who stood between Ronald Ackermann and his mother's life insurance money—his older sister and his stepfather—were dead by violence. His sister having been killed a little less than two years ago in an apparent robbery/mugging, his stepfather having been gunned down just hours before the coroner was scheduled to officially identify Madeline Chase's remains.

So it was Jane Craig we wanted. Maybe Ronald Ackermann too . . . but Jane Craig for sure.

It had to be.

Didn't it?

Unlike the living room, which was a disaster of disorder and squalor, the second floor was neat and clean. In the master bedroom's doorway I hesitated while Larry jumped right in. He and I have two distinctly different styles when it comes to searching a room. He tears it up, pulling drawers open and turning them over to spill their contents on the floor. I let things develop more slowly, soaking in the atmosphere, trying to put myself in the place of the room's usual occupant in order to understand just what the room and its contents might represent in that person's mind. As Larry rattled around, my eyes moved slowly over the objects before me.

King-sized bed with a canopy over it.

Satin sheets, all in purple.

Two night tables, one on either side of the bed.

Two dressers, his and hers.

Curtains, also purple, drawn over the single window.

Full-length sword leaning in one corner.

White-painted shield, with a red cross, hanging on the wall.

Ceremonial daggers, also hanging on the wall.

And . . .

The autopsy protocol for Allison Ackermann that had been included in the file T. W. Younger had left in my possession took sudden and detailed shape in my mind:

Allison Ackermann had suffered a severe impact injury to the anterior portion of her head, displaying all the classic results of a sudden and violent contact between her skull and an unidentified solid object, including lacerations of the scalp, fracture of the bone, contusions of the brain, and epidural hematomas. Due to the extensive vascularity of the scalp, she had bled profusely. Indenting of the skull at the point of impact, with resulting outward bending at the periphery, indicated that the blow had been delivered from behind, in a generally upward stroke . . . which, since it was a rather unusual direction for such a blow, had led the investigators to conclude that a baseball bat or similar object had been employed. But—and this was the significant point—the skull fractures had not been of the shattering variety, as one might expect, but, as I've already mentioned, of the compression type, meaning that they were concentrated around a single, circular depression . . . like what one might expect to be produced by the head of a hammer.

So the skull fracture, looking as if it had been punched into the bone, served to contradict the expected weapon, a bat, which would be drawn up from below in the classic baseball swing.

But now it made sense.

The object I had noticed hanging on the wall brought it all together.

Stepping over I examined the weapon being so prominently displayed, remembering that it had been Ronald Ackermann himself who had called me with the information that had led me to George Sacks, his boarder . . . and, by extension, to this house. It had been Ronald Ackermann himself. . . .

The thing on the wall was called a mace. It was about three feet long, had a steel grip on one end, a wooden length for its shaft, and a steel weight on its other end, studded with four protuberances that had rounded heads, each of which would concentrate the force of a blow into an impact point sure to break flat bone into a round, circular depression. The size of the weapon indicated to me that it could be swung with one hand from above, forward, like a hammer, by a large muscular person. Or should a person be, say, a little smaller of frame, it could be used like a baseball bat, with a stroke directed across the user's body, aimed slightly up, with the victim's skull acting as the "ball."

Just as I was about to call Larry Fizner's attention to the mace, he said, "Bill, check this out," making me turn to find him standing over an open dresser drawer, pointing down. I stepped around the bed and approached him, glancing into his eyes briefly before following the direction of his attention.

"If I wasn't such a naturally trusting person," he said, "I'd say that there was something funny going on around here."

I nodded.

"You buyin' it?" he added.

"I don't know," I replied, suppressing the urge to reach out and touch the cloth that Larry had found, in a dresser drawer, lying right on top. It was about a foot square, made of some stiff material, colored a rusty orange. But what was really important about it—that thing that made me simultaneously want to whoop with triumph and slink away, convinced that I had been had—was the oily, stained outline it bore. That outline traced the perfect impression of a gun—an Encom MP-45, if I wasn't very much mistaken, which I wasn't.

When my cellular phone rang I removed it from my pocket without taking my eyes off the rag, saying, "Hawley Funeral Home."

"I want to talk to a William Hawley, immediately," a terse voice demanded.

"This is Bill Hawley speaking. Can I help you?"

"Mr. Hawley, this is Jerome Larson. Paul Larson's son."

"Oh yes, Mr. Larson. How's your mother doing?"

"Pardon me?"

"Your mother. How is she?"

''My mother's dead, Mr. Hawley.''

''Oh, I'm very sorry,'' I said, immediately switching gears from snoop mode to funeral director as I fished out a pad and pen so that I could start taking down the death call information. ''Where exactly in Phoenix are you calling from, Mr. Larson? What's the name of the hospital your mother's at?''

''I don't know what you're talking about, Mr. Hawley,'' Jerome Larson said, his voice growing colder with every word. ''But whatever it is, it isn't going to work. I'm calling a lawyer as soon as I can. If not today, then first thing Monday morning. I'm going to sue you for everything you've got.''

''Wait a minute,'' I said. ''What's the problem? What's going on?''

''You know damn well what's going on! The police just told me that you dug up my father and cremated him . . .''

''But that's what you told me to do.''

''No, I didn't.''

''Oh, come on, Mr. Larson. You practically begged me to take care of things before your mom passed away, remember? You said that it was the only way she could die in peace. We were on the phone for nearly an hour. I'm not going to start playing games about it now. We had a verbal agreement . . .''

''My mother passed away nine months ago, Mr. Hawley,'' Jerome Larson said.

''What?''

''I said that my mother's been dead for nearly a year. I don't know what you're trying to pull, but . . .''

''Didn't you call me from Arizona? Didn't you tell me that your mother was terminal and wasn't expected to last out the week?''

''Mr. Hawley . . .''

''No, Mr. Larson, please. Just answer the question. Did you or did you not call me from a hospital in Phoenix, Arizona?''

''No, I didn't.''

''Mr. Larson, I'm serious . . .''

''So am I. I'm so serious, you wouldn't believe it. What you did is desecration, Mr. Hawley. There are no words for what you did. That was my father you burned. My *father*! How dare you? How *dare* you?''

"Mr. Larson . . ."

"You'll be hearing from my attorney . . . bet on it. That funeral home of yours is mine, pal. Along with everything else you've got. I want damages. I want compensation. You just wait and see what I don't want. You just wait, you son of a bitch . . ."

"Mr. Larson? Mr. Larson? Oh, sweet Jesus."

He'd hung up on me.

"What now?" Larry asked.

"I gotta go," I said, disconnecting the phone. "I gotta get back, right now. Mr. Fizner, we've got to leave . . ."

"We can't leave," he replied, surprised. "We've got to secure the scene until the cops can get a warrant. We've still got business here . . ."

"I've got to go!" I exclaimed loudly, striding out of the bedroom and down the stairs. Everything but what Jerome Larson had just said disappeared from my mind, leaving one concept, one simple, screaming, terrifying reality that seemed to have physical, solid substance reverberating ominously in my skull.

"Bill!" Larry Fizner called, following behind. "What the fuck . . . ?"

At the bottom of the stairs he caught me, grabbing my arm. I spun on him then, thrusting my face in close, ignoring George Sacks, who I noticed from the corner of my eye was still planted with his beer bottle in the easy chair near the computer console, watching me through a bleary grin. My intention, at that moment, was to spell it out for my partner, to describe the situation to him in a clear, logical manner that he would be sure to understand. I meant to say that Jerome Larson, the son of Paul J. Larson, the deceased gentleman that I had disinterred just two days before, was now claiming that he had not, in fact, asked me to cremate his father. Worse, he was claiming that he had not authorized me to do it.

Authorized!

After having implored me over the phone until I had agreed to bend the rules and forge his signature on the authorization the cemetery needed before they'd dig Paul J. Larson's casket back up, he was turning around and screaming about lawsuits, lawyers, and damages.

And what could I do about it?

My legs felt a little rubbery.

Just how the hell could I prove that he was lying? All I had was his word over the telephone. I'd never even met the man! One look at the authorization form that I had signed, and that my uncle Joe, the notary public, had notarized, as a favor to me, and a blind person would be able to tell that it wasn't an authentic signature. One handwriting sample, one signed check or driver's license, and I was cooked.

God!

I could see the headlines now . . . worse, I could see the jurors . . . JURORS! Oh, Jesus! How could I have been so stupid? Me, of all people? I know what good targets funeral homes make for legal action. I know that judges, juries, and the court of public opinion all traditionally weigh in against undertakers as a whole . . . that the unspoken attitude of almost everyone not in the business is that funeral directors are positioned only a notch or two above parasites on the evolutionary chain . . . that nearly everyone believes that what we really do is take advantage of grief to pad our own bank accounts, preying on defenseless widows at that one, single time in their lives when they are at absolutely their most vulnerable.

I know all that.

I've seen other funeral homes get slapped with unbelievable settlements for the most trivial—and often subjectively perceived, completely unsubstantiated—offenses. Never bend the rules, that's the dictum of our profession. Never bend the rules, because you never know who is going to turn around and bite you in the ass. You can never tell who's going to become transformed once the funeral is over into an entirely different person—a person making claims, pointing a finger, saying out loud for the whole wide, hostile world to hear, "This funeral director screwed me. My husband—or my wife—died, and look what this man did to me. I'm scarred. I'll never be the same again. For as long as I live, whenever I think of my dearly departed, I will think of this man, and what he did. How can anything as inconsequential as money ever make up

for my pain? How can money ever ease my suffering? Well
. . . maybe a *lot* of money might help."

I blinked, intending to say all of that, or at least something
like it, something more to the point, something succinct that
would explain my concerns. But when I finally did speak, all
that came out was, "I've got to leave. Come on. Let's go."

Larry looked at me, then at George Sacks, then up the stairs
toward Robert Ackermann's bedroom, presumably seeing in
his mind's eye all the evidence that that room contained. Then
he withdrew the keys to his van, handing them over as he said,
"Take the van. I'll catch a ride from Rubins later on."

"You sure?"

"Somebody's got to secure the scene while the cops are
getting a search warrant signed. Forensics are going to want
to examine that club, and the rag, and . . ."

He went on, but I didn't hear another word he said because,
at that moment, I suddenly realized I couldn't have cared less
about Robert Ackermann, or Madeline Chase, or T.W.
Younger and his life insurance company, or, for that matter,
Larry Fizner himself. I couldn't have cared less about any of
them because reality had just come crashing down atop me in
the person of Jerome Larson, with his lawyer, his lawsuit, and,
most especially, with the bag of dust that was now, because
of me, all that was left of his father. Oh, the shit I was in!
Nothing mattered anymore other than the shit that I was in.

Nothing mattered . . .

Nothing.

I drove in a daze, automatically, not really paying attention,
trying all the while to recall, word for word, what Jerome
Larson had said to me over the phone, looking for anything I
might be able to use in my own defense. Why was he doing
this to me? What could have possessed him to even conceive
of such a cynical, blatant scam? Worse, again, why had I fallen
for it? Why, oh why, had I forged that authorization? Pounding
the steering wheel in frustration, I made my injured fingers
howl.

I had like a million dollars worth of business insurance
meant to cover me in the event of a suit. But who could tell
if that would be enough? With some of the crazy figures I've

seen awarded lately in those now famous cases you read about in the newspaper, those remarkable cases, those cases in which people sue for goofy shit—like a restaurant having the temerity to serve coffee that was hot . . . imagine, the nerve. Hot coffee, of all things. Hundreds of millions of dollars, not one million, or ten, or twenty, but more.

Then I wondered if my insurance company would even pay, considering that I was provably guilty of obvious negligence. Or, depending on how you looked at it, it wouldn't be that much of a stretch to allege, given the circumstances, that I had deliberately set myself up, maybe even deliberately gone along with the whole thing specifically so my insurance company would have to pay. I mean, for me to knowingly sign somebody else's name to a disinterment authorization, and then to dig the body up and burn it? Christ, there was sure to be an investigation. New American Life had hired me to investigate one of their claims, offering me a fee based on how much I was able to save them from having to pay. Could I expect my insurance company to do anything less?

"I can't think about it," I said aloud. "I'm going to have an accident if I don't watch what I'm doing."

Maybe we could settle out of court.

Maybe it wouldn't be so bad.

Maybe if there was a bridge between me and the funeral home I should just drive Larry's van off it and be done with the whole fucking thing.

I found Nat in the office, standing at the desk, looking confused. As soon as I stepped into the room she said, "Bill, what the hell's going on? As soon as I took the call forwarding off your portable phone, some lawyer called to warn me that we were going to be served with some kind of papers first thing Monday morning. Do you know anything about it?"

I didn't say a word. Pulling to a halt in the office doorway I simply stood there, heart pounding, chest heaving with fear and grief, drinking in the sight of my wife, feeling so, so bad for what I had done, feeling worse for what it would mean to her. I was willing to take my punishment, to do whatever it was that I had to do to make up for being stupid enough to get myself into such a jam. But it wasn't going to be just me who was going to suffer. It would be Nat too. And my brother Jerry, wheelchair bound, also because of something I did. And my uncle Joe, who had notarized a forged document, because I had asked him to. And my dad, who had co-signed the mortgage on the funeral home I was about to piss away, using his own funeral home that he had worked so hard to build into the solid business it was today as collateral, again, because I had asked him to do it, and . . .

"Oh, Nat," I said, trying to stop the flood in my mind by lifting my arms and walking toward her. "I'm so, so sorry."

"What?" she said, holding me. "What's wrong? What did you do?"

I didn't even know how to explain it. I didn't know what to say. So I just stood there, hugging her, trying as I did to squeeze away my fears, eyes closed, thinking two diametrically opposed things at exactly the same time, which were:

Thank God for this woman. Without her, I don't know what I'd do.

And . . .

Christ, would a shot of vodka hit the spot right now.

The insidious way that the notion of booze just popped into my head like that jarred me back into motion. Reluctantly, I pushed Nat out to arms' length, looked her in the eye, and said that I had something awful to tell her. She sat down, watching me, eyes as wide as a little girl's. I sat down too. When I was done explaining, she sighed, deeply, and leaned back in her seat, rubbing one hand over her forehead as she said, "Oh boy."

"That's it?"

"What else is there?"

I frowned, stood up, went to the bar, and drank a glass of water. Elsewhere in the building, I heard a door slam. Glancing at the clock, I realized that Jerry had just gotten back from taking out the funeral that I should have taken, which was just one more in the ever-expanding list of things I had recently done wrong that I could feel bad about. Suddenly, I knew that I couldn't face him . . . not yet. Telling Nat had been hard enough; right now, telling Jerry would be too much.

"You tell him," I said, placing my glass in the sink. "I've got to be alone."

Just as I was leaving through one office door, I heard the other hissing open on the pneumatic tubes we had designed into the place when we built it. All the doors have these big, square metal buttons next to them so that Jerry can open them and roll his wheelchair through. Actually, the whole funeral home is entirely handicapped accessible. Somebody was going to be taking possession of a fine building, I thought, without meaning to. There was a lot of potential here.

I just hoped that whoever bought the place on auction after Jerome Larson took it away from me would appreciate all the effort that had gone into designing it.

Through the closed office door, I could hear voices as I walked slowly across the main foyer toward Parlor B, the largest of our three. All the lights were off in the building, and since we only have two narrow windows, one on either side of the front door, the interior of the place was very dark, and very quiet . . . which was exactly what I was looking for. It was in the big parlor, which is eighty feet long and thirty feet wide, that I broke down. There are a hundred folding chairs set up in rows that face one end, where there is a pair of torchier lamps and a standing candlestick for the head of the casket. There are tables with brass lamps and floral-patterned carpeting that my wife picked out. There are recessed light pots in the ceiling, and two huge overstuffed couches, light green, with big lengths of multicolored rope adorning each end, positioned with their backs to the wall, facing the foyer. I sat down on one of those couches, in the nearly perfect darkness, took off my glasses, placed my good hand over my face, and cried.

What the hell was I going to do? Just what in the living hell *could* I do?

My hand was trembling against my face. My eyes were hot and sore. My mouth felt funny . . . like my tongue had gotten swollen. Briefly, I worried that I was going to have a heart attack, because I got a twinge in my chest that straightened me right up on the couch.

I lowered my hand and blinked. "Think, Hawley," I whispered, seeing Nat in my mind. "You can't just let them take it all away. Now THINK!"

But it was hopeless. The pressing issues of my own culpability were smothering everything with images of bankruptcy hearings and long, sweaty explanations, in court, under oath.

As I've already described, the interior of the parlor was pitch-dark, and the curtains on the windows near the front door were all but completely drawn, making the foyer a shade lighter than the parlor. It was because of that desperate illumination that I noticed the silhouette in the closest of the parlor's two doorways, backlit by the grey-toned dimness behind. Jerry didn't move, but spoke from his wheelchair.

"Bill?" he said, into the darkness.

I didn't respond.

"Bill, I know you're in here."

Reaching over, I snapped on a brass table lamp.

Rolling toward me as I wiped the tears from my cheeks, Jerry stopped a few feet in front of me and said, "So, what the hell?"

I sighed, saying, "This is a big problem, Jer. A nightmare. I don't know what we're going to do, except maybe . . . uh, I know it's a weird time to ask, but how about doing me a favor?"

Jerry kept his eyes on my face, but he didn't say a word.

"What would you think of putting the business in your name?" I said. "That is, assuming that we even have a business to transfer after next week. But if, by some miracle, we should get through this thing with our skin, how about we put the place in your name, and take my name off the deed?"

"Why?" Jerry asked, knitting his brows, but not reacting nearly as vociferously as, knowing his temper, I thought he might.

"I'm nothing but trouble," I said, embarrassed at the whining, self-pitying tone in my voice but unable to do anything about it. "I've been nothing but trouble since I was a kid. You've always been the achiever. You should run the place, not me. I'm just going to blow it for all of us . . . if I haven't already."

"So that's it?" he said when I was done.

"Don't you get it? We're screwed."

"No, I mean, this . . . *this* is it? You're going to deal with it here? On the couch?"

I knew suddenly what he was about to do, and to avoid it I stood up, performing a karate chop kind of motion with the flat of my hand while saying, "Don't even think about it, Jer! Don't you dare even think about any pep talks. I don't want to hear it. I swear to God . . . I won't listen . . ."

"SHUT UP!" he thundered, silencing me where I stood. "Just shut the fuck up! My ass is on the line here too, you know. I've got a right, Bill. I've got a right . . . and you've got an obligation. Dammit. You owe me. . . ."

He stopped, his hands gripping the arms of his wheelchair, his face ashen with anger. At that moment a thought popped into my head, which said, He's going to get out of that chair someday. He's going to do it, and the doctors be damned. He's going to stubborn his way right out of that chair, and he's going to walk again, powered exclusively by his own force of will.

"You owe me," he repeated, his voice softer but still sharp. "I was on the fast track before the accident. I was making it."

He was right, of course. Before he broke his neck, he was a computer salesman for a company with its headquarters in New York and a division hub in Cleveland. At twenty-two, fresh out of college, he had earned sixty thousand dollars. The next year it was nearly double that. At twenty-five, he was being groomed for a management position. And then came the accident.

"I'm crippled," he said venomously. "But I'm not stunted. I can still think. I can still do that.

"You told Nat that the reason you took this case on in the first place was because we needed the money . . ."

"The case isn't what's important anymore," I said.

Jerry's eyes flashed as he replied, "Shut up! I'm talking now, and I'll start where I please."

I closed my mouth.

"Nat told me all about what you said," he went on. " 'We

don't have enough funeral business to pay the bills,' you said. 'It's taking a long time for us to catch on in a new town. We need some breathing space.' You said, 'The bills keep coming, whether we have business or not.'

"You actually told your wife that you needed to use your private investigator's license, not because you wanted to, but because you had to. You weren't doing it for you, you were doing it for us. It was a sacrifice . . . or at least that was the implication. You were just being a responsible adult, taking care of business the best way you could."

He paused.

"Bill," he said, "you're so full of shit . . . I mean, my God. Don't you see it?"

I opened my mouth, closed it, and shook my head.

"When was the last time you did any promotion?" Jerry asked. "When was the last time you went out and tried to introduce yourself, shake a few hands, become a part of the community? Who the hell's going to bring you business when they don't even know who you are? Don't you understand? Don't you get it? I was in sales . . . I was good at it! I know. You don't earn someone's trust by putting your company's name on a couple of shopping bags and church calendars. You've got to go out and earn it."

I frowned.

"It's all been an excuse," Jerry said. "This whole private investigator charade has been one big load of smoke from the start. You never wanted to be a funeral director. You never should have built this place. And now that there's a problem, you're just going to sit back and let the whole thing go. You never wanted it, so you're not willing to do anything to keep it. You're fucked in the head, Bill. And you're going to take us all down with you."

"Jerry, man, you just don't understand."

"Don't I? Then educate me."

"So what's the point? What are you trying to say?"

"You want it straight?"

"Yes."

"All your life you've taken the easy way out. That's all the booze ever was, whether you want to admit it or not. Nothing anybody's ever said or did made the slightest difference in the way you behaved. But this time, my ass is up for grabs too. I can't afford to let you just roll over and die.''

''You think that losing the funeral home in a lawsuit's going to be easy?''

''Yes, I do, for exactly the reason you just said.''

''What did I say?''

''In your mind, we've already lost. It's just a matter of time. No options. No hope. Since it's all out of your hands anyway, whatever happens from here on out can't be your fault.''

''But it is my fault,'' I protested. ''It's all my fault. If it weren't for me . . .''

''See, you're doing it again.''

''What the hell do you mean? I just accepted the responsibility . . .''

''No, you didn't. You accepted the blame. There's a difference. Responsibility is an ongoing condition; it demands that you commit yourself to behaving in the best interest of a particular thing. Blame is static, it can't be changed. Since all you can do is wallow in it, it's the easiest way out. Once you accept the blame, you don't have to do anything else. You're done.''

''You're talking like I've still got some other option.''

''You do. You've always got options. It's just that sometimes all the options are hard.''

''So what are you telling me?''

''That there are other things that you can do besides sit in the dark and cry.''

''Like what?''

''Like you can *go for it*,'' Jerry replied, his voice suddenly growing strong as he held a clenched fist up before his face. ''That's what I'd do. If you're convinced that it's already too late, that you're screwed anyway, no matter what you do, that the business is on the block and there's no way in the world to prevent it, then what in the hell have you got left to lose? What's stopping you? What are you waiting for?''

''But . . .''

''You bet your ass I'll take the funeral home,'' Jerry interrupted excitedly. ''I'll take it, and I'll make it a success. And

I'm not talking about just a break-even proposition. I'll make it a real, flag-waving success. Something we can all be proud of . . . something special. You just watch and see if I don't. But for me to do it, for me to even get my shot, there's got to be something here that I can work with. If you just roll over and give the place away, you're fucking me, Bill. You're fucking me . . .

"Again."

He said that last word after a pause that was almost imperceptible. But it hit me anyway, right in the face. There it was . . . after all these years. Jerry was finally telling me what I could do to make it up to him. He had always known as well as I that he wouldn't have even been in that wheelchair were it not, at least partially, for me. But he'd always refused to admit as much out loud. He had categorically denied that I bore any of the responsibility. It had all been a facade, and I had known it. It had all been a part of the wall that he had built around the core of resentment that he was carrying. Together, he and I, we had deprived him of the life he might have built, the career, the family. He resented it all right, as much as he denied it, he couldn't help but resent it. During all those years of paralysis, physical therapy, and dependence on me, his older brother and coconspirator in the purgatory his life had become, the anger had been there, festering.

Now, he was admitting to it. And, what was even more important, he was finally telling me precisely what he wanted as restitution. He was putting it on the line.

I want the funeral home, he was saying. I want my shot at being what I could have been. I want to be somebody. I want to *work*.

"Give me my shot," he said. "Don't blow it for me, Bill."

"But, Jer . . ." I began.

Jerry placed his hands on the tops of his chair's rubber-lined wheels and deftly turned around, with all the practiced precision of a pro. "Don't explain," he said. "Don't talk about it. Don't say a word. Just do it. From now on, you focus your mind on the things you know how to do, and I'll focus mine on what goes on around here. That's the deal, and it's nonnegotiable."

"But what about Ellie?" I said, feeling that I still owed him something on that score too.

"I already told you what you can do about her," he replied, rolling into the foyer. "But she can wait. If we all end up sleeping in a bus stop, it won't make a hell of a lot of difference about her anyway."

Then he was gone.

I sat back down on the couch, thinking about how right he was on the one hand. If I let what could be preoccupy my mind, then I was essentially surrendering myself to what would be without a fight.

But could he have been right about his other point as well? Could I, subconsciously, actually have been using Jerome Larson's threats of legal action as a convenient way to shed myself of a business that I had never really wanted?

I stood up, deciding that now was not the time to indulge in a lengthy bout of self-analysis. Now was the time, as Jerry had said, to act. So . . .

I turned off the light, a sensation of excitement running through me that made me feel clearheaded for the first time since I had been shot. Calling Jerry's name as I strode across the foyer, I found him sitting in the office, behind my desk, with the file folder for the funeral he had conducted that morning, open before him. For an instant it felt strange, seeing him in my place. Then I admitted that it felt exactly right. He looked natural, behind the desk . . . far more natural than I had ever looked, or felt, in that same chair.

"I think I've got an idea," I announced.

He put his pen down and asked what he could do to help.

"You're doing it," I said. "Tell Nat that I'm going out. I might be late, so she shouldn't wait up."

"Where are you going?" the lady herself asked from the doorway, surprising me.

"I'm going to fix it," I said with as much conviction as I could muster, which I found, to my own surprise, was quite a bit. "You just wait and see if I don't. I'll take the portable phone. Have Larry Fizner call me the minute he checks in. And, Nat, don't worry. We've got options. Jerry pointed out a couple, and I think I might have come up with a few more. There are things we can do . . .

"Holy cripe!"

As I was talking, I had caught sight of myself in the wall mirror we've got behind the desk.

"Jesus," I said, more to myself than not. "I look like hell. That's not going to make it. I need a shower."

Which is exactly what I did need. Before leaving the funeral home, I went upstairs, shaved, showered—with a plastic grocery bag over my bandaged hand to keep the dressings dry— combed my hair, and buffed the toes of my shoes. I selected a freshly pressed suit from the closet—black, naturally—tied my necktie in the sharpest Windsor knot I knew how to make, and examined myself in the mirror on the back of my closet door. Shooting my cuffs once for luck. I brushed some lint from my lapel before saying, "There, that's more like it."

From where Nat was sitting on the edge of the bed, she asked, "Feeling better?"

"Yup," I replied. Then, as explanation, I added, "I'm not going to let other people bounce me around anymore, Nat. I am what I am—and I'm tired of trying to be anything else. This is me." I spread my arms out at my sides. "And right now, I'm the best bet I've got going. I may lose. The way things are set up, I may lose no matter what I do. But I'll promise you one thing: even if I do lose, there's no way I'm going to let someone else win."

"What's that supposed to mean?" Nat asked.

"You'll see," I replied, kissing her on the cheek. "Wish me luck."

"What are you going to do?"

"I'm not sure. I've just got to do it before Monday morning."

"You've got to do *what* before Monday morning?"

Checking the thermometer we've got outside our bedroom window and deciding that it was cool enough for a coat, I replied, "I don't know."

"Bill, talk to me."

I sighed.

"Okay," I said, removing, for the first time since my father had given it to me, a black fedora with a silk band from where it had resided on my closet's shelf for so long that it was dusty. Brushing it off before slipping both it and my long, black cashmere overcoat on, I turned to face my wife, saying, "Something occurred to me while I was in the shower. I don't know what to do with it yet; I'm not even sure if it means anything. But let's see what you think, okay?"

"All right," she agreed.

"That casket I dug up . . . the one that Jerome Larson says he never told me to disinter, it had Madeline Chase's head in it. Right? Just her head."

"So?"

"So her head proves categorically both who she is and that she's dead, without question. With her head, all doubts are instantly removed. Since we know that Edward Craig cut her into six pieces after she died, I had a one out of six chance of finding that head, as opposed to say, some other, less identifiable part of her body—a one out of six chance; and that's over and above the absolutely remarkable coincidence of disinterring one casket out of a zillion and finding any part of her at all."

"So?" Nat asked again, although I could see a sparkle in her eyes that made me realize that she was already thinking along the same lines as me.

"So isn't it something that, just two weeks before Ronald Ackermann turns twenty-one years old, thereby qualifying him as the first heir to his missing mother's insurance claim, I should get a call to dig up the one casket in the whole world that has unequivocal evidence in it that his mother is, in fact, unquestionably dead?"

"And now Mr. Larson's son is claiming that it wasn't him who called you," Nat observed.

"That's right," I agreed. "That's what he says, that he didn't call."

"Assuming that he's telling the truth," Nat said, rising from the bed and straightening my necktie before tipping my hat forward a little and smoothing the brim down in front, "then it looks like somebody wanted to make sure that Madeline Chase was declared dead before Ronald Ackermann was old enough to collect her insurance money."

"That's exactly what I was thinking," I agreed.

"Everett Chase?" she suggested.

I shrugged, saying, "As far as I can tell, he's the only person around who stood to profit from my finding his wife's body—though I don't really understand why he'd decide to have her found now . . . almost five years after he successfully disposed of her the first time. But if he was the one who called, posing as Jerome Larson, he had to know what a god-awful can of worms he was digging up . . . so to speak."

"Maybe it was his only way out."

"Of what?"

"You never asked me what I did today," Nat replied coyly. "While you were out asking questions, so was I."

I had almost forgotten about what the girl at the college library had said about her leaving early to run an "errand" since it was such a slow Saturday. "Really?" I asked.

"That's right."

"Where?"

"The county auditor's general record program."

"Your computer again?"

"Of course."

"What did you find out?"

"Only that Everett Chase's restaurant, the Ivy Spring, is going out of business."

"Get out of here! The Ivy Spring's one of the hottest spots in town. It can't be losing money. Where'd you hear that it was closing up?"

"It's public record. Everett Chase filed for bankruptcy protection ten days ago."

"Bankruptcy?" I wondered aloud. "That's almost unbelievable. Did he cite a reason?"

"Insufficient funds to pay creditors. He apparently had a serious cash flow problem."

"And now he's dead," I mused. "And my funeral home's on the line along with his restaurant."

"So what are you going to do?"

"The only thing I can do. I'm going to cause whoever's

left with an interest in this as much grief as I can. Then we'll see what happens.''

''Well,'' Nat said with real concern in her voice, ''just be careful.''

''I'm always careful.''

Cocking her head to one side, she glanced at my bandaged fingers, lifted one eyebrow, and said, ''Then this time, maybe you should be extra careful.''

She had a point, so I kissed her again, told her that I loved her, and promised that I wouldn't do anything that might be even the least bit dangerous . . . which would turn out to be the first promise I had broken to her in a very long time.

TEN
■■■■■■■■■■

BANKRUPT? I THOUGHT, heading downtown on a nearly deserted freeway. Sprinkled across the opaque skyline toward which I drove, the lights of Cleveland sparkled in tiny white pinpricks, while overhead, street lamps flashed past like comets, leaving decaying tails of reflected light to play odd games in my glasses. Even if Everett Chase's restaurant were truly going out of business, could that really have been enough of a motivation for him to have risked having his wife's body discovered after all these years?

"Why not?" I said aloud. "He probably figured that since he didn't have that much left to lose, he had everything to gain."

Which, given my present circumstances, was certainly a point of view that I could appreciate.

Then I thought it through.

When I had first taken that phone call, I didn't know either Jerome Larson or Everett Chase from Adam. His was just a voice on the phone . . . a very persuasive voice, as it turned out. But still just a stranger's voice, so subtly distorted by the telephone's electronics that even after having spoken to both men, I still didn't think I could accurately differentiate between the two. As far as my legal standing was concerned, it probably didn't make a hell of a lot of difference whether it was Everett Chase who called me or not. I was still liable for my breach of conduct, regardless of my benign intentions.

Concerning Madeline Chase's remains, I had to assume that there wasn't much of a chance that the coroner would be able to accurately nail down her cause of death after the embalming process and five intervening years had both done their work. Without a handle on exactly how she had died, her body's main value was to serve as a physical testament to its own existence. Given the secrets her condition concealed, Madeline Chase had been effectively dehumanized into a simple, monetary quantity. Today, she was a financial transaction, an embalmed lottery ticket, the key to the treasure chest for whichever of her heirs was fortunate enough to be left breathing once the smoke had cleared. Had Everett Chase not been murdered, he probably would have already been declared the legal beneficiary of her insurance policy—a good two weeks before his stepson's all-important twenty-first birthday. Because of the success of that one fabricated telephone call, had he lived, both he and his failing restaurant would surely have found themselves financially solvent once more.

But what if I hadn't gone along with it? What if I had refused to disinter Paul J. Larson no matter how strenuously he argued?

Well, then there was always an anonymous tip to the police. Or a call to some other funeral director with the same story. Or, if worse came to worse, an anonymous call to the insurance company might even have done the trick. But Christ, he must have really been desperate for the cash. Ronald Ackermann and Jane Craig must have been squeezing him dry.

Now wouldn't that be something? I thought, unable to help but appreciate the irony of it. What if the underlying reason that Everett Chase had been forced to rat out on his wife's death was that he needed her insurance money to save his restaurant because his stepson had driven him to the brink of bankruptcy with his demands for hush money? But even if that should actually be the case, what good did knowing it do me in my present dilemma? Not much . . . unless . . .

I was thinking about Edward Craig's version of the story. More specifically, I was thinking about his contention that he had been hired by Madeline Chase to hide her body after she had taken her own life so that her children wouldn't be cheated out of the insurance money she felt they had coming. Again, as I had originally done in Craig's apartment, I tried to visualize the scene he had described, with Everett Chase driving the car in which his wife had committed her fatal act, late one cold winter's night, alone. Craig had said that Everett Chase had wanted his wife embalmed so that he could have a private viewing before her body disappeared forever. There was something wrong there, I thought, now that I was really examining it. Actually, it didn't hardly make any sense at all.

Why would Everett Chase want to view his dead wife when he was the one who had transported her body to where Edward Craig stood ready to cut it up? Why would he want to assume the added risk of keeping her around long enough to be embalmed, simply so that he could view a body he had already seen?

The whole idea just didn't add up, and I intended to find out why. But this time, I'd do it right.

We hadn't pushed Craig hard enough during our first interview, I decided, feeling a little ashamed of my soft, squishy middle. Larry Fizner and I had more or less taken the embalmer's word for what had happened, simply because he had sounded sincere. This time I wasn't going to be so easy to convince. And this time, I intended to do a little homework before I asked so much as a single question. I wasn't really sure what practical good this second shot at Edward Craig might serve, but, as I had already promised my wife, I had no intention of suffering alone. If I was going to be made to pay for a mistake that someone else had conned me into making, I was just enough of a vindictive son of a bitch to piss on the whole cake.

Larry Fizner called from the funeral home just as I was getting off the freeway, saying that once Detective Karl Rubins had secured a search warrant for the Standish Drive premises, the evidence found there had been forwarded to the appropriate labs for analysis. Now Larry was chomping at the bit to dive back in.

"Where are you?" he asked. "Where can we link up?"

"Sorry, Mr. Fizner," I said, pulling into the darkest alley I could find. "But I can't let you in on this one. There's too much of a chance that things will go sour."

"Bill," he cut in, "are you kidding? Don't be stupid. Tell me where you are. If we're gonna start fightin' dirty, all the better. I can help. Nobody in their right mind goes in on a bad job without backup. It's just not done."

"Well, then maybe I'm not in my right mind," I said, hoping to sound glib. "But I just can't let you take the chance. This is personal . . . it's between me and whoever's trying to screw me out of everything I've got. I lose that funeral home, I lose it all. I've got until Monday morning before some lawyer's going to be knocking on my door. With a timetable like that, there's bound to be trouble."

"Great!" Larry exclaimed. "Now you're talking. Gimme an address."

"Can't do it, Mr. Fizner."

"Bill, goddamn it! Remember what I said about thinkin' you're suddenly Superman?"

"Sorry, Larry, but thanks. I mean it. Now sit tight and keep an eye on Nat, okay? If I do stir up the bees, I don't want her getting stung."

He was still trying to talk when I hung up, turning off the little phone's ringer so that he wouldn't be able to call me back. No rules, I was thinking as I slipped the phone into its cradle between the seats. No time to lose; no time for rules.

Sammie's Taxidermy and Trophy Shop's front door was covered over for the night with a steel security cage. With its glass-block front window nearly as dark as the soot-stained brick, and the odd page of newspaper tumbling along the sidewalk out front, the place looked abandoned. That same description pretty much held for every other business on the street, except for a girly bar two blocks up that had a red, flashing sign out front over where some motorcycles were parked along the curb. This was not what you'd call the world's most desirable neighborhood. Actually, just the week before, the police had announced that soon they were going to double their patrols in this very section of the city because it had the highest incidence of drug dealing and street corner prostitution in town. With that in mind I checked my watch, found that it was almost exactly ten-thirty, and decided that, if I was going to find out anything useful about Edward Craig, I would probably do better to stay in the car.

Restarting the engine, I left the headlights off, pulled back out onto the street, and headed east, going slow. On my second pass I heard the first call of, "Hey baby, goin' out?" And, "Twenty bucks, honey. And you ain't even gotta get out the car."

Like cats from a shadow, two women slid from the girly bar's front door, waving as I went by. I looked them over, rolling past slowly, watching in my rearview mirror as they turned their heads as I U-turned over the curb and headed back their way. One of the women was white, the other black. Both were wearing very short skirts, very tall shoes, and puffy, fake fur jackets. From where they were standing Sammie's Taxidermy and Trophy Shop was in plain sight. Who better, I thought, to know something about a hideously scarred man living alone than the hookers who plied their trade directly in front of his residence? I didn't expect that Edward Craig would be able to get a lot of dates, looking like he did. But he was still a man. I was sure there had to be times when temptation prompted him to turn Jesus' picture to the wall.

Rolling to a stop in front of the two women, I lowered the automatic window on the passenger's side so that the black one could lean in and say, "So, what you want?"

"Just to talk," I said.

"Shit," she replied, waving me off and heading back inside. "Too goddamn cold for that."

I held up a fifty-dollar bill for the other girl, who, opening the door, said, "Honey, for fifty bucks, I'll sing the national anthem. Why don't you pull over there where it's dark, and we can talk all you want."

When I had us parked and the engine off, she turned toward me, taking the money as I said, "I meant what I told you. I really do just want to talk. I need some information."

She eyed me suspiciously. Even from where I was sitting I could smell the aroma of perfume, cigarette smoke, and bourbon she exuded. It wasn't an altogether unpleasant combination—but it wasn't roses neither.

"You a cop?" she asked.

"No."

"I didn't think so. Cops ain't allowed to pull out cash or their ying-yangs. That's entrapment, or some such shit. So, what you wanna talk about? Something dirty, I expect. You're one those, right?"

"No," I said, resisting the urge to ask what one of "those" was, exactly. "I'm a private investigator."

"Oh yeah, what you investigating?" she said as her right hand slid over to the van's door handle.

I popped the automatic lock, and she got suddenly upset.

"Oh no!" she shouted, fumbling for the lock. "Not this time, baby. No shit, not this time!"

"What the hell's the problem?" I demanded. "I already gave you fifty dollars. Why are you freaking out?"

She settled down a little, looking me over.

"Last week a girl I know got stabbed just down the street. Said that the guy who did it just wanted to 'talk' too."

"If you were so scared, why'd you get in?"

"I don't know. Slow night, I guess."

"That's a hell of a reason."

She shrugged.

"Got a light?"

I turned the ignition key on so that the cigarette lighter would work, holding it out for her when it was ready. She cupped one hand over it, touching my wrist as she did. Exhaling smoke, she said, "Okay. What you wanna talk about? I ain't got all night."

"I'm interested in a man who lives in the neighborhood. I figured one of you girls might know him."

"Why, he like payin' for it?"

"I don't think he's got much of a choice."

"Weirdo, huh? Likes it funny?"

"I wouldn't know. I'm talking about his appearance. He's not very nice to look at."

"You ain't talkin' 'bout Wang Chung, are ya?"

"Who?"

"Spooky guy who lives upstairs of where they stuff the animals. We call him Wang Chung—looks like a chink." She pulled the corners of her eyes into slits. "Got burned in Vietnam."

"Is that what he told you?"

"That's what he tells everybody."

"Isn't he kind of young to have been in Vietnam?"

"Maybe it was Desert Storm then. How the hell should I know how old he is?"

"How well do you know him?"

"Okay, I guess. He's pretty regular—once or twice a month, usually. But only once with me. I can't handle that face of his . . . gives me the willies. Why? What he do?"

She gave her cigarette a pull, looking interested. If her fear of being stabbed had been genuine, she had certainly shed it in a hurry.

I decided my best bet would be to make her think I was letting her in on something important. To that end I said, "Well, I don't really think I can go into that. It's pretty hairy."

"Yeah?" she said, holding her cigarette in midair. "Meaning what?"

I sighed loudly. To make her wait, I said, "What's your name?"

"Jazmine."

"Okay, Jazmine. You remember that guy in Milwaukee? The one who was killing boys in his apartment for like two years before he got caught?"

"You mean the one who was eatin' people?"

"That's right."

She watched me, smoking thoughtfully for a moment before she gave her head one quick shake and said, "No way. Not Wang Chung. He ain't *that* squirrelly."

"I didn't say that he was."

"You didn't?"

"I only mentioned that other guy because I wanted you to realize that sometimes people get away with the most awful things simply because nobody pays attention."

"But eatin' people?"

"I didn't say that he was eating anybody . . ."

"Now if anybody's eatin' anybody it would be Mooshy."

Despite myself, I asked, "Who's Mooshy?"

''This biker I know. He's sittin' at the bar right now. He bit a guy's finger off in a fight one time.''

''I think we're drifting here a little bit,'' I said, rubbing my chin.

''You brought it up.''

''Well, I'm un-bringing it up.''

''So what do you want to know? It's gettin' cold in here.''

In deference to her comfort I started up the van and set the heater blowing.

''Look, Jazmine, does this Wang Chung do anything that makes him stand out? Does he buy a lot of dope, have loud parties, see a lot of visitors, steal, borrow, or lend money? You know . . . what's the score on him on the street?''

''That's it? That's all you want for fifty bucks?''

''That's it.''

''Well, let's see.'' She poked a button with a painted fingernail, cracked the window, and pitched her cigarette out before rolling the window back up. ''Ya hardly ever see the guy, especially since they started makin' the customers use the back door. The way it was before, guys would pull up in a Bronco with a fuckin' moose tied to the hood, and Wang Chung would have to wrestle with it right out in the street. Later he'd be out there hosing blood off the fuckin' sidewalk. Folks complained until they finally started unloading behind the building, so I ain't seen Wang in months.''

Well, that made sense, I thought to myself. Dead animals scaring off the johns and crack heads could certainly put a crimp in the local economy.

''I been here almost three years,'' Jazmine continued, working the cigarette lighter herself this time. ''And Wang was already part of the scenery when I moved in. He buys a little dope, from what I know. Pot, mostly, no crack, which I guess you could say is weird since everybody buys crack. But I ain't never hearda him borrowing no money, which around here is weird too, I suppose. Ah, what else? As far as visitors go, other than his nurse, or whatever, there ain't nobody who comes round regular . . .''

''What nurse?'' I cut in.

''Oh, I don't know that she is a nurse for sure. Maybe she's his sister, or a social worker, or maybe she's his fuckin' parole officer. She's just some skinny blonde that shows up every once in a while. It's just that, other than the hunter/gatherer types, she's the only one who's ever come back, so I suppose that's why we noticed. You know, it's funny, but now that I'm thinkin' 'bout it, I guess I do know more about what goes on around here than I thought.

"So, how's that? I hope you got your fifty bucks worth 'cause I really do have to get back; Ziggy's gonna be pissed I stay out too long."

"Just a little more," I said, "then we'll be through. Tell me about this nurse—does she come alone, or does she bring somebody with her?"

"Like who?"

"I don't know. Anybody at all?"

"Not that I ever saw."

"How does she dress?"

"Like people dress: slacks and a blouse. Stuff like that."

"Do they go out together when she comes?"

"Nah. Like I said, Wang Chung don't hardly stick what's left a his nose out the door but for shopping and such."

"So what do they do?"

"Mostly, from what I can tell, they fight. In the summertime, when the windows are open, you can hear 'em all the way to the corner, which I guess is something else I never thought about. But I wonder why that woman would bother trampin' her ass down here just to spend a couple of hours arguin' with a freak?"

Once Jazmine had rejoined Mooshy and Ziggy in the bar, leaving my van so aromatic from smoke and perfume that I had to crack both windows, despite the cold, I sat, puzzling over what she had said. The only person associated with the case that I could see fitting her description of a "skinny blond nurse" was Edward Craig's ex-wife, Jane. But the idea of Jane visiting her ex-husband for any reason after the way he had described the ugly circumstances of their divorce just didn't make sense.

I needed to get into his apartment, I decided, watching the shop from the alley across the street. I wasn't sure why . . .

but it seemed like the logical next step. The only question now was, how? I was so absorbed with formulating a plan that when Larry Fizner tapped his ring against my driver's side window, the only thing that kept me from jumping through the moon roof was my seat belt.

"What the hell are you doing here?" I asked as he slid into the seat Jazmine had just vacated.

Slamming the door, he said, "Hey, she left the seat warm. Christ, it smells like Estée Lauder farted in here. Does your wife know what kind of women you hang around with when you're not home?"

"I asked you how you found me."

"Come on, Bill. After that bullshit story we got from the flammable embalmer, where else would you be? I was plannin' on checkin' up on him myself, just to see if I was right about him takin' off after we worked him over the last time—but it looks like you beat me to it."

"And here I was thinking that for once I was ahead of the game."

"Think again, sonny. So, what did your lady friend have to say?"

When I told him about Jane Craig's visits to her ex-husband, he nodded. But instead of offering an opinion, he asked, "So, what's the plan?"

"That's what I was just trying to figure. I want to toss Craig's apartment, but I'd rather he wasn't there when I did."

"Why you bein' so particular?"

"Because I'm not sure what I'm looking for. Him kicking up a fuss would be distracting."

"Well," Larry said, unfolding my portable phone, "let me see what I can do."

"Who are you calling?"

He ignored my question as he dialed and held the phone to his ear. Listening to it ring, he said, "By the way, Detective Rubins says hi. He wasn't too thrilled that we searched Ackermann's bedroom before we called him in. Said something about how it busts his balls when private investigators contaminate a crime scene. But once he and his boys started pulling shit apart, he shut up. Well." He hit the disconnect button before placing the phone back in its cradle. "That problem's solved. Craig ain't home. Come on."

"Maybe he's just not answering," I said, locking my door.

Larry waved off the suggestion, leading me across the street as he asked, "So what's the story with the Sam Spade outfit?"

"You mean the hat?" I said, following him into an alley along the taxidermy shop's east wall. "My dad gave it to me for my birthday a couple of years ago. I hardly ever wear it."

"That's probably wise," Larry muttered, pulling a tiny flashlight out of his pocket and running its beam over a series of garbage cans lining a decrepit picket fence. To me, it looked as if someone had been trying to keep the inside of the cans clean by throwing their garbage on the ground. Broken glass crunched beneath our feet as we pushed our way through a rusty gate set into a chunk of sagging cyclone fence that more or less encircled a kind of courtyard behind the building.

"You know," I said, keeping my voice down, "it wasn't too long ago that the cops said they were going to double their patrols around here."

"Yeah?" Larry replied, testing the knob on a door bearing two windows that were both painted over on the inside. "Then they'll never cruise by twice as often as they didn't used to. Christ, I don't think this door's been open in my lifetime. Bill?" he added, turning around and bumping into me. "Come on," he complained, "I'm workin' here."

"Pardon," I said, stepping back to give him some elbow room.

While I watched, he checked out a barred window before turning his attention to another cluster of trash cans, this one positioned beneath a kind of overhang made of rotten plywood. Something about the cans had apparently caught his interest, because, with a groan, he bent way down to examine the ground beneath them with his light. When he stood back up, his spine cracked, making him say, "Christ Almighty," through a grimace of pain. "It's hell getting old."

"Did Detective Rubins believe what George Sacks said about Jane Craig borrowing that Camaro?" I asked.

Larry shrugged, saying, "He probably won't even talk to him until sometime tomorrow morning."

"Why not?"

"Because, by the time the cops showed up at the house with a warrant, Sacks had sucked down like six more beers and was screaming something about having a right to a lawyer, due process of law, and the Eighteenth Amendment to the United States Constitution—which, if I'm not mistaken, is the one that repealed Prohibition. So go figure. Rubins decided just to read him the sheet and tank him until he sobered up. He doesn't want anything he says thrown out on a technical, so he's goin' by the book."

"When's he going to arrest Jane Craig?"

"Without Sack's statement, he hasn't got cause until forensics looks at the stuff they found in the bedroom. But even if the club turns out to be Allison Ackermann's murder weapon, he'll have to hook up with the Columbus homicide squad about who's got jurisdiction over what. It's a lot of procedural bullshit, but that's the way it's gotta be. Plus there's the little complication of nobody other than George Sacks knowing where she is. George Sacks, and me, that is."

"You?" I said, louder than I intended to. "How did you find out where the war is?"

From the inside breast pocket of his sports coat, Larry produced a folded piece of paper. When he shined his flashlight on it, I saw that it had "Ye War of the Spring" printed in Old English letters across the front.

"It's a brochure," he explained. "I found it in the night table next to Ronald Ackermann's bed. It's got a map on the last page."

Glancing from the brochure to Larry's shadow-darkened face, I said, "You really should have turned this over to Detective Rubins."

"You're probably right," Larry replied, smiling.

"What about Everett Chase's murder?" I asked, changing the subject.

"Rubins has still got his men looking for a witness to the shooting," he said. "But so far they haven't had any luck. Now step back a little. Go on, a little more . . . like all the way to the fence. When rats get worked up they'll bite anything in their way."

"Rats?" I whispered, freezing in my tracks. "What rats?"

"Watch," Larry said, producing a can of pepper spray.

Without further explanation he uncapped the can and directed a fierce stream of the noxious stuff at the base of the trash cans he'd been examining. Almost simultaneously I heard a terrible shriek and saw the ground at his feet come suddenly to life as a dozen or so screaming black shapes came tearing out from between the cans, moving faster than any living thing I had ever seen.

"Watch yourself!" Larry called back at me, still spraying as he did. "There's more here than I thought."

Okay, I admit it, I've led a pretty sheltered life. Until that moment, I had never seen a real rat. I had seen photographs of course, and, when I was in high school, the movie *Willard*, which scared the hell out of me. But I had never seen a live rat up close. And, truthfully, there were two reasons that I didn't get all that good a look at them at that moment. The first was that they were shooting past me at like a million miles a minute . . . and the second was that I was busy trying to keep both my feet up off the ground at the same time. My reaction amazed me with its simple physicality. For a period of what must have been five or ten seconds, I literally blanked out. No matter what I did, I couldn't think of a single thing other than staying the hell away from those rats . . . which I never did see as anything more than featureless dark blots racing along the ground in perfectly straight lines, right at, and past where I stood, too stunned to move.

As quickly as they had appeared, they were gone, leaving my heart galloping as I leaned on a fence, watching Larry kick a trash can a couple of times, as insurance that he'd gotten them all before he began moving the first of the ten or so cans off the rectangular pedestal of hollow-sounding steel plates upon which they had been arranged. There was a dark lump of what I took to be cloth bundled up between the cans, and, nudging it with the toe of his shoe, he said, "I hope there aren't any babies in here."

"Why didn't you warn me?" I asked, when I felt semi-composed.

"I did," he replied, kicking the rag nest away and returning his attention to the cans. Even though I couldn't see his face in the dark, I could still hear the glee in his voice as he added, "Now come on. Gimme a hand."

What he had found was a set of ancient steel bay doors set into a concrete frame that I recognized as being similar to the ones that the tavern my grandparents used to own had in its backyard. The tavern's doors had led down to a concrete chute into the cellar for coal and ice block deliveries back when the building was new. When we had cleared the cans away, Larry indicated a steel ring, saying, "Your turn, young man."

I handed him my hat, grabbed the ring with my good hand, set myself, and pulled. The door lifted maybe four inches before getting hung up on something hard. I dropped it, readjusted my grip, and yanked again, this time using my legs for lift. When I did, something gave out a loud snap and the door came free, officially heralding my second act of breaking and entering in as many days. Surprisingly enough, the realization that between the Peaceful Knoll Cemetery's mausoleum and here I had perpetrated two crimes didn't really phase me all that much.

No rules, I thought, opening the door all the way and letting it fall on the ground as Larry preceded me down a rickety set of wooden stairs. Glancing over at the discarded pile of rags he had kicked off the doors, I wondered briefly if there had been any baby rats in there, and if so, where they had gone. Then I wondered if and when the adults would come back. Then, placing my black fedora on my head, I followed my partner down into the dark cellar where Edward Craig did his bloody work.

ELEVEN
■■■■■■■■■■■■■

AT THE BOTTOM of the stairs we paused as Larry ran his flashlight's beam over first the floor, then the walls ahead. It was as cold as a morgue down there, and twice as dark. Consequently, the illumination provided by his little penlight was concentrated into a dim, slithering circle into which objects appeared, hovered, and were replaced. The things defined in that eerie shadow box were grotesque: rectangular racks made of metal tubing upon which animal pelts were stretched and drying, glittering stainless steel surgical instruments, a blood-stained workbench, spools of some kind of heap, chemical jugs, body parts on spikes. The air smelled of raw meat and formaldehyde. The concrete floor was mottled with dried drippings. There was the disembodied head of a boar lying on its side on a table near the far door, tongue lolling, eyes rolled back, with a little yellow tag bearing a claim number hanging from one ear. Next to the head was a hacksaw and rubber mallet.

"This what your embalming room looks like?" Larry asked, voice hushed to a rough whisper.

"No," I replied, just as softly. "We'd get closed down in no time flat. Come on, let's get on with it."

I probably should have looked around a little, but I didn't. Instead, I just shoved Larry into motion with a kind of nudge on his back so that we crossed the room in as straight a line as we could. At the door he removed his gun from where he keeps it under his sports coat, holding it with its barrel pointed straight up next to his face as he soundlessly turned the knob, opening the door just a crack before aiming his dark sparkling eyes my way and saying, "You know, we're sneaking around for nothing. All that's in this building is me, you, and what's left of Porky Pig. Craig jumped a Greyhound before we were six blocks away this afternoon."

"Just go easy," I whispered, wishing that, instead of talking, he'd move. "Even if he's not here, being careful won't hurt."

"You're the boss," he said, pushing the door open wide.

On the stairs leading up to the shop, I worried briefly that the place might have a silent alarm. If it did, we had already set it off, which would mean that the cops would be showing up any second. Then I tried to imagine how desperate a junkie would have to be before he broke into this house of horrors for the twenty or thirty bucks that might be in the cash register, deciding that, if the place were mine, I wouldn't have wasted my money wiring it.

In the shop we found the front curtains drawn and every light out. Without a wasted step, Larry led the way around the counter, up the back stairs to the building's second floor.

Even from the landing at the end of the upstairs hall, I could see that the door to Edward Craig's apartment was hanging half-open, still broken from when I had kicked it in earlier in the day. There was a light burning inside, but there wasn't any sound. Not a squeak. Maybe Larry had been right about Edward Craig taking off for Mexico with whatever cash he had on hand. In a way, the notion disappointed me, but not too much. What the hooker named Jazmine had said about Jane Craig's visiting her ex-husband wasn't sitting well in my brain pan. What the hell had she wanted? I wondered. Why did they argue? And if they did argue, why did she keep coming back? Like an apparition emerging from a mist, a possible explanation for Jane Craig's behavior began revolving near the corner of my consciousness, just beyond where I could see it clearly. But the brief glimpse I was able to catch told me that there was an altogether more sinister reason that this building was so quiet than Larry's conviction that it was empty. A reason that had more to do with Jane Craig's ambition than Edward Craig's admittedly tenuous emotional state. Pausing at the door, I drew a deep breath through my nose, exhaled, and sniffed again, this time closing my eyes briefly to help me concentrate.

"What's up?" Larry asked.

I held up my hand, saying, "After all those chemicals downstairs, I can't hardly smell anything at all."

"What's there to smell?"

"Maybe Edward Craig's body. Although he probably wouldn't stink yet. It's only been about ten hours since we were here before."

"What are you talking about?"

"He might be on a longer trip than you thought."

"Why?"

"I'll explain later," I said, taking a final sniff before placing my hand on the apartment's door. "I don't want to stay in here any longer than I have to. Just don't be surprised if he's history. We should have known what would happen the minute he got pissed when we told him about Everett Chase's murder. We've been stupid, Mr. Fizner. Dead dumb . . ."

Unlike the door in the cellar, when this one swung open its hinges let out a long, mournful squeal that sent a chill up my spine. From where we were standing in the corridor, the interior of Edward Craig's apartment was lit a pale amber by the single unshaded floor lamp standing about eight feet in front of what I took to be a closed closet door. The rest of the room was empty. I was going to call out, but when I opened my mouth Larry put his finger over his lips before stepping past me, gun held with two hands at the end of stiff arms. Like a dancer, he gracefully sidestepped his way across the tiny apartment, ending his silent performance by leaning into the bathroom, silhouetting himself against the tawdry pink light of the girly bar blinking through the window from across the street.

There was a piece of shower curtain on a rod stretched across the entrance of the kitchenette that Larry used his gun's barrel to push aside, checking every corner behind it. I was still standing near the apartment's doorway, looking at the floor lamp standing incongruously near the center of the room. What an odd place to put a lamp, I thought, trying to put my finger on what was disturbing me about its placement. Why had the shade been removed, exposing the harsh glare of the bulb? To my right, Larry opened a door, checking out the pantry, before moving back around the couch and coffee table toward the closet door near the lamp.

The closet door . . .

Wait a minute, I thought, my heart nearly freezing in my chest as the image of how I had seen my brother just a couple of hours before, backlit into a silhouette in the doorway to the funeral home's big parlor, popped into my head.

Larry stepped around the floor lamp, placing his hand out for the doorknob ahead, effectively putting the apartment's only light source behind himself so that, should the door not be a closet, whoever was beyond it once he had it open would be afforded a clear view of him, while being hidden in darkness and . . .

"NO!" I shouted, moving with sudden desperation.

Larry was no more than ten feet away, though it may as well have been a mile since I had only covered half that distance before the "closet" door exploded in first one, then two, and finally three splintering holes. Concurrently came a series of terrible concussions that overpowered my voice as a confused, pounding swirl of motion sent both Larry and me sprawling as my shoulder connected with his gut and we went crashing down in a heap.

"Holy Christ!" he growled, wrestling beneath me on the floor. "I think you busted a rib!"

"Shhhh!" I hissed, still on top of him, placing my hand over his mouth. When he was quiet, I reached out and yanked the floor lamp's cord out of the wall socket, sending the apartment into darkness.

My ears were ringing from the shots, and the smell of gun smoke seeped through the three bullet holes in what I now realized was the bedroom door. Unlike the popping sound I had heard when Everett Chase was gunned down, the confined nature of these shots had amplified each explosion into a veritable peal of thunder. What the hell kind of gun did Craig have? I wondered. And who did he think he was shooting? As if in answer to my second question he shouted from behind the door, "Jane, you get the hell away from me!" His voice was high and shrill. "I told you I wouldn't talk, and I meant it. Now go away!"

"Jane?" Larry whispered, having pulled himself over to a spot next to the bathroom door where he was sitting with his back to the wall, holding his arms across his stomach as if squeezing himself together.

"His wife," I reminded him quickly. "It's why she was coming here. She must have been using him to back up her threats when she and Ronald Ackermann pushed Everett Chase for money."

"What could Craig back up?" Larry growled.

As an answer, I raised my voice and said, "Eddie? Don't shoot anymore. It's Bill Hawley. Your wife's not here. She's gone off with Ronald Ackermann. She can't hurt you, so take it easy, okay? I know what's been going on. I know about your wife's threats. I know what Everett Chase did. . . ."

As I was speaking, I was also crawling past the bedroom door, placing my back against the wall, down low near the floor, close to the outside corridor.

"I know everything, Eddie. Let me help you! You can't spend the rest of your life waiting to be killed."

"Go away, Bill!" Craig replied, his voice breaking with strain. "Get the hell out of here. You don't know what she could do . . . you can't know what she's like."

"But I do know, Eddie," I said, trying to sound reassuring. "Believe me, I understand . . ."

"You can't understand! Nobody can understand . . ."

"I do, Eddie! Honest to God . . ."

"Why did you have to stick your nose in this, Bill? Why the fuck can't you leave shit alone?"

"Everett Chase fooled me, Eddie. He's the one who started it, not me. You told him the names, didn't you? You told him where you hid the pieces of his wife . . . right?"

"It doesn't matter anymore," Craig said, so softly that it was almost inaudible. "Jane'll get what she wants. She always gets what she wants. I can't . . ."

"Eddie, listen to me," I said, leaning my head back against the wall and closing my eyes, groping for just the right line of logic to talk him back down to earth. "You can't just wait in a dark room until she comes for you. You've got to let me help. Together we can beat this thing. We can't let her win. . . ."

"It's no use. She'll get me no matter where I go."

"That's not true."

"You don't know what she's like . . ."

"Eddie . . ." I began, opening my eyes to find that Larry Fizner had moved from his place near the bathroom to the floor in front of the bedroom door, where he was lying on his back with both his legs cocked over him, his arms still wrapped over his stomach. I was just about to call his name when he kicked out with both legs, hitting the bedroom door once, hard, yelping with pain as he did. The door rattled but didn't open. Edward Craig screamed something from inside, maybe my name, maybe not. I shouted, "Larry?!" just as he nailed the door again, this time popping it open so that it swung inward as Edward Craig started shooting again, and the whole place went momentarily nuts.

I rolled toward the corridor, out of the way of where Craig's shots were throwing chunks of plaster as they passed through the flimsy bedroom wall to embed themselves over the sink in the kitchenette, shaking pots and pans from their hooks to go crashing down atop some kind of glass as ceramic tile exploded into flying slivers. Larry, instead of rolling the other way, as I expected he would, sat straight up on the floor, lifted his gun, and fired back, fast, emptying his revolver in a quick, brutal series of pounding shots that silenced everything as effectively as if they had made me deaf.

Through that sudden silence came a quick *click, chunk, click-click* as Larry popped his gun open, dropped the spent cartridges from inside, and slapped a speed loader home. Then, almost immediately, came a heavy thud as Edward Craig's gun dropped to the floor a second before he started sobbing in the dark, saying pitifully, "Please. No more. Please. Please . . ."

I stood up, heart pounding as I reached my hand through the bedroom door, found the wall switch, and snapped on the ceiling light to find Edward Craig cringing on the bed, facing me. His back was against the headboard, his legs were drawn up protectively in front of him, and on the wall over his head was a nearly perfect semicircle formed by six bullet holes. I kicked his gun away from where it lay on the floor and turned my attention to Larry Fizner, who, despite the grim expression on his face, and the gun in his hand, had not gotten up.

"Larry?" I said, moving to him, frightened by the ashen quality of his complexion. "Larry, what's wrong?"

Instead of a reply he reached one hand up toward me, which I took, pulling him to his feet. He groaned, teeth exposed in a snarl of pain as he hunched over for a moment, holding his stomach and shaking his head. He still had his gun, and, as soon as he had taken a couple of deep breaths, a look came into his eyes that I had seen before, and that I knew meant trouble.

"Larry," I said, trying to keep myself between him and Craig. "Take it easy. That's enough."

He stepped toward me, reaching out one hand to brush me aside. I suppose I could have refused to be moved. I suppose that I could have planted myself in his path and blocked his advance no matter how hard he tried to pass. I was younger than he, and stronger. His ribs, at a minimum, were bruised where I had tackled him, and he was, at least theoretically, weakened by illness. But instead of pressing the point I allowed him to approach the bed. Since I didn't try harder to stop him, I guess I am at least partially responsible for what happened next . . . which is fine.

I had seen Larry Fizner's anger turn physical a number of times before that night. Once he had pitched a man down a flight of marble stairs; another time he had used a two-by-four on an aggressor twice his size. But there was something about the simple efficiency of his attack on Edward Craig that stunned me with its brutality. With three strokes he laced his gun back and forth across Craig's head, leaving the younger man senseless in a heap.

There were long tendrils of gun smoke turning slowly in the air between us. Larry wheezed a little as he breathed through his open mouth, his lips so bloodless as to appear blue. When I spoke to him, he didn't look at me. Instead he just stood there, arms hanging at his sides, eyes fixed on Craig's motionless body as if he were wishing that the younger man would try to fight back. But Edward Craig was beyond fighting. He was cleanly out . . . probably broken, bleeding on the sheets.

"Are you okay?" I asked.

Larry blinked.

"Mr. Fizner?"

"So Madeline Chase didn't kill herself," he said, voice rough, eyes still fixed on Edward Craig.

"No, she didn't. Everett Chase murdered her, and Edward Craig knew it."

"When did you figure it out?"

"I'm not sure. On the stairs coming up here, I think. But her teeth having been pulled before she died has been bothering me all along. If she had no idea that she was about to die, then the story Edward Craig told us about the way she planned her suicide was phony."

Larry finally looked at me as he said, "Is that why you thought we'd find Craig dead?"

"Yes. It occurred to me that if Everett Chase were paying his stepson and Jane Craig enough hush money to put the restaurant he loved so much out of business, then he must have had something more substantial to hide than just complicity in his wife's suicide. He had to be paying for a murder. And since he's the one who Chase paid to dispose of the body, Edward Craig must have known it. That's why his wife was coming here: she needed her ex-husband to back up her threats when she called Chase for money. Edward Craig was resisting, which is why they spent so much time arguing up here, but in the end greed was the one thing they had left in common."

"Then Craig must have had the goods on Everett Chase," Larry said, that frightening pallor of rage I had seen overtake his features slowly draining from his face. "He must have some kind of proof that it was Chase who committed murder."

I was nodding my agreement as Edward Craig moved for the first time since Larry had hit him. It wasn't much, just a half-roll of his head, but it caught Larry's eye. For an instant

I thought that Larry might go after him again, but instead he slipped his pistol into the holster he keeps clipped to his belt at the small of his back and said, "Help me," as he reached down and took one of Craig's arms. Together, we dragged him to the bathroom, where we stuffed him in the tub and turned the shower on, making him gargle and shout in protest before slumping into a wet bunch when Larry turned off the spray.

I gave him a few minutes to kind of get himself together before sitting on the edge of the tub and speaking down at him, slowly, so that he wouldn't miss a word.

"You could have killed us, Eddie," I said. "I'm sorry that Mr. Fizner hit you, but he was angry, and I really can't blame him. You're lucky that hitting you is all he did. He could easily have put those six shots into you instead of the wall."

"It wasn't personal," Craig mumbled, both his arms up, hiding his face.

"Oh, yes, it was," I said. "Everything's personal, Eddie. Get used to it. Now, what did you have on Everett Chase that your wife could threaten him with?"

"He murdered his wife," Craig replied.

"I know that," I said.

Craig looked up at me from the bottom of the tub, revealing an eye nearly swelled shut, bruised so vivid a purple as to be almost black.

"You do?" he asked. "Then why'd you come here?"

"I want to know what you had on him," I explained. "It must have been more than just your word. It must have been something physical. Some kind of proof that he was sure could have hanged him. Something that you could have shown him that would have scared him so badly that he would have given you anything you asked just to shut you up, and something that your wife could use to keep Everett Chase in line. Now, what was it? What do you have that could make Chase pay, even at the risk of losing his restaurant?"

"Jane'll kill me if I tell."

"Jane will kill you anyway. With Chase dead, she doesn't need you anymore and you know it. You damned near shot Mr. Fizner and me because you know that you're her last liability. As long as you're alive, she's at risk. Now get yourself together. Without me, you're sunk. Period. I can kiss or kill you, Eddie. It's your choice. What's it going to be?''

When he pulled himself into a sitting position in the tub, his hands finally came away from his face, revealing the extent of the damage Larry Fizner had done. It was hard, but I didn't let my face show the slightest change. Instead I concentrated on remaining unmoved.

He sighed, wiping blood from under his right eye with the back of one hand.

"I didn't hide the whole body," he said. "I saved a piece. Or at least that's what I told Jane."

"The piece with the wound?"

"Yeah."

"How'd he do it?"

"He shot her through the heart."

"So you saved her heart?"

"Her thorax."

"Here in the shop?"

"No. Somewhere else."

"Why?"

"As insurance, I guess. So that nobody could ever come back at me."

"About what?"

"I don't know. I don't know why I ever went along with it in the first place. I must have been crazy. But once it was done I guess I just freaked out. I got convinced that Chase was going to try to say that I killed his wife . . . you know, hang the whole thing on me . . . like I just murdered her and chopped her up."

"Did you?"

Rolling his eyes, he leaned his head back so hard that it bumped the tile wall as he said, "No. I swear I didn't. I swear to God."

"Then how was saving a piece of her supposed to prove otherwise?"

Instead of answering, Craig did something noisy to the inside of his mouth with his tongue. I got up and stepped over to the window, looking down on the dark street outside as I asked, "So where did you keep it, Eddie?"

"What?"

"The part of her body with the wound."

"At Noland's."

"Marsh Noland's funeral home?"

"Yeah."

"Weren't you afraid that Marsh would find it?"

"Find what?"

"What are we talking about here?"

"Wait a minute . . ." He was moving around in the tub. "Maybe I didn't make myself clear. Me savin' a piece of Madeline Chase's body is what I told Jane I did."

I looked at him.

"Are you saying that you didn't really keep any part of her?"

"What would I do that for?"

"Eddie, what the fuck are you saying?"

"Look, Jane knew about me hiding the body. All right? I should never have told her, but I did. That's what started everything. One minute she was the woman I married, and the next . . . I don't know. She was somebody else. She started talking about how there was all this money out there, and how we took all the risks and got shit for it. All of a sudden everything was *we*. Then her eyes got real big and she said that Everett Chase was gonna end up hanging the whole thing on me. She turned around and started pointing her finger, sayin' how I was a moron, and didn't I see what he was gonna do? She scared the hell out of me . . . so I made up this story about having insurance against anybody ever trying to set me up."

"What exactly did you tell her? What words did you use?"

"I said that Everett Chase had shot his wife to death, and that I could prove it if I ever had to."

"Because you had the part of her body that had the bullet wound in it?"

"That's right."

"What did you tell her you did with it?"

"I said that there was this crawl space down the basement of Marsh Noland's funeral home, next to the boilers, which there was. I told her that Marsh had changed the place over from forced steam heat to gas, which was true, so now nobody ever went down there no more. I told her that I had cut a hole in the concrete floor, put her in, and replaced the stone. I even said that I had sealed it up with concrete patch. Without knowing just where to look, nobody would ever know she was there. So if Everett Chase ever tried to cause me a problem, I could take him down with me.''

''Did Everett Chase shoot her?''

''Nah. She died from monoxide, like I already said.''

''Then she did commit suicide?''

''No way. She was murdered. There was never any question. That was Everett Chase's plan all along. He just didn't want no blood or nothing around, so, bein' like twice his wife's size, he just wrapped her up in duct tape, sat her in the car, turned on the motor, and went out to dinner in their other car. When he got home, she was toast. He brought her body over to Noland's just like I told you he did.''

''So he didn't shoot her?''

''No, he didn't.''

''And you didn't keep a piece of her body behind?''

''No, I buried them all, just like Mr. Chase hired me to do.''

''For the thirty thousand dollars in the pre-need trust?''

''Yeah. And everything would have been fine too, 'cept that Jane started showin' up here at the shop. She made me call Mr. Chase on the phone and tell him that if he didn't pay, I'd go to the cops. Jane would be sittin' in the room, and I'd say how I could prove that his wife wasn't really a suicide . . . and he wouldn't want me to do that, would he, and if he wanted me to keep quiet he better pay whatever I asked.''

''So you told your wife that you had a part of Madeline Chase's body that you could use to blackmail Everett Chase with, when you didn't. And when you threatened Everett Chase over the phone, he thought you were talking about testifying against him, which you weren't. That about right?''

''Yeah.''

Turning my face back to the window, I looked up and down the street. Not so much as a single living soul moved. If I didn't know better, I could have sworn the city was deserted.

With a sigh, I said, "Now tell me why Everett Chase wanted his wife's body embalmed? And don't give me any of that shit about good-bye kisses."

Edward Craig hesitated for an instant. Then he said, "He wanted her kids to see her."

"Her kids?"

"Yeah. Ronald and Allison."

"Ronald and Allison knew that their mother had been murdered?"

"No. Chase told them the story about how she had killed herself—he even showed them the contract she'd signed. He said that this was the way she had wanted it, and that the best thing that they could do for her, and for themselves, was to keep their mouths shut, 'cause if they made too much of a stink the cops might really push hard to find her. But if they behaved and looked appropriately sad for a while before just sorta lettin' things die down, then they'd split a bundle . . . which was what their mother wanted them to do."

"And they went along with it?"

"They were just a coupla kids. He brought 'em into a dark funeral home in the middle of the night, showed 'em their mother's body, and a contract with her signature on it, and said that they had a choice between answering a bunch of questions for the cops or havin' an insurance company write 'em a check for half a million bucks each. What choice did they have?"

"Why did Madeline Chase sign that contract?"

"She didn't, really. When she came to make her funeral's prearrangements I had her sign a blank, sayin' how I'd fill it all in later. Then I wrote what Mr. Chase told me over her signature. So . . . Bill, now what happens?"

I took a long, deep breath, held it, and turned my head his way, looking down at where he sat crumpled in the tub as I slid my hands into my overcoat's pockets, thinking about Everett Chase's worldview. His accomplice in murder had been extorting money with threats of a confession, putting his good name, and the business that he had committed murder to gain, at risk of ruin. But what exactly had Chase hoped to accomplish by posing as Jerome Larson and convincing me to dig up a grave full of evidence? Had he simply been upsetting the apple cart, or had he had something else in mind?

"You know, Eddie," I said, hoping that my disgust for him and everything he had been doing was clear in my tone of voice, "even with all the shooting that went on up here, there's not a soul outside who gives a good goddamn about it. Nobody's even curious. Nobody called the cops. Nobody came outside to see if anybody was hurt, or needed help, or whatever. Either they didn't hear, they're scared, or they don't care. Whichever way it is, I don't think that one more shot will make the least little bit of difference."

"One more shot?" Edward Craig asked, wide-eyed, glancing first at me, then at Larry Fizner. "What ya talkin' about, one more shot?"

Reaching to the wall switch next to where he stood in the doorway, Larry snapped off the overhead light. Then he turned on the tiny night-light stuck in a socket next to the sink, withdrew his pistol, and aimed it down at Edward Craig, who pulled his arms up as if to shield his face, saying, "Come on, Bill . . . you gotta be kiddin'! Why? For Christ's sake . . . why now?"

When Larry thumbed back the hammer, his gun made a loud, ominous *click.*

"Eddie, what you don't seem to realize is that you're not only a liability to your ex-wife, " I said, with Larry Fizner's long shadow distorted by the night-light's glow on the wall over the tub. "You're a liability to me too. Because of the way Everett Chase set things up, I've got an awful lot riding on the way this thing turns out. I can't afford to take any chances. You're in my way."

"Oh Jesus, no!" Edward Craig cried as I stepped across the bathroom, heading for the door. As I passed the tub, he reached out and grabbed my arm, holding me tight as he struggled up to his knees and pleaded, "Tell me what to do! Goddamn it, Bill. Please. Just tell me what to say. Just tell me . . ."

I let him have hold of my arm for what I considered an appropriately thoughtful moment before I glanced at Larry Fizner and nodded toward the door. With a dramatic lifting of his arm, he eased the hammer on his gun back down before removing himself from the room, leaving Edward Craig and me alone.

"All right, Eddie," I said, making sure that I sounded less than enthusiastic. "Maybe we can make a deal."

"Anything," Edward Craig said. "You name it."

"You'll have to lie for me."

"Fine. No problem. Jesus, Bill, I been doin' that all my life."

"And don't think that you can change your mind once I'm gone. If you ever say one contradictory word, I'll have Larry Fizner hunt you down, no matter where you go. Do you understand?"

He nodded his head so hard I thought his eyes would fall out.

"Now listen," I said.

He stared at me hard.

"Are you listening?"

"Yes."

I looked at him, saying, very, very slowly, "She killed herself. Got it? If anyone ever asks, anyone at all, ever, you will swear that Madeline Chase killed herself, categorically, without question, just like your contract said she did. The story you first told me about her husband bringing her body to you after she committed suicide is God's own truth, so help you by the blood of Jesus, and that's the story you'll stick to forever, no matter what. Understand? No . . . matter . . . what."

"Okay. Yeah. Absolutely."

I spent another moment looking down at him before extricating my arm from his grasp and saying, "Are you sure?"

He nodded.

I turned, and was already halfway across the living room before he called from behind me, "That's it? But what about Jane?"

"What about her?" I replied, picking up my hat from where it lay near the bedroom door.

"Don't you want to know about her and the Ackermann kid?"

"I'm not following."

"They're gonna get married. Ronald Ackermann asked her

to marry him. That's why she moved in with him after she knocked off his sister.''

I was dusting my hat against my leg, swinging it back and forth slowly as Edward Craig spoke, wondering if he was telling me the truth or making up another lie in an effort to convince me that he was fully on my side. Without breaking that ponderous rhythm, I asked, ''How do you know that it was Jane who killed Allison Ackermann?''

''She told me.''

''How did she say she did it?''

''She hit her with some kinda club.''

''What did she say she did with the club after that?''

''She didn't say.''

''And now she and Ronald Ackermann are engaged?''

''Yeah. So what about Jane, Bill? She's a demon, you know? She's mean. What should I do about her? With Chase dead, I'm nothin' but trouble to her now.''

Edward Craig was speaking from the tub. He had not followed me out of the bathroom. Instead, he was just hanging his head out so that I could see his face, side-lit by the nightlight near the sink.

''What you should do about Jane,'' I said, placing my hat on my head and running my fingers along the brim, ''is nothing. You should just go away. You got thirty grand waiting for you in that pre-need trust, and you're getting more of a break than a germ like you ever deserves. Find yourself a new place to live, preferably in another state, wait a month or so, and then send me your address. Better yet, send it to Larry Fizner's office—he's in the book. I'll make sure you get a certified copy of Madeline Chase's death certificate so you can cash in her pre-need account. I should think you could start over on thirty thousand bucks. No?''

''But . . .''

''Is there a problem?''

''No, but . . .''

''You don't sound so sure. Maybe I'm making a mistake. Maybe I should get Larry Fizner back up here.''

''No! It's fine. Anything you say.''

''When are you leaving?''

"I'm gone already. I been gone for days."

"Good."

"Bill?"

"What?"

"Are you gonna tell the cops what I did?"

"Yes, I am," I said, wondering where Larry had gone as I stepped into the hall. "At least I'm going to tell them part of it. So the farther away you go, the better."

As I stepped out onto the street, I found Larry bent over, with one hand on the taxidermy shop's brick wall, throwing up on the sidewalk.

"Are you all right?" I said, approaching him, my own stomach sour not only from the after-shock of my having very nearly been shot to death in Edward Craig's apartment, but from my distaste for the slack I had just been forced to cut the son of a bitch.

"I'm fine," he said, holding out one hand so that I wouldn't get too close. "Goddamn chemotherapy knocks me on my ass . . . and the pain pills make me nauseous. When you tackled me back there, you sent my guts spinnin' that's all. I didn't think I was gonna make it through without tossin' my cookies, but I didn't want that prick seein' me puke. Here, take this and hold it out in the open. And thanks for not lettin' me get shot. I owe you one."

Wiping his mouth on the back of one hand as he moved away from the building, he handed me his pistol, took a deep breath of cold night air, and stepped into the street. I followed, saying, "You don't owe me anything—we're a team. Now, what's the deal?"

"We're being watched."

"By whom?"

"By the local gang, that's whom."

"Where?"

"Everywhere. They know every little thing that goes down on their turf. Just keep movin' and keep my gun out where they'll see it. Now, what happened up there after I left?"

I filled him in.

"Shit," he said, fishing for his keys as we approached our cars, which, miracle of miracles, were still in one piece. "I should have popped him. I hate the thought of that asshole gettin' a break.''

"So do I," I said. "But I've got an idea. If it works, I still might need him."

"You think he'll play you square?"

"What choice has he got?"

"Fucker almost killed us, you know."

"He was shooting wild through a wall. I doubt if he even had his eyes open."

"That matters somehow?"

"Come on, Mr. Fizner. Ease up. The way things were before we broke in on him, Edward Craig was trapped and crazy. I just showed him a way out. He'd have to be nuts not to take it. Now, go home and get some rest. You look lousy."

"Don't worry about how I look."

"Just do it, okay?"

"What are you gonna do?"

"I'm going home too, after I make one quick stop."

"Where?"

"The morgue."

"Why the morgue?"

"I'll explain tomorrow."

"What's tomorrow?"

"Jane Craig."

Larry didn't like it, but that's as far as I'd go. So, grumbling, he took back his gun, got in his van, and drove away, leaving me smoking the cigarette I had bummed from him, sitting in my van's driver's seat, virtually vibrating, watching out of the corner of my eye for some indication of the surveillance Larry had insisted we were under. On my portable phone I dialed the county coroner's office, and when my buddy who works the graveyard shift on the receiving desk answered, I said, "Hello, Rusty. Is the Wolfman in?"

"In, and in a state," Rusty Simmons replied.

"Bad mood?"

"Surly, more like."

"Ah, well. See you in a bit."

I was dreading this, but there was no way around it. If I

was going to get where I wanted to go, I was going to have to call in every favor I could.

With a final glance up at Edward Craig's apartment window, I turned my van north, toward Lake Erie, the sick feeling in my stomach subsiding as I ran through a quick mental inventory of my own emotional state. I didn't like what I found. What bothered me the most was the big, empty hole positioned right where my sympathy for Craig's beating should have been. Larry could have killed him, plain and simple. Despite what popular entertainment portrays as reality, the truth is that a blow to the head is a dangerous, potentially lethal occurrence. Using his gun as a bludgeon, Larry Fizner easily could have given Edward Craig a concussion, paralyzed, blinded, or even killed him. And I hadn't felt a thing. Instead, I had used his pain as a point of argument to convince him to first run, and then, ultimately, if necessary, to lie to the police should they ever decide to ask him about what really had happened to Madeline Chase, which, now that I was thinking about it, might have bothered me even more. I was stepping way over the line on this one.

What the hell was happening to me?

And, more importantly, was I going to be able to live with myself if I let things go much further?

No rules, I thought.

No rules.

TWELVE
■■■■■■■■■■■■■■

"LOOKIN' SHARP!" RUSTY Simmons, my best friend at the morgue, and arguably the oldest friend I've got, said as soon as he caught sight of me stepping through the door from the morgue's receiving dock. "To what do we owe the honor?"

"Strictly business," I said, shaking his hand. "Where's the Wolfman?"

"In his lair," Rusty replied. "Though I don't suggest disturbing his royal highness."

"He's already disturbed," I said, heading for the elevator. "Talking to me won't hurt him."

Despite my false bravado, as the doors slid shut before me, I found myself silently wishing that I had the luxury of coming back at a time when Dr. Gordon Wolf's mood was a little brighter. This, I suspected, was going to be the moment of truth between the two of us, and I needed all the help I could get.

The doctor answered my knock from behind the frosted glass of his office door with a gruff, "What is it now?"

I opened the door a crack, stuck my head through, and said, "Dr. Wolf? Can I talk to you?"

He was standing at a blackboard, chalk in hand, an anatomical line drawing on the board before him. When he saw who I was, his furrowed brows rose on his forehead, and his expression softened ever so slightly. The Beatles' *White Album* was playing almost inaudibly in the background, "Birthday

Song,'' specifically. And, with a motion that I should enter, he said, ''Close the door behind you, Mr. Hawley. Favors are best requested in private.''

''How do you know I need a favor?'' I asked, removing my hat as I pulled the door closed.

''I've been expecting it for a long time,'' he replied. ''A fireman like you occasionally needs help carrying water.''

''Fireman?'' I asked.

The Wolfman shrugged as he placed his chalk down in the tray, brushed his hands clean of dust, and turned to face me. Overhead, a pair of light pots in the ceiling directed two harsh white beams down on his work, rendering the Wolfman's tall frame in distinct relief, all but slicing him down the center with shadow, making him appear twice as thin as usual. The effect was unsettling—when he moved he appeared skeletal, as if he should clatter like old bones; his jutting eyebrow ridge and high cheeks formed a veritable crevice of shadow over the exaggerated hollows of his eyes.

''I'm speaking metaphorically,'' he said, removing his half-rimmed reading glasses. ''A fireman is a person who spends his life running from problem to problem, solving each in a panic before moving on to the next—like a fireman putting out fires. The act of extinguishing serves to give you a sense of personal worth, a need so deep that if there's no convenient fire nearby for you to put out, you'll set one yourself . . . just to have something to do.''

''Is that how you see me? As consciously creating my own problems?''

''Essentially.''

''That's a pretty grim diagnosis.''

''Pathologists are like that. Occupational hazard. I think it might have something to do with our mostly dealing with terminal conditions.''

''Am I terminal?''

He looked at me knowingly, his amber-colored eyes absolutely alight with what I can only describe as suppressed glee. ''So, Mr. Hawley,'' he said, ''what can I do to square the books between us? I owe you a favor, as it were. And you're obviously here to make me pay.''

I told him what I had in mind.

"That's all?" he asked, eyebrows raised. "I thought it would be something difficult."

Moving to the desk to his left he removed a pen from his white smock's front pocket, clicked it with his thumb, and leaned over a sheet of paper, saying, "So it's your contention that Madeline Chase's cause of death is carbon monoxide poisoning?"

"Yes, sir."

"Very well," Dr. Wolf said, scratching his pen across a death certificate as he did. "I'll concur."

"Thank you."

"You must have quite a stake in this, to satisfy my debt so easily."

"I do. Though I honestly don't know if even your help will be enough."

"No?"

I shook my head.

"That's a shame," he said, looking up at me from where he was still bent over the desk. "But, you know, it will help matters considerably when we find the rest of the body."

"I'm sure it will," I said. "How's the official search going?"

He smiled.

"We've got some promising ideas."

"Dr. Wolf, can I ask another favor, in line with the rest of this?"

He cocked his head.

"Could it be Detective Karl Rubins who gets the public credit for cracking the case? This time, I'd like to stay as far off to the side as possible."

Dr. Wolf frowned for a moment before finally nodding his approval as he said, "When it's time, have Detective Rubins call me personally. I'll sign the disinterment orders myself."

"Thank you."

"And now that we have established poor Mrs. Chase's cause of death," Dr. Wolf said, pen poised, "all we need do is settle on the manner of her demise, and our personal obligations will be erased. Correct?"

"Yes."

"Suicide, you said?"

I nodded.

"Very well."

With a flick, he scratched an *X* over the appropriate box, signed and dated the certificate, stepped to the Xerox machine, and ran me off two copies, which he handed over with aplomb.

Just as I was about to take them, he pulled his hand back, saying, "For the record, this is all you wanted, correct? No more unspoken hold, no more silent gratitude, no more debts of honor?"

"Absolutely," I agreed.

"No more knowing glances?"

"No."

"I don't have to be nice to you anymore?"

"May I please have those, Dr. Wolf?"

"You know, Mr. Hawley, what I just did is highly unethical, considering that I haven't seen all of this case's blood work yet."

"If it helps," I said, hand still extended, "I promise that the lab results will be consistent with your findings."

"Then why did you use up your favor asking me to do something that I would have done anyway?"

"I needed to be sure."

"That I didn't make a mistake?"

"Frankly, yes."

"Well, then, as payment in full."

"Dr. Wolf?"

"Yes?"

"There is one other thing."

"I thought as much."

"It's nothing now . . . it may be nothing at all. But could you wait until Monday afternoon before you send the original death certificate over to city hall to be filed?"

"Why?"

"In case the manner of death has to be changed."

"From what to what?"

"Suicide to homicide."

Dr. Wolf's face went grim as he said, "Mr. Hawley, are

you going to cause me a problem?''

"No," I replied. "It's just that I need the certificate to say what it says for something that I have to do tomorrow. If things go the way I think they will, it'll stay just the way it is. The cause of death is absolutely authentic, I guarantee. The blood work on the rest of the body parts will back me up.''

"Then what's the point of the suicide finding?''

"To keep someone from profiting from a shameful act.''

"Really?''

"Really.''

"I won't lie," he said. "I won't do that. I'll bend the rules this one time. But I will not lie.''

"I'd never ask you to, Doctor.''

He looked at me, frowned, and finally nodded as he handed over the death certificate copies. As I took possession of them I had to consciously force my hand not to shake. Despite my effort, I think he saw more than I would have liked him to see, either in my face, or in my eyes, because he paused, looking at me carefully as he said, "This is genuinely important to you, isn't it?''

"Yes, it is.''

"Is there anything else I can do?''

"No. But thanks for the offer.''

A positive sparkle danced in the Wolfman's eyes as the moment passed. Then he said, "Well, in that case, given what has just transpired here, I'd appreciate it if you would get your ass out of my office. I've got work to do, and you're keeping me from it.''

Smacking my heels together like a Nazi officer, I replied, "Yes, your worship," before heading for the door.

I had just placed my hand on the knob when Dr. Wolf stopped me by saying, "By the way, Mr. Hawley.''

I turned.

"When do you think it would be convenient for you to reinter Mr. Larson's remains? He's been lying in the cooler for three days now. Casket and all.''

"Mr. Larson?" I said, my mind clicking crazily. "Paul J. Larson? What do you mean, reinter?''

"Bury," Dr. Wolf said, picking up his chalk and returning

to his work at the blackboard, his shadow contorted into elongated spider legs by the ceiling lights overhead. "When do you think you can pick him up and put him back in his grave? We need the storage space he's been taking up."

"But I thought he was cremated!"

"He was evidence in a questionable death investigation, Mr. Hawley. I ordered his body impounded and placed in isolation. It was unfortunate that we couldn't contact the dead man's son when you were first asked to dig him up, but that would have jeopardized the success of all the hard work we now know Detective Rubins has been putting into this ongoing investigation. Though he didn't exactly appreciate my explanation, I was finally able to bring Jerome Larson around to my way of seeing things when we spoke earlier this evening. Naturally, he would have preferred knowing that the police were in control from the beginning—but he said that since his father was never in any real danger, he can see how important our security precautions were. Now that I'm done with his father's remains, it's up to you to see that he is returned to his grave as quickly, and with as much dignity, as possible."

"Dr. Wolf . . ." I began, my voice catching in my throat as the magnitude of what the Wolfman had just said hit me, full force.

He had saved my ass! The son of a bitch had pulled me right out of the fire! My funeral home! My brother! My God . . .

"Mr. Hawley," he said, turning.

"Yes," I replied, too stunned to move.

"Go home."

I suppressed the urge to shake his hand, or hug him. Instead, I said simply, "Yes, sir," which made him nod, professionally, once, as just the hint of a smile returned to the corner of his mouth, making me realize exactly what he had done.

He had gone out of his way to make me acknowledge that by signing Madeline Chase's death certificate in accordance with what I asked my price had been met for squaring up our original debt, incurred when I had gotten him out of trouble last year. All the while he had been saving his surprise about Paul J. Larson's body. Mr. Larson's son, Jerome, must have contacted the coroner's office after he had told me that the police had informed him that his father had been illegally disinterred. Dr. Wolf knew how much trouble I was in because of what I had done. And he also knew what Paul J. Larson's disinterred body, still intact, meant to me professionally. All the Wolfman had to say was that, as the county's medical examiner, he had authorized Mr. Larson's disinterment in conjunction with an ongoing police investigation, and I was off the hook.

So the Wolfman had squared up his debt, while establishing a new one.

Now I owed him.

Which was just his way of doing business.

With things starting to get back to normal, I could now concentrate on what Ronald Ackermann had known, and when he had known it. In my mind, that pair of questions made all the difference.

THIRTEEN
■■■■■■■■■■■■■■■■

SUNDAY MORNING BROUGHT clouds, the threat of rain, and surprisingly high temperatures for the fifteenth day of May. It was over sixty degrees by nine o'clock, and, as Nat and I climbed into Larry Fizner's van, the weather took honors as the topic of conversation. We each had our own reasons for avoiding comment on our mission—though quest might be a better word—and I could tell by the way both Larry, who was driving, and Nat, who was seated to my right in the back, surreptitiously glanced my way, either making brief eye contact or using the various mirrors positioned around us, that I was the unspoken master of ceremonies. After I had told them about the one very important point left to establish concerning Ronald Ackermann, they obviously wanted to talk. I didn't. We were all nervous.

As we rode, an eerie sensation of unreality overshadowed my mind—a sensation that had started late the night before, at almost the exact moment at which Dr. Gordon Wolf had announced that the body of Paul J. Larson was gloriously not burned. By the simple act of still being intact, Mr. Larson's body, in itself, had freed me of the greatest single obstacle to complete concentration I had ever faced. With the fear of losing my funeral home effectively removed, suddenly things came back around to where I was in charge once again. That secret, private, detached part of myself that I think of as being who and what I truly am beneath my everyday ineffectual veneer was taking notes in my head again. The future was again filled with a promising abundance of days that I could anticipate and plan. And, most importantly, my brother would still get his chance. It was what he wanted, and I could still give it to him, which was such a thorough relief that it was like having my hands untied, throwing my arms out wide, and opening my eyes after having spent a month blind, all rolled into one marvelous moment.

A moment that, unfortunately, I wouldn't have very much time to savor . . .

"You're crazy," had been Nat's reaction when I had explained my plan to her, in bed, before we went to sleep the night before. I had gotten home from the morgue at a little before midnight, full of good news and hope. As my wife listened to my proposal, she frowned, but resisted the urge to argue all the way up to the part about the SWORDS Spring War. That's when she said, "Bill, sweetheart, wait a minute. Since Mr. Larson's body is all right, then the risk to the funeral home is gone, right? Why would you want to mess around with Ronald Ackermann and Jane Craig now? Let the police handle them. You've already done more than your share. . . ."

"But what about George Sacks?" I cut in.

"What about him?"

"He says that it was Jane Craig who took the Camaro, which is to say that she's the one who murdered Everett Chase . . . and me too, damned near."

"So?" Nat asked. "What of it? You provided the police with a witness who can put her and the car together—isn't that enough?"

"But Edward Craig says that his ex-wife is also the one who killed Allison Ackermann, remember? She supposedly killed Ronald's sister, and then she moved in with him after he asked her to marry him!"

"So?"

"In either case, Ronald Ackermann isn't involved. According to both witnesses, Ronald Ackermann, the one and only person left alive who will benefit from these killings financially, is cleared of any wrongdoing. Even though he's been living with Jane Craig since virtually the day his sister was murdered, and, according to Jane's ex-husband, is actually engaged to marry her, he supposedly doesn't know a goddamn thing about how she's been systematically removing everybody who stands between him and his mother's money. He's completely innocent. The unwitting benefactor of Jane Craig's treachery. A good boy in the clutches of an evil, older woman.''

"So what?" Nat asked.

"So, he's also the one who called Jane Craig the day Everett Chase was shot. As soon as I told him that his mother's body had been found, and that she was about to be identified officially by the coroner's office, he locked himself in that concession stand and called her on the phone. As soon as she hung up, Jane Craig raced off in a borrowed Camaro, with a stolen gun, to kill Everett Chase, thereby clearing Ronald Ackermann's way to the gold.''

"Is there a problem there?"

"Maybe. Don't you think it's awfully damned convenient that Ronald Ackermann should call Jane Craig so soon after finding out that his mother's body had been unearthed . . . while there was still time for her to do something about the health of the one remaining obstacle standing between him and the cash?"

"But who else should he have called?" Nat cut in. "If they're engaged, like Edward Craig says they are, then I would have thought it more suspicious if he hadn't called her with the bad news."

"That's true," I agreed. "But what if he knows that Jane Craig killed his sister? What then?"

"Are you saying that he deliberately asked the woman who murdered his sister to marry him?"

"Why not? If Jane Craig killed Allison Ackermann, she must have done it for the money. If that's true, then the minute Ronald Ackermann proposed he became the most important person in her whole world.''

"So you're saying that Ronald Ackermann asked Jane Craig to marry him because he knew that she was a murderess?''

"Right. With Allison dead, as long as Ronald Ackermann lived long enough to celebrate his twenty-first birthday, he was next in line to collect his mother's insurance. With Jane Craig slated to be his wife, then the one person in the world she would do anything to protect was him. Anything—including borrowing a Camaro and shooting down Everett Chase.''

"So what if you're right? What if Ronald Ackermann did know what Jane Craig was doing?"

"Think about what he did."

"You mean when he called you on the phone?"

"Yes."

"He told you about the Camaro."

"And what else?"

"Do you mean what else did he say?"

"No, what else did telling me about the Camaro do?"

"It put you onto George Sacks."

"That's right. It put me onto George Sacks, who, by telling me that Jane Craig was the one who had borrowed the Camaro, all but accused her of murder."

"My God. Are you implying that Ronald Ackermann was setting her up?!"

"I certainly think it's a possibility. There was an awful lot of physical evidence in that bedroom. Between the club on the wall and the rag with the imprint of the Encom MP-45 in Jane Craig's underwear drawer, both murder weapons were represented. Even Larry smelled a rat."

"So?"

"So, it occurred to me that if Ronald Ackermann did know that Jane Craig is a killer, telling me about the stolen Camaro on the phone was the same as telling the police what she had done. Either way, he gets rid of her, and keeps the money."

"But what if he's innocent? What if he really was just trying to help?"

"Then he's got nothing to worry about."

"What about him makes you think that he could be so cold-blooded?"

"A couple of things. The first, I think, is something that George Sacks said about how Ronald Ackermann is never scared of anything because he's always in control. Everything is part of a scenario, Sacks said. Ackermann's supposedly completely calculating in his actions. He thinks ahead, leaving nothing to chance. That's one thing.

"The other is that Edward Craig insisted that both Ronald and Allison Ackermann saw their mother's dead body before it was cut apart. They were there, in that funeral home, and neither one ever said a word about it. If Ronald Ackermann's kept a secret like that since he was sixteen years old, I don't think I'd put anything past him now that he's an adult. If he did know what Jane Craig was doing when she murdered his sister, then I'd have to say that he's perfectly capable of either going along with her plan, or of keeping what she did to himself without doing anything to interfere. Either way he comes out rich. And either way, he's a shit."

"But how can you prove it?"

When I told her how simple I thought it would be to find out whether Ronald Ackermann did or did not know what Jane Craig had been doing, she looked shocked.

"That's absolutely crazy!" she protested, sitting straight up in bed and sending Quincy, whom she had been brushing, scrambling to the floor. "There's a million things that could go wrong!"

"Have you got a better plan?" I asked.

She scrunched up her face, admitting finally that she didn't. "But that doesn't mean that I like it."

Sliding under the covers next to her, I reached out and pulled her close, saying, "You don't have to like it. You just have to back me up."

Now we were rattling along the freeway in Larry Fizner's van, which made me briefly recall that this wasn't the first time that Nat and I had been in this exact same situation: having Larry chauffeur us somewhere that neither of us really wanted to go. The first time had been when Larry and I had first met . . . a time that had ended with me sitting in a wrecked car, bleeding from the mouth, lucky as hell that I didn't have a handful of my own teeth to string into a souvenir necklace. I sincerely hoped that this time things would go more smoothly.

I suppose I should have known better.

I was also thinking about how I had bruised Larry's ribs when I had tackled him the night before . . . and about what he had said regarding his reaction to chemotherapy. Battered and weakened as he was, I couldn't help but wonder how he'd hold up if there was trouble.

I suppose that I should have known better about that one too.

As I was leaning back in the seat, my anticipation about what we'd find at the SWORDS Spring War brought my grandmother to mind. When I was a kid, Grandma didn't believe in television as a baby-sitter, so she taught me how to read when I was very young. Consequently, books have always been an extremely important part of my life, and there are things that I've read, images as strong and vivid as anything real I have ever seen, that have remained with me, becoming, in their own way, memories. The weird part about that is that some of those things that I read in the past, especially when I was really, really young, have been transformed in my mind into memories of events that never actually happened. They're fiction. Someone else made them up. And yet I integrated them into my consciousness as if they were actually a physical reality—an unassailable part of the fabric of my life.

For example, there's a passage in a novel by Howard Pyle called *Men of Iron*, which is about a boy coming of age in medieval England by avenging the wrongful death of his father, that sticks with me in particular detail. After serving as a squire, the boy eventually grows up to kill the evil knight who committed the book's opening crime, in lethal combat, under the king's watchful eye. The passage that I recall most vividly concerns a scene in which the story's young hero, along with his best friend, breaks into an ancient, unused tower in the castle where they live. There they find a bunch of old swords, shields, cloaks, and armor. Just as they are swearing an adolescent oath of fidelity to one another concerning the secrecy of their discovery, from over the horizon comes the blare of a trumpet announcing the approach of the king and his entourage. Together, the two boys watch the advancing army from a tiny window high atop that crumbling edifice, seeing the glint of a thousand silver helmets beneath the splashing color of even more lance-borne flags, red and gold, against the green of English hills and the blue of a country sky.

I remember that. I don't remember the passage in the book ... the physical imprint of black-and-white words strung across a page; I remember actually witnessing those knights marching over that hill as if it were me who was in that tower.

Now here's the funny part:

When I found a copy of *Men of Iron* a couple of years ago, I couldn't find the passage I just described. I found the part about the boys in the tower, but the approaching army didn't come over the hill until much later in the story. So there it is: a memory of something that didn't happen, recalled in a way that it never occurred. Somehow, I created my own version of events in my mind, in such detail, that I still find it hard to believe that there isn't a different edition of that same book out there somewhere that contains exactly the memory I've got in my head.

I mention this because, as we headed south to the SWORDS Spring War, the words George Sacks had used to describe the way the group's members cooperated to mimic some magical, bygone era brought to mind a Civil War battle re-creation that Nat and I had attended a few years back. I recalled the strange sensation I had felt on that particular fall morning when the hills had erupted with the staccato pop of musket fire and a brigade of blue-coated northern troops had answered the bugle call to charge. It was like an electric tingle that ran over me: it didn't last very long, but it was there for a moment. Then I had looked around at the other people standing on the sidelines with me, eating their hot dogs and cotton candy, and the tingle faded. But for just that instant I was transported in my mind to another time and place where the familiar was erased in favor of a new and exciting reality.

And I'd never really been all that interested in the Civil War.

But knights in armor ... when I was a kid, that was my kind of stuff. Even at thirty-five years of age, the idea of seeing a thousand knights clash in full battle gear, as George Sacks had promised we would at the war's opening battle, gave me a charge. I certainly couldn't see devoting my life to

being one of those knights. But being there to see it happen
. . . now that I could get into.

The ride took us a little over ninety minutes, which went
fast, considering my preoccupation. We were heading south,
which, in Ohio, will take you from the city to the country real
quick, if you take the right roads. Ohio's also flat, so there's
a lot of big, empty fields stretching in patchwork arrangements
on your every side. But there are also a lot of woods and hills
toward the central part of the state. As we followed the map
on the back of the SWORDS brochure Larry had found in
Ronald Ackermann's bedroom, exiting Interstate 71 South and
merging into the two lanes of Route 16, avoiding Akron, the
"Rubber City" of old, for the more rural bits of color between
the larger towns, we started seeing things that told us we were
getting close.

There were signs tacked to trees shaped like the arrowhead
of a knight's shield, with the tip aimed to the earth, painted
light blue and announcing, "SPRING WAR, Take Thee Ahead,"
with arrow symbols leading the way. There were also lengths
of light blue silk fluttering from fence posts; an occasional
staff stuck into the ground on the road's shoulder, also fluttering with light blue silk; and, the most obvious sign of all,
a van at a rest stop that bore a coat of arms on its side . . .
three leaping lions, gold, on a background of bright red, separated from a black falcon's head by a band of blue. The van
was ratty, rusted, and all but falling apart. But the coat of arms
was perfect. The lady we saw getting back into the van as we
raced past had her hand raised demurely lifting her long skirt
as she raised her foot and dipped her pointed hat, with its
length of fluttering silk, so that she wouldn't knock it off.

I got a twinge, seeing the juxtaposition of the two images:
a lady in a "garment" climbing into a beat-up, black Chevy
van, painted with a coat of arms and driven by a man with
tattoos and a beard. Inevitably it brought my first sight of Jane
Craig to mind, when I had privately dubbed her the Fairy Lady
because of the garment she wore, which made me finally say
out loud to Nat and Larry, "You know, we had all better start
thinking about who we want to be for the day. According to

the brochure, they won't let us onto the grounds unless we're in costume."

"What ya mean, costume?" Larry asked, without taking his eyes off the road.

"We'll have to rent something at the gate," I explained. "We can't enter the grounds in street clothes, or 'mundane garb,' as they say. It's against the rules."

"Peachy," Larry growled.

Making Nat smile.

I've never been camping, so I don't know what that's normally like. All I can say about pulling up to the site of the SWORDS gathering is that it reminded me of pulling into the parking lot of one of those carnivals they give on church property during the summer . . . the ones that have those ratty old rides, with those ratty old guys running them, complete with elephant ears, corn dogs, and games of chance that few people ever win. The lot outside the cyclone fence was gravel and grass. There must have been over a hundred vehicles, mostly vans, parked all over, some occupied, others locked and empty. The cyclone fence had razor wire on its top and a sign over the gate proclaiming, "RALSTON CONSTRUCTION COMPANY—NO TRESPASSING." Another sign, this one hand-lettered, read, "NO MODERN ITEMS PAST THIS POINT."

"That means you can't take anything inside that's not made of wood, leather, cloth, or primitive iron," I explained. "No wristwatches or kerosene stoves or anything like that. It's all got to be period, or you can't take it past the gate."

"What about eyeglasses?" Larry asked.

I replied that, according to the brochure, glasses were one of the few exceptions to the rule.

There was a man at the gate running a hand-held metal detector over a couple who held their hands up and giggled. Larry watched, saying to me through the corner of his mouth, "What about my gun?"

"Looks like you leave it," I replied.

He narrowed his eyes.

"You're kidding, right? You're not gonna let these fruitcakes search us like we was gonna get on a plane, are you?"

"If that's what it takes to get in, that's what we're doing."

"And costumes? Really?"

"Really."

Nat took my hand as Larry sighed, undid the holster from where he had it clipped to his belt at the small of his back, turned around, and did something under his van's driver's seat. "What am I supposed to do with my car keys?" he asked. I said that, since we needed the keys to get back into the vehicle, they were another of the exceptions SWORDS would make.

I was still looking at Nat. Though her eyes were sparkling, she looked apprehensive. "Are you all right?" I asked, confidentially, as we headed for the front gate.

"Yes," she answered. "If no one gets hurt, this looks like it could be a lot of fun."

"No one will get hurt," I assured her, hoping the forced confidence in my voice sounded convincing enough to mask my lack of sincerity. "How's your vest?"

"Hot," she replied, tugging at her sweater.

Beneath our clothes, we were each wearing a flak vest that Larry Fizner had provided when he showed up that morning. Without knowing the details of what I had in mind for the SWORDS war, he had anticipated that there might be trouble, insisting, "Hot or not, we wear 'em, or we don't go. Period."

I thought he was being overly cautious, but I went along with it, more so that Nat would agree to wear a vest, which she called ugly, than anything else. Now, as we were approaching the gate, I was glad we had them on.

When our turn in line came, I took the lead, saying, "We three would like to rent appropriate garb. We've never attended a war before. This is our first time."

"Do you have a persona?" the woman behind the desk inquired.

"Uh, let's see . . ."

"I am Natalia DeStahl, wife of Sir William of Hawley," Nat piped up from behind me.

"Sir William?" the woman at the desk said, marking something in a book. "Will you be fighting today, Sir William?"

"I certainly hope not," I replied.

She looked up at me quizzically.

"No," I said. "No fighting. This time I'll just watch."

"And you?" the woman continued, directing her attention to Larry, who all but scowled at her in return.

"He's Bilious Fiznus," I said. "My squire."

Larry squinted one eye virtually shut. The woman accepted my description, wrote out some ticket stubs, which she handed over, after I had given her two hundred dollars for admission and our various garment needs. As we stepped through the gate, Larry said, "Doesn't bilious mean lumpy or fat or something?"

"It means ill-tempered and sour." I smiled, glancing at Nat as I took her hand again. "It was the first thing I could think of."

The man with the metal detector ran it over me, then Nat, but when he got to Larry a strange thing happened. Just as he was bringing the device up toward Larry's chest, Larry folded his arms around over himself and turned away, saying, "Hey, watch it with that thing! I've got a pacemaker. What are ya tryin' to do, screw it up?"

The man immediately pulled the metal detector away, apologizing through a contrite expression.

As we moved away from the gate, I leaned toward Larry, saying, "Since when do you have a pacemaker?"

"Don't worry about it," he grumbled back.

So I dropped it.

There were storage buildings set up in a row about twenty yards from the gate, looking like Army barracks. Just as George Sacks had described, this facility was used to store heavy construction equipment, with even more identical buildings behind used as rental space for people with boats and R.V.'s. So early in the season, I imagined that those boats and R.V.'s were probably all still in their berths, with the construction equipment as of yet unclaimed for the season's work.

A man in a monk's outfit took our tickets, looked us over with a critical eye, pronounced our approximate sizes, and told us where we could go to select the costumes we would wear for the day. Inside building number four, which had a high ceiling and a concrete floor, there were dozens of rolling garment racks set up, with size ranges pinned to the ends. Nat went one way, to the "ladies' department," while Larry and I both stepped around to where the monk said we would find, "Attire to suit thee in thy station."

I thought Larry was going to deck him.

"Come on," I hissed when the monk had gone. "Remember why we're here. What, you've never been undercover before?"

"I ain't never been bilious before," he grumbled. He snatched the first thing his hand grabbed from the rack and said, "Let's just get on with it."

After I'd picked the stuff I was going to wear, the monk showed us to a line of empty Port-O-San booths, where he told us we could change. We could lock our mundane clothes in the lockers located near the building's rear exit, he said. And, "May thy stay in our land enlighten and delight thee."

I checked Larry on that one, just as a precaution, but I don't think he even heard. He was too busy monkeying with some leather cords to have been paying much attention.

When we were all changed and regrouped in front of the building, the first thing that struck me was how beautiful Nat looked in her gear. She had chosen a long dress of jet black with flowing sleeves. Simple, and on her, elegant. She had allowed her hair to fall over her shoulders and was standing, waiting for me as I came clumping out of the locker room, pulling at the crotch of the pants I was wearing, which were way too tight. She smiled when she saw me, extended her arms, and said, "My knight."

"My lady," I replied, going to her.

I was dressed in a pair of green stretch pants that went to my knees, with dark brown socks from the knee down, ending in light shoes with toes that curled up at the top. I had on a dark green shirt, over which hung a vest made from leather straps, crisscrossed and held together with little metal buttons. My arms were bare beneath where the tunic's short sleeves ended in an exaggerated saw-toothed edge. And I had a brown felt, pointed hat with a long peacock feather stuck in its band. Though I looked like I was preparing to play Robin Hood in some community theater production, what I felt like was a jerk.

"Where's Mr. Fizner?" Nat asked as I took her hands.

"He's coming," I replied. "Don't laugh, or he'll end up waiting for us in the van."

Larry came out fuming. The hanger he had chosen hadn't been a good one. He was wearing bright yellow nylon tights with short pants that were poofy and striped with bright orange, green, and black bands. He had on a red vest over his undershirt and was holding a three-pointed hat with bells on it, as well as a stick with a laughing clown face on top.

"What the fuck's with this shit?" was the first thing out of his mouth.

Even though I'd just told Nat not to do it, I couldn't help but laugh when I saw him . . . it was more his face than anything else. I had to grab him by the shoulders when he started turning around, saying, "That's it. I don't need this . . ."

"Come on," I coaxed. "It's a jester's outfit. You look fine."

"You do, Mr. Fizner." Nat smiled. There was something so sincere in her voice that both Larry and I turned to look at her, finding her face positively beaming with good humor. "It's really not so bad. Is it?"

"No," Larry pouted. Then, aiming an evil eye at me, he said, "But I ain't wearin' this fuckin' hat."

I shrugged.

Nat said that we had better get moving if we were going to find Ronald Ackermann's tent before the festivities got rolling.

The farther from the front gate we got, the easier I found it to allow myself to slip into a fantasy frame of mind where the details of the surrounding events fused into a new reality of their own. Once the storage buildings with their aluminum roofs and shingled sides were out of sight behind us, and the paths that had been worn through the woods led us first to a declining slope and finally down to a clearing from which we could see the vista of a valley before us, the illusion built upon itself until that final moment when the SWORDS vision greeted us from the valley.

We stood and gazed down at what these people had made

for themselves, and I must admit to a real feeling of amazement.

"It's beautiful," Nat whispered, squeezing my hand. "Isn't it, Bill? I mean, really."

I nodded, not trusting myself to speak.

Below us was the tent city of SWORDS. The tents were all tall and pointed, something like Indian teepees, but more elaborate, with striped sides and flowing streamers. There must have been a hundred of them, of every color you can imagine, and they were surrounded by the movement of people, made small by distance, but as brightly dressed as their colorful abodes.

Larry took the lead down the slope, and, glancing at Nat, whose eyes were sparkling, I followed, thinking that this was the craziest thing I had ever done in my life. I was also thinking that now was probably a good time to ask, "Are you two sure you've got your assignments straight?"

Larry and Nat both said that they did.

"What about you, Mr. Fizner?" I asked. "Are you going to be all right with all this walking?"

"I'll be fine," he glowered. "You just worry about yourself, sonny."

Hearing the gruff edge to his voice assured me somehow, since, whether I like it or not, over the years I've come to depend on Larry's leatherlike toughness. No matter how tight the spot, he has always come through. I don't know what I'll do when he's gone. . . .

I frowned, wondering why I had chosen this particular moment to think about my partner's mortality. Until then, even after he had announced that he had been diagnosed with cancer, I hadn't allowed myself to acknowledge him as anything short of impenetrable. It must be some masochistic part of my nature that demands that I recognize the realities of the stupid things I do, even as I'm doing them. It's as if I have to tell myself, "Yes, I know better. But I'm pressing on anyway." For good measure I remembered his recently revealed pacemaker, wondering why he had never mentioned it before.

"Bill?" Nat said. "What's wrong? You look like you're a million miles away."

"Nothing," I replied. "I guess I'm just tense."

"You want to turn back?"

"No. Do you?"

"Yes, but we're not going to, are we?"

"No."

Things were getting a little heavy, so, to break the tension, I started reciting what I had learned from reading the SWORDS brochure that Larry had found in Ronald Ackermann's bedroom. The tent city built by the people of SWORDS, I said as we covered the two hundred or so yards from the edge of the first ridge to where the city was located on a plateau overlooking the combat field, grew in size and sophistication every year. Some of the tents were stored in the buildings we had seen upon first entering the grounds, others were hauled back and forth, while still others remained up year-round. The people who occupied them spent a great deal of money getting them up to speed historically, using a number of textbooks as their models, though there were certain concessions made to modern comfort, such as the sanitary facilities, a number of freestanding outdoor arrangements that looked like any other tent but that met the codes dictated by the state for a group of this size camping out.

At the center of "town" there was a Maypole, a good forty feet tall, with dozens of streaming ribbons blowing from its top. The Maypole dance would happen that evening, after the war had begun, during the feast. Around the Maypole was a clear area called the courtyard, fifty yards around, that served as the central market where the members of SWORDS set up shop, doing whatever it was they had come to the war to do. Some gave leather craft lessons, standing in their period dress, while others sat on the ground trying to match whatever the teacher was doing with short lengths of cord. Others danced. Others sang. And others told stories. It was rather a lot like what I would image the first Woodstock must have been, though cleaner, more organized, and deeper in its scope.

Approaching the perimeter of the city I felt the first twinges of just how strange the atmosphere surrounding the place truly was; it was almost as if the people there radiated an aura that thickened the closer to the Maypole you got.

I guess the music is what I noticed first—it was everywhere, generally plucked out on some kind of string instruments, but here and there pounded rhythmically on what sounded like tambourines and bongos. Then came the smells—a lot of wood smoke and meat, I noticed—fragrant and, even to a confirmed vegetarian like me, seductively appetizing. Last came the impact of the people themselves, which was definitely the most profound.

Every once in a while they have exposés on TV about some cult or another that I can't resist watching. I'm a junkie for sensational, true-crime stories. I admit it. What I've often noticed about the people involved in cults and fanatical groups is that they have a kind of serenity about their faces, an inner glow. Really religious people have that same look sometimes. Like they know what's going on, while everyone not initiated in their group is in the dark. That look makes me nervous because, without understanding at least a little bit of how someone sees the world, I haven't got the slightest clue as to what they think they're accomplishing when they act. I'm not in on their motivations. Anything could happen, and I'd be at a loss as to how to respond.

The people of SWORDS had just that look. I mean, every goddamn one of them, including the kids. They were the happiest-looking bunch I had ever seen. I had just that second realized that I was uncomfortable, when Nat said, "Now remember, from here on out we've got to stay true to the period. If we break the mood of this thing, we'll have a problem."

"Meaning what?" Larry asked.

"Meaning," Nat replied, "that these people spend the rest of their year looking forward to the couple of weeks they spend here. Once they arrive, they try not to let anything interfere with the fantasy. The minute they're through those gates, they're totally into what they're doing. It's like a play, breaking period would be like turning a piece of scenery around in the middle of a show so that the audience could see that it was really made of canvas and wood. It blows the whole thing apart.

"Listen," she continued, reading aloud from the SWORDS pamphlet. " 'We, each member of SWORDS, depend, one upon the other, to strictly maintain the scenario. Imagine your time at the war as a great improvisational experience. Improvisational theater, taken to the extreme . . . performance art on a scale beyond any other spot on earth. At the war, what is performed is what is lived. Like a great web, our fantasy is held together by the integrity of its individual strands. One word or gesture out of place is like one of those strands going slack. It weakens the whole web. When someone trusts you with their dream, you voluntarily acknowledge your responsibility to help them keep that dream alive.' ''

''What's that supposed to mean?'' Larry asked.

''It means that you better let me do the talking,'' I said as our little band pulled up short at the end of the field, collectively hesitating, or so it seemed to me, before actually setting foot into the town. Somehow, crossing that line felt as if it were tantamount to accepting some collective challenge.

Nat was reading again, gesturing as she spoke.

'' 'Our town is called Glennwillows,' '' she said, sweeping her arm out before her to encompass everything that lay ahead. '' 'And it is divided into four sections, each matching a compass point, and each representing one of our Lords. At the edge of the city center, there is a different colored flag at each corner, demarcating each Lord's section. Members pitch their tents in the section belonging to the Lord to whom they have decided to support this time. Remember, when the war starts, it is treason to abandon your Lord.' ''

''How do you get to be a Lord?'' I asked.

''Apparently,'' Nat replied, ''it all depends on how much time you want to put into the club. According to this, during the year the Lords are responsible for getting the newsletters out and conducting meetings in their own individual districts of the country. The Lords pretty much stay the same because you need to have a fairly substantial side income to meet the obligations of the office. So the Lords are four older, retired guys, all of them ex-Society for Creative Anachronism members. They've got them listed, along with their highest ranking knights, on the back. See? Ronald Ackermann is called Rodant the White, and for this war he's pledged to the gold flag of the Earl of Brinewedding, which is, ah, that way, I guess.''

She pointed again. "His standard is a red cross on a white background. That's apparently what we look for on his tent."

"Okay," I said, having heard enough of the ground rules. "Let's stick together."

Nat squared her shoulders, took my hand, and was the first to actually step onto the soil of Glennwillows, realm of Lords. I followed, with Larry Fizner bringing up the rear. As we walked, I said through the side of my mouth, "I wish Larry had his gun."

Nat squeezed my hand as she replied, "How were you supposed to know they'd have a metal detector?"

"I, with care, should have prepared the way for thee, so that my lady's path would be as of roses and the softest leaves of spring," I said, trying out some prithee speech, since in a minute I'd be using it for real. To my unsophisticated ears, it didn't sound bad.

"Oh, for Christ's sake," Larry grumbled.

Nat punched him on the arm.

A number of people along the way greeted us, bowing, the men taking off their hats in sweeping motions and the women turning their heads in courtly propriety. According to the listing of Lords and knights, we were not looking for Ronald Ackermann, but the tent of the noble Rodant the White, teller of tales and warrior in the league of the gold Earl. There, amid the tents and banners, hearing the music and smelling the smells, listening to the way people spoke, and seeing how even the children stuck to their period ways, I have to admit to a certain feeling of discomfiture . . . a sensation of being of two minds so contradictory that I had to constantly remind myself of the purpose of my visit and the risks I was taking. The thing that brought me back down to earth the quickest, I found, was simply drawing up the image of Madeline Chase's head in that plastic bag . . . when I did that, SWORDS and all its strangeness looked suddenly silly, which, though it made me a little sad, cleared the cobwebs from my attic.

Ronald Ackermann's tent was the finest, next to the one that I assumed belonged to the Earl himself, in the gold district. All done in white and red, it had a fluttering silk streamer emblazoned with a red cross affixed to its peak, with a big, biker-looking guy in a kilt standing out front as a sentry. Clearing my throat and feeling simultaneously foolish and spooked, I said, ''I beg thee, good man, to inform thy knight of my request for parley this good spring morn. I am acquainted with him, and would have thee say the name of Hawley.''

The man nodded but did not speak, disappearing into the tent flap. When he returned his eyes were dark, and for a moment I didn't think he was going to let us in. But glumly he held the flap for us to pass, watching us warily with his hard blue eyes as we did.

Now, I want to get this one just right, because it would be easy not to. As unsettling as the rest of what I had so far seen was to my concentration, stepping into Ronald Ackermann's tent, actually being inside the thing, produced the strangest sensation yet. It was big in there, with the daylight diffused by the tent's fabric so that the interior seemed awash in a kind of pink glow. The ceiling was high and peaked. Jane Craig, wearing a long white gown, was sitting in a corner playing a lute. Two boys, no more than sixteen, dressed in short white tunics and baggy pants, were attending to their knight, who, dressed in his warrior's finest, was standing, facing away from us as we were ushered into his presence. When Jane Craig's eyes met mine, her fingers paused in mid-phrase, bringing the gentle strains of her music to a shrieking end.

The place looked and felt real . . . honest to God. It looked and felt as if we were, all of us, truly in the tournament residence of a knight of the realm, come to offer that good warrior luck before a joust. The atmosphere was so complete, each detail so thoroughly attended to, that I very nearly spoke, just to hear my voice. Jane Craig did not speak, but sat there, watching. The two young squires stopped what they were doing. And Ronald Ackermann, or Sir Rodant the White, turned, presenting himself to us with grim resolution.

He was perfect, I decided, far more comfortable-looking here than he had been even in the park where he had been practicing for this very event. George Sacks had warned me that the equipment Ronald Ackermann had been wearing in the park was only his practice stuff and that his real armor was both expensive and impressive. I should have taken him at his word, because what I saw Ackermann wearing that moment looked as if it should have been displayed in a museum, so closely did it match the suits of steel I had seen under a collector's glass as a child. It gleamed an almost iridescent silver, washed slightly pink in the tent's interior light, with a skirt of chain mail, a breastplate of steel, and tubes of matching metal on the arms and legs. I don't know the proper terminology for the individual pieces of his outfit. I suppose I could have looked them up since then, but I didn't know them then, and it didn't really matter . . . actually, it made what I was looking at all the more intriguing for its unfamiliarity. Ronald Ackermann's head was bare, jutting up from the top of his breastplate, hanging with his long, darkly curled hair, his brown eyes looking predatory and poised as he gazed down upon us . . . which is when I realized that he was standing on a pedestal. He didn't say a word. He just looked.

"My Lord," I said, bowing slightly at the waist.

Ronald Ackermann acknowledged my greeting with a nod, saying, "Sire, what brings thee nigh?"

Oh Christ, I thought, rolling my eyes.

"I beg of thee a private word," I said.

But Ronald Ackermann protested, "A call has come from my earl of treachery and attack. I have not time for parley. I have time only for my duty."

"Duty my ass," Larry piped up, making all heads flash his way.

"What sayest thou?" Ronald Ackermann said.

"Excuse him, sire," I cut in before Larry could speak again. "For he is old and knows not what he says."

Larry scowled at me.

Ronald Ackermann was just opening his mouth to speak again, but I didn't give him the chance.

"Sir Rodant," I said, "it is well that thou should treat thy duty as of import, but take me at my word when I say that, without two minutes of thine time, myself and my companions will, without delay, bring thee to ruin."

Ronald Ackermann's eyes darkened, and he looked, so help me, just like a true knight of old. With a frown and a grand sweep of his iron-clad arm, he said to his two squires, "Take thee away, my sons."

The boys piped up their courtly protest, saying how Ronald would need a few adjustments to his equipment if he was going to be ready for the coming battle. But he cut them off by slamming a steel glove down on the table next to him and shouting, "I said away with thee. And thine lady as well. Away, I would have thee fly!"

They flew all right. While the boys and Jane Craig gathered up their stuff and headed for the tent flap, I was looking at the helmet next to where Ronald Ackermann had dropped his glove. It was a gorgeous thing, tall, with a visor that was pointed in front, and holes drilled through the lower portion for ventilation, with a slit cut across the top through which the wearer could see. Atop it was a huge plume, probably two feet long, half-red, half-white. Leaning against the table was Ackermann's shield, painted white with a red cross. Next to that was his sword, carved wood with a metal handle wrapped in chain. And next to that leaned a very authentic-looking longbow and a leather quiver full of arrows.

This was definitely just too weird.

At the tent flap, Jane Craig paused, turning her upper body half around and aiming her face right at Ronald Ackermann. She didn't so much as open her mouth, but her eyes were staring at him so hard that I could feel their power all the way across the tent. If I hadn't known better, I would have sworn that the two of them were communicating at that moment . . . sending messages silently through the air, like married couples do, speaking with their minds. It made me remember that they were in fact going to be married, and also, I don't know why, but it culled up in me the notion that Ronald Ackermann had attended his mother's viewing, late at night, in a locked funeral home, after his stepfather had told him that she had taken her own life. I decided to play with this creep for not a second longer than was absolutely necessary.

When Jane Craig and Ackermann's two squires had made their exit, closing the tent flap behind themselves, I said, "Mr. Fizner, you and Nat can wait outside too, please."

Hearing my own voice, speaking normally, was soothing

somehow, but Ronald Ackermann obviously didn't like it.

"What the hell's going on, Hawley?" he demanded, stepping down from his pedestal and laying his other glove on the table. He looked so big in that steel suit of his, I thought. And when he moved he jingled and clanked, like the tin man in *The Wizard of Oz*.

"Come on, let's go," Larry said, taking Nat's arm.

Ronald Ackermann was staring after them so hard that I thought he'd pull a muscle.

"What the hell's going on here?" he demanded the instant they were gone, stepping toward me menacingly, rattling his armor when he did.

I held up my bandaged hand, saying, "Don't even think about it, Mr. Ackermann. Not another step." Then, with his eyes watching my good hand, I reached inside my tunic and produced a folded piece of paper, which I let fall open so that he could see what it was without touching it. That was important . . . I couldn't let him touch it.

His eyes jerked back and forth as he read. Then they grew wide. Then they moved to me as he said, "Where'd you get that? Who gave that to you?"

"You knew, didn't you?" I asked, waving the contract that Edward Craig had given me from behind his picture of Jesus, the one that spelled out his mother's expressed desire to end her own life and have her body hidden from the world forever. "Your mom didn't disappear, she killed herself. You knew that all along. You were at her viewing. You saw her body. YOU KNEW!"

He opened his mouth, but I shut it for him.

"Did you do the shooting, Ronald?" I demanded, trembling all over now that I was facing him, seeing him, remembering what had happened just two days before when I had seen his stepfather die. "Did you shoot Everett Chase, and me? Well? DID YOU!?"

"I don't—"

"You played along with him, didn't you?" I cut in. "When Everett Chase told you to shut up about your mother, you did . . . and so did your sister. You kids wanted the money. Your mom was already dead, there was nothing you could do about

it, you were young, and your stepfather was telling you that
it was a suicide. He showed you the body. The embalmer
backed him up. I can understand all that, I suppose. I might
even go so far as to forgive it, maybe, if I tried. . . .

"But not the other, Ronald. Definitely never the other
thing."

"What other thing?"

"You went right on keeping quiet, even after you were told
the truth about your mother's death."

"What are you talking about?"

Outside the tent there was sudden activity. It wasn't a particularly great commotion, and no new individual series of
sounds indicated what was going on. It was just movement
developing. Something was starting to happen out there, but I
didn't let it in, I forced it to stay out. I didn't have time. Like
Jane Craig had done, I was sending every ounce of my attention in Ronald Ackermann's direction, hoping, to be perfectly
honest, that I might sheer the skin off his lying face with the
pure, psychic heat of my anger.

"He told me," I said, low and mean. "Edward Craig told
me what he did. He admitted it. He admitted that your stepfather had murdered his wife, and that he had been hired to
dispose of the body. It's all been a lie, the whole pathetic
charade. Edward Craig knew it, so did Everett Chase, and so
did Jane Craig . . . your dearly betrothed. The only question
left is, did you know it, Mr. Ackermann? Your stepfather's
been giving you so much money that his restaurant went under
from the drain. Did Jane Craig tell you why he was being so
generous? Or didn't you ask? That's the last thing I want to
know, Mr. Ackermann. Just how much of a shit are you exactly?"

He was looking at me now. Really looking. Sizing me up,
I could tell. If he charged, I didn't know what I was going to
do. My only consolation was that, in that stupid steel suit, I
could surely outrun him.

"Shaking down your stepfather with threats of exposing
your mother's murder is called blackmail, Ronald," I said.
"And not reporting that murder is a crime too, you know. It's
called conspiracy . . . which makes you an accessory. So,

whose idea was it to shoot Everett Chase, Ronald? Was it yours or Jane's? Did she do it on her own, or did you send her out to kill?''

Outside a trumpet sounded and there rose a cheer, long and loud. Ronald Ackermann's eyes flickered to the side in response to the sound, and he seemed momentarily torn. Then he looked back at me and said, in a surprisingly reasonable tone, ''What can I do? How is this going to work, Mr. Hawley?''

''I want the details,'' I said. ''I want the truth; I want it now.''

''Yeah, okay,'' he agreed. ''But Jesus, not here. Not now. That's the trumpet call for the war. The first battle's just going to start. This place is going to go nuts. There's no way we can talk here, and there's no way they're going to leave me alone if I stay. I'm supposed to be there, you know. I'm leading the gold flag's charge this year. They'll be looking for me. We'll be interrupted. Can't this wait, just a couple of hours?''

''No.''

''Goddamn you, Hawley. Have a heart.''

''Now.''

''Okay. But listen. Meet me up on the entrance grounds. Okay? Give me that much. Half an hour, in building one-eleven. Okay?''

I looked at him, letting my suspicion show.

The trumpet blasted again, and this time the movement outside the tent, the bustling of feet, and the murmur of voices grew loud enough to fill the air around me, making Ronald Ackermann have to practically shout as he said, ''See what I mean? How are we going to resolve anything like this?''

Grudgingly, I agreed, saying, ''Half an hour, building one-eleven,'' using the paper bearing the prearrangement agreement that Edward Craig had forged to spell out Madeline Chase's intention to commit suicide for emphasis.

''Thanks,'' Ackermann said, turning and beginning to undo some kind of strap. ''You won't be sorry. You've got me all wrong, Mr. Hawley. Really. I can see why you're confused. But believe me, once I've had a chance to explain, you'll see how straight I've been. It's all a big mistake, really. You'll see.''

''Half an hour,'' I repeated, heading out of the tent into the bustle and rush of the war's growing momentum.

Glancing around, I found Nat and Larry by a tree, trying to stay out of the way. Knights of all sizes were emerging from their own tents, some in armor very nearly as spectacular as Ronald Ackermann's, others in equipment barely a cut above what Ackermann had worn to practice, all of them accompanied by squires who followed and fussed with last-minute preparations, held swords and shields, and talked excitedly. The trumpet blasted again. The knights almost all had helmets tucked under their arms.

''Well?'' Nat asked.

''We're cooking,'' I replied. ''You guys go ahead and get lost. But keep your eyes open. This is it. So be careful.''

They both agreed solemnly, and as Nat went by I kissed her. She paused, then she kissed me back, holding me against her. When she drew her face away she said with an earnest look in her eyes, ''Watch your ass, Bill. Please.''

Watching her leave, I couldn't help but smile. God, I love her, I thought. And silently I swore an oath to myself that, if things turned out right, I'd never do this to her again. I'd never make her worry or put her at risk. I turned to say something to Larry Fizner but found instead that he had already performed that same vanishing act that I had seen so many times before. Even dressed like a court jester, with yellow tights and a red vest, Larry Fizner had faded into the crowd virtually before my very eyes, leaving me to get my bearings as to which way I needed to go to find the entrance grounds, and building number 111 where, I hoped, my quest would finally end.

FOURTEEN
■■■■■■■■■■■■■■■■■■

I WAS HEADING against the flow, skipping between people dressed in the most outrageous costumes, dressed outrageously myself, and hurrying to what could very well prove to be a real mess. I felt as if I'd been sucked into one of those old movies my dad and I used to watch in our basement rec room when I was a kid—*Ivanhoe* or *Prince Valiant*, period pieces full of clanging steel and noble deeds. My noble deed was based primarily on deceit, with the simple goal of learning an ugly truth.

I crossed the field of tall grass at a trot, the soft bottoms of my funny shoes finding every stone. Where the main path that led down the slope from the construction company's storage yard was cut through the foliage on the hill I paused, glanced around, and decided to make my approach from a different direction. It was slower going as I struggled my way up the hill about thirty yards down, but the effort would be worth it, I thought, if it would bring me up at a spot from which I could get a view of the storage buildings without being seen. Ideally, I wanted to beat Ronald Ackermann to our rendezvous. That way, maybe I could anticipate his behavior, since his motive for setting up a meeting in an isolated spot could only be that he either wanted to honestly talk in private, or do something that he didn't want anyone else to see him do. Everything rested on his behavior during the next few minutes. Whether it was he, or Jane Craig, or the pair together, I was the biggest single problem in the world. What I wanted to see was how the problem that was me would be handled.

Behind me, as I worked my way up the slope through thick trees and undergrowth, the sound of trumpeting had gone from a fairly regular series of heralding blasts to a kind of mournful tune, the notes of which were modulated by the undercurrents of breeze rolling up from the valley into a random vibrato that seemed to hang and sway in the air before decaying into the next long note. My tight pants proved ideal for the climb since the branches and prickers around me slid off without hanging me up. And in what seemed like a very short time, I found myself at the rim of the slope, hidden behind low-hanging leaves, crouched, examining the yard.

Had I beaten him? I wondered.

More than likely I had. There was no way Ronald Ackermann could have slipped out of that clunky costume so fast. And he sure as hell wasn't going to make that climb, even on the path up the slope, carrying all that steel. Still, I wanted to be sure.

The yard was deserted, I saw through the leaves. Nothing moved. The front gate was closed. But from my vantage point I couldn't quite tell if it was chained or not. Behind me rose the roar of so many voices that, despite myself, I had to turn, just in time to see the two opposing armies of knights as they marched into the valley beyond Glennwillows, moving like two long lines of ants, one on each end of the tent complex, separated by a crowd of spectators, disappearing over the plateau's edge. I strained to see if Ronald Ackermann was among them, searching for the red and white that were his colors, wondering if he had stood me up. But I was just too far away for that kind of detail. My eyes weren't that good.

Oh well, I thought. I'll just have to take him at his word. But still, I'd be careful.

The storage barn closest to me had the number 113 painted on its side. Next down the line was 112. Then 111. The fronts of the buildings faced away from me, pointed at a second row of buildings, forming an alley down the center of the yard. There were twenty buildings on either side of the alley, forty in all.

I took a deep breath, wondering what to do next. I didn't have my wristwatch, so I didn't know how much of Ronald Ackermann's half hour was gone. I had taken a few missteps at first, and my exit from town wasn't as direct as I would have liked it to be. But still, I hadn't lost more than five or ten minutes, so I was fairly certain that I must have gotten here first.

Give it another couple minutes, I thought.

Then move.

Before I did, I picked up a stick.

Crouched like a cat burglar, I emerged from the cover of the trees and ran to the rear of building 113, carrying my stick in both hands, across my belly like a rifle. Carefully peering around the corner at the front of the barn, I scanned the alley between the rows, looking for motion. Then I checked the front gate again. Now I could see that, though the gate was closed, the chain and padlock were hanging loose over a post. The table, called the "Troll Booth" on the sign taped to its front and sides, sat empty. The woman with the notebook and roll of tickets was gone, as was the monk who'd been watching the costume racks. They were at the war, I thought. Naturally they were at the war . . . it was the first charge, the big event they had all come to see. Where else would they be?

That's when I really felt alone, with a brief pang of regret emphasizing the absurdity of my position. I should probably just turn around and go back, watch the war with Nat, make a day of it, and go home. Let the cops sort this mess out, I thought. Let Detective Rubins do his own dirty work. But then Madeline Chase's milky-eyed stare found me from the recesses of my memory, and I moved into the open, my purpose renewed, my heart pounding as if it would explode.

It was eerie, having gone from the commotion in the valley to the stillness of the yard. The sound of my shoes crunching gravel was horribly loud as I ran, still in a crouch, hugging the building fronts, toward the barn numbered 111. The rest of the buildings had their doors shut. One-eleven, I saw as I folded myself in at its corner, had its door open. A big, sliding wooden door, nearly as tall as the structure itself, probably twenty feet wide, yawning empty, afforded a perfect view of a big dark nothing inside.

A drop of sweat rolled off my nose. I wiped my face; it was wringing wet. Where the hell was Ackermann? More to the point, where should I be when he got here?

There was precious little cover where I was, so I decided that it would probably be best if I were inside the storage shed when Ackermann did finally show up. Strategically, that would put me in the dark, looking out at him in the light. I'd see him, but he wouldn't see me . . . which appealed to me somehow. To that end I started for the open barn door, my eyes scanning the gravel yard around me as I moved.

What happened next happened quickly, in virtual silence. I hadn't taken even a full step around the corner, heading for the open barn door, when I heard a dull, innocuous thump, directly behind my head . . . and I do mean, directly. Whatever it was, it brushed my hair, and without even thinking I dove for the door.

The second arrow hit the concrete floor as I rolled. This one, unlike the first, seemed to make a whistling sound as it approached, and, as I tumbled into the dark, its metal head struck the stone behind me and ricocheted off, producing a mix of sharp cracking sounds and sparks.

I came up and scrambled, expecting darkness and getting it only in strips. There was a pair of skylights in the ceiling. The building didn't have any windows, but it had the skylights overhead, and they cut the darkness inside into nearly perfect bands of black and white, illuminating the stuff contained therein in such a way that everything looked strangely truncated. Like it was all cut into pieces, and thrown in a heap.

A third arrow hit, this one on the sliding barn door, going right through and sticking there so that its nasty steel tip—real steel, not the harmless soft wood of the other weapons I'd seen—jutted like a tooth, catching the light and throwing it off in a sparkle. I put as much distance between me and the doorway's opening as I could in three seconds, found something big to duck behind, and parked myself there, looking at the yard through the open door and seeing absolutely nothing . . . remembering the longbow and quiver I had seen just a short time before, leaning against the wall in Ronald Ackermann's tent.

Safe, for the moment, I thought. But what if getting me inside was exactly what the person with the arrows wanted to do? I turned, expecting to find the archer's cohort looming over me with a knife . . . or a sword . . . or a mace or something. . . .

Hold it, Hawley, I thought. Hold on!

I was crouching behind something that was covered with a tarp. It looked to be about the size of a riding lawn mower or a snowmobile.

When I turned I found that the whole barn was loaded with similar objects—things covered with canvas sheets to form misshapen lumps that did nothing to betray what they actually were, and that were made all the more confusing by the windowpane-patterned light cutting down from above.

My stick suddenly came in handy as I moved back between some big pieces of equipment. I used it to poke stuff, jabbing at the hanging canvas as I glanced every couple of seconds back at the door.

I just couldn't get it straight in my mind.

Where had the arrows come from?

Then it hit me—the roof of the building in front of 111.

The bastard had been waiting for me on the roof.

No wonder I hadn't seen him. But . . .

No!

There was just no fucking way that Ronald Ackermann could have gotten out of his knight suit, beaten me to the yard, and gotten into position for his ambush so fast. It was impossible. Maybe he could have beaten me to the yard if he had left immediately after we met in his tent. I had been distracted by the motion in Glennwillows and slowed momentarily by the lay of the land. But he sure as hell hadn't heaved himself up on that roof in that tin can outfit he was wearing.

No way.

It couldn't be Ackermann. Which could only mean one thing. . . .

My stick made thumps as I rapped it against the canvas, raising dust as I went. There was a corner to turn at my left, but I didn't take it, preferring to edge my way straight back along the aisle so that the sunlit doorway would remain firmly in sight.

There!

I froze.

Someone had slipped through the door. Goddamn it, but I hadn't looked away from more than a second. Still, I'd been distracted by my fear of not being alone in the building, and it had taken just that long for the bitch to move in, fast, way too fast for me to get even the hint of a visual fix. The figure had been little more than a flicker in my eye, a shape flashing from the comparative brightness outside to the absolute darkness of the shadows created by the edge of the doorway. I still didn't know what was behind me, but now I knew at least one thing positively.

I sure as hell wasn't alone in the building now.

Someone was in there with me.

And that someone wanted me dead.

"Jane?" I called from where I finally settled, pulled into a ball on the floor with my butt stuck in as close as I could get it to the tire of some kind of truck. "Jane? Talk to me. What do you want?"

Nothing.

After that first glimpse of the figure sliding into the shed there hadn't been so much as a shuffle. Maybe two minutes had passed, minutes I had used by recklessly rushing back toward the rear of the building, seeing the area around me getting progressively darker as I went, doing all I could to chase that darkness and make it my own. Maybe she had been moving around during that time and I hadn't been able to hear. She could be anywhere by now. So I decided it was time for me to be quiet, and wait.

Jane Craig!

It had to be one or the other. I had taken great pains to ensure that, before the day was out, I'd find out which it was. Now I knew . . . or did I? I hadn't actually seen her. I'd seen someone. But was it her? For sure?

It couldn't be Ronald Ackermann . . . there simply hadn't been enough time.

Had there?

Dammit, THINK! I screamed at myself in my head.

Suddenly, I became aware of my own pulse, pounding in my wounded fingers. The pain was cleansing, in a way. Clarifying. I looked down at my hand in the gloom, thinking about the evil that must be inside a person to be able to just shoot at someone from a moving car, wondering what I could possibly say to such a person that would make a difference. I still hadn't heard so much as a footfall from my pursuer. I glanced up, almost expecting another arrow to come whistling in at me from above, only to find the skylights near the center of the building, hanging with cobwebs and dust.

The rumble that came next startled me into pressing my back even harder into the truck behind which I was hiding. It took me a second to identify it, and when I did, everything I had been thinking about who it was that I was facing, armed with a stick, went out the window.

It was the barn door.

Someone had just closed it.

Then I thought . . . no, maybe it's not somebody outside, maybe it's whoever's inside with me making sure I can't get out. Or maybe it is somebody outside, trying to keep us both bottled up in here. . . .

Jesus.

Something moved, sounding far away, and to my general left. Slipping off my shoes, I tiptoed, knees bent to a virtual squat, moving along the truck until I got to the cab door, which I tried, and found locked.

I was breathing hard, and my left nostril was whistling. I stuck my finger up it to make it stop, which it did . . . just before my right one started. I ran the back of my hand over my eyes to clear the sweat away, readjusting my grip on my stick once I did. Then, without a clear purpose, I pitched the stick as hard as I could, overhand, aimed high so that it would clear the tops of the equipment stored around me. It came down with a clatter somewhere on the other side of the barn.

Nothing.

Shit.

"Dammit, Jane," I called. "What's this going to get you?

Another killing? You've got to know you'll never get away with it.''

''I want that paper,'' she returned from somewhere out there, God knew where. It was Jane Craig's voice, and it hit me so hard that my stomach turned over. ''I want that contract Ed gave you.''

So it was her!

Jane Craig!

''You're the one who shot me,'' I said, moving again, purposefully, so that she'd hear my voice moving and have to concentrate on keeping herself focused. ''Ronald Ackermann called you from that concession stand, and off you went to do his dirty work. Come on, Jane. Don't you see what he was doing? Don't you get it? He was setting you up. First he tells you about his mother's body, and then, after you take care of his stepfather for him, he calls and tells me about George Sacks and that Camaro. Don't you see it? He gets the insurance money, leaving you with what? Nothing but an engagement ring you can wear while you're serving your life sentence.''

''You think I don't know what he was doing?'' she returned. In the dark she sounded closer, on my right side now, just over . . .

I lifted my head and looked. In my line of sight I saw a lunar landscape of sheets and canvas tarps, dusty and grey, upon which fell a spray of sun rays, cutting through from the skylights, hazy with gold and silver.

Then I saw a motion and ducked, slamming my chin on the fender of the car I was hiding behind as a sound like escaping air went *sssnitt* over my head. I've always thought of arrows as primitive, essentially harmless weapons. They've never instilled any fear in me. But the speed of the shots Jane Craig sent at me was terrifying. They were like long, winged bullets. And when the one she had just shot hit, somewhere behind me, it smashed glass.

''I want that paper, Hawley.''

''Sure, and then you'll just go away.''

She moved, and so did I. It was almost ridiculous. She went

one way, so I went the other. Not once, but five or six times. We were getting nowhere fast.

"Is this how it's going to go, Jane?" I called. "Hide and seek? How long do you think it'll be before somebody comes back up here?"

Nothing.

"Maybe we could make a deal."

Still she didn't speak, but she wasn't moving either. I held my breath. Finally, she asked warily, "What kind of deal, Hawley?"

"I'll split it with you, fifty-fifty."

"Split what?"

"The insurance settlement. We'll finish what you started. I'll help you, then we'll split the cash."

"Exactly what did I start?"

"Come on, Jane. Don't you think I know what you were doing? You did all of Ronald Ackermann's killing for him, and in return he promised to marry you so you could share in the inheritance money as his wife. You did wax his sister, didn't you? That's what your ex-husband told me. He said that it was you who killed Allison Ackermann, not Ronald—and you know what? I believe him. It couldn't have been Ronald because I don't think that he's got the balls."

"What's this got to do with a deal?" she called.

"You killed Allison," I barreled on, determined to finish it. "Then the two of you just sat back and waited to become rich, milking Everett Chase for an income by blackmailing him with what your ex-husband had told you about Madeline Chase's murder. The trouble was, your ex-husband was lying, Jane. Everett Chase didn't shoot his wife. He killed her with carbon monoxide. Not only that, but Eddie didn't have the piece of her with the bullet hole in it stashed away, because there isn't any piece of her like that. As long as you had Eddie making the threats for money on the phone, everything was fine. He could keep Chase scared shitless simply by saying that he knew what he had done and that if he didn't pay, he'd spill the beans. But then something happened to tip Everett Chase off. Something happened to tell him that you didn't really have anything on him at all. What was it, Jane? How'd Everett Chase get wise?''

''I don't know what you're talking about,'' she called back. And that's when it hit me.

''You called him, didn't you, Jane?'' I said, excited. ''That's got to be it. Did you get tired of arguing with Eddie about it, or did you just decide that he wasn't worth splitting the money with?''

''Fuck you, Hawley!'' Jane Craig shouted. But there was something underlying her voice, something revealing, that told me that I was right.

''You called Everett Chase yourself, it must have been . . . oh''—I thought of when I had gotten the call to disinter Paul J. Larson's body, which had been about ten days ago—''a little more than a week ago. That about right? You called Chase yourself. You told him that you wanted more money, and to make sure he paid up, you gave him the threat. Too bad you didn't know not to mention the shooting. As soon as you opened your mouth about him shooting his wife, he knew that something was up . . . he knew that it was all a load of shit. You didn't have anything on him, because you had the killing wrong.

''How about that, Jane? Sound about right? Everything was fine until you tipped Everett Chase off about how things really stood, and he decided that he didn't have anything to lose by having his wife's body dug up. If she was found, he'd get you off his back, and he'd get all the money he had paid to you and Ronald back, with interest. So he called me to dig up the casket with his wife's head in it. Then, when Ronald found out about it, he called you on the phone, told you what happened, and off you went to take care of it . . . again. You did so much for Ron . . . and then he turned you in. . . .''

''Bullshit, Hawley,'' she suddenly announced. ''Ron wouldn't do that to me!''

''No?'' I said. ''Then why did he call me about that Camaro? Huh, Jane? Explain that one to me.''

''Fuck you, Hawley! I want that contract . . . and I want it NOW!''

"So that no one will ever know that Madeline Chase was a suicide?"

"She wasn't a goddamn suicide!"

"That's not what your ex-husband is going to say. I got to him Jane. He'll do exactly what I tell him."

"What?"

"There's not going to be any money, Jane. I might not have the evidence to prove that you and Ronald were in this together, but I can make sure that neither of you ever see a dime of that insurance."

"Then you're not getting out of here," she shot back. "I'll kill you, and I'll kill your wife. I'll kill you, you son of a bitch! I'll cut your goddamn heart out!"

Her voice was hard, and cold . . . filled with a hate-crazed intensity that made me understand that she was capable of anything at this moment. She wasn't the soft-spoken, doe-eyed woman who I had dubbed the Fairy Lady in my mind. She was a flinty, hard-hearted, manipulating bitch who would do anything to get what she wanted.

And I was locked in this stupid barn with her!

And Christ, was she ever pissed. . . .

That was it!

I panicked.

I was running before I fully realized what I was doing. The door was the only way out and I was heading for it, running as fast as I could in the maze of junk surrounding me, barefooted, trying to be quiet. I don't think Jane Craig understood at first. I think she probably expected to do some more negotiating before she finally put an arrow through my head and relieved me of the precious paper that she thought was the key to her fortune. But I wasn't interested in playing anymore. There was this rush of something supercharged shooting up from my gut and sparkling into clean, pure, animal terror behind my eyes. All I could do was feed that fear. All I cared about was getting my ass home.

How well can she aim on the run? I wondered as I moved beneath the skylights at the building's center. I had half the building's length yet to go. Behind me I could hear Jane Craig's running feet.

I started shouting, loudly, almost hysterically, "Nat! Nat! Open the goddamn door!"

The barn door didn't move.

"Nat, for Christ's sake!"

The door only started opening when I was less than twenty feet from it.

If Craig shot now, I was a goner, I thought, visions of my body falling through the crack in the door with an arrow in my back assaulting my mind. But miraculously she didn't shoot. I heard her, behind me, shouting something that I couldn't make out. But I kept running. I think I might even have been shouting too.

The crack of light toward which I raced widened as the door slid. I sucked in my shoulders, turning my upper body sideways as I skipped, slipping through the door into the yard outside, my momentum taking me onto the gravel as I shouted, "Okay! Close it! Close it!"

Then the pain hit me. Against my bare elbows the sharp gravel felt like fire and made me prance involuntarily, lifting my knees high, back and forth, as Nat, instead of closing the door like I'd asked her to, continued opening it, pausing only long enough to do a second, even more weird thing:

She pitched me a gun.

"Bill, here!" she said, throwing a pistol to me underhand before returning to the job of opening the barn door.

"NAT!" I shouted, catching the gun and finally settling myself, the gravel hurting my feet, but my attention caught by what I saw inside the storage shed.

Jane Craig was standing there, clear in the light pouring through the now fully open door, shadow stretched out ominously behind her, arm pulled back as far as it would go, arrow aimed directly at my chest.

Nat was standing off to the side, her back to the building's wall, staring at me, eyes wide.

Jane, with the eye of a hunter, was looking at me too.

I had the gun Nat had pitched to me aimed back at Jane, held in both hands, sighted right between her eyes . . . though whether I could hit her, even from where I was standing, was anybody's guess.

The moment stretched, but no one moved.

Then a sound came from behind me.

Click!

Then again.

Click!

Then came a whole series of *clicks* as I saw, in my peripheral vision, the arms of men raised and steadied as their thumbs pulled back the hammers on blue-black pistols that were all aimed, with mine, into the barn. I glanced around, finding several policemen to my left, even more to my right, and behind me, though I only caught the briefest glance, I could hear the crunching of wheels as cruisers bounced through the main gate through clouds of dust, sirens off, lights revolving.

I looked back at Jane Craig.

She was still holding the arrow aimed at me, her arm trembling from the strain of holding the cord. The tip of that arrow still steady, sharp, and precise.

I moved my eyes from the arrow to Jane Craig's eyes, paused, lowered my gun, and said, "Don't be stupid."

For a second nothing happened . . . which was just long enough for me to think that I had said the right thing, and that everything would be okay. Then, as if in a final act of denial and defiance, Jane Craig relaxed her fingers, the bowstring sang its terrible, single note, and, for the second time in three days, she shot me.

I wish that I could say that I remember the experience in detail, but I really don't. I just recall that look in the woman's aiming eye as the sun glinted off what might have been a tear on her cheek, but was more likely a bead of sweat. Then there was that *twang* of the bowstring. And then something hit me directly in the center of my chest so hard that it was like being kicked by a horse.

With an "Ooph!" I went down backwards, landing hard on my ass, sure that I would soon be dead. Incredibly, I had a flash of myself bleeding, with my wife holding me to her as I died. There was immediate movement in two directions around me; the cops came forward in a surge, heading for Jane Craig, guns still drawn, shouting like mad, and there was Nat, coming at me, arms out, screaming.

In the barn's doorway there was a scuffle as the cops gang-tackled her, shouting for her to, "Get down on the ground! Get down!" Meanwhile I rolled my eyes, waited, and finally, after what seemed an eternity, coughed out a terrible strangling sound as my recently emptied lungs inflated, pulling cool air down my throat. Nat was kneeling over me, just as she had been in my brief dream of death. I was reaching up for one last embrace. Everywhere there was commotion. But then, instead of a dark tunnel leading to a white light, or angels, or nothing, Nat was helping me to my feet and Detective Rubins was slapping me on the back, saying something like, "Sorry I'm late, Bill. But we had a little delay with the paperwork, being out of jurisdiction and all. . . ."

Nat was smiling as she pulled the arrow out of my chest and said, "The next time Larry says wear a flak vest, I promise I won't argue at all."

My mouth was hanging open, but I couldn't think of anything to say. Instead I probed the hole in my shirt where the arrow had been, blinking.

"Do you think you'll have much of a bruise?" Nat asked.

Finally, I said, "Who cares?"

As they led Jane Craig past me, her hands cuffed behind her back, she glared, her long blond hair blowing over her face, her eyes sparkling with loathing. I turned my face away, choosing instead to concentrate on my wife—feeling her, squeezing her, loving her so much, and so proud of her at that moment. . . .

Opening that door after I had asked her to close it behind me must have been the hardest thing she had ever done. But by opening it she had revealed Jane Craig as the cold-blooded killer she was to a dozen police officer witnesses. It must have been hard, but she'd done it.

"That's my girl," I whispered. Then I added, "You stuck right with her."

"That's what you told me to do," Nat said in my ear. "I was scared, Bill."

"She talked to Ackermann?"

"Yeah. As soon as you were gone she slipped back into his

tent.'' Nat pulled away, watching my face as she spoke. ''She wasn't in there more than two minutes.''

''And Ackermann?''

''I don't know. Larry's on him.''

''Where'd you get the gun?''

''It's Larry's. He smuggled it in. That's why he said he had a pacemaker. He was keeping the guy from finding it with the metal detector at the gate. Do you want to keep this?''

She was holding the arrow.

''No,'' I said, taking it from her and pitching it away.

As we started walking, Detective Rubins was shouting questions at my back, but I ignored him. My heart was racing, and the gun Nat had given me felt heavy in my hand. A terrible notion filled my head, roaring in there, pounding, calling out for me to use it. That insistent indicative persisted all the way across the highgrass of the field at the bottom of the slope as Nat and I walked, quickly, urgently, hand in hand, in grim, purposeful silence. Nat didn't ask where I was going. I think she knew. I think she understood exactly what that period of two minutes that Jane Craig had spent in Ronald Ackermann's tent meant to me . . . and to her . . . what it meant, period. Detective Rubins and a couple of his men were following behind. I think they were afraid of what I might do. Rubins had seen the gun. There had been a very powerful instant that his eyes had rested upon it before I had turned and begun the descent down the path. He'd called my name, but he hadn't tried to have me restrained. I didn't know why, but he didn't do that. He just followed, trying to talk me out of it all the way.

The battle was winding down on the field below Glennwillows. Everyone was pressed along the rim of the valley, cheering their champions. A number of knights, already having been ''killed'' apparently, had joined the crowd. No one paid any attention to Nat and I as we walked through town and approached the action from behind. But someone finally did notice as I started walking down the hill from the spectators' area to the battlefield itself. Before I started down the hill, I saw Larry trotting up to meet me. There was a table I was passing . . . a metal worker's table, covered with bits of steel, lengths of leather, some kind of tongs, and an assortment of other tools, including a very modern-looking claw hammer, which I picked up as I passed. At the rim I pitched Larry's gun to him, nonchalantly, without explanation, just pitched it, swinging the hammer at my side with my other hand. I could hear Nat following behind me, and I let her. She deserved to be there. She had earned it.

They were playing out there, on the field, hundreds of full-grown men, playing at banging and hacking each other, maiming and cutting and brutalizing each other with pretend swords and axes, playing at death. As I approached the battle, stretching out all across the field before me, the first thing I noticed was the way the sun glinted off their armor. Then I heard the sounds of their conflict, coming in on me, cutting through the din in my own head . . . the shouts and screams and clanging of confrontation, the grunts of athletic exertion, and, incongruously, the subdued babble of discussion passing between the combatants regarding rules and points.

It was stupid.

It was sick.

There's nothing fun about killing.

Nothing.

NOT A GODDAMN THING!

Nat stopped at the periphery of the battle, preferring not to step between the knights. At first, as I made my way along, they didn't seem to notice me, so concentrated on their fighting were they that I had to push my way between them. When they saw me, unadorned with armor, there were a few startled questions, as well as a few indignant exclamations. But when they saw the police officers at my back, their outrage quieted.

As I progressed deeper into the fray, it was like I was a teacher on the school yard. The fighting stopped in direct relation to where I was, voices fell silent, arms stopped waving, the knights parted the way as I moved toward the tall staff about forty yards ahead that bore the fluttering gold flag of Ronald Ackermann's Lord. Finding him once that flag was in sight wasn't hard. The knights parted for me, and I found him fighting, his back to me. The man he was fighting, seeing the police behind me, stopped. Ackermann pulled up short when his opponent did, apparently watching the other man, who simply motioned my way. Ackermann turned, his helmet gleaming, his shield white with its red cross protecting his upper body, a long, wooden sword poised aggressively in his gloved hand.

I didn't even pause, but strode toward him, the anger in me bubbling to a boiling point. I heard Detective Rubins at my back say, "Wait," maybe to his men, maybe to me. I kept walking. I didn't speak. I didn't do anything but close the distance between me and the son of a bitch who had ordered his fiancée to come and shoot me, the son of a bitch who had known all along that Jane Craig was killing people, the son of a bitch who, thinking he was some kind of genius, had been playing out his own special scenario, one that would make him rich, put the woman who would be his wife in jail, and leave at least two people dead . . . not to mention what had happened to his mother . . . chopped into pieces . . . cut into fucking pieces . . .

"You KNEW!" I shouted when I was within ten feet of him. The sweat was running down my face, and the effort of my shout tore at my throat.

Ackermann obviously knew that I meant business. When he spotted the hammer, he lifted his shield as he assumed a fighting stance, sword in hand.

"You asshole!" I shouted, wading into him with the hammer, swinging it as hard as I could, viciously contacting the metal of his shield, then his shoulder, then his breastplate, driving him back.

It must have been the fury of my attack . . . or the fact that this was real, not play, that made Ronald Ackermann all but fold before me as my hammer clanged out great dents in his precious armor and the sound of my ringing blows chimed faster and faster as he stumbled, yelped, and fell with a smashing clatter, his sword going one way, his shield going another, his helmet banging the ground so hard that the visor over his face rattled.

"You knew . . . you sent her to kill me . . . you son of a bitch!" I shouted, standing with one foot on either side of the felled knight's chest, bent at the waist, swinging the hammer down and down again, smashing that stupid suit, making him scream inside it as I finally, with two vicious strokes, took the visor off his helmet, revealing his sweaty, terrified face. When I saw that face, something happened to me, and I stopped hitting him—I simply stopped.

I was standing over him, looking down as I reached into my tunic, then I lowered myself by bending my knees so that I was sitting on his chest, looking down at him from so close now that I could smell the odor of his sweat rising up out of his suit.

"Not a dime," I said, opening first the contract Edward Craig had given me. "Not a fucking dime. No blood money, Ronald. No money at all." I opened the second paper, which was the death certificate Dr. Gordon Wolf had signed for me the night before—now with a hole through its middle where Jane Craig's arrow had struck—and thrust it into Ronald Ackermann's face, saying, "You sent her to kill me! You picked up the phone and you sent her out to shoot me and your stepfather down. And in your tent I only told you about the contract. She didn't know a thing about it until you told her . . . and until you told her to kill me. Well, read this, you asshole. Read it! This is your mom's death certificate, and it's official. She killed herself. The county medical examiner says so. She's a suicide. . . .

"No murder, so no insurance, no nothing. Life insurance won't pay for a suicide. You lose."

"But she didn't . . ." he began, but stopped and widened his eyes when he realized what he was about to admit.

"Yes, she did," I said, standing. "She killed herself. She wasn't murdered. No insurance. Forget it."

I pitched the hammer away from myself, suddenly feeling a little sick as I turned to find Detective Rubins standing there, looking at me. His face was drawn, almost blank. I couldn't read it at first. Maybe it was because I was so worked up. Maybe it was because he had spent years practicing making just that face and had gotten good at not allowing his emotions to show. But whatever the reason, nothing registered as we faced one another. Nothing. Finally, with just the corner of his mouth moving up ever so slightly in the tiniest, most private smile I had ever seen, he asked, "You finished, Bill?"

I glanced back at where Ronald Ackermann lay, prostrate on the ground, his armor covered with dents.

"Yeah," I said, returning my attention to the detective. "Thanks."

Then Nat was walking toward me, arms extended, smiling as she said, "My knight."

"My lady," I replied weakly.

Nat hugged me as I put my head on her shoulder, closed my eyes, and just pushed it all away. Everything else but her, I pushed it all away. Or at least I tried. But that's when I noticed my hand—I was bleeding through the gauze on my fingers. It didn't hurt, but there was blood running down my arm.

"Nat," I said, still holding her, feeling her hair against my face, "I think I popped a stitch."

"You can say that again," she replied, misunderstanding me.

And that finally did make me smile.

EPILOGUE
■■■■■■■■■■■■■■■■

"YOU KNOW, THEY'RE still pointing their fingers at each other," Detective Rubins said, placing his coffee mug down on my desk as he rose from the recliner in the corner of my office. "They're still each saying that it was the other one who did it. What a pair. For the past few years they've been playing lovey-dovey, while each was plotting to send the other to jail. Christ Almighty, ain't love grand?"

"What did George Sacks have to say?" T. W. Younger, the New American Life Insurance Company's president, who was also standing in front of my desk with a coffee mug, asked, conversationally, with a tone that implied that, at least as far as he was concerned, it really didn't matter.

Detective Rubins shrugged his shoulders as he replied, "He's not saying anything, just this minute. He came up with some kind of hotshot lawyer who's telling him to button up for now. But we'll get to him. He's got a daughter to worry about. He'll be straight. He'll want us to drop his burglary charge, which we will. But I'm sure we can count on him as a witness for the prosecution."

"What about Madeline Chase?" Mr. Younger asked.

"Now that Bill gave me the names of the people Edward Craig used to hide her body, we'll get her dug up and back together as soon as we can. According to our source, we've got five disinterments yet to perform. Isn't that right, Mr. Hawley?"

I nodded.

"So," Detective Rubins concluded expansively, "all that's left for us is to fill in the blanks as best we can . . . which shouldn't be too terribly hard. Not with Ronald Ackermann's house being as full of evidence as it is. Plus we've got more motive than anyone could need. Nobody gets away without a trace, Mr. Younger, no matter how carefully they might plan. Once a piece of a crime is dug up, so to speak, we can usually uncover the rest. We'll nail her all right . . . it just might take some time."

"Her?" Nat said from her seat by the door.

"Sure." Rubins nodded. "She was the killer, and Ronald Ackermann was her Rasputin. Or at least that was how he must have thought of himself. What a mess. Fucking squirrel cage . . . I beg your pardon, Mrs. Hawley."

Nat smiled.

Rubins turned to me one last time.

"But you still don't have any idea what ever happened to that embalmer, Edward Craig?" he said. "You don't know where he went? We had some men visit the taxidermy shop on Carnege Avenue, and they said that he apparently took his stuff and left late Saturday night."

"Sorry, Detective," I replied. "But I haven't got a clue."

"Don't know anything about the bullet holes in his apartment, huh? That still your story?"

"Yes, sir."

"And you're sticking to it?"

"Until the end of time."

Rubins frowned as he said, "Oh well." He shrugged. "I guess it's not that important. We've got bigger fish to fry, and besides, even if we did find him, who knows what he'd say?"

"That's true." Larry Fizner nodded importantly from his seat next to Nat. "It's probably better that we not know."

T. W. Younger snapped his briefcase shut.

"Well, again my thanks, Mr. Hawley," he announced. "And now, I'll be on my way."

I was standing next to him, holding the check he'd given me in my good hand—$138,462.09. Ten percent of the total funds remaining in-house due to the suicide clause in Madeline

Chase's life insurance policy. I wasn't sure that I deserved it. But if I didn't, who did?

I folded the check and slipped it into my shirt pocket, shook Mr. Younger's hand and escorted him to the door. Before he left, he turned his face to mine and said softly, as if he didn't want Detective Rubins, who was standing less than ten feet away, to hear, "Can we call you again, Mr. Hawley? If we should ever need to?"

"Of course," I replied.

When he was gone, I asked Detective Rubins, "When will Madeline Chase be released for burial?"

"End of the week," he said.

"Can I do it, gratis?"

He smiled, saying, "Dr. Wolf's already got your name on the release."

"Fine."

Then he was gone too, but not before saying something gruff and macho about how my dad, his old friend, should be proud of me.

I'm starting to get used to that . . . having people change their opinion of me from one end of the spectrum to the other in just a few days. It used to make me kind of intellectually seasick; now, I guess it's not so bad.

After Detective Rubins, Larry Fizner took his leave, pausing long enough to point at the pocket in which I had deposited T. W. Younger's check as he said, "I'll be expecting my cut of that."

"Coupla days." I smiled.

Larry punched me gently on the shoulder as he passed.

"Well," Jerry announced from where he was seated behind my desk, "that was fun. But now it's time to get to work."

I glanced at my brother, finding him suited and groomed to perfection. He looked strong and in charge. If it weren't for the handles of his wheelchair jutting behind his shoulders, you wouldn't have known he had any handicap at all. The change in him since I had first offered the idea of stepping aside and letting him be the funeral home's manager was profound. It still made me feel a little funny, having him sitting in my place, preparing for the family of the body we had gotten late the night before to come in and make arrangements. But I didn't mention it. Instead, I just said, "I'll catch the phone," as Nat stood up and I took her hand.

On the way up the stairs to our living quarters, she said, "The hot tub's available."

It was Monday morning, just past ten o'clock. We had spent all afternoon Sunday and late into Sunday night giving our statements to what seemed like every cop in Ohio, individually, again and again. We had slept less than two hours. The hot tub sounded great.

"Then a nap?" I suggested.

"You're a wild man," my wife replied.

The phone rang, I picked it up, spoke a few words, and hit the hold button. On the intercom I asked my brother, "Is your family in yet?"

"No," he said.

"Then you've got a call on line one."

"Who is it?"

"You're the manager, right?"

"That's right," he agreed.

"Well, then, manage."

I hung up.

"Who was that?" Nat asked, entering the living room with a bottle of sparkling white grape juice and two champagne glasses.

"Jerome Larson," I said. "He wants to know when we're going to bury his father again."

"And you gave him to Jerry?"

"He's the boss."

Nat considered that, and nodded, saying, "Good. When are you going to talk to his girlfriend?"

"Not today," I said, rising from the couch and leading her to the patio. "A promise is a promise. Ellie Lyttle and I will definitely have a heart-to-heart sometime soon. It just won't be today."

As I sank into the steaming water, with the birds singing and the blue of an early spring sky easy on my eyes, an airplane crossed my line of sight, moving slowly from my left to my right, heading for the airport near our city. I watched that little plane for a moment, thinking about how there were, inside it, hundreds of people, concerned with their own lives and troubles, as far removed from me and mine as Jane Craig and Ronald Ackermann had been from each other, even when they were sleeping in the same bed. I could hardly accept it; and the notion that they had been living in that nondescript house together, on that nondescript street, made me briefly wonder how many other houses contained how many other secrets. . . .

Secrets that, for at least the moment, I decided that I would rather not know.

Or that airplane . . . flying so far overhead, a tiny speck full of people and their lives. How many secrets were on that airplane?

How many plans?

Keep going, I thought. At least for today, just keep right on going.

Nat slid in at my side and I placed my arm over her shoulder, pulling her in tight and whispering that I loved her. Returning my eyes to the plane, I watched its tiny white tail following it across the sky, blissfully unaware that just such a plane, at our airport, not five miles away, would soon . . . very soon, come to play a momentous role in my life.

At that moment, what was overhead was still a secret.

At that moment all was warmth, and love, and my wife.

At that moment, I was happy.